# The Regent

## Charity Mae

On this the princess had to lie all night. In the morning she was asked how she had slept.

"Oh, very badly!" said she. "I have scarcely closed my eyes all night. Heaven only knows what was in the bed, but I was lying on something hard, so that I am black and blue all over my body. It's horrible!"

Princess and the Pea

# Contents

# Chapter 1

The contest is over, but the real game has just begun. I don't feel any of that, though. Not yet.

The morning after the public announcement, I wake up in my room at the palace bursting with happiness. I won! I am engaged to the love of my life, Prince Gavril, and today is the first day I will truly get to experience that freedom.

I smile at the sunlight filtering through the curtains of my bedroom. I had experienced many heartbreaks in this room, but today none of that crosses my mind. Today, the world is perfect. It will not always be, but at least today, I can enjoy my win and finally find some happiness in these struggles.

As I sit up, my three maids enter the room to help me prepare for the day. Vivian, my head maid, beams to see me sitting up with a soft, pleasant, and content smile on my face. Flur and Ro smile at me, delighted to see that light in me.

Vivian doesn't comment though, and the others follow her lead. She walks over to the curtains and opens them to let in the full sunlight of the day. There's a break in the rainstorms we'd been experiencing. Not even it could reveal a hair out of place on Vivian's head, however, as she goes about her work.

"Ready to start your first day of transition?" Vivian asks me brightly as I get out of bed.

"I am." I sigh, happier than I have ever been inside this palace, perhaps ever.

The only break in the normal routine is that Damian, my attendant, doesn't show up. I am not too surprised but a tad disappointed. He is the Merlin's brother. He'd have to leave soon if he hasn't already, too heartbroken to survive a proper goodbye. I'll survive either way. Not saying goodbye will undeniably be a sore ache in my heart for the rest of my life, but I understand it if that's what he had to do. He has missions far bigger than me.

The palace is its normal bright, ocean-themed self, and for once, the brightness of it doesn't bother me. The first thing that is different is the dining hall. It's strange not to have at least one long table for all the Chosen girls. But now I'd won, it was just me, the queen, the prince, and Princess Zelda as our royal guest. Isla had gone to stay with Rose at her embassy. The royal table is now a simple round table with more space for the staff breakfast at the far side of the room. I never realized how smashed into the back they'd been with the long tables.

Princess Zelda looks happier than I've ever seen her, engaging in conversation with the queen, a smile on her face. Perhaps the Enthronement had felt as entrapping to her as it had to me. Her blonde hair is different too, done into a nice braid that goes below her waist. The Hyvian-style dress she wears is freer and more relaxed, unlike anything I've normally seen her in. Her green eyes sparkle in the joy of relief.

Gavril looks up at me as I come in and beams, his amber eyes gleaming in delight to see me looking so bright and myself. I beam back, admiring his strong form as he stands to greet me. He's such a perfect combination of his parents, his father's warm smile and demeanor coupled with the royal power and grace of his mother. My heart flutters as he draws closer to greet me.

I can't stop smiling as he kisses my cheek. I resist the urge to grab him and kiss him harder, but the queen would object, so I behave as Gavril pulls out my chair for me.

He sits beside me, returning to his food but still smiling as he resumes his breakfast. As acting king, he probably has a full day ahead. Though I now know his father survived the assassination attempt (though just barely), Gavril still has much to do, likely under his father's orders.

A sliver of uncertainty wiggles into my stomach. If he's busy all day, what am I supposed to be doing?

"So how is Sage faring?" The queen asks Zelda, snapping me from my worried thoughts.

"He insists he's fine when he's not. He winces every time he moves and fights taking any painkillers, insisting he's fine and the doctor won't let him leave because the doctor hates him." Zelda giggles. "But he'll be alright. I think he's still resisting the hope he might actually have something he wants."

"I can imagine." I frown in sympathy. After what happened with the last girl...

"He'll get over it. He's crazy enough to love you," Gavril assures her. Zelda gives him a look and makes a mocking face at him, which he returns.

"Gavril," the queen scolds and even gives Zelda a look. I think I am finally seeing what Damian said about Gavril and Zelda's relationship being much more like siblings than lovers.

"Minnow," Zelda hisses at him when the queen isn't looking.

"Blonde."

I have to cover my mouth to stop myself from losing it laughing. Minnow?

Gavril spots the clock and jumps up. "See you later," he assures me, kissing my cheek. "I have an important meeting." He winks at his mother, who rolls her eyes.

"Are you not also in that meeting?" I ask the queen.

"Not allowed until other work is done," the queen replies.

I frown at that, but Zelda then asks if I want her help with anything.

"Uh... like what?" I ask.

"Oh." She blinks. "Well, if you do, let me know."

"I imagine the staff will be her hands just fine." The queen smiles.

"Staff?" I ask.

"Well, I imagine Lady Hydie will help give you a rundown of what needs to be prepared for the wedding and coronation," the queen explains. "She'll work with your team to get it all ready."

"So, she'll help with the transition?" I ask.

"Well, part of it. I imagine your attendant will do most of it." The queen smiles at me.

Not with him leaving soon, if he hasn't already. So, it's down to Lady Hydie, the chief of the palace staff, to help with the transition. She helped me at the very start of the Enthronement. So at least she's not a stranger.

When I leave the dining hall, Lady Hydie accosts me in the hallway. She's a bright, happy woman with blonde hair that curls at the end of her ponytail, perfectly matching her Purerahian blue uniform. She wore a skirt on the day I met her, but today, she's wearing the work pants worn by my maids.

"Good morning, Your Highness." She bobs me a curtsy with the biggest smile you could imagine on her square face. "I hope you rested well; we have a lot to do today," she says brightly. "I took the liberty of preparing the Ladies' Chamber for our uses today. If you'll come with me." She's still beaming as she waves a hand for me to follow.

I follow, feeling strangely anxious, but I have no reason to be.

When I walk into the normally familiar Ladies' Chamber, I blink in surprise. It's not arranged the way I'm used to. Normally, it has a few armchairs and sofas gathered around tables throughout the room, or it has a row of student tables and a whiteboard at the left side of the room ready for lessons.

Instead, there's one long table with a chair on the far side, with stacks of papers, binders, and other supplies. There are a few books as well. Something about the individuality of the one chair makes uncertainty and loneliness prickle in my chest.

"The chair is for you, My Lady," Lady Hydie chirps brightly. "There is much to go over. We have many things to get ready. And the sooner we get started, the better." She puts a hand on my arm and smiles. "Go on, Your Highness."

Something about all this has dispelled my happy bubble and set a heavy weight into my stomach.

*I'm not Princess yet*, I think, but I am too busy trying to process this sudden change to reply as I sit down.

I start slightly as an unseen gentleman-in-waiting comes forward to push my chair in. In appreciation, I give him a smile and nod of thanks. He returns the smile as he nods back.

I look back at the table, steeling myself for whatever surprises the enthusiastic Lady Hydie has in store for me.

"Before we get too far into things, I wanted to congratulate you again." Hydie's blue eyes twinkle as she smiles at me. "We have a lot to get ready before the big day, which I'm sure will factor into picking a date. So, I put those items of business at the top of the list."

Picking a date? No one had ever given me a choice in such events. And now... out of nowhere? Would I have to do all the planning myself? I had managed the festival well, but I'd never planned anything like this. Where did I even start?

Hydie is holding a leather portfolio with a clipboard on the front. "A copy of the to-do list is right there in front of you. It's ordered by items to be completed with their accompanying sub-tasks. They must all be finished before we press forward."

I look down at the first stack of papers. I expect the to-do list to be perhaps the first few pages, but when I pick it up, it turns out to be a long, folded piece of paper. The bottom falls into my lap and still has some folds. How big is this list?

My eyes bug out as I scan it. At the top of the list are staff assignments with five or ten smaller tasks under them. Then there's bedroom preparation, office preparation, wedding event organization, which has so many subtasks I can't see where they end.

"I believe we will need to get the team together first," Hydie says, beaming as I stare at my list. "And then we can work on the events leading up to the event, and, of course, the event itself. Oh, and on the sixth fold, you'll see the coronation plans as well."

Sixth!?

But as I'm thinking this, Hydie nods at the guard by the door. She opens the door, and two menservants and four maids walk into the room, line up in front of me, and bow or curtsy respectively.

Hydie is beaming. "May I present you with new staff."

"What!?" *No!* "You're reassigning my maids?" They can't do that. Damian was being taken from me; I can't handle them taking Vivian, Flur, and Ro too.

"Oh no, no, of course not. But as princess, you'll need a full staff. A Chosen only needed an attendant and three maids. A princess will need her valet, or lady-in-waiting, as well as a full staff."

"Full staff of what?" I ask, brow and eyes creased in worry at Hydie. Gavril is acting king, and he doesn't have a full staff.

The line of servants is casting apprehensive looks at one another, likely concerned about being dismissed. A twinge of sympathy wiggles in my chest as I look at them, but I don't understand why I need so many.

"Did... didn't you cover this in your royalty lessons?" Lady Hydie's beaming smile slips into a frown.

"Cover... what? I learned politics and... etiquette. Why do I need nine staff members in total?"

"Actually, twelve," Hydie gently corrects me. "You will retain your three current maids and gain one extra for personal needs. Then your two groomsmen and three maids will act in various positions, and you'll need one court liaison, and two security. We'll want to get started on looking for a court liaison right away. We're already getting applications, including some former Chosen, so we'll want to get started on that."

"V-various positions?" I stammer. Gavril hadn't even personally chosen his valet or court liaison. Why am I suddenly choosing from this random group and applications for my court liaison!?

"Yes. We do not get a say over the two guards, of course, but I'm sure the head of security or Custods will work that out shortly," Hydie says brightly. "But you choose the rest. Oh... and I have a note saying we'll need to find you a new attendant as well." Hydie picks up the note in question that was stuck to her clipboard. "But that must be a mistake." She laughs.

My heart sinks. No, that's right. And a greater lost emptiness fills my chest without that guide to help me figure this out, as he had so many times. Could I do this without him?

I can't think like that. Of course, I can. I won for a reason. I repeat this several times in my head, which gives me the strength to say through a sad kind of murmur, "No. No, that's correct."

"A princess doesn't need to mumble." Lady Hydie beams at me, trying to cheer me up. "You have every right to pick someone else if you choose, Your Highness. No need to be ashamed or embarrassed."

It has nothing to do with choice. I shove those gloomy thoughts aside as best I can to try to tackle this sudden obstacle tossed in my path, tripping me up just when I thought I only had to sprint the last final steps.

I'm overwhelmed. I had no expectations for how this day would unfold, but it certainly was not this. A million sudden choices to make all on my own. I suddenly wish with all my heart Gavril was there to give me the courage that I could do this. I don't let myself wish Damian was there.

Once again, I remind myself that I won for a reason. I am a true princess, and a true princess can do this. I look down at the to-do list. A nine-fold to-do list? A little despair leaks into my heart. Just a day in the life of a princess. This attempt at comfort fails.

Hydie must sense my overwhelm but also underestimates it. "It's quite alright to take time to adjust. This time yesterday you didn't even know if you'd be princess!" Lady Hydie laughs a little. "There's no guilt in taking your time. We are expected to treat you with that respect. It's quite alright."

She glances at the jittery-looking staff with just her eyes. Uncertainly betrays itself in that rapid glance. Guilt bubbles in my stomach. I certainly won't send them away, but I don't have a clue what to do with them.

"So... why do I need so many, exactly?" I ask again, trying to quash the lost and confused feelings nosing around in my chest like blind little mice after a cheese that isn't there.

While fighting those feelings, I take deep breaths. I am the winner. I am good at this. I have to understand this. I can understand this. I just need a moment to digest, that's all.

I pick one thing to focus on. "What do I need all this staff for? The prince just has his two."

"I'm sure he'll hire more in time." Hydie waves off. "And it depends on what kind of princess you choose to be."

"Kind?" I frown. What does she mean? I'm to be the crown princess. Being next in line for the throne is the job. What does she mean, kind?

Hydie explains, "There are numerous traditional variations, of course. For example, you can be extremely involved with the court and politics and be what some might call the Court's Princess." Hydie giggles a little.

"Or perhaps, you'll be more of an activist version, where you deal more with being the face of the people to the royal family. Many common ladies turned royal will go this route, making them quite popular with the people. Though in a nation like this... that comes with its own risks.

"Then there is the more 'hostess' model where you don't touch politics or policy on either end but handle the events and that alone. This is what many born princesses end up doing because when they start their duties at a young age, they don't know what policies or political angles they wish to pursue.

"Not to put words in your mouth, Your Highness, but I would presume you'd like to be more of a mix of the three rather than actively trying to be one or another." Lady Hydie beams at me again. "And your staff assignments reflect what pursuits you wish to seek, such as if you went with the ambassador/hostess angle, you'd have two scheduling staff members, one correspondence, and the fourth would be your personal shopper."

I swallow. "So... what if I don't even know what jobs I will want them for yet?"

"Are you sure your teachers didn't cover this?" Lady Hydie asks tenderly.

"Quite sure." I nod, feeling stupid and underqualified in equal and growing degrees.

"I see. Well, not to worry, perhaps as we make plans, you'll figure out what you'd like." Lady Hydie's sparkling smile twinkles across her face once more. "If I may make recommendations, not that I am an expert on political aims even if I am on staff, I would suggest at least one correspondence person and one scheduler who handles your agenda. Someone you trust and communicate well with would be ideal for that position, as they will tell you how your day is going to go. It is your choice, but they arrange the schedule for your daily approval."

"Daily?" So, I'll have to spend time every day reviewing the next day's schedule for approval?

"Yes, and more or less as needed." Hydie smiles once more. She is always smiling, and it is feeding the unsettling feeling in my chest. "But of course, you can work that out as you like. From my limited experience with princesses, I think that would be the minimum for now."

"I see." How did I know who I communicated best with before I truly knew them?

"And of course, as the head of all hosting events, the princess is considered the queen of the staff." Hydie beams at me. "So, we'll work together often."

*Oh great, lovely.* I think with sarcasm, but don't say it. Her never-ending smile is intensely unsettling now.

"So, this afternoon, I've scheduled time to meet with all the heads of the various staff departments over the palace." Hydie beams.

For what? What does that have to do with being princess? Have I really misunderstood my role? Would I be little more than the pretty hostess until I was queen? That is not what Gavril or Damian led me to believe.

"And I thought we'd assign your new staff this morning, but as it seems your teachers failed to prepare you for this, how about we instead go over what needs to be done during the transition?" Hydie offers. I nod numbly.

Hydie has one of my new groomsmen bring her over a chair to sit next to me. She then covers the basic structure of the royal household, which is about what I'd have expected. Then she gives a straightforward, but confusingly highly detailed lecture on what I would need for my staff.

I'm so lost I don't even know what to say.

"Then I think preparing your new living quarters will be most important, as you can't have the wedding until you have your royal spaces to move into." Hydie giggles. "As well as, of course, planning the wedding itself. Several top-line designers have offered to make mockups for you." She beams. "And you could choose to split some of the budget for the wedding and transition to accepting their design and letting them build it." Hydie finishes going over so many options, making my head spin, and says, "They would be honored to make designs for you."

I was so certain just this morning I could handle anything the royal life threw at me, but now... I'm starting to question what it is they all expect me to become.

# Chapter 2

Hydie goes on and on through lunch that's brought up for me before we start our rounds with the staff. I am so unsure what it is I actually need to do, I let Hydie lead completely.

The first stop is the kitchens which Hydie says are quiet, but to me, it still seems crazy. Roughly twenty people are darting around the large room. Ovens line one wall, sinks occupy another, and long tables or counters fill the room's center. On the side nearest the door that leads up a set of stairs into the dining hall are open counters and shelves for placing food on to send up and serve.

The main insanity at the moment are the sinks. Every single sink has people manning it, washing, drying, or putting away cooking dishes, serving dishes, and whatever else. Some wear regular staff uniforms while others wear the neater ones of serving staff with aprons over them to keep them neat.

The clatter of dishes, the rustle of flowing water, and the stomping, shuffling of feet fill the air, accenting the chatter of voices. It smells of soap and dirty water with just the lingering hint of frying oil lingering from lunch.

"Make sure all used towels are sent down the shoot to the laundry," a lean man reminds some of the serving staff doing the drying.

I'm unsure if it's a good idea to interrupt the madness that is the kitchen, but Hydie clears her throat loudly to announce us. The man who'd called out immediately rushes our way while calling to two others to join us. Two women with stern looking expressions come over.

Once they're near me, though, they all put on dazzling smiles. "Thank you for taking the time." Hydie is beaming as always. "P—" Hydie chuckles, "I mean Lady Kascia, let me introduce your lead kitchen staff."

Hydie introduces me to the head chef, Chef Cora; Mr. John, the kitchen manager; and Ms. Camilla, the head of serving staff. They bow or curtsy in a proper but eager manner, expressing more thanks than necessary in their attempt to gain my favor.

To try to alleviate the knot in my chest, I look over their work and suddenly recall Flur's mother works in the kitchens. She makes my sleep tea for me every night. Seeing Flur's mother again would certainly help the anxious knot in my stomach.

I open my mouth to ask as my eyes search for her, but Hydie speaks first. "Would you like to explain what it is you do?" Lady Hydie offers the three leads.

They take an hour to explain in detail what it is they do and why every single member of their staff is needed. I'm reeling as I wonder why I need to know all of this, but I am too anxious and scattered to figure out how to politely ask why I should care.

I do my best to take note of each of their positions and what they do, trying to figure out how that might help me later, until finally Hydie drags me off to the next station, which is the cleaning and decorating staff. Hydie herself leads this, but she takes what feels like another hour explaining why each and every member of her crew is needed.

My mind is spinning as I try to remember it all and figure out why it's relevant to me as princess when I'm pulled off yet again to our next station.

She takes me to a new room I'd never seen before. Hydie explains it's the laundry room as she almost pulls me down the stairs by the hand and opens the large door to this underground space.

The laundry room is a rather depressing room with no windows. It's right under the kitchens and with the loud thunks of the machines cleaning clothes, the hammering stains, and rush and flow of water, in addition to the footsteps from the kitchen, join together in a painfully loud clatter. Not only that, but it's also rather dark, only lit with lamps which only offer a dim flickering light. I can see why Ro desperately wanted to avoid working down here.

The laundry department comprises ten staff members and the head of laundry, Mr. Dudley: a short, portly man who has the biggest smile yet. He praises me, calling me "Highness" nonstop after kissing my hand. I can't help but notice Hydie's disgusted expression as he does that.

I don't know why. He's perfectly polite, a little over the top maybe. Mr. Dudley does smell harshly of several different kinds of soap, slightly of dirty water, and his hands feel a bit clammy, likely as they are wet most of the day, but I don't have a problem with him. His poor uniform already has dirty water marks all over it. For some reason I rather like him.

Rather than lecture me on how important he and his staff are, he happily gives us a tour, showing us where two staff handle ironing, another four tackle folding, and two work on getting stains the washing machines miss, and the last two rush around, gathering laundry from the shoots or running about the palace collecting the laundry bins. They also man the machines, making sure laundry moves between them as quickly as possible, sorting them into the right color and type, and checking them for stains when done to hand to the stain staff.

It's a mesmerizing scene. Their movements are precise and almost rhythmic. Their dull expressions are the only things proving this isn't some kind of dance. The shuffle of their feet, the pounding of the hammers, all of it come together in an elegant pattern.

"Then I move about helping in all places. I also personally handle the things that must be hand-washed like ballgowns." Mr. Dudley beams at me. "I ensure that is done to perfection."

I smile back. "I'm sure that's a lot of work. Thank you." I really like him.

"Yes well, we have many others to see," Hydie dismisses him with a slightly haughty air and takes my arm to guide me away.

Honestly, a little disappointment drips into my chest. I'd have been happy to talk to him more. He was less uptight than the kitchen staff. He only looks sad for a second before he waves me farewell and thanks me for the half an hour I gave him. I hear him say to one of the other staff he thought I'd not stay so long for a tour.

The guilt intensifies. He thought that was plenty of time when Hydie gave the kitchen more than an hour?

I open my mouth to ask her why she pulled me away so quickly, when we re-enter the kitchens and we're accosted by Chef Cora, asking what I'd prefer for dinner.

"Uh... wh-whatever you normally like. I've never been unhappy with your meals," I stammer, surprised at how quickly she raced up to me. I am so overstimulated I can't come up with any other answer.

"Are the serving arrangements to your liking?" Mr. John asks.

"I-I wouldn't change a thing. Y-you did fine for me." I don't understand why they didn't ask this before we left.

"The princess has others to meet with. We'll make one-on-one meetings if you need." Lady Hydie smiles.

I can't help but feel they're muttering about my uncertain stammers as Hydie pulls me away to keep us on schedule. My staff won't even respect me as princess with my deer on the rails reactions to this overwhelming shock.

It is just past three, and I'm sure we have a lot more to cover, but do I really need one-on-ones with them tomorrow?

"Will there be one-on-ones with all the heads of staff?" I ask.

"Not all, of course not. You don't need to worry about *all* of them," Hydie says. "Just those you'll do the most with so they can get a sense of your style. Princesses are the hostesses, and in many ways, the real head of household. The kitchens will be one of your biggest tasks. Then, of course, the cleaning staff is big too, but I manage them, so you don't need to worry about all one hundred of them."

*That's a lot of cleaners.*

"Though I'm sure you've met them, you may want to talk to the medical staff. I don't know if Hellen can handle all your needs. Perhaps you aren't comfortable with Dr. Stephen as your main doctor. After all, with the wedding and what comes after, you may want more... specialized doctors."

I turn red at her hint.

"Oh, and we do need to have that physical done for you as well before the wedding. It's been a year since those tests." She laughs.

I hate that idea. When she brings me into the medical room, Dr. Stephen stands up from his desk, smiling. He's the miracle working doctor who saved Jake and the king's lives after being stabbed in the chest, not to mention how he helped me save Gavril's life during the first presentation attack.

"You made time for me? I can hardly believe it," Dr. Stephen teases warmly. "I'd like you to formally meet my nurses though." Dr. Stephen invites the other two over. "This is Mr. Edvard, we call him Ed, my first nurse, and Ms. Hellen, she's our second nurse."

Ed is a strong looking man with an impressive beard and smile. Hellen is strong looking too but more motherly in appearance with light red hair slightly going white on the sides.

"Nice to properly meet you." I smile. They had checked on me after the gas attack, and probably when I was ill, but I don't really remember that.

"Honor Your Highness," the lady smiles. "We hear all about you from your father of course."

My heart drops. I glance at the door that's hiding my father from view. He is still recovering from the wound I had given him. I'm not sure I'm ready to trust him yet, but part of me longs to trust him, to rush in there and feel his comfort like I used to. I could use it on this confusing day.

Maybe if I was brave, I could visit Sage, but that's still different. Besides, Zelda is likely in there with him anyway.

"We were thinking that perhaps now we have a princess that you may need—" Hydie begins to say.

"I'd rather worry about that another day. Plenty of time." I cut her off, turning pink. I'm not sure what I want for that moving forward, but I'm not ready to discuss it.

"Oh? Would you rather set up a proper meeting?" Hydie asks.

"Um... let's wait until I have a scheduling staff to worry about that." I surprise myself with how fast I come up with an excuse.

"Oh, good idea. So many you need to talk to." Hydie beams. "We certainly will need more help now we have a princess to handle these affairs."

I notice Stephen's frown of worry, but Hydie must have too because she says if I don't want to talk about it now, there are others we need to see.

"Changes?" I hear Ed ask worriedly as Hydie drags me away. I don't want to fire anyone. With our limited budget, would I have to if I wanted another woman? I know with the royal family being broke we couldn't just hire one more, but I couldn't imagine getting rid of the team Stephen likely chose. I'd seen Stephen pull off some impressive feats. I can't imagine firing him.

We then go outside to a garden house I'd never seen before. We meet a sweet older man named Ramos who's handling taking care of the very rain-soaked gardens. He looks like he could be related to the Queen with his complexion and small smile for Hydie. But the big smile he gives me is much more like the King. Maybe he's Gavril's long lost older brother. Though he's too old for that.

He is more friendly too, calling for his ten staff members to come and bow to me, ask me how I like the grounds and if I want to make any changes.

Once more, I just stammer that I think they're doing a great job. But Mr. Ramos is kind and understanding, thanking me. I manage to smile and just start to calm down, when Hydie jumps and declares we're running late, takes my wrist once more, and yanks me off.

Why is it when I'm finally feeling comfortable that we have to rush off? This time, we're meeting the stable hands. We have a surprising amount of them: ten, then Ms. Rosalind who is the head of the stables. She proudly introduces me to a horse named Starcoral, or Coral for short, who she has picked for me to learn to ride on. She also shows me the horse they acquired for Gavril named Pirate. Now we could do lessons together. That idea comforts me slightly before I'm yanked off once more.

I wonder why Hydie is in a hurry as she pulls me inside. Normally, we'd be heading to prepare for dinner around this time, so I wonder if that's why Hydie is worried about time.

Instead, she takes me back to the kitchen and puts a finger to her lips. "I just thought you'd want to see what a pre-meal rush looks like."

"I-I'd rather leave them alone to do their jobs," I confess as she opens the door as quietly as possible.

It is a madhouse, like I expected. But it's better organized than I thought, other than the yelling across the room. The team division was evident now, with some members maintaining cleanliness, six cooks preparing food, and the serving staff ensuring its presentation, while others rush up and down the stairs to the dining hall. Why does she insist I see this? Not a person in the entire kitchen is idle? The room does smell better with the scent of cooking. The sizzle of cooking food and clatter of stirring join the rest of the kitchen clatter.

"Well, that should wrap up that portion," Hydie says after a painfully long time watching the insanity. "I hope that helps give you a better idea. Tomorrow, we can go over staffing lists, get started on the wedding plans so you can set a date, and discuss positions."

"Uh," I don't have an answer.

Once more, Hydie takes my arm, leading with our arms linked like I'd often done with other Chosen girls and escorts me to my room, expressing her excitement about it all.

But once I shake her off and reach my room, I want to hide from all of them. Tomorrow would be more of this? I'm not prepared to take on running a palace on top of all the other things I was told a princess would do. And they expect me to make adjustments? It all seems fine to me. And the one I don't know how I feel about I *don't* want to think about. It was bad enough last time I had to do the full physical to get into the Enthronement. Being forced to consider it honestly makes me angry.

This wasn't what I was promised. I want to cry but not in sadness. These tears are hot. But is it really their fault I misunderstood what my duty was? Had I misunderstood what a princess was and all I'd thought I'd do isn't until I am queen and who knows when that will be?

I'm so overwhelmed and struggling to process everything, the last thing I want to do is go down and pretend to be chipper at dinner, but I have no choice. It's only day one. I can't show them that I can't handle the pressure on the first day!

I stand with my back to the door to keep Hydie out for a long time as I take in deep gulps of air. My maids only come in after I've stood away from the door.

It's like the world is in a constant state of frantic rocking until they come in. Vivian, for the first time, looks rather disheveled as I let them in.

"Sorry, we've been busy," Vivian pants. It sounds like all three have run here. I should have realized it was odd when they weren't waiting for me as they always had before.

"Makes two of us," I mutter.

All three of my maids frown. "We didn't mean that, miss," Flur says. "It's just been wild how many people have wanted our attention." The new staff were skeptical of my ability to handle my role and sought reassurance from the staff that knew me they weren't getting fired I'd bet.

"Let's get you ready." Vivian smiles warmly. "That can be normal."

I barely pay attention to how they dress me. I smile in thanks to them and head down to dinner, almost feeling guilty for how much fuss they had to go through for the meal. Being hyperaware of what's going around me with the staff, suddenly, the nearby staff table looms at the other end of the dining hall. It was like I was never truly alone.

Zelda's excited mood is in stark contrast to my frantic state. She's talking about her plans to explore Purerah more now that she's not obligated by the Enthronement and what she'll do when she gets home with Sage and how happy she is that it all worked out in the end.

Meanwhile, I'm using all my acting skills just to smile and get myself to eat. The anxiety rolling in my stomach is making it hard to want to eat a bite. I keep looking over at the staff table, which only makes the knot in my stomach worse.

All I want for that evening is to escape from the army of staff I have and get this anxiety out of my chest. But I'm not even sure how to do that at this point.

I try to retreat up the stairs after the meal, but a voice calls out to me. "Hey," Gavril catches me before I get to the staircase.

I stop, knowing I have little of a choice. Gavril is frowning before I even turn around. "Something wrong?"

"No." *Just a horrid surprise.*

Gavril's studying me. "Kascia... you don't have to hide anything anymore. You can't get kicked out now." He smiles.

But I can make him want to get rid of me.

Though I'm pretty sure Gavril can't read minds (or maybe his magic is that good), his expression drops as if he had. "You alright?" he asks again.

"Just... been a long day," I excuse.

"Well... you can do whatever you want." He smiles. "What do you want to do?"

"I have to go back to my room."

"No, you don't." Gavril smiles.

"What do you want to do?" I ask in resignation.

"Uh... I didn't have a plan." His frown deepens.

"Well, I have to be with you or—" Gavril's laugh cuts me short. I scowl a frown, annoyed. I'm not wrong. While I may have been mistaken about many things, I was not mistaken about this.

"That was the Enthronement rules. But it's over." Gavril smiles comfortingly. "This is your home now. You can do as you please."

"Not even you get to do that," I remind him.

"Well, I can now," he chuckles. "What is my family going to do? But that's beside the point. You need to talk?"

"I'm just getting used to this. It wasn't the day I expected." I hug myself.

"I guess adjusting to the game being over will take longer than I thought." Gavril comes closer to me. I don't want him to, but it'd be rude to back away.

He must have felt my reluctance because he frowns again. "What's wrong? It's been a while since you've shied away like this. You can tell me anything; you know that, right?"

"It's nothing you've done," I assure him. "I just..."

"Retreat when you're upset." Gavril nods. "I've come to figure that out. It's not my intention to force you, you know. I just want to help, remember?" He smiles. "Damian got annoyed."

I do smile at the memory. "He's not here to do that now."

"He's running errands; he didn't elaborate." Gavril shrugs. "He'll be back."

"I hope so."

"Okay, what happened today? I won't make you spend the evening with me or anything, but you're acting off. What is it?" A sliver of anger penetrates his voice.

"Going to beat up whoever hurt me?" I ask dully.

Gavril sighs in frustration. "The game's over. You don't have to impress me. You can melt, get mad, stop being perfect. If you don't want me to bug you, say so, and vene, push me away if you want. Why do you keep trying to put that broken mask back on?"

The way he says it gets to me, and the tears fill my eyes. "I didn't make this one."

"Okay. I... if you really don't want to talk, I won't make you, but seriously, you need to talk to me or tell me to go away. Don't... play secrets anymore. There's really no need." Gavril's doing his best not to be exasperated with me, but he's not doing a great job. "Think it will be easy when we share a room?" he jokes.

"Yeah, let's do that and not bother with the princess's suite." I snap.

"Uh?" Gavril's perplexed crease in his eyes and the studying dart of his eyes says how he is trying so hard to understand. "Sure? Would you please, um... explain a little more?"

Not in the hall, I can't. He notices me looking around. "Want to talk alone? That's not hard. Your room, mine, I don't care."

"I don't want to talk." I don't want to repeat all that happened today.

"Okay... do you want me to help at all? Go away? I'm dumb. I need help here."

That makes me laugh. It does break a little something in my frustration.

Gavril smiles. "I'm sorry this transition is hard. Did no one cover the fact you're not bound by any rules anymore?"

"I don't even know what they covered." I release a weary sigh. "It's been a rush of sudden realization of what this all really means."

"Ah... you weren't as prepared as you thought?" he asks.

"I... had no idea what being princess meant to the palace, I guess." I force a smile.

Gavril nods. "Want to blow off steam, then? Could play some games. Hide from the staff in my suite?"

"That sounds amazing," I confess.

Gavril smiles. "Let's go."

Spending the time with Gavril alone certainly helps me forget what a rough day it had been and makes me dread going to bed that night even more, but tomorrow would be worse if I didn't. So, I drink my tea, internally thanking the Maker for the sweet old lady who makes sure I have it each night (though I wish I used some of the time in the kitchens to meet her) and try to have good dreams about all the things I'd looked forward to about being royal and not what I was now hating.

# Chapter 3

Getting ready the next morning feels like preparing for battle with no strategy. I can't keep floundering like this. I won't survive life like this, but I don't know what else to do. *It's just until the wedding*, I tell myself, *then I'll adjust to the kind of work they'd prepared me for.* That makes it easier to keep hope and focus.

First, I have to stay firm to what I want and not let them pull me around. But how do I fulfill my duty and lay down the ground rules? This question plagues me as I get ready and throughout breakfast.

I don't know where Lady Hydie expects me to be, but I'm sure she'll find me if I'm not where she wants. The queen is all bubbles and happiness over the wedding, and she and Zelda spend most of breakfast discussing what a fun event it will be.

Gavril, on the other hand, notices I don't join in. His concerned eyes go from my silence to the others a few times. But doesn't draw attention to it. He simply takes my hand under the table, so no one notices, and keeps eating.

As I expected, the next meeting with Lady Hydie is in the Ladies' Chamber once more. I let her twitter her plans. First, we'll go over plans for the princess's suite, have a one-on-one with the head staff we need to speak to, then I can work on a short list for which of my staff I want in each position.

"Before we go into... that," I begin, unsure how this will go. "Can't we... simplify the plans a little bit?"

"Simplify? How much simpler can it get?" Lady Hydie asks.

"Well... it seems that everything has to be done *now*, but I'm sure that's not the case. Can we tackle what *needs* to be done now rather than... trying to eat the whole pie at once?" I try.

"We are, My Lady." Hydie sounds surprised. "Think I wouldn't streamline it for you? I assure you; I'm doing my best to adapt to what you're ready for."

"Of course not, but perhaps it just appears that we need to do all this first," I try again.

"Well, your room must be ready before the wedding, so we'll need a report from those who will make the changes to know when it will be, so we can pick a date. Wedding-wise, all is on hold until that is done," Hydie says with a hint of surprise. "So that will be the morning, I imagine. We looked over your options, so now we can make some choices. That will be fun." I can tell she's trying to help me enjoy this.

She sits next to me this time, still beaming. "We could always see about those designers who can choose for you. That would give them full control, but it leaves you free."

I sigh. I don't want to waste funds on that. "Can we not find... less costly ways to make this list easier?" I ask, giving a dark look at the huge list of things we need to do.

"Well... perhaps we can give some tasks to staff once you've assigned them," Hydie hesitates. "But that really is a duty for you to fulfill."

"Haven't you all done just fine without me until now?" I demand.

"Are you sure you're ready for this? Perhaps we should give you more time and training before we move forward." Hydie looks genuinely concerned for me, not judging, just feeling sorry for this commoner suddenly thrown into power.

I resent it, though. I let out a heavy breath. "No. It seems like a big ask for anyone to do so quickly." I could do this. I won for a reason, right? My confidence is slipping, and I'm doing all I can not to let it drop. I thought I was done with this.

"Well... this is an average list. Would you like to see examples? I'm sure Sir Godwin would be happy too—"

"No need for anything like that," I cut her off. "I just... never mind." There was no need for Godwin or anyone else to "save me" from this. *I can do this. I won for a reason. I can do this.* "What do we have to do first?"

She goes over color schemes, arrangements, and the like. I recall discussing options with Gavril, so I bring up some of his suggestions, but Lady Hydie seems concerned that I'm not worried about making my space my own. I should have my own bedroom, after all.

"I will. It will be our room." My frustration is mounting. She leaves me so overstimulated I can't make a choice. Then when I do, she spends the whole time questioning it.

"Of course, I was referring to your own room when you may want to get away," Hydie amends. "But of course, it's up to you. It's just that royal couples often find themselves wanting their own space, so we designed the rooms for that purpose. I'm sure the king and queen even had their times when they wanted it."

I hold back the retort. She thinks Gavril and I will be that bad? "I still think that would be the best arrangement to give me my space. If I'm stuck in my room for a long time again, it has all I need in one place."

"Just not a space to yourself," Hydie almost mutters it, but doesn't argue it again.

"I do have space for myself," I insist.

"I suppose." Hydie frowns. "But it's up to you. Just... be ready, I suppose." She gives me a winning smile.

But that's more than enough for me. I'm ready to scream. "You're that sure we're going to fight on our wedding night, so I'll want my own room?" I let slip.

"Of course not!" Hydie gasps in horror. "It's about more than the one night though, of course."

I'm done. I'm going to lose my temper like I did after Dahlia tried to blame me for the Japcharian fiasco.

"If you think you know what to do better than me, do it yourself," I snap, shoving the books and notes and whatever else at her as I stand up.

"Oh, I'd never presume to know what you'd like better than you. This is your home. This is your only chance to make it exactly what you need. I said if you like that better, then do it. I just think you may want your own retreat, that's all." Hydie's eyes are wide in surprise as she gapes up at me. She'd clearly missed my frustration.

"Maybe you should have joined the Enthronement. You seem to know the job better than any of us did." I shove the endless papers away from me as I turn to leave.

"Your Highness, please—"

"I'm not princess yet!" I snap. "Just do whatever you want." I turn for the door.

"My Lady," Hydie jumps up, a bit panicked now.

I ignore her and leave the room, slamming the door behind me. I ignore anyone between me and where I'm going. Making my way down the stairs, through the entrance hall, I finally step out through the front doors.

I expect guards to stop me, but they don't. Perhaps even they can sense now is not the time to mess with me. I'm getting out, and I'm tired of letting people stop me. I thought once I won, having to cave in and play the part was over. But everyone seems to know better than me. If they all know better, then why not do it themselves? What do they need their precious winner for?

Shielding myself from the chilly breeze by crossing my arms, I turn right and head to the beach, passing through the rose garden and other stunning sights that are beginning to bloom into spring. Finding a rock to sit on not too far from the surf, I sit on it, resting my chin on my arms that rest on my knees, ignoring the hint of more rain in the air.

I let my eyes rest just above my arms as they almost glare out over the ocean's gray waves in the cloudy morning.

This was not what I had been prepared for. Even less than what I'd wanted. I understood I would play the role of hostess often, but... at the moment, being princess feels like a glorified head of household.

I was never the backstage girl. I wore the dress and used the sets; I was a dancer, an actress. I took action, not... planning and preparing like this. I didn't sell the life I'd wanted at least three times to become a glorified party planner. I signed on to help my people as princess and marry the one I loved, not just be bound to a coworker.

And that thought makes me angry. I feel lied to. Being royal wasn't what they taught us in lessons. It wasn't what my father or Jake or the rest of us expected. And I was sure I'd understood it after seeing the struggle of the surrounding royals I cared for. Not this. I was lied to again. Again! Just like Father lied to me about everything. This is not what I was promised.

I fight hot tears. I hate that I'm an angry crier. As I watch the waves, I try to hold back the hot tears. A few animals jump out of the waterway out to sea. I don't recognize what they are, but I'm sure Gavril would. The thought of his smile and light in his eyes as he'd tell me brings a little light to my heart and a soft smile to my lips.

Would that little spark go away, like Hydie insisted it would, so fast? I'm being told trusting in a good relationship is foolish. Maybe they're right. I'd fought with Gavril, sure. We had differences, and there are things about him that drive me crazy, but the joy is worth it. Maybe once real royal duties set in, I would do anything to get away from him.

I don't want that to be the reward I fought for. This isn't what I'd disciplined myself for. This is not what I'd changed my mind, heart, and soul for. And I can't let them change it or take it again.

But how do I stop them from changing my role? I am in power, but I also am not. Not yet. And even if I was, I see how those higher than me keep Gavril under control.

I can't give up now, but I'm at a loss for what to do. What if I'm not good enough for this? What if I really am going to let Gavril down? I gave in to save his life. Was that a mistake? Not saving his life, but giving in. I could have gone back to my old life once the dark magic was gone, and he healed.

It's not the answer I want. I trust him. I won for a reason, right?

Perhaps I just have to persevere until I am crowned. And that still makes me angry and feel weak and powerless. But it won't be too long. I still have the win. I just have to hold on a bit longer until I can receive the power, the literal crown.

I frown a bit and abruptly get up, brushing the sand from my skirt and head directly to my room, which is mercifully empty.

I pick up the tiara and look at it, shining in the dim light. It is beautiful. A rare blue pearl rests at its crest with sapphires and some pale, teal-green gems in a beautiful, flowing wave pattern. It's not as heavy as I would have expected. I study it, thinking about how hard I worked for this.

I overcome my own anxieties and delicately place it on my head. It fits perfectly. I don't have to adjust my position at all to ensure it stays secure. It's not even as heavy as I thought it would be.

Then why is all this so hard so soon? I turn and look at the room that soon won't be mine. I had questioned my fate so many times in this room, and though I thought I never would again, here I am. And that sets my heart ablaze. I will not be bullied anymore. I am going to save myself.

Placing the tiara back on the desk, I am determined this time not to fear my temper but to use it to get free of all of this.

Maybe I am not what they wanted. But I am what they got. And I have to conquer this like I had everything else. The only doubt that wiggles in my chest is I don't know how.

I try not to let on during lunch. I excuse myself sooner than necessary by stating that I have a lot of planning to do.

"You need help?" Gavril asks when I don't pause to let him kiss my cheek or anything, as he normally does before he got up.

"You have more important things to do." I smile. And that would look great. I need his help to do what *I'm* supposed to do.

"Okay. But if you really feel you need it, just ask," Gavril says. "Don't want to neglect you, either."

"Who said you were?" I smile before turning out the door.

"Well, no one, sorry. I'll see you at dinner then," Gavril says as I step out the door, sounding a bit uncertain.

"She's just trying to find her own. It's not against you." I hear the queen soothe her son. Well, that is true. It isn't him. I just have to find my power without relying on him or anyone else.

But it is pointless. I still can't find Hydie. Angry, frustrated, and fighting not to feel defeated, my feet guide me and take me somewhere I don't expect. I'm standing in front of the laundry room door. I don't know what I expect to do here, but I step inside, choosing to trust whatever instinct I have that brought me here.

"Your Highness." They all jump to attention to see me, all in surprise.

Mr. Dudley, though, is over the moon excited. "What can we do for you?" he asks, bowing to me and even kissing my hand.

"I... I don't know," I admit. "I just..." I smile a little. "Liked visiting before."

I don't know if I could have said or done anything to make him look happier. I can't help but smile wider at how his muddy brown eyes widen and light up. "Want to see how it works?"

"What works?" I ask in honest curiosity.

"I didn't show you the line," he says. "Do you want to—"

"Yes," I say before he can finish.

He laughs in delight and goes over to the long wall with buckets full of dirty laundry. Many of them are lined up by the laundry chutes that deliver some laundry. Other piles of laundry are clearly hand-delivered by the neater and far more organized piles they were in compared to the crumpled heaps of those tossed down a shoot. Some baskets had straps that the workers would use to strap them to their backs. I picture Godwin doing that. Reinold would likely have fun trying to toss crumpled shirts into it.

"Ah! Here's a fun one." Mr. Dudley finds one of the ballgowns on a hook that Damian had made me, needing to be washed.

I spend the afternoon watching in honest interest as he shows me how he uses some non-water solvents (whatever that means) and unique techniques like pounding to get spots out of the delicate dresses. Something about seeing the work helps soothe me, and the innocent and unpretentious behavior of Mr. Dudley is a breath of fresh air. Unlike everyone else, he has no ulterior motives.

"Ready for the princess to wear again." He beams at me as he puts it into a garment bag for my maids to fetch later.

"How can you be so happy down here?" It's dark and depressing.

"I enjoy taking care of my people and taking pride in my work. You can see what we do. You can measure it. It's not shallow or intangible," he explains. "The kitchens may think they're the best, but what they do is the same every day. My tasks can be a challenge. A dress with more gems may take a different angle entirely or need a tricky repair. I like what I do. Even if everyone thinks it's easy."

"It's not easy to stay cheerful down here. Are you too deep for a window?" I ask. Even the kitchens have windows.

Mr. Dudley shrugs. "I never asked."

My expression turns into a frown. I wish I could make it better. Anything to make it brighter. "Your work is valuable. They shouldn't treat your work any differently." Perhaps that's why I felt drawn here.

I too feel like I have much to give and am being ignored for not being what they want.

Perhaps I can change that. Perhaps that's why Hydie had shown me around, to try to fix the inequality in the castle staff before I tried on the larger kingdom. It wasn't her plan but fate's.

"Maybe not. But I doubt any clothes would come out cleaner and better than after we work on it." Mr. Dudley smiles at me. "We make them better than anyone else could."

I return it. "Well, I better get to dinner." I sigh. "Thank you for showing me."

"The princess just gave us the afternoon. It's us who thank you." He waves happily as I leave. I chuckle and wave back before I hurry to my room to change. Never before have I admired the softness and clean smell of the dinner gown as much as I do now. I am proud to receive his work.

But the anger returns in a rush as I go down to dinner and hear a worried Lady Hydie's voice. "I've looked all day. If we don't find her, the prince is going to make sure we're *all* fired instead of just a few."

So that's what's going on. Unknown to me, I have to make staff cuts once in power, and they all are trying to be needed. I may have to choose who goes or stays. I assume they recruited extra staff for the Enthronement. As princess, I have the responsibility to choose who stays. That's not what I signed up for or agreed to.

I do my best to hide my hurt and frustration at the dreaded task that will soon be mine and how much it crushes my spirit. How could I dismiss someone when I am fully aware of the challenges of finding a job these days?

I force a smile for my new family as I join them at the table.

"There you are." Gavril smiles and kisses my cheek as I sit down. "You smell good."

"What?" I hadn't put on perfume or anything.

"You smell like some kind of new soap. Trying something new?" he asks. I smile. I must smell of the rose solvent Mr. Dudley let me pick for the dress he was cleaning.

"This life is pretty new." And not what I'd expected.

"Guess not." Gavril chuckles. "Long day?"

I sigh. "You have no idea." And I have no idea how I'll handle it tomorrow.

I try to be part of the conversation at dinner to help pick up my spirits, but it doesn't work very well, and I'm quieter than I wanted to be. Gavril takes hold of my hand under the table, which helps, but I want to be good at this without help. I'm not sure how to balance that.

As we all go our own ways for the evening, Gavril catches up to me again. "Sure you're okay?" he asks quietly, in case anyone is listening.

"I'm fine." I lie.

Gavril frowns a bit. "You sure?"

"Would you all stop questioning everything I say?" I give him a bit of a glare that deep down, I know he doesn't deserve. He's not who I'm angry at.

Gavril pauses. "I'm sorry. You just don't seem okay, and that reply honestly makes me sure you're not. Kascia, you were off yesterday too. What's going on?"

"So, I'm the problem?"

"No." Gavril frowns deeper. "I never said that. I just said you seemed off. What's going on?"

"Nothing," I insist.

"Kascia, we don't have any secrets anymore. You can't be eliminated. You can be honest. No need to put up a front with me or anyone," Gavril reminds me gently.

"Who said I was?"

"You're not acting like you."

"If I was putting on a front, how would you know?" I demand.

"I-I didn't say that either." Gavril frowns, hurt and confused. "D-did I do something wrong?"

"No." I turn away. It isn't really his fault. "Figure anything out with what's next yet?" Maybe having that will help me solve all this mess in my head and shut up the doubts in my heart.

Gavril's brows draw in confusion. "For the kingdom? Not exactly... mostly been working with the state and the court... Kascia, what happened?" he asks, concern and confusion still in his tone.

"Nothing." And that's the problem. I got nothing done today. I should have been more productive to complete the wedding tasks, but instead, I spent time making footprints in the sand, washed away by now, and observing how a dress is cleaned, which was irrelevant to my duties.

"Should... were you expecting me or something?" Gavril asks, still more confused.

"No. I told you. Nothing happened. I'm sorry. I just should have done something." I shake my head. "I should make up for it." Rising on my tiptoes, I give him a kiss on the cheek and then turn to go, recognizing the need to make up for my display of anger today. That would help me feel better.

This is why I fight so hard not to get angry. I was never very good at handling it.

"Wh— wait." I think Gavril stammers, but it's hard to tell with how he's stumbling over his words as I turn and go to get to work. I have to prove I can do this, even if it's not what I signed up for and I am bad at it. If I have to do this before I get what I want, fine. I can prove to be exactly what they want and more.

I go right up the stairs, but don't go to my room. I go to the princess's suite and take in what's there and make choices on what to do. I hate to give in on this, but I do agree to at least install a bed in the main bedroom, which we were converting into my study, so that my current study can be turned into my dance studio. Gavril had suggested that first. And I liked it and trust him. Then at least I'll have the space to "get away" like Hydie insists I'll need. Then I'll prove I'm not stupid or naïve and still get what I want, at least. And I am going to make changes to the staff like they expect, just not the ones they're hoping for.

# Chapter 4

Upon waking up, my determination is to stand firm and to change how the staff view each other. I can do this. I have to. With great determination, I struggle to hold back the hot tears as I contemplate it. I hate being a crier.

My maids set about their work, once more apologizing for not being around. "We're keeping the court and others at bay who want your attention. With Damian busy, they come to us instead," Vivian explains.

"But call us if you need us, please," Flur reminds me.

"I will." I don't know what I'd need them for, though, but I do know I can count on them.

Once I'm dressed and ready for the day, I go down to breakfast, full of determination to not let them run me over. The others are there before me, as seems to happen most of the time.

"See? Told you all is fine." The queen smiles at Gavril, who is standing and turns mid pace to face me, his brows drawn in worry, perhaps wondering why I am taking so long. Perhaps in my mood, I had taken longer than normal.

Gavril gives me a smile when he sees me, but it's not as open as it had been the last few days. He pulls out my chair for me and pushes it in, but he hesitates before kissing my cheek, kissing my head instead. I smile at first, but as Gavril sits down, that strikes me as odd.

I give him a sideways look as he settles into his seat and starts to eat. He hadn't touched it until I'd arrived. I think he had begun his meals before I arrived in the past... perhaps I just hadn't noticed until now. He reaches for my hand and squeezes it under the table like usual, but even that feels tentative after his hesitation for intimacy before.

I look at him again after he pulls his hand back, but the fact he doesn't look at me seems odd as well. Maybe I'm just oversensitive because I'm fighting to prove I'm not rattled. But Gavril is quieter than normal, too.

When he's first to get up, despite having started on his meal last, I get up, not caring about my unfinished food, pretending I'm done. I take his hand to go out into the hall.

"You... you busy?" I ask, stealing a cautious glance at him from the corner of my eye.

"I have an about average day." Gavril looks at me much the same way I glance at him. "Something wrong?"

"I was hoping for a moment."

"Anything." He nods towards his office, and I don't mind at all.

Godwin looks up as we enter from the front that passes through Godwin's office, or maybe the reception room is a better name for it. Though Godwin's desk and files are in use, there are also chairs for visitors to wait.

A hint of surprise crosses Godwin's eyes to see me enter with the prince. "On hold?" he asks Gavril. Gavril nods firmly. "Very good." Godwin nods and opens the office door for us, smiling at me and bowing his head as we step into the office.

The room is lit with the natural light reflected from the light dome, which is the pride of the palace design. When I first saw the room, the shutter was closed tightly over the light, but Gavril has kept it open ever since. I'm sure the open feeling comforts him.

Once inside, Gavril lets go of my hand and turns to me as Godwin secures the door behind us. "What is it?" he asks gently.

"Are you alright?" I ask.

"Why wouldn't I be?"

"You... seemed off at breakfast," I admit. "Perhaps I'm reading too much into it, but... you didn't seem yourself."

"Hm, yet when I say that to you—" I miss the rest of what he says as it strikes me like a ball to the face. Now I look back. I had been rather abrupt with him last night. Sure, I was open and honest about what bothered me, but that still might have been abrasive, even if I didn't see it at the time.

"Oh Gavril, I'm so sorry. I didn't realize... without context, I suppose it was just a confusing mess." An aching guilt writhes in my stomach like battling snakes.

"At the time, I thought I was being open and honest. I really was complaining at you more than venting, I suppose. Without context..." I pause. "I shouldn't have been so abrupt."

Gavril smiles a little. "I understand you're under a lot of pressure. I don't blame you in the slightest."

"But it still hurt you." I'm not stupid. Even if his mother and Zelda missed it, I still see it. I had accidentally hurt him by not explaining and simply complaining. "And I didn't mean that at all. I should have seen it in the moment. Being under a lot of pressure is not an excuse. I'm sorry. I will try not to do that again." Determination fills me once more. "But I have it handled now, so it won't."

"Can... can I ask what happened?" Gavril asks tentatively.

I give him a sad smile. "Of course you can. I didn't realize... I wanted to just forget it the first day, and last night... I almost forgot you're not like Damian and just know everything." Gavril laughs. "I'm so sorry. I should have explained. You deserve better than that from me."

"Kascia, really, it's not you that hurt me or really upset me," Gavril assures. "I was fine letting you remain silent the other night because I knew you didn't want to talk. I thought perhaps it was a mistake with how you seemed worse yesterday and pushed you too hard in chasing you, perhaps."

"But I hurt you. I really hurt you." I frown. It is clear to see in his stiffness at breakfast and the furtive frown and crease in his eyes. "What did I do? It's deeper than just being snippy with you, isn't it?"

"I'm—"

"Please be honest," I gently beg. "I can take it. I know I hurt you. I want to know how badly."

"Kascia, as I said, it wasn't really you," he says slowly.

"Then what was it?" I plead.

Gavril lets out a heavy sigh. "I just expected for a small moment, even if it was just a day or two, it would feel as good as I expected. We'd get a reprieve. I suppose a honeymoon from the Enthronement, at least, you know? The happiness of the game being over and finally being engaged to who I love most, and we'd get to enjoy the success for even just a moment. But... that's not what happened. I shouldn't have expected one moment to just fix everything between us like that. I was angry; I didn't get it. I was hurt; I knew it might never happen. We still have to take the time to fix the habits built by a contest like the Enthronement. I resent it."

"Me too." I'd thought almost those exact things yesterday on the beach. "I knew I'd be busy, but... this." Tears fill my eyes, and it feels good to let them out. "This completely blindsided me." Oh, to safely release the frustration and anger with someone who feels the same.

Gavril's frown deepens. "Kascia... are you alright?"

"I... I don't know," I say, surprised that I really don't know the answer. "I think I feel the exact same as you."

Gavril's face falls, and he hugs me tightly. "I love you," he whispers, and I latch onto it. I need to feel that right now. It would have been foolish of me not to. I suppose I spent the evening with him the first night, but it's still different.

"I want to be good at this," I almost squeak out. "I *need* to be good at this. I can't let you, them, or the prophecy down. I thought I was going to be able to handle this. The fact I'm so confused and lost... I must be good at this," I say desperately.

"Kascia, you are. How can you doubt again?" There's nothing but love and compassion in his question, though.

"That's just it. I don't, but at the same time... I trust you. I chose it. So why am I questioning it?" With my eyes shining, I gaze up at him. "I don't understand why the doubts keep coming. I thought... I really thought I was going to be good at this. Not that it would be easy, but I'd be good at it at least, and I'm not."

"Why do you think that?" Gavril asks me, leading me to sit on the loveseat that's along the wall beside the door we'd entered from.

I tell him everything. What frustrated me, the stupid doubts, the annoyance that they kept coming up when they shouldn't, the determination, all of it. "I can do this. I have to. I must be the one." Tears fill my eyes again. "I have to be. I want to be so badly... I can't let you down. I can't let them down. I want it so badly." The desire burns inside my chest and the uncertainty I can makes my heart ache with the acid-like desire.

"Kascia, you don't have to fight for it. You have it already," Gavril assures, stroking my cheek. "It may not feel like that. And as we both are painfully feeling the pressure, just because I put a tiara on your head doesn't make all the past and habits go away. It doesn't magically go away when you get what you want. I think we both have to accept that. You'll get there. It's alright to stumble and to be unsure. You've doubted for over a year, perhaps longer. It will take time. I'm just sorry it has to hurt so badly to be disappointed. We both got that slap."

I sniffle slightly, then hug him tightly. "I didn't mean for you to feel it like... like that." I'm ashamed of such a big misstep, but at least I can catch it, talk to him, work it out anyway.

"I know. It's alright. I don't blame you." Gavril stiffens a little, the way he does when he gets angry and tries to restrain it. "I have others I might blame."

"Don't." I sigh and pull back a little. "They already are so afraid of being fired."

"Excuse me?"

"They're just trying to help me and keep their jobs because it's so hard to get one out there," I say, a sudden firmness coming to my voice. "You can't fire them." I have other plans.

"I didn't say I was going to, even if I wanted to," Gavril mutters the last bit. "But," he takes in a deep breath through his nose, trying to keep calm, I suspect, "that's not her job. She shouldn't be dragging you around the palace, questioning you. She's not your advisor. She's just the only person we have who can help plan an event like this, and it sounds like she wants you to do it all."

"She's just trying to make sure it's all exactly as I like." In the hope I'd keep her, I suppose.

"Doesn't matter! Not if she's instead slowly stripping you of your confidence," Gavril snarls. "We need your new attendant as soon as possible. We need that buffer." And to my surprise, Gavril stands up.

"Where are you going?" I stand too.

"I need to check the status of—"

He's cut off by a knock on the door. Godwin steps in. "Pardon, Your Highness, but I have Miss—"

Someone pushes past Godwin, and a petite, rich-toned girl steps in. I normally see her assisting Hydie. "Lady Kascia, we've been worried. We're ready to get started. Lady Hydie sent me to fetch you."

"She can wait," I say firmly. I have to take care of my husband-to-be first. Hydie could wait.

"But My Lady, we don't have a lot of time to—"

"I'm busy at the moment. She can wait her turn," I say stubbornly. "You can tell her I'll be with her when I'm done."

"But my—"

"I'll be with her when I'm done." I give her a firm look. "I will go when I'm ready."

"Lady Hydie will—"

"She will wait," I say deliberately and slowly, not backing down. "She can handle what she can in the meantime, but I have more important things to take care of right now. You will await me. Now go and tell Lady Hydie that this instant."

"But..." The girl looks stunned. "There's much..."

"I will attend to her in time," I say with a bit of an order in my voice. "You will tell her you found me. I'm busy and will be there when I'm done."

"Yes, My Lady." The girl curtsies to me and leaves. Godwin looks annoyed as he closes the door. I think I hear him telling her off for pushing past him.

A happy bubble of delight in myself rises in my chest. That was easy, easier than I thought it would be. I can do this. I proved it to myself, and that's all that matters.

I turn back to Gavril, expecting him to be proud or impressed. But he just smiles normally. "Well?" I try to get it out of him.

"Well, what?"

"Are you impressed?"

"Why would I be?" Gavril chuckles a little.

"I... I just gave her an order." I deflate a slightly.

"And?" Gavril is still smiling in amusement at my little bubble of pride.

"And I was struggling to order them around before." I frown.

Gavril blinks. "Why?" He sounds a bit dangerous.

I sigh. "Please, Gavril, don't do anything to them. I didn't know what I was doing with the surprise of the changes in what was happening. Having to follow the staff's orders to stay in the game, I became accustomed to trusting them. I know better now, so please don't rip their heads off for it.

"I'm done with that. I thought I'd never be sure enough to know how to do that." I can't stop myself from smiling again. "But that wasn't so bad." I am really proud of myself.

Gavril smiles gently. "Of course, it wasn't. You have this. You can do this." He steps forward and takes my hands in his. "Sorry I'm not as excited as you, but that is just the command of royalty that you've always had. You'll use that often. You've seen me do it plenty."

"I suppose I have." I smile, searching his eyes. He genuinely seems better, the normal light back in his eyes, and that makes a new bubble of happiness rise in my chest. With him still holding my hands, I reach up and kiss him.

He latches onto it, kissing me back and wrapping his fingers at the base of my neck. We both sigh in contentment, happy to be hiding here in each other once more. "I love you," I whisper between our long, intent kisses.

"It's so good to hear you finally say it." Gavril smiles, and with a low kind of growl in his voice I greatly enjoy, we resume our kissing.

I put my arms around his neck, letting my body curve with his as we fall into our slow, intent rhythm with one another. This is the man I'll spend the rest of my life with, and that is the best feeling in the world. I truly do love him, his temper and passion, his keen observation, how he adores me. I love him, mind, body, and soul.

A knock interrupts our happy moment. Whoever it is doesn't enter right away this time though, forcing me to slide back down to let Gavril give the knocker permission to enter.

Godwin steps in. "Sorry if it's a bad time, but I have about three appointments backed up now." Then he looks at us. "Never mind, I *should* have barged in."

I giggle as Gavril sighs in annoyance. "You can send them in order in a moment."

"Yes sir." Godwin bows and steps back out.

"I should let you get to your work." I sigh and straighten out Gavril's waistcoat and jacket across his chest.

"And it sounds like you have to calm Hydie." Gavril sighs too and gives me one more kiss before pulling his arms out from around me. "You'll be okay?"

I smile and nod. "I have this."

"Good. I'll see you at lunch." He kisses my forehead. "Feel free to leave out of your office instead of the front entrance."

The lady's chamber is vastly different from the day before when I walk in. It's cluttered. Instead of having a long table with tons of papers on it, someone has placed a sofa on the left-hand side of the room, facing the long side. There are boxes, rolling racks, and covered display easels all around the room.

I frown a bit and look around. "What is...?"

"Your Highness!" Hydie almost squeaks, relieved and happy to see me. "I was so worried. I'm glad all is well. We are falling behind, but that's alright; we'll help you." She beams that smile. "I'm glad you've finally arrived. I didn't mean to overwhelm you so much," Hydie apologizes to me. "So, I thought we'd take a lot of it off your shoulders."

"And how—"

An excited woman comes up next to Hydie, beaming. I notice the other staff in the room do the same, getting into positions as if getting ready to present. They aren't wearing the castle staff uniforms.

The woman introduces herself as Madam Adelinda, a master wedding planner. I frown slightly. I wanted to prove I could do this myself.

Hydie is still beaming though. She explains she thought it would help lessen the pressure on me, and Madam Adelinda had volunteered and seemed the best match.

I cannot dismiss the woman out of my foolish pride, so I accept it. Though I quickly realize this woman's real job is more like taking Hydie's job.

Madam Adelinda takes me step by step through what choices I need to make for her to prepare for the wedding, showing me her ideas for theme, decoration, and so forth. It's a million times more helpful than Hydie just tossing the list at me.

It doesn't take long for her ideas to spark a mix of themes into my mind, which I try to explain to her. She thinks she understands them and asks for a moment to prepare a few mockups to check she understood me correctly.

Hydie looks greatly relieved as I turn to her, letting Madam Adelinda work.

Hydie helps me make a list for all those who should be in my bridal party. This I'd totally forgotten about. I expected a secret wedding until the Enthronement, so I hadn't considered such a thought.

To my relief, the girls who I wanted in the party perfectly fill it up. Hydie questions my three maids about being in the party, but I hold firm. It's the least honor I can give them for all they've done. I want them there in my party. Though I'm unsure if some of the former Chosen who I'd like to ask will want to be part of the party. I can only hope, I suppose.

"If you're ready," Madame Adelinda calls, having finished her mockups.

I get up and go back to the sofa. When she shows them to me, my mouth drops open. It's perfect!

She'd used gold and sand-colored decorative pieces; the flowers are coral red, purple, and Purerahian blue, working together perfectly in a way I didn't expect to look good, but choosing the coral red made all the difference rather than deep rose red, even though they are so close in color.

The dress options are either dark lavender, teal, or coral red. The men's suits are sand gold and white with either of the three colors as neckties.

But it's her quick watercolor of the ballroom that takes my breath away. I can't decide if it looks like the stunning night sky Gavril showed me on our stargazing date with the way the star-like lights work together, streaking the darkness with its most brilliant blues, purples, and pinks, or if it's an underwater scene with the hints of the teal, purple, and coral red decorations bringing a real coral reef to my mind.

"It's stunning." I finally manage to say, then smile. It's perfect. It's us.

Madame Adelinda is thrilled to pieces at my praise. "Then that is what we'll use. We'll make designs and show them to you to approve. Most of the time, I'll try to show you two or three options and you can choose between them. Hmm," the madam looks at her sketches, "this might be one of the most beautiful and unique themes I've done. I approve."

Hydie, on the other hand, appears to be in shock. "You're sure?" she asks. "That's... it? You chose a theme?"

I smile and nod. "Yes. I'm sure Gavril would like it, and I know I do."

"Excellent." Hydie sounds pleasantly surprised. "Excellent indeed." She laughs happily.

"Well, I believe you have an appointment in your room before lunch." Hydie smiles at me. "And we'll work on this here."

"And after lunch?" I frown a bit.

"I'm not sure. Your staff will let me know," Hydie assures me and waves me off.

That seems odd, but I go up to my room nervous, but also a bit glad that at least I could work without fighting Hydie the whole time.

# Chapter 5

I step into my room, and my maids are there, smiling. Why do I feel like they are about to bomb me with a surprise? Do I want this surprise?

A few moments later, the door opens behind me, and I hear a very familiar voice. "Good afternoon, ladies."

I gasp and turn around, a smile splitting my face. "Damian?"

It's him! Looking no less than perfect, as usual. Damian's smile matches my own as his emerald eyes beam at me. "Hello, Kascia."

"I thought I wouldn't see you until the wedding." I rush forward and hug him.

He accepts my hug and holds me tight for a moment. "And miss all the fun?" he says with a smile in his voice.

"No, you didn't miss any fun." I smile as I pull back to look at him. "Where have you been? Can I ask?"

"But of course." He beams with a bit of a wink. "This may be the easiest way to put it. I believe we are both painfully aware that my time here is coming to a close. But I can't have you short staffed simply because my unique situation puts you in a tight spot, so I've been out and about interviewing to find you a replacement."

"Oh." I blink in surprise. "Thanks, that takes a load off," I confess. Damian would find the best person.

"I hope so." He smiles a little. "And... I believe I have found just the person. I have her on good recommendation, and I've already cleared it with Prince Gavril, but you have the final say. Would you like to meet her?" A soft smile rests on his lips as his eyes glisten with hope and a subtle excitement.

"Yes, of course." I'm caught even more by surprise. I hope meeting her will be as good as seeing him.

"Flur, if you wouldn't mind bringing her in. She's waiting in the hall," Damian says.

Flur bows her head and goes to the door. I wait, nervous but hopeful. I have no idea who he would have gotten or if I even know them. The knot drops into pure shock when Flur stands back with the door open, and the woman steps in. I look at Damian, mouth agape. It can't be.

Damian grins at my reaction as he raises his arm to present her to me. "Princess Kascia, meet your new assistant, Lady Bella."

I can scarcely suppress the happy bubble. I beam and rush forward to embrace Bella. She laughs as she hugs me back, surprised but undeniably happy. "And I thought the competition coming to stay might annoy you," she teases.

Of course, she is the obvious choice. She sewed many of her own stunning dresses, often only outdone by Damian's work. She had always wanted to steal Damian's notebook, and she had been so protective of me even as a competitor.

"I can't believe you said yes," I say as I pull back. She looks great: her black hair pulled back, her smile big, and she just seems... freer, happier. I can't put my finger on it. Her dark blue eyes are shining in excitement against her dark hair, but her smile is still the brightest thing she wears. "I don't know if I could have come back after losing."

Bella waves it off. "I had time to get over it. Clearly, it was not meant to be. I'm so excited. I was afraid you'd not want me."

"Of course, I'd want you!" Why wouldn't I?

Damian chuckles and claps his hands together. "I take it you approve then?"

"Yes. Absolutely yes." I beam at him. "You always know best," I joke.

"I could hardly believe he came in person to offer." Bella grins at Damian. "I'm honored, humbled, and so excited. Your look will go down in history."

Damian chuckles warmly. "That's all set then. Bella already has her room, and the rest of her belongings will arrive shortly," he assures her, then turns back to me. "I'll be instructing Bella periodically until I leave. She and I took the morning to start working and get acquainted with the new staff, but I want to arrange an afternoon where you can meet them properly." He smiles. "Once we settle that, I'll be spending much of my time behind the scenes as we work on preparations. With Bella's help, of course. You can help me finalize the designs for the coronation dress." He smiles at Bella.

"Really?" Bella's eyes light up further in excitement.

"Absolutely. Who knows, a fresh perspective may make it even better." Damian smiles.

"Thank you, Damian." I smile gently. The idea he'll handle the minor stuff I'm overwhelmed by... "So, you've seen the list?"

"I have." He nods. "And Hydie wanted me to give you your list for the remainder of the day." He extends the paper towards me.

"Oh." I eye it nervously but take it. Bella frowns behind me and looks at Damian. I notice the list is not as thick, and when I get a look at it, I notice it's not the same list. It's far too short. "You... got this from Hydie?"

He grins. "Technically, no. But she did give me *a* list, and I took the liberty of removing some of the more menial tasks for you. She also noted that there was a disagreement about the princess suite that needed to be resolved." He frowns. "But we can discuss that if and when you have the time."

I frown and nod. "Yeah... I took care of that and left notes in the room for the workers." Then I figure I should fully confess. "Hydie hired a wedding planner, so... guess that handles part of it."

"Oh. That will help, as I've not planned a wedding in two thousand years," he chuckles. "And if the queen inquires, inform her that the expenses are taken care of." He gives me that gentle, reassuring smile.

I relax a little. "Thanks." Even if I still feel guilty about that. "At least that isn't a problem." Bella seems confused. I'm sure she doesn't know yet. "There is a lot to fix. Sorry, so much of it falls to you."

Damian smiles gently. "I highly doubt it falls on me, My Lady. But I will help you bear the burden and ease it where I can. Though... perhaps you can answer a question for me. Why did Hydie fill your afternoon with individual appointments with the kitchen staff?"

"What? Individual?" I frown. "I met with them as a group the other day." And my annoyance at the reminder tinges my voice.

"So I heard. On the list she gave me, she had a list of one-on-one appointments for you to get through. You may have noticed I removed them all from the one I gave you, but it does make me curious."

"She... was hoping knowing the staff I was ordering about would help me calm down. And... trying to save jobs, I suspect," I confess. "Guess I'll have to start cutting staff soon."

"Honestly, that is ultimately up to the king and queen, a discussion you and Gavril will take part in, I'm sure. In which case, I suspect that much like with the courtiers, they are hoping by buttering up to you, you'll put in a good word for them. But that's politics, I'm afraid: truly, a beast." He rolls his eyes and shakes his head. "And this is why I went into the theatre."

"Well, I had no idea and thought it was important, so... I went along with it." I look down. I was supposed to be good at this and reading this stuff.

Damian smiles, then puts his knuckle under my chin to get me to look at him. I meet his emerald eyes with my own. "Hey, it was your first day, and I'm sure you had a very different image of how it would go. They took advantage of that. Anyone would be overwhelmed. What happened is on them, not on you. And even so, one day does not a failure make. You only fail when you give up."

"I'm not giving up," I say stubbornly. "I won for a reason."

"Yes, you did." Damian smiles and pulls back. "But I'm sure you're hungry, and it is almost lunch."

"Oh, right." I almost forgot.

Bella beams at me. "Don't worry. We'll have this for you." She still is as excited as ever. "Do we need to meet up later?" Bella looks at Damian.

"Well... how did your meeting with the wedding planner go?" Damian asks.

"We got a theme going, and they're working on it," I express candidly. "I'm sure there's a lot more to do though... just not what I'm familiar with."

"I'll talk to her and set up your next appointment," Bella assures me.

"Brilliant. Shall we meet you here after lunch?" Damian smiles at her and looks at me as if for approval.

"Of course." I smile.

"I'll handle my end and meet you here." Bella smiles. I notice she sneaks glances at my maids. She must think she should get to know them, and if they had lunch here, that would be perfect.

Damian leaves her to it and turns to me, offering me his arm. "Shall we get you to the dining hall?"

I beam, happy to be escorted by Damian and accept his arm. "Let's." I missed him more than I realized. As Bella begins talking with my maids, Damian leads me out into the hall.

"Thank you," I say once we're alone. "Surprised it took you so long," I tease.

"You are, of course, welcome." Damian gives me a warm smile. "And I had to help her pack and make sure she got here safely."

"I see." I smile again. "Thought you'd just hide in the back until I called for you or you had to say goodbye."

He chuckles. "I'd never do that. You're more than a job to me, Kascia. And regardless, I don't leave things half done." Damian smiles gently. "During this transition period, I know you need me now more than ever, so I won't be going anywhere until after the coronation."

"Whenever that is." Dread for him leaving mixes with the joyous anticipation of my wedding. "I wish I'd done better on my own. I did a pretty bad job."

He gives me a sympathetic look, our footsteps providing a background rhythm. "That's how everything feels at the start. Hydie certainly did not help, but I have every confidence in you, night angel."

"Everyone seems to, and they should, but I still slipped." I let out a deep sigh. "And I know I shouldn't... but..."

"But what?" He tilts his head.

"I do," I confess.

"We all do. It's a natural part of life," Damian says with tenderness as he watches me. "Life is filled with hills and valleys. The valleys can be dark, and it feels like you'll never see the light over the hill. It gets worse after you have been on a hill and fall back into the valley. But you are not horrible because you fell. Nor are you any less of a person because the darkness of the valley blinds you to the path out. Sometimes we just have to hold on to what we know and feel our way through the darkness. But you don't have to do it alone. We have each other to lean on and support us during the climb. Even the Merlin needed that support in his dark times. And even he slipped after making it to the top. It took years for him to get back up, but he did. And so can you."

"I don't even feel like I got on top," I admit. "But I can do this. I have to. I won for a reason." And I hold to that.

Damian nods. "That you did. Do you know what that reason is?"

"No. I just trust that Gavril does. It was that or watch him die. I made a choice. I'm holding to it," I say, infecting my voice with as much stubbornness as I can.

Damian thinks for a moment. "Do you remember when he first said that he chose you?"

"When he first said it? At the harvest ball, he said if he could, he would." But I was so unsure then. I didn't truly believe it until he backed it up at the Celeste Ball.

"And what did he say that made him believe it was you?"

"Then? I... I don't really recall him saying anything then," I admit. The way my father attacked shortly after might have caused me to block it out.

"Well, then... What did you do at the first public interview?" Damian asks.

"I spotted his father struggling to breathe." I recall that vividly.

"And what happened after they got the king into the palace?"

"I helped Gavril go back out there to distract the press."

"And in the conservatory?"

"I assured him he could do this."

"Exactly. You believed in him when he didn't even believe in himself. You give him strength and help him channel his temper and make him a force to be reckoned with. You empower him, just as he inspires and empowers you. Together, you will be the change this nation needs."

I smile a little. "I suppose that's true." He certainly makes me better. "I just have to have hope in it."

"And I shall hope you hold to that." Damian smiles with that shining pride in his eyes. "I have missed you."

Despite my sadness, I force a smile. "I missed you too." It's only going to get worse.

He holds my gaze for a moment then looks ahead with a sigh. "The road ahead might not be as smooth as all would hope. And I have more I would say to you, but this isn't the place or the time to discuss it."

"I'm guessing there is a lot we'll need to discuss." At least he'll know how to warn me and prepare me for what I don't know.

"That is one way of saying it." Damian returns the smile. "But it has little to do with yesterday or the day before. But I will not say more here. Just know that how you reacted to Hydie's 'guidance' is perfectly understandable. We all have those experiences. I wish you could have seen King Rox's face when several people tried to arrest me falsely. The man had no clue what to do. He was panicking," he chuckles. "And he'd been king for over four years by that time."

"Well, if it was before today, I may have gotten you arrested too." I smile a little.

He returns it. "So would he, had his wife, Airabelle, not said something. I think Princess Rose got her judgment skills from him." Then he frowns and looks at me. "Don't... tell her I said that."

I chuckle. "Don't know if I'll get a chance."

"Why not? She'll be here for the wedding, and you are a princess now, same as she. I'm sure you'll have plenty of time at future summits."

"That's true. Just doesn't seem real I suppose." I smile. "Just been so focused on the wedding and coronation, and then on Japcharia."

"That I can perfectly understand." He nods with a smile.

"I just have to get through them." I nod with a deep breath.

"And you will, dear angel. You will." He grins assuredly. "Look, we're almost to the entrance hall," he says as if it is some grand accomplishment as we reach the bottom of the stairs.

I laugh. "Thanks, Damian." I needed the laugh.

He nods. "Anytime." He leads me to the dining hall and lets go of my arm at the door.

"Right." I sigh. "Can't just hide with you?" I joke.

He arches a brow. "You'd rather hang out with an old relic like me than have lunch with your fiancé?"

"But the rest of it is in there too," I point out. "And this 'relic' is going to vanish soon." Chatting with Damian felt normal... nothing had felt normal in so long, or so it seemed.

"True, but we'll have plenty of time to talk before then. I'll make sure of it." He smiles at me warmly.

"Alright." I pause. "You... have work to do?"

Damian gives me an understanding smile. "Would you like me to escort you to your seat?"

"If you wouldn't mind."

"Of course not." He smiles back and takes my arm again then opens the door and guides me to my seat.

"There you are." Gavril smiles at me and then at Damian. "Ah good." He relaxes a little. "Good to see you."

"And you, Your Highness." Damian bows his head to him.

"Would you like to join us?" Gavril invites.

Damian seems to debate for a moment, glancing at me then smiles and nods. "Alright. Thank you, Your Highness."

The staff react by bringing an extra seat before Gavril finishes the request. Damian chuckles and thanks them with a nod.

"Nice to see you." Zelda smiles at Damian. "Keeping busy?"

"Quite." Damian smiles. "And how is our Sage doing?"

"Better, but not as fast as he'd like. Think we'll have to chain him down too." She smiles. "His mother says we can do that to keep him on the boat if needed." Gavril laughs most out of any of us at that.

"I'm sure that will help." Damian laughs too. "And you, princess?"

"Well, thank you. Much easier to explore now." She genuinely sounds happy.

"Glad to hear it." Damian smiles with a nod.

"While the rest of you are working?" She hints at Damian as the reminder makes my stomach knot.

"Well, I did a bit of exploring myself these last two days, as Gavril knows." He nods to him then lifts his head to look at him. "And I'm happy to report that her new attendant is already settling in well."

"Excellent." Gavril beams and grips my hand under the table as he often does. "We'll settle into it in no time." His eyes and relaxed shoulders express his relief.

"New attendant?" Zelda frowns. "You... oh." She frowns with an apology.

Damian smiles sadly. "Yes, my time here will be ending soon, as will Cedrick's." He glances at the queen.

The queen nods solemnly. "Ah, I see. It will be sad to see you go, but I understand he's asked you."

Damian smiles, but it seems more to himself. "Yes, I suppose he did."

I am fighting a smile as I look at Damian. He still got out of that. Gavril is grinning at my repressed smile.

"But you'll be pleased to know that Lady Bella will be taking over in my stead," Damian informs the queen with a smile.

"Thank you for handling it," the queen says, and she clearly means it.

It's Zelda who has the big reaction. "She's here?" Zelda almost talks over the queen. Damian chuckles and nods then looks to me as if asking if I want to add anything.

I chuckle too and nod at her, smiling. Zelda looks delighted. "She's working at the moment. Perhaps we can pull her over for lunch tomorrow or something."

"This finally feels like a vacation," Zelda says, making the rest of us laugh.

"So, you'll be helping with the preparations then?" Gavril asks Damian. "Or just helping her figure it out?"

"A bit of both," Damian confirms. "You'll likely see me off and on until the coronation. Cedrick, however, may choose to stay clear of most circles."

"Sounds like him. He doesn't like the attention or the pets," Gavril jokes.

Damian rolls his eyes. I giggle.

"Well, there is much to do to prepare for these changes." The queen smiles. "I'll speak to my team about it." She means the king, I'm sure. Gavril shakes his head in amusement. Clearly, he thinks everyone in the room could know.

"Of course, Your Majesty." Damian bows his head to her.

She bows her head to Damian and gets up to get started. Zelda sighs with contentment. "So, do we have a date at least?" she asks Gavril and me.

I don't like that Gavril looks at me. I shrug. "Working on it," I confess.

"Well, I'm in no hurry." She smiles. She really does look happy.

"Makes one of us," Gavril chuckles.

Damian smiles and bows his head but doesn't comment. I completely know the feeling!

"Whatever you need." Gavril kisses my head. "I'm sure we'll work out when you'll drag me in there. Meanwhile, I have to do what she isn't."

"Told Rose," Zelda jokes, making me giggle.

"Be nice," Gavril teases us before leaving.

Damian smiles then stands and offers to get Zelda's chair then mine. "So, to work?" I ask Damian.

"Thank you, Sir Damian." Zelda beams. "You two off to work as well?"

"Uh..."

"You'll learn to handle your schedule soon," Zelda assures me. "It took me years." I hope I don't take that long.

"It took Rox the course of his natural life." Damian rolls his eyes. "That may be exaggerated *a little*," he says to himself, looking up at the ceiling.

"It couldn't be that long, could it?" Zelda is surprised. "You're lucky I respect you, or I'd pick your mind all day."

Damian laughs. "Lucky me. But no, he simply took a while to learn he didn't have to bend to his people to be a good king."

"That can be hard," Zelda agrees. "Easier when you know some of them are wrong." She smiles as if to make sure that doesn't scare me off. "I'm sure it will be fine."

"In time," I agree, eagerly looking forward to it being over.

"Indeed." Damian gives me a firm nod. "But for now, I believe Bella is waiting for us, and if you have already chosen a theme, I believe the next step is sending invites to the bridal party. As we await the availability of the groom," He smiles a little.

"Ah, sounds interesting." Zelda gives me a look.

I smile. "Yes, of course."

"I wasn't going to ask." She defends but wears a bright smile.

Damian smiles between us. "We'll make it fun," he assures me. "If we get through that, perhaps we can move on to dresses and the like."

"Well, I have a tentative list, just... not sure," I say honestly.

"Oh, well... that part may go fast then." He smiles.

I manage a weak smile. "It's all we've done," I confess.

"Well, if you're going to make dresses and a full party, might as well bring as much of the wedding party as you have." Zelda teases.

"I don't mind if Kascia doesn't. Might be helpful to have another opinion in wedding planning. Lord knows the last time I planned a wedding." Damian chuckles.

"Your daughter," Zelda says confidently. "Sound fun?" She raises her brows at me.

"Sure. If Damian and Bella don't mind," I agree. Zelda beams in delight.

"I doubt she will. Come with me, Your Highnesses." He grins and bows to us both.

Lovely, Damian is doing it too, but I ignore that, and we all go up to my room where Bella is looking over things with my maids.

As Bella smiles and greets me, she catches sight of Zelda over my shoulder. She squeals like she did at our reunion and rushes up to give Zelda a hug. They laugh and enjoy a moment to catch up, and Zelda congratulates Bella on the position.

"When do the other girls get their jobs?" Zelda asks me.

"Um... no idea," I confess. I glance at Damian.

He chuckles. "You really think I know everything."

"You're running the show," I point out. He always was. "You made the new list."

"To help you focus on what was happening today. Mine was more of a schedule, really. Eventually, scheduling your day will be between you, Bella, and other members of your staff. My part in the Enthronement was to help you." He grins with genuine warmth. "I have no say in the jobs for the other girls. Besides that, I'd be far too biased. Were it up to me, there'd be a few girls that ended up in a dunghill."

All of us laugh. He has a good point. "I just meant when we're getting to it." I smile.

"You'd have to talk to that fiancé of yours, but likely next week or the week after. Or they may wait until after the wedding." Damian shrugs.

I nod a little. "Makes sense, so there is your answer." I smile at Zelda.

"So, what are we working on today?" Bella asks Damian.

"Did you get the notes from the wedding planner like I asked?" he asks back.

"Yes." Bella goes over to my vanity and picks it up. "This is what she left: the color swatches, fabric suggestions, and images to help us see the theme." She offers them to Damian.

Damian takes it from her with a nod. "Thank you. So, it would seem we need to narrow down the bridal party, then we can start on the more enjoyable parts."

We go over the lists, apologizing to Bella that Alsmeria will kill me if I don't let her be maid of honor, but Bella doesn't mind. She'll be busy enough without it. I hand Damian the list I'd made earlier for him to look over.

He takes it, looks it over, and smiles. "I think we can handle that." He reaches into his jacket and magically pulls out his notebook.

"Ooo, I can't do that." Zelda admits. I laugh.

Damian laughs too. "It took me a while." He smiles as he flips it open.

"I'm better with light magic." Zelda chuckles uneasily.

"I'm better with none," Bella jokes.

"Gavril works with water." I smile.

"What?" I forgot Bella didn't know. She didn't see it at the attack.

"Yeah, he has finally been able to control it for a while. Good student," Zelda comments.

Bella laughs. "Of course he does, the little fish."

"Minnow," Zelda whispers to herself, making us both giggle.

Damian shrugs, looking down at his notebook. "I'd have gone for Nemo."

We all laugh. We actually have a good time, going over basic sketches to have ideas and colors. Bella and Zelda have too much fun joking what kind of fish or stars we should look like until we're all giggling and throwing throw pillows at one another. Damian doesn't seem to mind until a pillow grazes his pen, almost forcing him to draw an ugly line across his notebook page where he's making out a sketch. He freezes in shock, braced for it to happen again.

Bella and I throw Zelda under the wheel and point to her. She'd thrown the offending pillow.

"Maybe we should calm things down," Damian says as he slowly relaxes.

"Likely," Zelda agrees. "Sorry, I made it crazy."

"I'd hate to see how nuts your sisters' parties are," Bella says. A giggle escapes me.

"I blame Cedrick," Damian says as he pulls out his watch and checks the time.

Zelda gasps. "That's right. I am his direct heir in Hyvil." She grins teasingly.

"Remind me not to be around for that teasing." I sigh.

"No, worse, he'll be annoyingly cutesy about it." Bella shakes her head. She has a point.

"Sounds about right," Damian says as he puts his watch away and stands up. "Well ladies, it has been fun, but there is something I must see to." He then pushes his notebook toward Bella. "You can keep working on that in the meantime."

"Sorry for the craziness," I apologize.

"I should check the post. Working arrangements with family." Zelda sighs too.

Damian smiles understandingly, then looks back at me. "It's quite alright. Don't forget you have a meeting with Gavril in his suite at three."

"I do?" I hadn't seen that anywhere.

He smiles good-naturedly and nods. "Yes, you do. And that might be a good time to talk to him about a date."

"Okay." I nod. I didn't mind. I don't recall Gavril mentioning it. Maybe he didn't have it planned yet either.

"Ladies, until next time." He bows to us and leaves the room.

Bella smiles. "Well, shall we work until your meeting?"

I nod, and Bella does a few more sketches and ideas, explaining why each one might be good, but then it's time for my meeting. My emotions are a blend of excitement and nervousness. I don't know why I'm nervous. It should be easy.

# Chapter 6

When I get to the meeting, Gavril greets me with a kiss on the cheek, which I return with a kiss on his lips. It makes him happy I initiated it. He perks up slightly, a gentle, contented smile resting on his face and a softness in his eyes make him as handsome as ever in his happiness.

"Well, I'm guessing we have a lot to go over?" Gavril asks.

"Yes, Bella helped with a list for us." I say, reaching into my pocket as he takes me to the sofa, and we sit down.

"Damian will join us a bit later, but we'll worry about that when he shows up," Gavril says.

As I sit down, Joy, Gavril's red and white husky puppy, yips a hello at me. She doesn't jump up at me, returning instead to a mouthwatering bone. She is growing up. She looks more like an adult than a puppy now.

I pat her as she sits with us, and Gavril and I start with the wedding date, as we're under a lot of pressure to have that set. In order to have the coronation as quickly as possible, we settle on three weeks from now to hold our wedding. The coronation will be held the day after the wedding.

Then we arrange the details for the rehearsal dinner, which is less about rehearsing and more about creating a political event so that the actual wedding day will belong solely to Gavril and me.

"We'll check with state to make sure we didn't miss anyone," Gavril says as we make a final note. "Who do I talk to about your schedule?"

"Uh," I frown. "Haven't... Damian, I suppose?"

Gavril chuckles. "I'll figure it out." He turns back to the calendar.

"I'll be happy to coordinate anything you need," I hear Damian say as the door opens.

"Ah, there you are. Everyone make a big mess?" Gavril teases lightly as he invites Damian to sit.

"Not everyone, thankfully," Damian chuckles as he comes over and takes a seat in the armchair near us. "Though I did have a certain princess nearly force me to ruin my own work." He can't help but smile.

"It wasn't that bad." I flush.

"What did you do?" Gavril laughs at me.

"It wasn't her. It was Zelda." Damian smiles wider.

"Okay... what did Zelda do?" Gavril raises a brow.

"She... hit his pen while throwing a pillow at Bella," I confess. Gavril snorts.

"About ruined the whole sketch." Damian smiles teasingly.

"I didn't throw it," I defend.

Damian chuckles. "I didn't say you did."

"Glad you had some fun." Gavril squeezes my hand. I manage a smile.

Damian nods, then pauses as he sits back. "Well... I did have to douse a bit of Hydie's fire. She is... an excitable woman."

"Normally helpful for us. She's eager to please." Gavril is fighting to keep something repressed in his voice. Great, Gavril really does want to fire her.

"Which can be helpful at times. Others, not so well. I swear, my brother Rox would never have survived her." Damian smiles a little.

"So, you'd have fired her," Gavril jokes as staff come over with a tray of tea, cakes, and crumpets. Honestly, I just feel guilt in my stomach.

Damian gives him an amused smile. "I don't think I would have the power to. And she does have her positive traits. Though I suppose," he looks up to one corner of the ceiling as he thinks, "there was a man who was equally as eager as Hydie. He was assigned to help Cedrick work through some... mental coping methods after the war with Heklis. We ended up disagreeing." He frowns.

"And him you fired," Gavril jokes while I'm wondering if I was going to accidentally get half the staff fired.

Damian smiles at him. "Actually, Cedrick's wife did. She was the one who hired him, after all. But yes, for his safety, he was removed from the position, but I'd rather not go into that."

"Alright, but you called for this meeting?" Gavril leans back, puts an arm around my shoulders, and crosses a leg nonchalantly, as if we do this every day. I fight a smile.

"I did." Damian nods. "However, before we move into that topic, I wanted to ensure that ones already at hand have been addressed." He looks between us, but mainly at me. "I know we spoke in brief this morning, but there wasn't much time to address it in full," he says, hinting his question to me, basically asking if I am feeling better about the last two days without actually asking.

"I'm... getting there." I give him a smile. "Just taking time."

Damian smiles gently and nods. "And that is perfectly alright. Just give yourself time and moments to breathe. Admittedly, I worried that I may have accidentally done you a disservice in never consulting you in my projects, but at the same time, I have to remind myself that you told me that is what you wanted, and it would have been insubordinate of me as your attendant to have pestered you further about taking a larger role in your look when you already gave me clear directions to 'surprise you'." He smiles a little. "In that, you already had the role of leading your team the way you wanted. And you had more than enough to worry about without stressing about approving your look every time, which would have slowed your work and mine. I suppose, what I'm trying to say is, you are already good at knowing when to delegate more minor tasks, so you can focus on what is important without even thinking about it, and as you are 'figuring things out' it is perfectly alright to tell your staff to 'surprise you'. So don't let Hydie, or anyone else, tell you otherwise."

I smile and nod a little. "I'll try to remember." Being reminded of what I had accomplished brings me solace.

Damian beams at me. "I am confident in you."

"Thanks."

"We all are." Gavril secures his grip around me, making me smile.

Damian takes another moment, then sighs. "Well, as true as that is and as much as I'd love to dwell simply on that, unfortunately, that is not why I arranged this meeting. And I doubt this topic will be welcoming, but it must be done." He takes another deep breath and looks at us. "Kascia, you remember how afraid you were to have Gavril or anyone else learn about your past?"

I bow my head and nod. "Yes." Gavril once more tightens his grip.

"But how do you feel now that he knows?" Damian asks.

Gavril smiles before I do. "Safe," I admit. "There's nothing that will change it now." Gavril beams.

Damian shares our smile. "And for that, I am glad. I want that for you, for the both of you, for the rest of your lives. However, if that is to continue and not be marred again by fear, the truth must be heard. Kascia," he looks down and sighs, "I know how difficult what I am about to ask will be for you." He then meets my eye. "But you must tell them, the press and the people, about your past," he says with urgency and love in his voice.

My face falls. "What?"

"You're suggesting we go public with it? In what way?" Gavril asks, leaning forward in concern.

"Simple. Arrange an interview with Fabian. We can present it as the two of you simply wanting to share your love story, but the true intent would be to share why she entered the Enthronement, how being in the palace and meeting your family changed her mind, and how you learned who she was and why you chose her as your princess," Damian says. "I know what I am asking is... that it feels frightening and unbearable, but it is what is best for your marriage and this kingdom. But it must be done before the wedding if it is to be of any benefit."

"You don't think revealing we have one of the rebel leaders under lock and key and naming him won't be a threat?" Gavril asks, studying Damian. I'm impressed by how he reacts. How he analyzes it. He's in ruling mode, and it's alluring.

"Only if you present it that way. It can also be seen as merciful because if you were truly tyrannical rulers, he would have been taken out and made an example of. I have seen it many times." Damian smiles sadly. "Instead, you are giving him his life. Showing that even though he showed you none, you are not without compassion, and that you want to work things out with other rebel leaders. If you show that you are making efforts to restore him to health and are willing to talk to him, others will see that and may become less aggressive."

Gavril nods a little. "I see." He pauses, thinking. "We don't think that will make them angry and want their boss back?"

"Well, you also have to consider that after the last attack, you have most of them in your prisons." Damian smiles a little.

Gavril chuckles. "True. So, you don't think that won't cause more attacks?"

"If they are a part of that group, trust me, they already know. Any attacks will have already been in the works. So no, it will not spur more attacks, even if it seems like it did."

"And that won't spur other rebels to action?" He looks at Damian, then at me. I swallow, realizing yes, he knows I might know.

"Um," my voice shudders. "D-depends if the Loyalists are still as committed to uniting the two rebellions as they once were."

"So really, it changes nothing, letting the world know we have him and who he's related to."

"Not in that sense, no," Damian agrees. "But it will help those who are not as rebellious to you and your family, and *that* is my main concern."

"So, people see that their new princess understood them, agreed with them, and saw different and now is the royal family's greatest defender?" Gavril recaps.

"Yyyeeess." Damian leans into the word. "And no." He straightens up. "Picture this. Say you don't make any kind of announcement. The two of you marry, Kascia is crowned, and for a while, everything feels right. But then, Fabian, or another member of the press, starts poking his nose in places you don't want him to be. He is curious and hungry for the next exciting story, and you begin to worry that the story might just be where Kascia came from and why she was fighting in the attack at the first presentation ceremony. So, you have to play ring-around-the-rosy with the press, trying to find new ways to distract them as years go by. All the while, the both of you go back to living in fear of 'what happens when they find out the truth' and doing all you can to ensure that does not happen. One possible end is that you are successful in keeping it hidden, but you never rid yourself of that growing fear.

"The other, and the more likely end, is that something happens. Someone says something they shouldn't, or the press finds the bit of evidence they need to at least spread rumors, if not confirm their suspicions. One way or another, it all comes tumbling out all without your say so or control. I suspect at such a point, many will feel betrayed and lied to. There could be more uprising and people who were neutral before may start picking sides. You may be able to calm them, but it will be hard to regain their trust. *That* is my fear if you do not come forward now."

Gavril listens with a set to his lips, eyes down and moving as he thinks it over.

"And they aren't going to be sure I cheated to win and throw a riot anyway?" I point out. "And that betrayal feeling just comes sooner." If the people don't trust me, how can I be what I need to be?

Damian smiles compassionately. "Not if we handle it right. Remember, you have done nothing wrong. You were manipulated, but you learned to see through the lies. Because of the nature of the public interviews and the Enthronement itself, there was never a time where you felt safe to come forward with this before now. If you take charge, show them who you are, all of who you are now, and we show Gavril knew who you were before he declared you the winner, those feelings of hurt and betrayal will never arise. You are not crowned yet, and that gives us the perfect opportunity.

"During the coronation, there will be a time where you will be presented to the people to be accepted as the heir to Purerah with Gavril. If you can give them the ability to accept you knowing all that, they will not only be understanding, but I think you'll find you will receive a deeper love for them and they for you. While technically, the people can't choose whether or not you become princess, that act will unite you in mind and heart. But only if you allow them to know you first."

"And after winning, the people's approval rating of you is going to be as high as it ever will be." Gavril gives me a look, compassionate and worried. "Which makes it easier for people to accept flaws because it's easier to forgive who you like."

"And you think they'll still like me after?"

"I still liked you." Gavril shrugs.

"That's different," I insist, heart racing now.

"Kascia." Damian reaches out and touches my arm. I stop and look at him. He meets my eyes with firm confidence and compassion. "Trust me. I would not suggest it if I wasn't certain it would be for your best interest. I want to ensure you are happy long after I am gone. And if that is to happen, it is time to cast aside the mask your father forced you to wear. You are a star because of who you were and who you are now. It is frightening, I know, but that doesn't mean it will end poorly. Have faith. You mustered enough to save Gavril. Now, have a little for yourself."

"They're going to eat me. Fabian at the lead." And then he'll dig for any evidence that I was the wrong choice and throw up any and all he finds.

Damian gives me an amused but sympathetic smile. "No, he won't. With your permission, I will speak to him to set up the interview. He is not without heart. If we ask him to treat this with seriousness and sensitivity, I am confident he will."

"Fabian?" I question. He loves to make things crazy.

"You do recall he is the one who would and likely still does, write a yearly piece to support the poor guards and troops fighting this war," Gavril points out to me.

I pause. I didn't know that.

Damian nods. "And recall, he was up north at the start of the Enthronement because he wanted to report the real news, that which is important to history. He only came down because he saw something in you that inspired him, that made him believe real change was coming. He wants to see an end to the fighting, and he believed you were the one to make it happen. Yes, he likes a bit of mischief now and then, but he believes in you. Trust me, he'll be on your side."

"Do it." Gavril nods at Damian. My mouth drops open, and I look at him. He smiles at me and squeezes my hand. "We have this."

Damian smiles confidently with a nod. "Yes, you do." And he stands. "My Lord and Lady." He bows to us.

"Thank you, Sir Damian. You do more than you have to." Gavril smiles and stands to see Damian out.

"I do what I can." Damian smiles meekly at him.

I sit there, unsure what I just got pulled into as Gavril sees Damian out.

I lose any semblance of certainty every time I find it. *I was the right choice,* I remind myself over and over, but now I have to reveal the whole truth to the world. And... I don't trust them to be as understanding as Gavril. In fact, I'm expecting it to start a fresh wave of attacks.

I don't know how long I sit there, anxiously twisting my engagement ring around and around my finger in my apprehension before Gavril comes back in. He pauses, looking at me with a slight frown on his face.

"Darling, you alright?" he asks slowly, coming over to me.

My lips twist into a soft smile. I like that pet name. I don't think he'd used it before we'd been engaged. It was peculiar to grasp that I had the freedom to be more open with him, yet I hadn't fully embraced it.

He settles down next to me, studying me. "I'm sorry if that was too abrupt for you, but if he's to catch Fabian by the end of the day, he had to go sooner than later. I really do think this is the right thing to do."

Biting my lips, I nod and avoid looking at him, instead focusing my gaze on my lap. "I trust you." I trusted him this far. It would be foolish to throw that trust away. But it feels like every time something goes right, it makes a sudden sharp turn to precariousness.

"But you're still scared?" Gavril asks gently.

I nod. "They're going to eat me."

"No, they won't."

"They will." I turn to Gavril. "You don't know what they're like. I recall how it felt when you heard someone turned on you, on the cause. It made you furious. Every rebel out there will hate me even if they liked me before. I was among them, Gavril. I know what they're like."

"We have most of those men locked up, as Damian pointed out." Gavril tries to soothe me and moves to take my hands, but I pull away and get up, hugging myself and start pacing.

"He can't have brought all his men, and the Loyalists are worse," I say with a hint of franticness to my tone that grows with each word. "Jake can tell you. They're the most vehement. They'll forget all about their original slights and their anger will grow because someone stole their ticket to the royal assassination because I changed sides. If I hadn't been sure Jake cared for me, I'd have been sure he would be just as hurt."

"Would you have worried he'd hurt you?" Gavril asks carefully as he stands up with me.

I swallow, pausing in my pacing and nod. "If I hadn't held onto the hope he cared about me." My shoulders drop, and I look up to meet Gavril's eyes. "So those that never cared for me will be worse. I'm sure of it."

"Even if that's true, it will be a lesser amount." Gavril puts his hands on my arms, locking eyes with me. "It's going to do far more good than harm."

"You don't know that."

"Would Damian suggest it if it would?"

"He cares about freeing me from my secret by letting it out sooner. In that regard, it will be exactly what he hopes. He's just saying we don't wait to be surprised by it. He's not wrong, I just..." I drop my head. "If it has to come out, I agree. Let's control it. I just... wish we didn't have to."

"I may not have experience with people in person, but I do see public response and backlash or lack thereof. Trust me. Most of all with how your numbers look, you're going to be fine." Gavril pulls me into an embrace. "Besides, we would never let them hurt you. I value you above my own soul. I will not let them get to you."

"I'm afraid of the damage it will cause." As I hold tightly to him, my frown deepens a little. "What if I do make it worse? What if I bring it all down?"

"Your secret won't make it any worse than it already is." Gavril smiles a little.

"If the Enthronement helped the people feel part of something, this coming out may break it all," I point out.

"And if it does, we'll be back where we were before the Enthronement with the public. And recall, the Enthronement never was for them. It was to fulfill the prophecy. So, if it goes back, it's not a tragedy. It would be great if it didn't, but if it does, I'm not worried."

"How can you not be?" I ask.

He kisses my head. "I found you," he says in that low voice that makes my heart race with joy. "And that's all it said I had to do. The rest will work itself out as we fight for it. I'm not afraid. My only concern when it comes to your secret is keeping you safe from it, and I do believe revealing it now will protect you best from that. Whatever else happens, I'll handle it. That was the promise. I find and marry my princess. That's the promise."

"So, we tell them after the wedding," I say dryly.

"Very funny." Gavril kisses my forehead. "I know you're scared. But I will not let you do this alone. I'll make sure those who need to know before are told, but you already told my parents which is most important. We can even practice to help you know how you'll react to help you control it better." He huffs a laugh. "Though with your acting talent, I doubt that will be needed."

"I was trained to cry when I want to, not to not cry when I don't want to." I point out.

"You hid your fear well from the other girls, and you did a good job with me for a long time until I got to know you." He holds me tighter. "It's going to be alright."

"When do we get to the fun part?" I ask.

Gavril's demeanor slumps a little. "I have the same question." He meets my eyes. That doesn't make me feel better, but what he says next does. "But the fact it's safe to tell you is a huge step, isn't it?" His smile makes my heart glow. "No more secrets, no more pleasing other girls. It's us, and we hold no more secrets. We can finally be open with each other, and... be us. Perhaps that doesn't help you, but it does me. That's the biggest 'fun' part we have not reached. It is a bit disappointing."

"I wouldn't hide things—"

"You've pushed me away the last two nights." Gavril's amber eyes flick to mine. "You didn't want to talk, so I gave you space and helped you forget, but when I thought I'd get answers the next night, you pushed me away to... work, I guess."

As I lower my gaze, I nod in agreement. "I suppose I wasn't as clear as I meant to be. I really thought I had expressed it."

"Hard when you gave me no context." He kisses my forehead once more. "But that's alright. We're learning. I shouldn't have expected it to get better magically because the game was over. Habits die hard, and you've had to hide every imperfection for a long time. Forgive my disappointment and anger at it not being as I wished as soon as I wanted."

"I'm sorry. I didn't pause to make sure I was communicating."

"You caught my mood later though. That's an improvement." He smiles. "We'll get there, and it will be easier when we don't have to be separated so much." He takes my hands, which he'd been fiddling with the way he likes to when we talk like this and kisses them. "But before long, we'll have the space we need."

"Unless Hydie has her way," I mutter.

"What?" Gavril's tone changed so much I actually laugh. His tone went from soft and tender to... I don't even know what to call it, indignant? Annoyed?

"Just what I lost my temper over," I confess. "She highly suggested I'd want my own space just in case, and... I liked what we talked about before."

"Which was?"

"Turning the bedroom into a study, the study into a studio, and then we could just share a room."

Gavril beams like the sun. "So, we'd update my room for ours."

I nod. "If you still are—"

Gavril stops me with a quick kiss. "Of course, I am. I... you don't want your own space?" He sounds honestly surprised.

"Why would I?"

"You retreat when you're upset." Gavril gives me a sheepish smile. "I just... presumed."

"You really thought we'd have our own bedrooms... most of the time?" My expression turns into a frown. I really hadn't given him the confidence of how much I loved him. I looked forward to not being alone. I'd never shared a room, and sure, it might be annoying in some ways, but I also felt like my room wasn't fully private with staff always coming in and out and working in there. So, sharing with him would be an upgrade.

Gavril nods apologetically. "Sorry. I just know how you've run away from me, upset."

"I only did that because you weren't promised to me, and I was scared it would only hurt my chances," I argue.

"Not last night."

My heart drops. "Gavril... can you do something for me I know you won't like?"

"Sure."

"Don't let me do that." My eyes meet his as I look up. "I fully agree we shouldn't hide anymore, but it's harder for me to get out of that habit than I thought. I want to be better. I don't want you to feel like I would want my own space, forget needing one. I don't want to hide from you. I really was sure you understood. I was distracted, and it was unfair to you. Don't let me just run off next time."

"Then what should I do?"

"Stop me. I-I don't know."

"What if I'd offered to help you with it?"

I frown a bit. "Then... I don't know if it would have helped, but from now on, yes. I'll know what you're doing now we've talked about it."

"May I ask why it wouldn't have helped before?"

"I want to be good at this." Even saying it raises desperation in me. "I want so badly to be right and good at this, just like you expect of me. I didn't want your help because I wanted to prove I could do it on my own, not really to anyone else, but to myself. I know you picked me for a reason. I believe you were right, but I keep doubting. I wanted to give myself evidence without any outside changes to help my faith when it slips."

Gavril nods with a small kind of "ah" sound, but it wasn't really saying it. "That... explains everything." He smiles gently and kisses my forehead. "I think I said it before, but for the record, that stuff Hydie is asking of you is not what your duty will be like."

"What will it be like?" I blurt out. Gavril stops, pulling back to look at me. "I thought I knew, but now I have no idea."

"Well, part of that will depend on you, but remember our talk after the Dragians threw a fit?" I smile and nod. "Was that fun?"

"I felt guilty for taking your time." I confess.

"No." He strokes my hair back. "I needed it. The time with you, your open discussion, your support, all of it. That is what it will be like."

"Only you don't leave at the end." I joke.

"Do I still get that supportive hug at the end?"

I laugh. Gavril beams and holds me close as I laugh. He likes to do that. When I'm in the middle of a good laugh, he'll hold me close as if he likes the feel of my happiness against him.

"Or can I ask for better?"

I turn my head to meet his eyes, only to have his lips meet mine. I relax a little and return the kiss. He could ask for better, and I kiss him a bit more intently.

"Hey, I'm giving you one," Gavril teases me, making me laugh, and he kisses me again, deeper. I playfully return it as if trying to one-up him. We play this little game for a few moments before his almost fierce kiss knocks me off balance, and we fall onto the sofa.

I giggle as Gavril grins like the little troublemaker he is and kisses me more tenderly. I wrap my arms around his neck and pull him closer.

"Oh come on, you two!" We both jump at Godwin's voice. "You were alone... what, half an hour?"

"We weren't doing anything," I defend. I had done far worse with Jake and not crossed the line.

"He was going to get on top of you," Godwin insists as he goes over to Joy. "I come in here to take care of the puppy and stop you two making a puppy."

I lose it laughing as Gavril leaps over to Godwin and pulls him into a headlock. "You don't call my heir a puppy." Gavril is smiling as Godwin begs for mercy. I can't stop laughing. They look like brothers.

# Chapter 7

I'm in a better mood by dinner. After Gavril finished "schooling" with his staff, we'd taken Joy for her walk in the garden until dinner. It had rained a little, but Gavril simply twirled me in the rain while Joy jumped up, trying to catch the rain in her mouth.

As we're eating, Gavril asks if I want to play some more games after dinner. "Damian will probably want to come let us know how it went with Fabian," he explains.

"You just spent all afternoon working on wedding plans." The queen smiles at us.

"And I can't have more time?" Gavril mocks aghast.

"You're not married yet," she reminds him.

"So?"

The look she gives her son makes me giggle. Good thing Godwin isn't there to make his point.

After dinner, Gavril tells me to change into my nightclothes, then meet him in his suite. "Our?" I say hopefully.

He smiles and kisses me. "Ours," he agrees.

My heart is a flutter as I go and let my maids do the normal nightly routine before I pull on a robe and slippers and go up to the suite. Gavril is already in night clothes. His hair is damp. He must have taken his normal night shower. I enjoy playing with his hair as I lean on him and watch him play a more action-packed game.

We enjoy this until Reinold steps over to us to let us know Damian is ready to speak with us.

The man himself enters a moment later with a gentle smile on his face and his hands clasped behind him.

"Hello, Damian," Gavril greets him warmly. "How did it go?" I brace myself for it. Gavril has done a good job making me forget, but now the terrible moment has arrived, and the fears all rush tightly into my chest.

"Good evening, Your Highness." Damian nods to him. "It went well, I think. He was very understanding. Though he had a suggestion I'd not thought of. Because there is no doubt to be an editorial about the interview, one way or another, he wondered if we should hold a private interview first where he will listen and ask questions to make sure he understands your story. Then he will write his piece, explaining it to the public, encouraging them to ask questions which will be addressed in a public interview."

"That might be a good idea. That worked well for the features." Gavril glances at me. "We could do the in-person interview tomorrow, then he can help us find the best day to air it."

I bit my lip. "The one-on-one might be easier to start with," I agree.

"Then you don't have to repeat the whole story in front of the world. Just answer questions," Gavril agrees. I still may end up telling the entire story, but Gavril has a point.

Damian smiles a little more for me. "That was my hope. Fabian promised to treat the matter with care, and, as he will be the only one listening, you can be freer with your words. If there's anything you don't want him to write, we can strike it from his notes."

"And that we can use to practice." Gavril nods. "What do you think?"

I swallow and look at him then at Damian. "If that's best."

Damian watches me for a moment then, almost like switching roles, his formality he'd been using with Gavril melts off as he kneels next to me and places his hands on mine. "I won't force you to do this," Damian says tenderly. "Yes, I think it is the wisest course, but I'll not make you if you don't think you can."

"I've trusted you this far." I force a smile. "I just... he'll try to rip me apart."

"I don't think he will, most of all, for a one-on-one," Gavril assures me, wrapping an arm around my shoulders. It feels so safe with the two men I trust most on either side of me like this.

"And neither of us will let him." Damian smiles, glancing at Gavril then back at me. "I'll rip him apart first."

"He's getting the exclusive of a lifetime to sell his paper. I think he'll cooperate even if he's as heartless as you think," Gavril assures me. "We can get ready tonight, and then meet with him in the morning hours so he can write it. That leaves the rest days for the reporters to collect questions and responses."

"Okay." That seems the safest bet.

Damian frowns. "There is no need to rush *that* quickly. He'll likely have gone home by now, so I won't get to speak to him until morning. But I'll try to set your interview for the afternoon."

"Alright. I just feel bad for him having to write it that fast." Gavril chuckles. "I suppose it could be easier than I expect."

"Could be. I'll see what he says about it tomorrow when I arrange it. Though there is one thing you should know." Damian looks between us, but mostly at me.

"What?" I frown. It couldn't be worse, could it?

"In order to help him understand the seriousness of the matter, I told him who your father is," Damian says. "But I have his word that he will tell no one else."

"Well... soon he has to tell everyone." I force a smile. "You think he'll be quiet?"

Damian smiles assuringly and nods. "I trust him to be a man of his word. And besides that, where is the benefit of letting it slip earlier? It'd be like punching a hole in his own sail and expecting it to still catch wind."

I take a deep breath and nod. "Okay. How... did he take it?"

Damian thinks a moment. "Surprised. And concerned. He said he could see the need for delicacy."

"That's a good sign." Gavril tries to comfort me.

"Yeah... yeah, that is." I put on a small smile. "And doing it once before will be helpful."

"I agree. Which is why I brought someone with me tonight whom I think should be told before most others," Damian says. "That is, *if* it is alright with you."

"Oh. Sure," I say, surprised.

Damian smiles a little, then looks to Reinold. "Show her in."

Reinold bows his head and steps out to fetch whoever Damian has brought. I glance at Gavril, who just smiles at me. Damian stands and watches the door, waiting for Reinold to return.

A moment later, Lila, my head of security during the Enthronement, walks in. I frown and look at Gavril. He looks confused too.

Damian smiles at her, then at me. "You, of course, know that Lila is a Custod."

"Yes. I ensured that." Gavril smiles a bit as I give Lila an unsure smile.

The connection clicks in my head, gushing a tentative tension in my stomach. "Why should... she know first?" I ask.

"Lila, please tell them who your father is, if you don't mind." Damian smiles at her gently.

"My father is Tolan Custod." She frowns a little. "I'm not sure... what this has to do with anything."

"Just... trust me. You will," Damian assures her. "And did he have any siblings?"

She swallows as if embarrassed. "Yes sir."

Damian smiles again and approaches her. "It's alright," he says, his voice full of compassion. "No one here will judge you. But I'd like you to name your father's siblings for us. Please."

"My aunt Namura and... his brother Peodrick." She almost winces, expecting us to be upset, I imagine.

Instead, Gavril blinks before his mouth drops open, and he looks at me. In complete disbelief, I find myself staring at her. I had thought about my father's side of the family when I filled out my application, but it hadn't really crossed my mind since. I have a living aunt and an uncle? And...

"You're sure?" I ask, still a bit in shock.

She nods, still nervous.

"But that..." What were the odds? Likely not that high until taking into account that Cedrick was here and there are a lot of Custods, but perhaps not that many. I glance at Damian; how long had he known?

"Well... that means you're in a perfect place." Gavril tries to help break the moment up for me, so I can explain.

"Perfect?" Lila frowns.

"Lila... h-he's my father," I get out.

Lila blinks more rapidly than I had. "What?"

I take a shaking breath. "Peodrick is... m-my father."

Lila is too stunned to respond. She looks at Damian, likely worried about the possible security hazard.

Instead, Damian just smiles. "It's true. I've wondered it for a while now. Mostly because you two have similar characteristics."

"We do?" Lila frowns. Gavril chuckles.

"You have the same smile," Damian says with one of his own.

"What?" I'd not even noticed that.

"This is why we're not assassins." Lila sighs. Gavril laughs.

"It's quite alright. We don't need that many," Damian chuckles.

"And you figured it out from that alone?" I ask, impressed, but should I be? He's good at everything, being over two thousand years old. And besides that, I had always looked at Lila and felt I'd met her before. Now I know we're related, I can see her cheeks and jaw remind me of my father, and the rather serious expression she wears on duty is like his too.

"Not quite. There were a few minor details that led to my overall conclusion." Damian shrugs. "But that is beside the point. Don't you think you should give your cousin a hug?" He smiles.

Oddly, Lila looks more uncertain than I do. "Um... she's still my charge," she points out.

"Does... that matter?" Gavril frowns. Lila gives him an exasperated look. "What? Sage liked to pin me down and pretend he wasn't when he thought I was being extra stupid," he defends.

"Oh, that's quite literal." Damian nods affirmatively. "He would flop on top of him, as I heard it."

"No... he shouldn't do that." Lila frowns.

"He's an assassin. He makes rules; he doesn't follow them." Damian shakes his head with a smile.

Well, I don't want to make Lila uncomfortable, but the overwhelming relief of having some kind of family on that side is a wonderful feeling: hopeful and like being buoyed up on warm waters. She had also been nice to me. She'd done just what a guard should and mostly stayed out of my way, but the few exchanges we had, like when she picked me up at the start of the Enthronement, had made me always like her. The idea she's my cousin... I have a cousin. It's almost as good as finding a sister. Are there any others? I'm reeling, excited yet nervous about what they might think of me.

"Well, I doubt those rules apply to family," Gavril reasons, glancing at Damian as if for help.

"Absolutely not," Damian agrees. "And frankly, if the Head disagrees, I'll stick him with Cedrick. Though I seriously doubt he would."

I'm not sure Lila is comfortable still, but that's enough for me. I get up and walk up to her, but I still give her permission to turn it down. Looking at her, afraid if she does turn it down, I'll know how the rest of my lost family will react to me. I desperately need the assurance. I'm scared but hopeful.

As Gavril stands behind me, Lila's hazel eyes meet my longing, and she finally lets go of her hesitation to give me a protective hug. There's a warm kind of love in it. I imagine this is what it feels like to be hugged by an older, protective sister. She doesn't want to let go at first, so the hug is longer than I thought it would be, but I have no complaints about that before she pulls away, smiling.

"So... he's here?" Lila asks after looking at me for a long moment. I think she put it together just like Sage had.

"Well... he's in the infirmary under lock and key," I admit.

Lila relaxes. "And he talked you into this?"

I nod.

"And you told him no?"

I nod again.

"I see... Father won't be too happy when he finds out." She frowns a bit.

"I doubt anyone is." I sigh heavily, hugging myself. Lila frowns and rubs my arm reassuringly.

"Not happy with your father, perhaps. But I'm sure he'll be thrilled to meet his niece." Damian smiles warmly.

"Once he's done deciding if he'll even show up to deal with his brother," Lila agrees. "After what Uncle put you through, I doubt he'd have a problem with you at all."

I smile. I hadn't feared that, but now she said it... would any of them dislike me?

"And Grandmother will lose her mind." Lila sighs. "She's... a doting grandmother." I'm not sure what to make of that.

"Well, we'll make sure they get an invitation. We'll leave that to you if you don't mind," Gavril says to Lila.

"Of course, Your Highness." She bows her head. "Who else knows?"

"We'll go public soon," Gavril says. "But perhaps you can help Kascia explain to her staff. I'll handle those on my staff who don't know and need to know."

"Does Sage? He'll feel so bad." Lila grins as if that's a bonus for her.

"He knows." I nod.

"Did he apologize?"

I smile and nod, recalling watching him unload his weapons just to prove it.

"Profusely." Damian smiles with a chuckle. Lila laughs.

"When?" Gavril asks.

"When he talked to me about it," I say.

"Which was?"

Oh right, Gavril didn't know Sage knew about my parentage before he did. I don't want to tell him. "After he found out."

Gavril doesn't push it. If he's upset, it's at Sage, not me, so I let it drop as he does. "We'll have to make sure the Custod head knows as well, I'd imagine. If he learns in a news article, he may be upset."

"I don't know. He seems pretty chill about that. I do not think he will care, as long as he does not have to handle it personally." Lila glances at Damian, clearly thinking he'd know better than her.

"I would imagine so. But it might be kind to invite him to the wedding, as it is a Custod marrying a Potentate." Damian smiles.

"Doesn't he always get invites to royal weddings?" Gavril asks.

"Usually." Damian nods. "Just as you would invite the high king."

"Then I'm sure state is already on it." Gavril sighs with a weighty exhale. "As fun as that is," he mutters to himself.

"Hmm... in that case, I'll make a point to do it myself," Damian says. "Personally, I don't fancy the grand duke 'accidentally' forgetting to invite them."

"He wouldn't. He wants the heads to like him." Gavril shakes his head.

"He's the state rep?" I frown.

"Yes, Mother put him over state." Gavril shakes his head. "Just before the Enthronement started, I think."

"I heard we must be careful with him." Lila glances at Damian, who probably gave the warning.

"Exceptionally," Damian says. Then he does the most Cedrick-like thing I've ever seen as he looks to Gavril with a begging look. "Can he be uninvited?"

Gavril laughs. "Well... you could try. Might be a political nightmare, but if you think it's worth it, I'll have a go."

Damian half frowns. "Be better if he simply stopped existing. Sorry, I shouldn't say that, but it's true."

"I wouldn't mind." Gavril grumbles. "But until there's an heir, we kind of need him."

Lila loses it, giggling. It takes me a second before I catch on and turn pink. Gavril looks quite apologetic.

Damian chuckles with a smile. "I wish you luck in that. But on that note, it is quite late."

"Right." Gavril checks his watch. "Sorry, we were enjoying a late night. Would you like to escort her to her room? Not that you need it," he reminds me with a smile.

"But of course," Damian smiles and offers me his arm.

I smile and take it.

"I'll see to the night watch." Lila smiles and bows to us all before leaving.

Damian shakes his head at her with a smile. "I wonder if she'll ever get over that."

"I think she's trying to do an extra good job now." A small smile forms on my face. "Help family, you know?"

"I suppose." He smiles, then looks at Gavril and bows his head. "Good night, Your Highness."

"Good night," he wishes Damian. He then kisses my cheek and wishes me the same before turning to go to bed himself. I smile softly as I turn to go back to my room.

# Chapter 8

Bella has put together a binder of all the wedding planner has done so far, so I can review it in peace until Gavril finishes his work. I decide to curl up with the binder in the loft within the conservatory to enjoy its cool quiet, with the gentle tinkle of the water as the only break in the peaceful silence.

I feel calm for the first time in a while.

Browsing through the binder proves to be a delightful experience, showcasing its impressive organization despite the limited time, and offering detailed sketches of decoration ideas, cake designs, table arrangements, playlists, and styles. Then towards the back, they have menu suggestions, invitation formats, and a list of the political points we need to cover with state later.

After a few hours, I take a break to stretch my legs, enjoying the coolness of the conservatory and the sound of the running water, watching the fish swim and splash about.

I'm near the entrance, thinking this will be my last loop before I head back to work when the doors open and the grand duke steps in. I pause, trying not to scowl at him.

He and I do not have a good history. With the pretense of being my ally, he made every effort to get me kicked out. He then started to hit on me, to the point that he assaulted me in the lift when I couldn't escape, kissing me in front of Gavril to try to get the prince to eliminate me. I hadn't spoken directly to him since, other than his awkward attempts to apologize.

"Ah, Your Highness, I didn't expect to find you here." He smiles warmly, but it never seems to reach his eyes. He's handsome enough, but he'd always felt off to me. His dark tones, coiled hair and beard, and noble gait do make him fit the tall, dark, and handsome stereotype, but he still has always creeped me out. "Taking a well-deserved break?"

"I was just heading back to work just now, thank you," I say, a hint of stiffness in my voice, and turn to go.

"I shall escort you. Where were you going?" he asks pleasantly.

"Back to the loft," I say dismissively, hoping he'll take the hint.

As I suspected, he does not. No one has ever shaken him that effortlessly. "I shall assist you. Were you planning on staying there? It is frightfully cold for that this afternoon, well morning still, is it not?"

"I don't mind it," I say as I turn to go, the grand duke still following.

"We wouldn't want you falling ill again." The grand duke smiles at me in a friendly way I'm not falling for.

"I'm just fine. Thank you for your concern," I say.

"I'm truly glad he chose you." The grand duke smiles. "Though of course there is a part of me that... Well, I had stated my intentions. I hope that doesn't make things awkward between us. Serving you as my princess and future queen makes me proud." I don't miss the slight twitch he tries to hide, as if calling me his queen is bitter on his tongue.

"I doubt that," I say honestly. After he'd pinned me to the wall, straddled me best he could and kissed me in a way I did not give even a hint at permission for, all to get me eliminated, I doubt very much he is willing to have me as his queen.

"I told you I didn't believe he could make a better choice. It's the one I would have made. But you have my assurance, I will not be pursuing that any further or misreading what you try to communicate in that regard, My Lady."

"I hope not and expect as much. Is that all you wanted?" I ask as I reach the staircase and start to make the climb up to the loft where I'd been sitting.

"My Lady, please let me assure you I have the utmost respect for you, and whatever has happened never once changed that. I seek only to assist you, as I always have the royal family." The grand duke is trying almost too hard to calm me. I think he can tell from my stiff demeanor I still don't trust him.

"So, what are you really after?" I ask, picking up the binder, but not sitting down, hoping he'll take the hint that I want to be about my business and that he should go away.

"To assure you, I am your ally and always have been. I'm sure your attendant has done all he can to insist I was only trying to have you eliminated, which is far from the truth. I... can you forgive my attraction when the prince could not resist?" He gives me an attempt at a sheepish smile. "I will certainly see you as my princess and constituent only from now on. You have my word. And you'll need me."

"I'll need you?" I seriously doubt that.

"Of course. Just because you did manage to win does not mean all the fears and weaknesses we've discussed just go away." He smiles warmly. "No one expects them to. I'll be a most helpful guide for you moving forward."

"Because you've guided us all so well so far," I reply, scathingly, deciding I'll have to end my lovely morning. I pull the bell to call for a member of staff to help put away the tea and the throw pillows and blankets. I can't recall if they are always in the loft or not.

"I beg your pardon." The grand duke frowns in confusion.

"All you ever did was try to make me doubt my ability to be princess and so I'd choose to rely on you," I point out. "And it was just to ensure you stayed in power or gained it by taunting the prince by claiming the one he wanted but couldn't have. You tried to get yourself made the queen's ruling partner by calling a vote of no confidence."

"I merely wanted to help the prince through a hard time." The grand duke's face reddens. "I never suggested being the ruling partner in the prince's place at any point."

"It's what you wanted. Don't play innocent." I shake my head. "You shouldn't have shown your true intentions to me in the lift that day. I know what you are. And though I cannot have you thrown out, if it wasn't a matter of national security, I would."

"I meant no offense by it. I simply was attracted to you," the grand duke insists.

"And even if it's true, you assaulted me," I reply. "And I'm not bound to behave just to make sure I'm not thrown back to my father anymore. You better prove you aren't lying, or so help me, I'll make sure you're nowhere near my line of succession."

"What are you going to do? Have too many children for me to outlive?" He has the gall to laugh.

My only power is giving Gavril heirs? "You shouldn't underestimate me because I'm soon to be 'crown princess' instead of 'lady'. I will use what power I have to eliminate you. If you prove disloyal and power grabbing again, I will have you thrust out, even if it is a risk to our national security."

"Don't overstep your bounds, My Lady." The grand duke finally starts properly arguing with me. I don't miss the lower title use. "I am vital to this kingdom, even if you dislike it. There is nothing you can do to dismiss me, anyway."

"If I have to go to the high king in person, and beg him on bended knee, I'll do it," I snap. And I will. I don't know how to get there or how easily I can beg it of the high king, but I'll do it.

"There's no one who could replace me," the grand duke mocks.

"I think several Chosen girls in need of an influential position to be appointed would prove otherwise," I warn.

The grand duke pauses as if realizing something, then nods. "You misunderstand why they need me. It's not just the position that must be filled."

"I know you're next in line after us. You've just been trying to skip over Gavril; now you have to skip over both of us. You and your team can scheme all you want, but if I get wind of malice behind our backs, I promise you will never gain the crown."

"I'm vital to your management of state with the war and I help manage relations with other nations. You'll need me for the Japcharian summit as well as the world summit. You cannot send anyone else. You go to the queen with it; she'll never allow it."

"You better hope so. Or if you don't improve your act, I'll be begging at that summit," I retort. "I'm not afraid of you. You may think they need you, but they don't. And all it will take is one more slip up and they won't let you near their meeting halls with a ten-foot pole. Now, I was trying to enjoy some quiet work. Leave."

I impress myself with my firm command. I'd *never* had this kind of authority. Maybe with my staff, but that felt different because they respected me. I had the power to order him about now. He disliked me, but I still have the power. It's a fun yet terrifying feeling.

The grand duke frowns. He knows he has been firmly dismissed. And he risks raising my ire further if he dares stay.

"But of course, My Lady." He's barely concealing a scowl as he turns and leaves.

I let out a heavy breath once I'm sure he's gone and plop onto the bench, looking down with a slight frown at the binder I'd let fall onto my lap. *Well, that went well.* I'd already threatened the first member of court I'd officially dealt with. But it also felt amazing.

"Well, you've not had the quiet morning you hoped for."

I jump and look up to see Gavril smiling at me. My face falls. He heard that?

"What's wrong?" he asks as he sits next to me. "You did amazing." He kisses my cheek.

"What?"

Gavril is still smiling. "Kascia. You did great. You put him in his place. And that, not this," he taps the binder on my lap, "is what a princess does all day. Unless you truly avoid it, which I doubt you would, that is what the princess does day after day. And for your first time doing it as official princess-to-be, you did perfect. Isla would have been too scared to tell him off as you did and should have done. Zelda would have laughed and not even taken him seriously, which she should as he is a threat. You did perfect. You're perfect for this, even if you won't always be perfect when you handle it. You can do this. You didn't even realize you were, did you?"

"Well, no." But he has a point. If I want to help fix this mess of a kingdom, I'll be doing work like that more than anything. I hadn't needed extra help to deal with the grand duke. Perhaps I am not so hopeless at this.

"And you have proven you know how to do the party side of being princess as well. You planned the festival, remember?" Gavril is still smiling. "You did it perfectly. You do not need to doubt."

I smile a little, looking down at the binder still. "I suppose I don't."

"Doesn't make this afternoon any easier." He frowns a little. "I was hoping to help you calm down a bit to be ready to practice. Then he'll be here in the late afternoon. What would you like to do?"

I frown a bit, unsure of what I want to do. "Hide," I say honestly.

Gavril chuckles at my tone. "Well, this is one of the best places to hide." He sits back, and I recognize his invitation for me to lean into him, so I do, tucking my feet next to me as he puts an arm around me.

"I don't know if I can keep composed."

"I'm not worried about that."

"It will matter once impressionors are on," I point out.

"That's a problem for tomorrow or not even then. We have a few days. Let's just worry about the private interview phase first." He smiles as he enjoys how I lean on him.

"He'll pick on what a blubbering mess I am." I frown.

"No, he won't. We won't let him for one, and for another, he really does want to record the makings of history, and this is one of those moments. He may like a good scandal, but the more comfortable and caring he is to you, the better his chances are to get the full story and our trust to let him have the deals in the future. It won't be long before other reporters start getting envious of all his exclusives. Most of all, after he gets this big one. He got to cover the Enthronement fine, but they'll see us handing him this one as another sign they need to up their game to get any good stories from the palace first. He'll behave."

"I trust what you all tell me. I'm still scared, though," I confess. "I struggle to trust doing the right thing always equals the best thing for me right now."

"I can understand that." Gavril puts his arms around me. "How about we get straight to how much to tell?" I nod, and we make a few choices, such as how to handle Jake's part in the story.

But Gavril can tell I'm still unsure. "We could ask Damian," he offers.

"But... We can't always." Should we really rely on him when it won't last long?

"I suppose, but since he's still here to help, why not?" Gavril gives me a warm smile and hugs me tighter, and I'm happy to hide in the hug. "It's going to be okay. I know you fear it causing everyone to hate you, but I honestly think, if anything, it will only help. And those it makes worse were going to not like you sooner or later anyway, and they can't hurt you. The way the people think of you does not change your position. You cannot be eliminated now. I chose you, and that's that. You're mine, no matter what anyone else does."

Gavril grins mischievously and nuzzles his face into my hair, so he can whisper into my ear, "I will be there no matter what."

I giggle at his references, and he laughs and pulls me closer and hugs me playfully, almost like I'm some plush toy. I laugh too and turn my head and twist my neck just right so my lips can meet his, even with how he's hugging me from behind.

He returns them, teasingly at first, but then gradually the kisses become more tender, then deeper. A kind of heaviness fills the air around us. But when we both move to adjust our positions to make it easier to reach one another, it's like we pop the bubble enough to realize what we are doing.

Gavril's chuckle is more embarrassed than my happy little giggle. "What?" I say as he goes redder and sits up more to get some more space. "It's not even close to the line. I've gotten much closer with Jake."

"Hey! That's not fair or allowed. What could you have possibility do—"

I don't let him finish. Instead, I turn and kiss him fiercely, not even hesitating to have to get onto his lap to do so.

Poor Gavril is so caught off guard all he can do is return the kisses, his hand getting tangled in my hair as I continue to tease him, loving the rush. It is far superior with him than it had been with Jake.

Finally, Gavril gently pushes against my body that has his pinned to the seat. I realize he's slowly begun to slide down the bench. I grin and pull back. He's still blinking stupidly. "That's what we did. But..." I lean into his ear. "This is better." I whisper before locking lips with him again.

"Oh..." A very embarrassed little call breaks us apart.

Gavril is far more embarrassed than I've ever been at being caught, even though I could have been eliminated for behaving that way before. He doesn't try to push me off, though. He clears his throat and brushes his hair back.

A poor maid, who likely came because I rang the bell before, is as red as a robin's breast and doesn't seem to know what to do.

I bite my lip. Although I'm sorely tempted to tell her to be about her work and tease Gavril some more, even with her there, I know that's not the best course of action. I am thoroughly relishing how embarrassed Gavril is, yet he still won't force me off.

"It's alright. You can clear up," I tell her and coolly slip back onto the bench next to Gavril.

"Y-yes My Lady," the maid stammers and quickly gets to collecting everything onto the tea tray to run away as fast as she can.

Gavril can't speak for a moment before he finally looks at me. "And you did that with him... all the time?"

"Not all the time," I defend. "Just when we'd get carried away sometimes."

"How often was sometimes?"

I shrug. "I don't know. Not every time we met up in our private spot, but every now and then."

"And it was never more than that?"

"Maybe for longer. No one ever found us," I admit.

Gavril smirks. "Did your father know?"

"I'm sure he did."

Gavril nods a bit, still smiling to himself as the maid leaves. "How about we go practice for our interview, then we'll have lunch, and Fabian will arrive shortly after."

I exhale deeply. "Alright." I'd rather stay there and tease him some more. Instead, I was in for a very long afternoon. I hope my makeup is waterproof.

# Chapter 9

We practice for a while before going to lunch. When it's time, we wait for Damian. He doesn't make us wait long. Before we get started, Damian asks to speak to Gavril privately for a moment. Gavril looks nervous at first, but then smiles and nods more certainly. He appears unchanged when they come back.

"Anything we should cover?" I ask Damian, looking up at him from where I sit restlessly.

Damian turns and checks the door, then faces me with a smile and nods encouragingly to Gavril. Gavril returns it, then looks at me. "There is one thing I'll cover." I nod. "We're going to tell them about the prophecy."

"What?" I thought his family had tried hard to hide that.

"Damian thinks it's the safest plan. And he makes a good point. There is no reason not to explain it, and it only helps your cause. Can't hurt your chances, right?"

"No, I suppose not." Though the doubts plague me, I do my best to hold to the faith I have in Gavril's choice. His belief in the prophecy allowed me to save his life, so it is powerful enough for this interview.

"It only helps you," Gavril points out again.

"And it will help the people understand why the Enthronement was needed in the first place," Damian says.

"So, I'll start the story on my end with the prophecy, then we'll start on your end where it is along the timeline." Gavril smiles comfortingly. "So, you have time to get it all straight."

I nod. "That might be helpful," I admit.

"Then that's the plan." Gavril smiles comfortingly.

"A-anything else." I look at Damian. We should have asked him before this point of no return.

"No, I believe we are ready if you are." He smiles at me gently.

"As I'm going to be." I sigh.

Gavril smiles and sits next to me, taking my hand and squeezing it to assure me. I force a smile back.

"And don't jump on my lap again," he teases. "I don't care how nervous you are." It does make me laugh and drop some of the tension. Even Damian chuckles. His smile asks, "Do I want to know?"

I giggle. "See? She doesn't even feel bad." Gavril keeps up the teasing. "Had to make sure we flirted with the line better than she did with Jake. Poor maid." I can't stop smiling. "See? Not ashamed at all," Gavril says to Damian, clearly trying to keep that smile on my face.

Damian chuckles and can't help but smile. "At least it wasn't me."

"Be thankful for that," Gavril agrees just as the door opens.

"He's here." Godwin nods at us.

I take a deep breath and nod. Gavril accepts that and nods at Godwin to let Fabian in.

Fabian doesn't come in bouncing off the walls like I expect. He defies my expectations and doesn't even glance at Damian to make sure he isn't overstepping the rules Damian set for this interview. Instead, he bows to us both and thanks us for trusting him.

Godwin nods him to his prepared seat situated across from Gavril and me on the love seat. Fabian takes a moment to get out a notebook, a pen, and oddly, a stack of sticky notes he puts at the top left of his notebook.

"Anything you all want to say before we start?" he asks. The normal, almost giddy, playfulness that comes from him is missing. Instead, his warm eyes are gentle and more serious. Though his windswept hair is about the same. He looks at us then at Godwin and Damian. I think he's making sure there aren't more rules he should know.

"I get to hit you for every rude comment," Godwin jokes, making us chuckle.

Damian smiles gently. "I don't believe there is anything to add, except that I am holding you to your word and that if anyone asks you to strike out something they said, you will honor it."

"Yes sir." Fabian's smile is much more like his old ones before he turns back to us. "So, for today, I'm going to keep the questions as few as possible. I'll try to wait until the end to ask. If you could just tell me your story, however, that would be easiest." He meets eyes with me first, trying to comfort me.

I swallow and manage a smile. He is the same man who'd talked to me so openly in the safe room and hadn't used a word of what I said in an article, keeping it all off the record. He wouldn't really throw it all at me, would he?

"Good. So where do you want to begin? With your side or the beginning of the Enthronement?" Fabian's eyes stay on me until mentioning the Enthronement , and his eyes flick over at Gavril.

"The latter," Gavril says confidently. "And though I know your impression is that you'll be hearing our story, you're going to get a little more than that. Starting with why the Enthronement was held in the first place."

"Oh, hold on." Fabian makes some adjustments on his note layout. I think he adds another box or something before he nods at Gavril to go on.

"Well, I'm sure many wonder why it took my parents so long to do something like this with how long I've remained single." Gavril gives Fabian a knowing smile. "And why they chose to run it as a contest at all. The answer lies back when I was a baby being presented as the heir."

"Way before I was on the scene," Fabian jokes. I think he's trying to get me to laugh just like Gavril was before.

"Well, maybe learning how to write your first articles in the mud outside," Gavril jokes back. "Or maybe teaching Godwin his ABCs." Godwin rolls his eyes. "But on that day, as the papers at the time reported, there was a... disturbance. The people argued that they should just kill me then and there.

"In the midst of the fighting, the Merlin appeared in flame and chided the bloodthirsty crowd for wanting to murder an innocent babe. But then he gave a prophecy."

Fabian pauses and looks up at us, then at Damian then back again. "About you?"

"About us." Gavril smiles and takes my hand.

Fabian's eyebrows go up, and a huge grin splits his face as he rapidly takes note. "Go on."

"It said..." And Gavril actually pauses and glances at Damian.

Damian gives him a smart smile then looks at Fabian. "As many will bless the child, so will I, with a special promise. This child will grow in strength and wisdom. He will be the one to finally bring unity and peace again to this land *if* he finds and marries a true princess. If he does not, he will not be able to bring the peace your land seeks. And perhaps, no one will." Damian makes a face as he finishes. "Not very poetic, but that's Cedrick for you." He shrugs.

Fabian laughs at the last comment. "Can I quote that last bit?" He'd written down the whole thing until he stopped to laugh at the extra comment.

Damian smiles and shrugs again. "Sure. I don't see why not."

Fabian chuckles and notes it down before looking up at Gavril. "So, the judge that mattered was you? I'm sorry. I'm getting ahead of myself, go on."

"Well, as you can imagine, that prophecy has shaped my life ever since." Gavril picks up without missing a beat. "And even with that in mind, my parents didn't really start the search in earnest until I was about twenty when most princesses are engaged at the very least. They arranged meetings with them, corresponded with them in most cases, and tried to figure out who the prophecy meant, but they had little luck when it was hard to compare them.

"So, they finally were able to arrange a visit with Princess Zelda, but even after spending a short time with her, they could not figure out who the princess was. They decided a test was in order. At first, it was just bringing all six of the eligible princesses here. The test would be done more discreetly.

"But that changed. While in a meeting preparing what kinds of tests would be appropriate, the Merlin showed up once more, much more secretly, and hinted that we had a true king who was not born a prince, so why did a true princess have to be born a princess? They'd never thought of that, and the fact the Merlin appeared again shook them up, so they created the Enthronement as we know it today."

That's my cue to start telling my side. Fabian asks a few questions to get more details on exactly what Father's plan was to make sure he had it straight. We somehow manage to dodge his questions about my former fiancé. I'd really rather not have angry mobs wanting to kill Jake. (Even if I'm sure every other person in that room would love to do exactly that.)

I tell Fabian about how anxious I was about the whole event as it drew closer. Gavril takes over as he can tell I need a break.

"Meanwhile, I was seeing the piles and piles of applications and honestly had to go for a run to control my breathing before I threw up. I know it might sound like fun to get to date all those lovely girls, but I felt the pressure and knew I'd end up breaking hearts and one of those broken hearts would likely be mine if I formed feelings for a girl who wasn't the right one."

"Did that ever happen?" Fabian asks Gavril the painful question. At least it means he likely won't ask me.

"Not... really," Gavril says slowly. "It's a bit complicated, but how about we tell the story in order. That will make more sense."

"Sorry. I'm trying to avoid asking too many questions. I don't want to get ahead or miss anything." Fabian smiles.

I then go on, thankful for the break, explaining how meeting the king and queen made me question my assumptions and made it all that much worse for me trying to untangle the truth. I try not to throw my former attendant Yarrow under the wheel, but his treatment of me certainly contributed to the anxiety that drove me to run away to the grounds that night.

Gavril picks up as I explain how easy it was to use the balcony to slip away. "I had been confined to the royal floor, terrified of running into a girl before I was supposed to. I was under a lot of pressure knowing the woman I'd marry could be any one of them down there, and I had to figure out who it was supposed to be, yet I couldn't search for the qualities I wanted in a spouse, I had to search out what the prophecy wanted. I talked my guard into letting me take a walk outside. It's not like I'd run into anyone out there." Gavril smiles.

"You didn't." Fabian is grinning widely.

"I didn't even suspect he was the prince," I admit.

"And I was terrified I was meeting one of them and wasn't supposed to." Gavril laughs. "And she ended up yelling at me."

"I didn't yell," I defend. "I just... he was so nice. He understood how trapped I felt and was so... well, understanding about it. I couldn't understand how someone like that could work for the tyrants, so I asked him how he stood it."

"And how did you reply?" Fabian couldn't help himself as he looks at Gavril.

"I admitted I didn't know how bad it was. I'd been so sheltered with everyone out to get me and being the prophesied last chance... I knew very little," Gavril admits. "So, I admitted I didn't understand but wanted to... I wanted to know what it was really like so badly it was what I wanted more than anything."

"And that touched me. Honestly, I felt I finally found a friend in this madness," I confess with a small smile. "So, you can imagine how crushed I was when I learned the truth a few days later when we officially met."

"And you didn't kick her out after asking such rebellious questions?" Fabian was impressed.

"I wasn't going to get rid of my best chance to understand my people's struggle. Plus, I'd have to admit I snuck out when I shouldn't have." Gavril smiles, and Fabian laughs. "I won't say it was love at first sight, but she certainly intrigued me. I wanted to understand her anger. How could she be here but hate us so much? I had to understand. And I told her as much in our first official one-on-one conversation. And that is how it all began, I suppose."

"And it was just... easy after that?" Fabian asks.

"No," we say together, even though that wasn't scripted, and Fabian laughs.

"Throughout most of the Enthronement I had a list in my head of girls I thought likely to pass and the ones I wanted to pass, and thankfully most of the time, those lists matched, at least most of the names, but... I don't know when it was for you." He glances at me. "But there was a moment that was particularly hard. I wasn't expecting to have to wrap up the first round of interviews before you came," he adds to Fabian to clarify what he meant. "And Kascia was the only one who noticed I needed help and was there, even if all she could give was moral support. No one else even noticed or thought to try to fill the role, and she didn't do it to outdo the other girls. She cared that I struggled.

"We spoke after, and... I just knew. After thinking over what we'd said and done, and as I stood there with her... I knew. I was almost frightened of how sure I was. Even more so when she pulled away."

I bow my head. I try to explain why I never thought it could be me with my past, and the struggle of knowing if I should go through with what Father wanted me to do.

"That's why it was hard for you to get close to the prince just yet?" Fabian guesses and also helps me go on.

I nod. "And I was starting to be seen as his favorite."

"That was my fault," Gavril confesses. "I rather unintentionally made a bit of a scene. After she pointed out that I couldn't just pick a girl like that, I decided I would try to find a second pick, so to speak. I went out with the other girls I felt likely to win and tried as hard as I could to see if they would react the way Kascia did or capture my interest like Kascia had. They didn't, no matter how hard I tried to help them be more like Kascia or how hard I tried to feel something for them.

"I was in this mode when the rebels broke in, and we were all in the safe room. Some rebels got into the safe room, and Kascia killed one who was trying to... take advantage of one of the other girls. And my inexperience with the cluster of emotions spurred by how much her actions excited me, in a rush I honestly had never experienced and have learned to curb since, I kissed her right there and then in front of the whole room."

"Ah, the rumor was true." Fabian smiles.

"In part." Gavril taunts, but he deflects Fabian's attempt to clarify.

I thought it would get harder as we talked about the Harvest Ball, but it wasn't as bad as I thought. I explain how I drove Father away, and though I made my choice, I still questioned it for a long time.

When Fabian jumps in to ask if all was smooth from there, we both laugh and Gavril steps up to share more of his side.

"I was being pressured into trying to find anyone who could at least be a happy second choice next to Kascia... in all honesty, it just made me surer it should be her," Gavril admits. "No matter how close I made myself get to the others... it just assured me more that it should be her. And I did my best to prove that to her... I was really bad at it."

We all laugh. "But that wasn't all his fault... I never was able to get up the courage to tell him of my past."

"When did you tell him?" Fabian asks.

"Only after I knew the truth." I bite my lips.

"Which was?"

"After the final test," Gavril says. "Because we thought it would get us down to one girl. It didn't. Princess Zelda, Lady Isla, and Kascia all passed. It was then we knew we had to tell them the truth about the prophecy."

"Were the other girls rewarded?" Fabian asks.

"Lady Isla is now the Princess Ward of Purerah, making her royalty in all but being in a ruling line. Princess Zelda is heir to her land. Not much we can reward her with." Gavril gives Fabian a half smile.

"Fair. So, when did the girls learn about the prophecy?" Fabian leads us on.

Gavril explains how his mother finally decided that Gavril should make the call on which of the three it should be because if they all passed, they must be true princesses. But he felt sure the prophecy meant one of them.

"And to be honest, I still was sure it was Kascia, but I'd never really sought confirmation of my own. You know? I didn't ask for direction like I should, so I asked them to wait while I confirmed my choice. I almost regretted that deeply. But after I spent most of the day pondering and in dedication to get my confirmation, I had a thought. We hadn't tested what the girls would sacrifice for their people. There I was, willing to give up the woman who meant the world to me if I was wrong, but we hadn't once tested to see what the other girls would give up. I had already told the three of them the truth of the prophecy before I asked them for time."

"And I was sure it couldn't be me." I bow my head and rub my arms. Gavril puts an arm around me. I struggle through explaining how guilty I felt. How I wished I'd told him the truth sooner, so he wouldn't have his heart ripped out. I had to tell him the truth. He could not choose me. When I explain how that fear drove me outside, even in the storm, Gavril takes over.

"And I'd maybe been in bed an hour or two," Gavril picks up. "After I had my revelation on the final test to put them to so I could be sure, I decided it was whoever pulled out of the game first. Who would choose to give up their chance to win first? I'd wait as long as it took. I got maybe two hours sleep before I was being woken up to be told Kascia was in the storm, refusing to come inside until she convinced me she couldn't win."

His smile could rival the sun for brightness. "So, I went out, and she explained everything. But none of it worried me. It only proved me right with how much she was willing to give up. And honestly, she understood the enemy better than anyone else in the Enthronement. That was a plus, not a problem. I knew I could trust her with anything. She was not the threat or guilty of treason like she seemed sure she was." He gives me a look which I just smile sheepishly.

"How in creation did he change your mind?" Fabian looks at me, impressed.

"Well... it wasn't until after the attack at the first attempt to announce it I even realized he was going to choose me," I confess.

We had carefully planned how much to share on this. I explain how I had to fight my father off. How he tried again to convince me to come back to him, but even though I lost Gavril, I was not going back to his web of lies. How the only way to protect them was to kill him and how I thought I had.

We keep private how I had to choose to have faith in Gavril's choice to save his life. It just felt too private, too sacred to share, and perhaps in the future, we'd be willing to, but it didn't feel needed for now, so we just make it sound like the time alone in the safe room did the trick. Fabian doesn't question it.

"And happily ever after," Fabian jokes, though his tone indicates we all know full well it is far from over.

"Pretty much." Gavril smiles.

Fabian asks a few questions, mostly about when I learned I wasn't an active Custod. I'm careful to make it sound like I made Mother tell me just in case that got her in trouble with Father.

"Well, that gives me a great place to start." Fabian smiles at us. "I'll get this written up and submitted as soon as I can. Then we'll have public reaction as well as any more questions I might have for the interview, for which I'll also write a summary. That sound like a plan?" He looks at us then at Damian.

"Any heads up on questions ahead of time would be helpful." Gavril indicates with a serious look at Fabian.

"As many as I can," he promises. "I understand having a heads up will help with emotional reactions."

"Thank you, Fabian." Damian nods. "And any questions the people send to your paper after the article is published, please have them forwarded to either Godwin or myself."

"Of course." Fabian nods. "Is there anything else I missed?" He looks at us again. I shake my head, and Gavril does the same.

"I believe that is the long and short of it." Damian smiles gently.

"Well, then I'll get started. If I have any problems or questions I need to finish this, I'll reach out to... you or Godwin?" Fabian checks as he stands to leave. Gavril and I stand too. Standing helps let a lot of the tension out.

"Please do, to either one of us," Damian says as he stands as well.

"Thank you for the trust and honor. I won't let you down," he promises us and gives me in particular a smile. I return it.

Damian nods to him. "I'm sure you won't," he says with a small smile.

"Enjoy the rest of your day, Your Highnesses, My Lord." He nods to us, then Damian and leaves with Godwin seeing him out. They start some kind of teasing, but I can't hear exactly what they're saying before they close the door.

"See? You were fine." Gavril smiles, giving me a sideways hug and kissing my head. I smile a little as I accept his praise, but I don't really have a response to it.

Damian smiles reassuringly. "You really were brilliant. I know it was hard, but you handled it exceptionally well."

"Thanks." I manage a smile for him too. But I have one more very painful round to go.

"It's going to be fine. You'll see," Gavril assures me. "Meanwhile, I'm sure there's some more fun work we can do?" he suggests. I take a deep breath and nod. Gavril looks at Damian as if inviting him to take the time he has.

"Well, as I heard how well you did at helping Gavril set up his office, I thought you might like to see how things are coming with the princess suite and make any changes or suggestions you like." Damian smiles.

"Oh alright." I nod. Gavril smiles and kisses my head again, excusing himself as he has to check in with his advisor and tells me to have a good time.

The progress looks great, and it's comforting seeing how well Damian knows me, and even somehow seemed to know some of Gavril's ideas about the space that I'd liked and was using them, it was just nice to spend time with him like nothing had changed, most of all when I go down to dinner and recall soon he'd be gone. But not yet. There was hope ahead, and I just have to make sure it doesn't slip away from me.

# Chapter 10

I wake in the morning feeling better, but still with a twisted knot in my stomach. It is a rest day, but I know Fabian will spend the day working on the article to be released tomorrow. I don't know how to not be dreading it all day.

My maids come in, just my normal team, and help me get ready. Though Vivian teases me that now I'm supposed to have four personal maids, but I haven't picked the new girl in their soon-to-be quartet. I assure her we'll get to it. I just don't know when now it's a rest day.

I wonder if Gavril will try to take the day to just have fun, as he seems so intent on trying to enjoy our victory. With a disappointed frown and begrudging scowl, he informs me at breakfast that he has some work to do that morning, but he proposes meeting up whenever he finishes if I am alright with that.

Hoping I can find another way to keep busy, I nod. I still have the binder Bella gave me. Perhaps I can review it and see if I have more work to do there. The grand duke wouldn't bother me in the conservatory two days in a row, would he?

Thankfully, he doesn't. I spend about an hour or so going over everything when Damian tentatively walks up to me, making sure I don't mind the interruption.

"Ah, I thought I'd find you here." He smiles at me warmly.

"Hello Damian." I set the binder on the side table. "What can I help you with?"

He smiles gently as he looks down. "Well, I have someone I'd like you to meet, if I'm not disturbing you."

"Again?" My shoulder blades tense in nervousness. "I don't mind. Bring them over, or do we need to go somewhere?"

"Here is perfectly fine," he assures me. "But this is... Well, I guess I can't promise it will be the last. But if you wait here, I'll be right back."

"Alright." I smile, curious and intrigued. He smiles with a bright hopefulness though there's a slight hint of worry, as if he really hopes I'll like this new person and leaves, only to return a few moments later with a man in tow. I frown a bit as I stand, trying to recall why he's familiar. We'd met.

The man is older, tall, with blue eyes and white-gray hair and a friendly warmth about him that's familiar in more than just that I'm sure we've met. I take a moment to recall I'd met him at the king's memorial. He'd come with the Athadinians.

"Lady Kascia, this is Sir Purillian Custod," Damian says, gesturing to the man.

I smile a little. "Hello again."

Sir Purillian smiles back, but there's something in his eyes. A worried wavering look of hopefulness as well as a nervousness. Is he wondering what this is all about too?

Damian smiles to see his hopeful yet tentative smile, then looks at me with tenderness. "I'm glad you remember, but Kascia... he's your grandfather," he says with a warmth in his eyes.

"What?" My eyes dart from Sir Purillian to Damian.

"I asked him to come," Damian says. "It was the other part of the reason I was gone those two days. But I'll let you two have a moment to talk." He then steps back.

I mouth saying "but" to draw him back, but I don't. I'm a bit overwhelmed with a tight yet empty knot in my chest. Although I knew there was a good chance I still had a grandparent alive, Lila even mentioned it, meeting them like this hadn't really crossed my mind. And perhaps I wanted my father back and this man perhaps was my chance at that now my substitute father, Damian, had to move on to helping others. Though more likely, it was because I had such a tumultuous relationship with this man's son, I fear having just as messy of a relationship with him.

I let Damian step back, though, and look back at Purillian, my mouth still slightly open. His warm blue eyes are studying me with a soft smile on his face. He seems as nervous as I am. "I'm sure your father... has said some things." He finally dares speak. I want to invite him to step closer as there is quite a gap between us still, but I don't really know how. And I'm too shy to step closer yet.

"You must really resent us for leaving you in this." Purillian forces a small, uncertain smile. "And I wouldn't blame you. I always wondered... well," he chuckles to himself, "I should let you speak your mind first, I presume."

I don't really have any thoughts; I'm still reeling, wondering exactly how I feel and why this overwhelms me after learning Lila is my cousin.

"I suppose I might not know what to say either." Purillian sighs heavily. "I never thought..." He smiles with that small uncertain smile with that warmth in his eyes still. "You're even more beautiful than I imagined."

My cheeks tinge slightly pink. "Imagined?" I don't know why that's what I decided to repeat back.

"I don't know what your father told you about us." Purillian gaze drops as if in mourning. "But none of it is true, I'd bet. We were all here assigned to the Purerahian conflict: me, your grandmother, father, uncle, and aunt. Your father was not long off his test when he started getting frustrated. When it came out what he was doing, they held a full trial and stripped him of his rights. The family is supposed to step back. If they want to earn their rights back, they must do it alone to prove they want it because they are truly penitent, not for family pressures.

"We didn't want to leave. As you've likely guessed, I and your grandmother took the offered assignment to assist the Athadinian court and have been there since. Your uncle took various guarding duties over the years, and your aunt became a provider after all that happened, focusing on medical assistance, becoming a minor healer. She travels about too, but most of the time, they'll come back to Athaduina to see us. I don't think any of them apart from Lila have come to Purerah since."

Purillian pauses, watching me with a slight concerned frown. "I say this not as an excuse, but as an explanation of why you never saw us or heard from us. Also, your father chose to disappear. We weren't even sure if he was still in Purerah or was running his little rebellion from another nation. Honestly, none of us ever guessed he'd never leave. Well, for a short time, he did, so we presumed he never returned. I hope you can forgive us for accidentally cutting you off as well."

"You didn't have a choice." I was aware how the family was supposed to step back from a disinherited Custod. They could run into trouble for bothering them too much.

"We would have if we knew about you." Purillian frowns as his eyes fill with a longing regret.

"You didn't know?" Of course not.

Purillian shakes his head. "You'd be an excuse for us to get involved if so." Then his expression falls a bit more. "Though... I suppose I wasn't... entirely clueless," he admits with a guilt-ridden expression that stirs pity within me. "Not too long after we finally settled into this new life, and most of all, my wife had finally let Peodrick go, I got an... unmarked message in the post. My wife never saw it, and I never let her, but I kept it... unsure if it was his or not."

I frown. "I-I don't understand."

His eyes meet mine, full of shame. "I know this will sound impossible, but I've loved you long before I even knew if you were real. I couldn't be happier or prouder to find you as you are. And you may not believe this with all that's happened to you, but I love you deeply and have loved you long before we ever met."

I still don't understand, so I stand still, waiting for him to explain, wishing he'd close the gap but the fear in my heart prevents me from crossing it myself.

With a slow hand, Purillian reaches into his breast pocket and slips out an old but well cared for bit of paper, unfolding it with trembling hands, looking at it tenderly a moment before finally coming closer and offering it to me.

"My wife doesn't know I have this. No one does. I rather hoped... your father may have sent it or perhaps your mother. So, I held onto it, but if I was wrong... I didn't want to bring it all back up when my wife only just got over the pain of what Peodrick had done."

I look into his pain-tinged face, which now I look, is rather like Father's, but it's hard to tell as my father sports a beard, and Purillian does not. I take the paper and turn it upright to study it.

The texture feels like someone has kept it safe in some kind of pressed book, the paper and it's folds crip yet delicate like old paper, but the rest of the paper remains as pristine as if it had just been pressed.

It's not even faded. The color on it is hardly changed from the date it was impressed. It's of a small babe, maybe a few weeks old, eyes surprisingly open and with a huge toothless smile, as if she'd been laughing her little head off. I know the color of those eyes. The hazel ring in the center of the blue is the same I see in the mirror every day, though not yet the more round-upturned shape they'd become. I also know the blue and white blanket with yarn ties all around it well. It was mine.

"And though I didn't... know, I knew. I just never expected to actually find you. And I knew without proof that you were real and not just some... lost mail, I'd never get permission to try to find you. So, I didn't even try. Just... prayed and hoped he was taking as good care of you as you deserved and too afraid to admit I even had this impression." There's still more guilt than anything else in his voice. "I'm sorry. I should have tried harder. You deserve better than whatever he put you through."

"You..." I don't know what to say to this as I finally look from the distraction of the impression up to his face again.

"I understand if that only makes you angrier. But you deserve to know. Just please don't mention it to anyone else. My wife, in particular, will be furious and likely never forgive me."

I fight a trembling lip and hope that I cling to, yet I am afraid to keep. I offer the impression back to him. It means far more to him than it ever will to me. "You... even not knowing if it was true still..." He still loved me from afar with no idea. I can't even imagine what that would be like. He loved me as his own without ever having met or known me. Just an impression to *hint* that I existed.

"I love you more than anything, even unsure you were real. It's a strange feeling to care for someone so much you've never met or could hope to meet. I never would have guessed in a million years... this is where you'd end up." He chuckles. "Your mother picked your name?"

"Um... I don't know. I think my father did." I admit.

"Really?"

"I think they mentioned something about it." I can't fully remember, just that I think that's what they'd said. His questions aren't helping the twist of emotions dancing in my chest.

"You may recall when we met, I said I liked your name because my wife wanted to name a daughter that." I have a vague recollection of that. "We compromised with your aunt's name, as it's a family name. My wife would tease me about the fact we didn't have another to give the name to. I thought perhaps your mother thought it kind. I... but if your father chose it." He pauses as he thinks that over, but then shakes himself. "Either way, it's dazzlingly perfect."

"I suppose it is." I manage a smile, still overwhelmed but in a very different way.

Grandfather smiles at me and hesitates a moment before putting a hand to my cheek. "I'm sorry we couldn't find you sooner."

I don't care. My shining eyes reach up to meet his. At this moment, I'm not sure I could care less. He's here now, and that's more than enough. Overflowing with these fresh emotions, I skip over any sense of priority and embrace him, holding on with all my strength, tears pricking at my eyes.

Grandfather just smiles and clings to me. "I love you, Kascia. I loved you before I knew you. And it won't change now that I know you now."

That unconditional love without feeling like I have to pull them into it or fight to create it is only making this warm pool overrun the sides more. Damian is truly the only person who I feel loved me without compulsion or trickery. Father's love had been a conditional lie, though I never thought it was. Mother's was confusing with all the secrets, and the whole Enthronement made Gavril unsure until recently. But I barely know this man or he me, but he cares for me much like Damian does.

I don't want to cry, but I can't stop the tears dancing in my eyes anyway as I hide in this grandparent I didn't even know I wanted. Honestly, I thought he'd judge me. He knew better than anyone Father most likely tricked me into this. Or maybe he didn't yet, or maybe he didn't have to figure it out, and Damian told him. He didn't care. I feel that in his secure hug as surely as I felt in Damian's or Gavril's.

Grandfather gives me a moment, likely wanting to just enjoy the moment too before he strokes my hair. "Used to stare at that picture and wonder if you were real or alright with whatever your father might have put you through. Honestly, I wasn't sure if you even were a her or a him."

I laugh at that and pull back to wipe my eyes on the back of my wrist. He smiles too and helps dry a tear. "I imagine he'd be harsher on a son."

"I'd guess." I laugh a little, still pulling myself together. "M-mother mentioned something about worrying about that."

"So..." I understand what he wants to ask before he forces it out.

"It was just after. Mother wasn't even sure if she was already expecting me or not when it happened."

Grandfather nods a little. "I see. That lines up with when I got the impression. It might have even been old then." He looks at me again. "I wish I'd been sure sooner."

"Everyone in my family has had to refrain from telling me or doing something for me. That's Father's fault, not yours." My father forced my mother to lie to me. Father preventing my grandfather from finding me seemed less of an insult in comparison, and I had no trouble forgiving my mother. I know how Father can be.

"That doesn't make it right or not unfair to you." Grandfather's brows and eyes pinch. "And that shouldn't be an excuse."

"It makes it easier to forgive, though." I meet his blue eyes. I guess I got my blue from him.

He smiles slightly. "Maybe it does." He hugs me again, and I enjoy it without as many tears this time.

"So, I got an overview from the papers, and I met you at the memorial, and my royal family has been very interested." He glances at the bench, contemplating whether to invite me to sit, but also realizing that might be improper etiquette.

I smile a little and lead him over by the hand so we can sit.

"But you tell me. What happened?"

I frown, but at the same time, I want nothing more than to tell him everything. I tell him what it was like growing up, about Jake, about how I knew Mother disapproved but never would speak against it, about how I felt when Father tried to push me into the Enthronement, I even tell him about the horrible pictures from the battlefront (which I hadn't even told Gavril); I tell him about every high and low of the Enthronement, the horror of learning the truth, Father's use of the prophecy against me: everything, and I don't hide the feelings either. Allowing myself to become angry, allowing tears to cascade down, just releasing it all, yearning, needing his understanding. No one could ever be as good as Damian at understanding, but I could let Grandfather try. I release all the pressure in my chest to him like pouring out a jug full of pressurized water.

Grandfather doesn't stop me to ask questions at any point unless it is helpful to prod me on. But that doesn't mean he just sits there. He'll laugh, frown, give me small hugs, and wipe my tears away, but I think he wants to understand as badly as I want to explain it.

When I finish, he doesn't speak right away, too busy studying me to make sure I'm alright. When he's sure I am, he just smiles. "You're one strong young woman, Kascia. I'm not sure I could be prouder of you. Your father has made many, many mistakes, but you aren't one of them. Even if how he handled you was a mistake."

I laugh away the last bit of tears. "And he will not do that again. I'll be here with you. I'll assist you as well as I ever did Athadina or any other nation I've worked for." I laugh a little again. "And we'll figure out what to do with him."

"I wish he'd just have listened." My face falls again.

"Me too. You gave him every chance to turn around. I'm so proud." He can't help but hug me again, making me laugh as I hug him back.

It occurs to me to offer him tea just as I hear some rather loud and hurried voices from the main entrance to the conservatory. I frown and look for Damian to see if he knows what all that is.

He isn't where I expected him to be. Instead, I spot him further away, closer to the entrance, talking to two women: one is my mother.

Grandfather smiles as he sees me light up to see her. I hadn't seen her since the funeral. Based on her gray hair and the way they are conversing, I would assume that the woman with her is my grandmother, not that I'd recognize my grandmother. I'm a bit surprised Mother gets along with her husband's mother so well.

We wait for them to join us up on this floor, and I jump up to greet Mother without hesitation. She laughs and hugs me tightly. "I'm so proud of you." She sighs and pulls back to look me over. "You look good."

"Thanks. I've missed you." I sigh and hug her again.

Grandfather gets up, but he does nothing else. Grandmother is hanging back, smiling at us and is likely waiting for a proper introduction.

It takes Mother a moment to realize she's waiting and chuckles at herself. "Oh, of course. Kascia, I see you met your grandfather." Mother takes my arm and brings me closer. "This is your grandmother, Rosetta Custod."

Before I can decide how to react, which likely would have been just a hug, my grandmother reacts first, coming forward and hugging me too quickly for me to return it before pulling back, twittering even more like a blue bird than Hydie did, which is saying something.

"I can't believe this is real. You're so pretty. I never would have guessed." She gently frames my face with her fingers before letting them rest under my chin like many an actor had done for a scene presenting or examining a character. "We're so proud of you. Oh Kascia, what a perfect name, too." She gives me that quick hug again before kissing my cheek. She's so fast I'm too stunned to speak.

"And soon, our princess. We couldn't be prouder. Your father did you no favors," Grandmother sighs. "But you've overcome that. Just stunning and ready for this. I'm just so happy to get to meet you. We had no idea." Grandmother hugs me again, longer this time.

I return it sheepishly. I notice Grandfather look at Mother and pull the picture ever so slightly from his pocket and raise his eyebrows in question. Mother smiles back softly and nods a little, tapping her chest to say she sent it. Grandfather just smiles and mouths, 'thank you', avoiding attention from Grandmother, who is still squeezing the life out of me.

She's even more overwhelming than Grandfather had been, but in a very different way. I don't know what to say. It's a bit like when Yarrow was praising me and trying to decide how to make me better. "Th-thank you?" I manage at last.

"And of course, the voice of a lark," Grandmother declares and kisses both my cheeks. I wonder if she's Purysian.

"Well, we had a good chat while you two were busy." Grandfather comes to my rescue. "Apparently, it wasn't Chrisa's idea?" Grandfather raises a brow at her.

"Her name? Actually, Peodrick suggested it, and I loved it." Mother smiles. "Why?"

"Nothing." Grandfather shakes his head with a smile, but Grandmother goes into a rapid explanation, the same that Grandfather tells me, and actually pinches my cheek just a little.

"It's perfect. With that name, it's as if she were one of ours already," she says.

"She is your granddaughter. Don't think her name being what you'd have named a second daughter makes her yours." Mother chuckles.

"I wholeheartedly agree." Grandfather gives me a smile, clearly able to tell I'm overwhelmed by Grandmother. I think he's trying to say she isn't normally so bad. I suppose she must be excited.

"This is all better than we could have hoped. I lost all hope of us ever coming together again, but we'll all be here for the wedding." Grandmother goes on.

"I don't know if you'll get Tolan to come after all that happened," Grandfather warns my grandmother, but she will not be deterred. She goes on and on about how we'll finally be together, and it's thanks to me and my bravery, and she kisses my cheeks again while I quickly realize forming a bond with my grandmother will be a lot harder than with my grandfather.

"Tolan was pretty upset with his brother, likely more than anyone." Grandfather tries to remind my grandmother, but she won't hear of it.

Mother sighs as Grandmother twitters on and on. "She's too happy to accept it won't be perfect."

"We'll see. His daughter Lila is here, so that may help." Grandfather sighs. It's hard to listen to them while Grandmother is so excited, but honestly, I can't even understand all the high happy sounds my grandmother is making while looking at me and touching my face and hair now and then.

"Be that as it may, the wedding is still a while off, and I think Lady Kascia would like her face back in the meantime." Damian steps up with a half joke.

"Hmm?" Grandmother looks over at Damian, which allows Mother to pull me back a little with a soft smile.

"But in that stride, why don't we go find the lucky guy?" Damian smiles and pulls out his golden watch and checks the time. "This time of day, he is usually in his office, if I'm not mistaken."

"You'd know better than me," I admit.

"Would he though?" Grandmother smiles.

"I wasn't allowed to bug for his time before winning, so I wasn't familiar with his habits."

"And I have an extra pair of eyes wandering about the castle." Damian smiles, amused with himself. I laugh.

"Extra eyes?" Grandmother glances at his watch, the one they say connects him to his brother. I giggle.

"He keeps a low profile, so I doubt you'll see much of him. But shall we pester the prince?" Damian smiles too like his brother and gestures the way with a half bow.

"I think that would be a great idea," Grandfather agrees. Grandmother beams and starts chattering again. Mother takes the attention though, so Grandmother coos over me, but to her instead of me. Grandfather indicates I go first, so I follow Damian.

Damian smiles and offers his arm. "My Lady."

I smile and accept it. "Thanks," I say to him as we head down the stairs.

"Anytime." He smiles and leads the way.

"I meant for finding them. You didn't have to do that." I smile.

"Of course I did. I had to be sure you will be cared for in the many years to come, whether your father comes around or not," Damian says with a soft smile. "You are my daughter, Kascia. I can't leave without knowing you will be safe."

"Or you could stay," I tease, though I know the answer.

"I'd have to convince Cedrick." He smiles, a bit amused by my joking attempt. "And frankly, I think he wants to see his wife." He chuckles.

"You don't want to see yours?" I tease, trying not to be sad at the idea I'd not get to meet her.

"I do, and I think she'll be sad she will have to wait to meet you. She would have loved you." Damian smiles warmly. "Though... she also liked to bake and would have tempted you far too many times with treats."

"I won't dance much anymore, so perhaps it doesn't matter." I giggle, but pause. "What did you mean by 'yet'?"

He smiles. "It's a long way off for you."

"Oh." I see what he's saying. "I can only hope so." I suppose rebels will want to assassinate me now too. It's odd to use the word assassinate when referring to myself. "It must be weird going back and forth like that."

Damian shrugs. "It was for a long time. Now, it's just life."

"It must be nice once you get used to it." I nod a little. "Still, it helps a lot."

Damian nods. "It does. Though I want you to remember something."

I look at him, listening.

"Just because you won't see me doesn't mean I'm not there."

"Really?"

Damian smiles. "I promise."

I smile and kiss his cheek in thanks as we reach the royal offices. He returns it as he takes us right up to the prince's office and knocks.

"Come in." Comes Godwin's voice. Damian opens the door and lets us in.

Godwin smiles as we enter his office. "Ah, oh... you have a party." He looks us over. "I... aren't you from Athadina?" He tries to recognize my grandparents.

"Assigned there." Grandfather smiles.

"Previously assigned." Damian corrects with a smile of his own. "And being reassigned." He turns to Godwin. "This is Sir Purillian and Dame Rosetta Custod. They are Kascia's grandparents."

"Oh. Lovely." Godwin grins. "Going to introduce the in-laws?"

"He's met me," Mother defends playfully. Godwin laughs.

"And the other at the announcement battle." Damian chuckles a little. "But yes, that is the idea. Lord and Lady Custod, this is Godwin, the prince's valet."

"Honor." Godwin bows to them. "He's just working on little things. I'll let you in."

Godwin goes to the other door, knocks, then opens the door. "Sir," he calls. "Kascia's got someone for you to meet."

"Let her in." I hear Gavril's voice, and Godwin steps aside, holding the door for us. Damian lets go of my arm and ushers me and my family forward.

I walk in first. Gavril is already standing and comes over to embrace me and gives me a quick kiss before looking up to see who else came in. He greets Mother, then tilts his head a bit.

"Ah, Sir Purillian... what a surprise to see you here. Hello Damian." He nods as Damian comes in last.

"So precious!" Grandmother can't hold it in. Though I'm arm-in-arm with him, she walks right up to Gavril, and no joke, pinches both his cheeks. "You're both so darling!"

Gavril blinks rapidly, controlling the temptation to slap her away. Grandfather winces in apology. Damian does too.

"Dame Rosetta, please." Damian almost begs. "We haven't even made introductions."

"Sorry, it's just..." She beams and straightens out Gavril's jacket before stepping back. Poor Gavril is trying so hard not to react.

Damian lets out a sigh and gives Gavril an apologetic look. That makes Gavril look at him with a begging look to know what is going on.

Damian sighs. "Prince Gavril, Sir Purillian and Dame Rosetta Custod, Kascia's grandparents." He gestures to each as he says their name.

Gavril blinks once more and looks at them again, then at me. I just beam in excitement. That tells him this is a good thing, and he greets them warmly, kissing Grandmother's hand (rather reluctantly though, but she doesn't notice) and shaking Grandfather's hand before Grandfather pulls him into a hug that Gavril does not mind even if he's caught off guard.

"You're very lucky," Grandfather tells him.

"Trust me, I know that more than anyone." Gavril smiles as they pull apart. "I don't deserve what they gave me."

"You're so sweet." Gavril pulls away this time before Grandmother gets there as Grandfather and I laugh.

"And of course, you already know Lady Chrisa." Damian smiles at my mother.

"Pleasure as always." He kisses her cheek much more easily. "So, you got them here."

"No, it was all Damian." Mother smiles at him.

"Ah." Gavril chuckles. "So here for the wedding?"

"Actually, if you don't object, the plan is to be reassigned here," Grandfather says. "We're negotiators, after all."

"Oh..." Gavril pauses. "We've not had that in a while. If the head approves."

"Well... after what happened when we were here before." Grandfather explains.

"I see." Gavril nods. "You're more than welcome."

"We'll all be together again." And Grandmother just stops herself from going for Gavril again by hugging her husband's arm.

"All?" Gavril frowns.

"At least for the wedding, she hopes our other children show up." Grandfather's tone makes it clear he doesn't believe they will. She waves him off. Gavril gives Damian a questioning look, wondering what's wrong with this woman and how I am related to her. I laugh.

Damian gives him an amused apologetic smile. "On that, we'll have to see. But the head won't object to the reassignment. I wrote him myself."

"Then I'm sure all is fine." Gavril smiles. "You take good care of her for me." And there's something in his voice.

"Admittedly, Your Grace, my actions were a bit more selfish than that," Damian says with a slight hint of sadness in his tone as he glances at my grandfather then to me.

"I know. But you still do more than I can ever thank you for." Gavril smiles slightly.

Damian smiles and bows his head to him. "You are indeed welcome. I simply do what I can."

"So, how much of all this are you planning?" Grandmother asks Damian.

"Of what?" I frown.

"Well, the wedding, coronation, I suppose, all of that." She smiles.

"Currently, none of it. But I believe our dear Kascia and her new attendant, Lady Bella, have it well handled." He beams at me.

I smile back. "I think we've figured it out." Gavril smiles at that.

Then Grandmother goes into a rush, talking about the other weddings she's helped with as well as her own. Her excitement is palpable. I glance at Gavril in apology. "Mother will love her," he whispers to me, making me giggle.

Grandfather smiles, and Gavril doesn't miss that the two of us meet eyes after I look away from Gavril. He smiles a bit wider.

But soon it's time to go to lunch and Gavril invites them all along. I'm sure the queen will enjoy that. I glance at Damian, wondering if he'll vanish again.

"Well... this is the most important thing on my list." Damian smiles at me. "Of course, I'll join you." He nods to Gavril.

"Excellent, shall be a great time," Gavril says and opens the door for everyone else to leave first, apart from Damian, as I could have told Gavril. He hesitates a second before he catches on that Damian was waiting for us, so goes out first. I'm giggling. Damian smiles, nods to me, then follows me out.

The queen is surprised to see so many of us. Zelda is delighted. We tease the queen at first, making her guess. Damian chuckles and jokes, "Honestly, you all get it from Margorim."

Gavril says he didn't, but Damain reminds him that Margorim was King Roxorim's father as well as Cedrick's. That would explain all the endless teasing we're doing.

But then I take pity on the poor queen, who is smiling, amused by our playfulness, but still unsure why these guests are here. "They're my father's parents."

"Oh." The light goes on in the queen's eyes, and she starts to gabber on with Grandmother and Mother almost instantly. I smile a little. Damian smiles at me. I return it, not sure what it's for, though.

Grandfather just relaxes as the "moms" start to bond and enjoys his meal. Gavril looks unsure if he should try to engage him in conversation, but Zelda beats him to it, and he doesn't seem to mind one bit. They're going to fit in just fine.

# Chapter 11

I get a surprise on the devotional day. Being a part of the royal family now, I sit in that section with the queen, which feels odd. During the Enthronement, I normally sat with my friends or maids. It is nice to be closer to Gavril, though. I notice Mr. Dudley and his staff sitting towards the back and smile as they beam up at me. I confess, I wave back.

After lunch, I get another surprise. Cedrick drops in unannounced. My first instinct is worry. What mess will he throw at me? I'm already in the middle of one. But instead, he has good news for me.

"It's about tomorrow," he says, his electric blue eyes twinkling.

"What's tomorrow?" The article had come out that morning. I hadn't had a chance to look at it yet. I am far too afraid. Gavril had made sure to keep me busy. My maids tricked me into sleeping in until it was time to get ready for breakfast and go to services.

"It's Damian's birthday." Cedrick grins.

"Oh." I had no idea. Of course, as I'd been here almost a full year, the odds of crossing his birthday were high, but I'd not even thought about it. Funny. Mine is the day after. I'd almost forgotten.

"And I thought you might like to take the chance to do something. So rare we get the chance." Cedrick smirks.

"Well, it's not like we did anything for your birthday," I remind him. I know full well his birthday is on Christmas Day. He'd spent it ill. Likely because he ate all those cookies and drank all that milk children leave out for him when he drops off gifts.

"No. I like to keep it that way." Cedrick nods. "It was not a happy time for me in my life, and frankly, the attention is terrifying." I giggle at the idea. He is happy to make people laugh, but he doesn't like praise.

"And honestly, it wasn't exciting for Damian either, but he insists on celebrating my birthday regardless and did the same for your husband, so I thought you could return the favor. Unless you don't want to. You have a right to choose." Cedrick grins. "Just leave out the catnip if you need me."

I giggle as he bows to me, which feels really weird. He is the Merlin, the most powerful enchanter, the one who sacrificed his life to stop the darkness, only to learn as a phoenix he could not die, so he used that time to keep helping us, but here he is, bowing to me. "Good day, Your Highness."

"G-good day, sir," I reply, unsure if that is the right title.

It seems to be. Cedrick beams at my acceptance of his respect. I realize most people likely insisted on honoring him. I had permitted him to treat me as higher, and I'm not sure I could have done anything to make him happier. "There's a reason it's you," he compliments me before leaving.

I'm not sure *he* could have done anything to make me happier.

When I catch Gavril that afternoon, we make hasty plans to prepare a fun day for Damian. My time with the staff proves helpful, as I have to inform them of what we're planning and need their help with.

I also, once again, see the clear hierarchy they have formed among themselves. Laundry staff is the bottom of the pole, for sure. Those who work in the kitchens hold the highest positions, and within that staff, there is a rigid system. Once I'm princess, if that means being head of staff, that will change.

The next day, we treat the morning like it's normal so as not to make Damian suspect anything, but as soon as I ask him to the library, I'm sure he's figured out something is up even though I'd just asked for his help with an assignment.

He enters the room ten minutes before the time I asked to meet. He enjoys being early to things. Cedrick is the only punk who yells "surprise" to which I give him a look.

"What?" Cedrick defends.

Damian chuckles and shakes his head. "Of course."

"A *quiet* party was the idea," I remind him.

"He never let me get away with that," Cedrick says as if surprised that was my plan, but he knows full well that's all we wanted.

"That's fair." Damian nods with a smile. "Though it was mostly Cena who arranged the party. My job was simply to get you there."

"Alright." Cedrick shrugs. "I did get away with it this year."

"True." Damian smiles. "I'll have to double down for next year," he teases him and ruffles his hair.

"Okay," Cedrick pouts in a child's voice.

"Just a quiet luncheon serving the food he likes. Chatting is our only activity on the itinerary. You don't have to do crazy things." I sigh at Cedrick as Zelda giggles.

"Sounds excellent." Damian smiles at me warmly. "Thank you, night angel."

"You're welcome. Though no one was supposed to say surprise." I give Cedrick another look, to which he gives me a guilty smile.

"So... I can ask you about anything now?" Zelda asks with a smile.

Damian chuckles. "If you wish."

"Me first," I insist playfully, making Zelda giggle and agree as we get the tea and treats Damian likes before sitting around the nice fire relaxed with the books and tea. It's wonderfully cozy.

We have tea and cakes and bring in the dinner Cedrick said Damian would like best when we get to that point. It's perhaps more fun for me than Damian as I sit by him, and I ask questions, and he tells me about the first performances of my favorite shows, his experience putting them together, and more. Zelda asks about historical events, but eventually, she asks Cedrick her questions, so I get Damian all to myself the rest of the day until it's about time for bed. I don't want to go. I'd rather enjoy more time listening to Damian's stories about the original theater.

I completely lose track of time, and before I know it, it's getting late. Zelda grows tired by the fire. "Happy birthday." Zelda wishes Damian with a kiss on the cheek before leaving.

I sigh heavily. "Sorry it has to end."

"All endings mean a better beginning is already on its way." Damian smiles warmly as he stands, then offers me a hand to help me up.

I accept it and stand up.

"I'll talk to you all tomorrow." Gavril wishes us good night, kissing my cheek before leaving too.

Damian gives me a smile. "In that case," he offers his arm, "may I escort you to your room, My Lady?"

"Of course." I smile, sure Gavril had done that on purpose.

I take Damian's arm, and he leads me to my room as he often has before. "I wanted to thank you again and apologize if I bored you at all." He gives me a small smile.

"No, not at all!" I cry. "It was wonderful. I really am sorry it had to end."

"Well, it has to end. Or else how could you have your day tomorrow?" He smiles.

"I almost forgot," I say honestly. "Father tried to make my birthdays special, but..." Perhaps that's why I forgot. "Well, he's not exactly safe to be around, is he?"

"I understand your fear, but he can't hurt you anymore, Kascia." Damian gives a gentle smile. "You are a wise young woman, and physically, he literally can't hurt you. No one is going to force you, but if you'd like to, I don't see the harm in seeing him."

"I know. But..." I sigh. "I just don't know if I can ever trust him. Not that he's up for anything, anyway," I joke. "I'll be fine. I'm not a kid anymore."

"No, you're right; you are not. But does that mean you don't want your father's love? Personally, I certainly hope that isn't the case," Damian says. "You don't have to forgive him today or any day soon. What he did to you hurts beyond measure, and it will take time to heal. But it can heal, if you are willing to show him you still love him regardless of his mistakes, someday he may just come around. He may never fully agree, but I hope you know that deep inside him, there is a man that still loves you very much, even if he didn't always show it the way he should."

"I just... wish I could trust him. Share my life with him." I desperately wish for that. My heart aches, but I try to suppress it.

"And perhaps you can, at least in part." Damian gives me a little smile. "If you share part of it with him, it may help him decide if he'd like to be a part of it and choose to make choices, so he can. However, you will have to bear in mind that it remains his choice whether or not he is willing to change."

"And that's what I'm afraid of," I confess. "I offer it, he refuses, and what... d-damage he could do?"

"Honestly, it'll hurt. I won't pretend it won't. But could you live with yourself if he died in his current state? You didn't at least try to include him and love him?" Damian asks, watching me.

"And if he hurt Gavril or... the king or queen?" That's what I'm afraid of. If I try and that attempt causes damage beyond repair.

"He won't," Damian says with certainty. "He isn't physically capable at the moment, and he is currently under house arrest. It is illegal for him to have a weapon, and he is guarded at all times. He cannot hurt them. I swear to you, they will receive no further harm at his hand."

"He'll recover eventually. I couldn't... I couldn't handle it if he did something." I swallow hard. "I want to trust him so badly, but I can't."

"I understand," Damian says sympathetically. "And even once he heals, he will still be unarmed and under guard. They will be fine. I swear it." He smiles reassuringly.

"I hope I can believe that one day." I force a small smile. "I just... if I lost Gavril to him..." I'd break. I'm sure of it.

"You won't." Damian meets my eyes. "Gavril is much stronger, faster, and frankly, wiser than him. And that's not to mention that Gavril can use magic. He'll be fine."

"I'll try to trust it." I promise. It will be easier after we're married, so he has no hope of stopping it, but then does he just get more desperate because I'm the heir if Gavril dies?

"I hope you will, but I can't say I blame you for worrying." Damian smiles a little, then he sighs. "Would you like to see him tomorrow?"

"How do you handle not being able to trust your own father?" I ask as we reach my room.

Damian is quiet for a moment, then musters a smile. "Do your best to love him and to show that love. And if he rejects it, take time to grieve and remember that you have so many others to support you. That's what got me through it."

"I forgot it was hard with your father too. He... b-betrayed your brother." Then I recall. "U-unless you mean your biological father."

Damian nods as we stop just outside my door. "I do. And I spent many years bitter and angry about it. Kascia, I let it destroy me. And it was a long time before I learned to forgive and move forward with my life." He touches my cheek. "Whatever happens, please, don't let it destroy you. Can you promise me that?"

I nod. "I won't get bitter. I have family to help, and... honestly, I think I'll just..." I swallow. "Get my heart broken, I guess." I chuckle as I look at my bedroom door.

Damian smiles sadly. "I know. It is hard to put your heart on the line. Know that no one will force you to."

"Again," I agree. "But... I should let you get to bed." I smile a little. Flur is preparing my tea.

Damian chuckles a little. "Well, sleep and I have never been friends, but I can certainly try."

"Really?" I pause. "You... you're like me?" And he'd never mentioned. I'd have remembered.

He chuckles again. "I suppose I never did mention that, did I?"

"No." I smile. "With your war history, I'd never have guessed."

"Perhaps not, but since I was a child, I have dealt with sleep issues. I've even been known to sleepwalk." He blushes a little.

"I'm glad I don't have that one." A smile appears on my face.

"I would imagine so." Damian smiles too. "It caused me a fair bit of trouble when I was younger."

"Like what?" I ask, feeling guilty I should let him go to bed, but I want to know.

"I once rode my horse to a town I didn't know, among other things," he admits. "But I really shouldn't keep you up talking all night." He smiles and opens the door for me.

I sigh. "I know. It's just been a fun day." I walk inside.

"Tomorrow will be another. Just you wait and see." Damian smiles as he glances over at Vivian. Vivian smiles back.

"I guess so." I smile and kiss Damian's cheek. "Thank you. For everything. It was supposed to be your day."

"It was, and it was perfect because I was able to spend it with you." Damian beams at me.

"Really?" I hope he's not just saying that.

"Without a doubt." He smiles. "It's tied for the best day I've had in my time here. Actually, it's tied for the best day I've had in the last millennia." He beams at me.

"Tied?" I tease.

Damian smiles widely, as if he'd been hoping I'd ask. "The other time was the day we performed *The Phantom* together."

"Of course." I smile. "I'm going to miss you." But for once, it's not as sad. I can think on the happy memories with a smile.

"As I will you, night angel," he says softly. "I'll see you in the morning."

"See you in the morning." I smile as I notice my maids waiting. He takes my hand and kisses it, then leaves. I wear a smile the whole evening as I get ready for bed.

# Chapter 12

And though I loved my day yesterday, I'm not sure I'm as excited for my turn as I wake up the next morning. Damian comes in before Bella, first time that has happened in a long time.

"Happy Birthday, Kascia." He beams at me. "Ready for your big day?"

"Big day?" I repeat. "What's so big about it?" My maids burst into giggles.

"It's your birthday, is it not?" He smiles with a laugh in his voice.

"Yes, but what makes it a 'big' day?" I ask.

"You'll just have to wait and see." Damian smiles warmly then offers me his arm. "Shall we?"

I smile and accept his arm with full trust. "I'd very much like that."

He beams, then nods to my maids. They smile and slip off while I go with Damian. I can't help but wonder what they're up to. Gavril must have decided I'd want a last day with Damian, and my birthday was the best chance.

He takes me back to the library, only this time, there is a little table set up with tea and pastries. There is a table set for two. I smile. Breakfast for just us. I don't think we've ever done that, and I love the idea.

Damian beams to see my delight, then lets go of my arm and pulls out my chair. "My Lady." He smiles at me.

"Thank you." I smile and accept his help. "Just a quiet breakfast?" I ask.

"If that's alright with you." He smiles as he pushes my chair in, then takes his seat.

"I love it," I assure him. "I don't know if we've ever done this."

"No, we haven't." The smile remains on Damian's face as he picks up the teapot and offers to pour it for me. I nod my thanks.

We enjoy a lovely brunch, talking like we had the night before, only just the two of us: telling stories, mostly talking about theater life and the things we'd experienced. Damian tells me more stories about his family and life: most helpful for me getting ready for marriage. Smiles and laughter filled the air.

After a couple hours of this, I notice we've eaten most of the food, and Damian seems a little less talkative, as if trying to wrap things up. I don't mind; I finish and wait to see what he has planned. There's no doubt he's waiting on something.

As I set down my fork, Damian smiles. "Well, I did have one more thing planned for this morning if you are finished eating."

"I am." I smile, ready to see what he has ready.

He grins wide, then gets up and helps me up from my chair. Excitement spreads across my face, eager to see what he's up to, following his lead. From there, he takes me to the practice room where a stack of papers awaits on the piano.

"Damian, you're brilliant," I cry in delight, excited for what he had planned.

Damian laughs. "I haven't even said anything yet."

"No, but whatever you planned is clearly perfect," I say, still smiling.

"So, I take it that you'd love to do a bit of singing and 'rehearsing' with me?" Damian grins.

"One hundred percent," I declare.

Damian beams and sits down at the piano. "Brilliant. Would you like to choose a song?" He nods to the stack.

"Sure." I walk over and look through the pile. I pick one I think Damian would like to start with and offer it to him. He grins and nods as he puts it on the piano, then starts to play.

It's more fun than the rehearsals we'd done as we experiment with all kinds of songs, playing, laughing, just like times playing with my mother or friends at the theater.

Just as we were finishing the latest song, there's a knock at the door, and Damian gets up and opens it. Bella comes in, smiling. "On time?" she teases Damian.

He nods. "You couldn't have timed it better." He looks at me. "I hope you don't mind if we have a few others join us."

I shake my head that I don't mind, wondering what Damian is up to. Bella steps in, and she's not alone. Six others follow, and they seem familiar, but I can't place it. I look at Damian with a half teasing smirk. What is he up to?

"Seeing that you'll be working closely in the future, I thought it might be a good idea to, as they say, 'break the ice'." He smiles warmly.

"Oh?" I raise a brow as my three maids enter last, and Flur closes the door.

"Why don't you choose one we can all do as a group? Then we can make introductions and assign parts." Damian smiles.

"O-oh... I don't know any that big," I admit.

"Hmm..." Damian puts a hand to his chin, then looks at the six new people. "Any of you uncomfortable singing?"

Everyone seems comfortable having a part, but when no one jumps up to take the first part, Damian looks over the room with a glance. "Alfreck, would you mind taking Barnum's part?"

"Sure." He steps forward confidently. Okay, he's the more confident one.

Damian smiles a thanks. "Would you mind introducing yourself to the lady?"

He gives me a sure smile and a slight bow. "My name is Alfreck. I suppose you could call me one half of the strong arms." He chuckles slightly. He's handsome, square jawed with light brown hair perfectly cut and styled in a rather relaxed yet formal look with happy light green eyes to match.

Something about the joke makes me pause and look the group over, including my maids and Bella. That makes...

"So, do I get to choose who I pick on?" Alfreck jokes to Damian.

"If you like." Damian nods to him with a smile.

Alfreck smiles and turns to the others. He looks over the list of parts Damian has and picks the other man, whose name is Clement, and who is more reserved than Alfreck, with light red hair and a smattering of freckles rather like Reinold and Godwin. He also pulls in a smiling blond named Jean and a slightly more reserved Helena who looks Athadinian to me with the rich brown hair and gray eyes their people often have.

Damian nods approvingly. "The rest will be chorus members if that is alright, but would you mind introducing yourselves?"

Alfreck seems to be some kind of leader, or at least, they look to his comfort and advice as the one who introduces herself as Briana glances at him before speaking as if for assurance. She rather reminds me of Flur, though she seems more intimidated than shy. She keeps her dark brown coils in the staff bun better than Flur does her blonde hair.

Last is Penelope who is reserved but not because she's shy, but because she likes to keep to the schedule. Her friendly voice is the first thing I notice and how big her warm smile is, rather like Alsmeria, my best friend at the theater. She even jokes in a mock whisper, "hiding in the chorus is just fine with me." It makes Briana giggle.

Damian seems to notice but makes no comment as he looks at my maids. "Now you."

Why do they need to introduce themselves? Vivian has no problem at all introducing herself and her role. Ro doesn't either, big and happy as always. Vivian has to lure Flur out to introduce herself, flushing pink the way she does. Damian gives her a reassuring smile, then looks and nods at Bella.

She smiles and introduces herself much as Vivian did, saying she's my attendant still learning with Damian's help, giving him a smile. He smiles back, then looks at me. "Would you mind?"

"Me?" I laugh a little. I look at them all. "Why?" It's not like they don't know who I am.

"It's to help everyone get to know one another and be confident working with one another," he says with a kind smile.

I pause, unsure what Damian means, but I've learned if I just do what Damian asks. I'll figure it out faster than asking. "I'm... Lady Kascia. I... Well, everyone knows I'll be the new princess in a few weeks." I honestly don't know what else to say. It makes me feel very silly when they know who I am.

Damian nods with a smile. "Thank you. I know this is all rather silly, but I have found silly situations often help build stronger relationships. As for me, I believe most have learned to call me Sir Damian, but just Damian is fine, if it fits your fancy. Now that you have gotten the chance to meet your 'cast'," He smiles at me. "Shall we start?" he asks with his hands at the ready.

"I think we are." I look around, and they all nod, holding their respective papers.

I can't say they're the best singers in the world, but most of them makeup for it with a lot of energy. Alfreck and Penelope in particular aren't shy about getting silly and get most of us to laugh quite a bit. They seem to have some kind of connection. I would guess dating or married with how they'd smirk at each other. Briana and Helena are on the shyer side, Helena even rivaling Flur's shyness, and I thought she was the shyest person I'd ever known. But even she laughs with us, and she isn't completely silent. They all seem to build off of Alfreck's energy, with Clement being the most animated as we follow Alfreck's prodding.

Damian plays his part and sings as well as he ever had, adding to the energy in the room. When we go to pick a new song, he assigns Penelope a lead role. She doesn't seem to mind one bit, playing it up despite her saying at least they got to hide before. I am sure it's all trying to impress Alfreck. He is handsome. Perhaps most of these ladies are trying to impress him.

After a few hours of this, Damian stands up. "Well, I believe it is near lunchtime. Thank you for humoring me." He smiles warmly.

"Humoring you?" I smile in amusement. I think even the shy ones had fun.

"Well, it isn't like their duty is to act and sing with the princess-to-be all morning." He smiles.

"It could be," Alfreck says in a dramatic voice that makes the others at least chuckle, even if a few look uneasy at the idea, and Penelope hits his arm.

"That's for Lady Kascia to decide." Damian chuckles slightly.

"True. But it could be." Alfreck shrugs. Clemont chuckles uneasily, telling Alfreck to knock it off.

"In any case, thank you. You may go." Damian smiles at them.

They all bow to us and leave. Something about all that was odd, but I couldn't put my finger on it. I look at Damian. "What was that about?" I ask as Bella giggles, the only one who hadn't left.

"I'll tell you in a moment. But first, let me ask, what did you think of your new staff?" Damian smiles wide.

That makes it *all* make sense. "Why didn't you just tell me?" I laugh. "That..." I have to pause to look at them that way. "Was a nice way to take Hydie's pressure off." It made it much easier.

"You're welcome." Damian gives me a short bow. "And I thought it might help with the birthday fun to have more people." He smiles.

"It was fun. Though I'm always happy with you," I assure him. "I really expected a more public display for all this."

"You mean for your birthday?" Damian tilts his head.

I nod. "I suppose Gavril's wasn't very public, but we had a delegation arriving."

"True. And we may have to do another celebration for the public, but today is all for you." Damian smiles.

"Likely one of the last days like that." I sigh. "But I suppose it's lunch now?"

He nods and offers his arm. "If you'd like me to escort you."

"Of course." I accept it. He beams, and instead of taking me down to the dining hall, he takes me up to the royal floor and knocks on the door of the second born suite.

Jake opens the door. "Ah, there you are." He bows to the two of us and steps out of the way.

"Lunch with the royal family?" I guess as Damian leads me inside.

He smiles and nods. "After all, King Aster still isn't up for much of a party."

"I'm glad they thought of me." I smile.

"I'd make sure if they didn't," Jake teases behind us. I wish he'd shut up. We could potentially be friends, but I'm not sure I'm ready to pretend nothing happened just yet. I would. Just not yet.

"Sounds like a good way for a guard to lose his position." Damian throws him a look and a half smile.

"By reminding them to make her birthday special?" Jake grins at Damian. I notice Jake has tried once again to remove the stubble on his face and failed.

"By overstepping his bounds as a guard and trying to 'make' the royal family do something," Damian says with a side look. It may have a hint of warning in it.

"I'm not going to force them." Jake defends. "Just make sure they don't make a mistake." Jake smiles at me. "And happy birthday."

"Thanks." At least he can pretend it's normal. I guess my misunderstanding what he said before the latest rebel attack unnerved me more than I thought. I shove away thoughts of what he and I were doing a year ago today.

Damian sighs, then looks at Jake. "Is he awake?"

"Yes. I believe the queen and prince are there as well." Jake nods. "Well, the prince arrived. I think the queen has been there since before I got on shift."

Damian nods, then opens the door into the bedroom. I smile and step inside.

"There you are." I try not to laugh that the king says almost exactly what Jake says. "Happy birthday, beautiful."

"Behave," the queen sighs.

"Means I don't have to," Gavril jokes as he gets up to greet me. I can't help but giggle as he taunts his parents more than me by kissing just below my ear with my arm still on Damian's.

"Gavril." The queen sighs.

Damian chuckles and unlinks my arm from his. "I'll take that as my cue to leave."

"I'll see you later?" I check, wondering if he'd try to vanish again.

He smiles warmly. "Without a doubt."

"Okay." I kiss his cheek before letting him go. He smiles, then takes my hand and kisses the back of it before he releases it, bows, then leaves.

Gavril smiles a little and leads me over to join the little table they'd set up for us to eat at so the king can join in. It's the most relaxed I think I've ever seen the royal family. I should expect this as now I'll be part of the family, but something about it still feels strange. I feel that close to Gavril, no hesitation, but his parents, perhaps, aren't quite as ready yet on that account. The lunch mostly comprises the dumplings I like so much, which is a fun treat as well.

We're enjoying little birthday cupcakes when the queen nervously offers me a small gift which surprises me. I hadn't expected anything knowing the budget. "Normally, we'd present you with some kind of tiara, but... giving you one made of fake gems felt... cheap," the queen confesses nervously. "You should at least receive something real. At least for your first gift as part of the family."

"You didn't... have to do anything," I reply, accepting the small package.

"It's actually quite the tradition." The king tries to help me understand. "Traditionally, it's a hand-me-down tiara of some sort."

"And most of the real ones were sold to try to repay debts long before I came around." The queen forces a smile. "And faux jewels feel too small."

"I wasn't expecting anything like that." Although she may feel bad with the tradition being lacking, I don't mind at all.

Lowering my gaze, I proceed to unwrap the package. The first thing I notice is how soft the fabric is, as the first item almost falls into my hand. It's buttery smooth, thin but not too thin. The workmanship is beautiful too. It's an impressive collection of handkerchiefs with lace at the edges and Purerahian roses and the country's emblem done into one corner. I knew princesses were expected to carry handkerchiefs at all times. It is a common gift to a lover to carry into battle or a contest.

The gift is a set, large enough to make sure I don't run out. I'd never felt a finer material for one and the way it just... looks like it's mine. Like someone would look at this and assume it was mine because it looks like something I'd have with the roses and the emblem. Then I notice in the same blue within the roses are hidden pointe shoes.

"They're perfect." I smile softly, admiring how they feel. This isn't a tiara, but judging on the craftsmanship of the handkerchiefs, I can tell they have given me the best they could afford. They may feel like it's too small or insignificant for me, but it has just the right amount of personal touch, thoughtfulness, and being a gift beyond fit for a princess. "I love them."

I put it up to my face and catch their amazing scent. It's lightly scented like the salty, floral scent of the Purerahian roses. I smile at the smell and how wonderful that feels against my face. "I love them."

"Thank you, but—"

"No, really." I meet the queen's eyes. "I love them." For a moment, I hold one almost like a blanket before placing it down with the others. They make quite a stack of them, for lack of a better term. "I can't wait to use them."

The queen smiles, touched but clearly unsure it is good enough and I am not just being nice, but the king seems to recognize I mean it and looks much happier.

We continue our happy chat for a while longer. The king starts to look tired after a while, so the queen takes that as the excuse to shoo us off to whatever is next. "Mind if I have a second?" the king asks me. The queen doesn't try to talk him out of it at all, but before she leaves, she reminds him to rest.

"I'll see you in a bit," Gavril assures, kissing my head before leaving too.

I look at the king, a bit more nervous. "Don't worry, not formal." He smiles. "I just wanted to give you one more thing."

He nods at the side table with several drawers for me to dig it out of a drawer as he really still struggles to twist his torso or bend over. I follow his direction and open the drawer to find the package. It's rectangular and has a rather tall and sturdy feel.

I tilt my head just a bit as I bring the package into my arms and sit back down, placing the gift on my lap. It's beautifully engraved or carved white wood or marble or something like that. The bottom half of it has grooves in it for something, but the main feature is a quote across the top that reads, "We are all stars, but only a few are given the spark to burn." With what looks like a handwritten note, not by the original creator, that reads "royal" which changes the quote to "We are all stars, but only a few are given the royal spark to burn."

"My father-in-law added that note." King Aster nods at the personalized bit. "Think he knew I wasn't sure I was up for this job, though he thought I was. I suspect it will get far better use on your desk than mine. The grooves are for shelves; they'll put the organizer back together for you. It's where your staff will put your briefings and other reading material you'll be assigned, which will be a lot. It's the most used piece on my desk."

I bite my lips, once again touched by the gifts they think are so small but mean so much to me. I often forget the king is more like me. He just seems... ready to do this. I know I only knew him long after he'd adjusted to the role, but still. He knows how frightening this was better than anyone else in this palace. He'd been where I now sat, minus a prophecy to fulfill.

"Thank you." With a smile, I finally look at him. "I'm sure I'm going to need the reminder." I wonder if he knows how much being called a star would mean to me after Gavril's many star-related nicknames for me. Or perhaps this is just fate's way of assuring me this really is all meant to be.

"I think we all doubt ourselves when we step into this, when it's not our expected calling." He smiles warmly. "Happy birthday, Kascia."

"Thank you," I say again, recalling he needs rest, so stand up, holding the plaque to my chest like I was holding a book, as if it needed to be kept safe. "Rest well," I wish him to which he thanks me before letting me go.

"Ready?" Gavril had waited in the main suite for me. I nod. "You should drop those off, then get dressed."

"Dressed?" I frown.

"You'll see." Gavril smiles and takes my hand.

My maids put my gifts on my desk to make sure they're properly handled for me before dressing me in what is clearly a swimsuit and swim dress, putting my hair in a lovely braid.

"What are we doing?" I ask with a smile.

"We're having fun," Vivian says as she scoops up her bag, her own hair done into a braid, uniform with the other girls' braids. "A princess can't properly celebrate a birthday without a party."

"Private party." Flur makes sure to clarify as she picks up a second bag that I think is for me. I'm right, as she gets me to toss it over my shoulder and pushes me out the door.

I'm hurried outside and to the royal beach where a full party is all set up. They set up a few long tables with food, an honestly intimidating collection of gifts, and ocean-themed decorations protected under little tents with many sand blankets spread out and shade structures set up. It has been quite warm lately, normal for this time of year here, though. It's just the start of the beach season.

There's a cheer from those already there to welcome me: my new staff I'd met early today (all wearing their own beach dresses and suits), Bella, Damian, Cedrick, most of the members of my castmates back at the theater, my mother and grandparents, Princess Rose, Azalea, Isla, Zelda, and Lilly.

The last one makes me pause. Everyone else is smiling, waiting for me to notice. I haven't seen Lilly since she'd left just after the delegations finished when she was assigned to become the Japcharian ambassador.

Many laugh when they spot my face as I notice her. "Lilly?"

She beams. She looks... so grown up. In a green and black Japcharian-style patterned swim dress that clasps around the neck like a halter top, with her long black hair done into a fishtail braid down her shoulders, she looks more mature. However, it's her gait and smile that catch the eye. It's the confidence she carries that she's never had before.

It shows even more when she doesn't shy away from my excited hug at all. Once I initiate the movement, she takes over and covers the distance, hugging me and smiling. She seems taller than she was too, though I know she isn't.

"It's so good to see you," Lilly says happily, her voice brighter than I've ever heard too. "Oh, Your Highness," she recalls, bobbing me a quick curtsy before giggling and hugging me again, making me laugh too.

"When did you get here?"

"They made sure I arrived in time for your birthday. I had to come for the wedding anyway, right?" She smiles brightly.

"Of course," I agree.

"Figured this would be the best birthday plan." Gavril's voice comes from behind me. I think the loudest giggling comes from my former castmates as I turn around to face him, only to be given a swept-off-your-feet style kiss, dipping me ever so slightly and getting quite a whoop from the guests.

"Happy birthday," Gavril wishes me yet again as he pulls away, kissing the tip of my nose before letting me go.

It's a thrill to be able to just enjoy the whole afternoon with all my family and friends. I'd never done anything like this before. I get a bit of time to talk and catch up with most everyone, laughing in our various groups, enjoying the talking, snacking, and exchanging of stories. And eventually, when the day is at its hottest, we enjoy the water and even a bit of wind surfing which I've never done before and am not brilliant at, but doing it with Gavril makes it more fun, even when I make us fall over into the waves.

At some point, all the guys decide to set up volleyball which is hilarious to watch because I think only my grandfather and a handful of guys from my troupe had ever played, making a hilarious game many of the girls decide to watch on the sidelines. The onlookers are relaxing and laughing at the hilarity of the game. The athletic feats at least are nice, even if the moments of dumb as those who aren't as familiar with it make comical mistakes in how to serve or return the ball.

There is so much for everyone to do. Some enjoy looking for shells, a few wander the tide pools, build sandcastles, sunbathe, fly kites in the wind: a bit of everything.

The picnic-style dinner on the beach is fun too, with a bonfire lit to keep it warm as it gets a bit cold. That's when we have cake and I endure the awkward giving of gifts. As I predicted, it is quite royalty-themed.

Though everyone is having such fun, all to soon it's time to wrap up as it gets dark. The staff handle the cleanup as I give each friend and family member a hug since many must return home. Those who live near enough that is. I thank them for coming and tell them I'm so happy to have seen them all.

That's when I notice Mother is planning to head home, and I point out she could stay in the palace and travel to work free of charge. I know our house is closer to the theater, but my grandparents are living in the palace. I see no reason she has to go home alone to that empty house. The thought makes tears want to rise.

Mother argues I'm becoming a royal, not her, but after Grandfather insists she take the extra room in their suite and I order my maids to assist her in packing back at our house, Mother agrees. Ro is as insistent as I am that she leaves with Mother to help her get her things.

That will be a good combination to help her adjust to sharing the royal life with me. Most of all, with Father around or, rather, his not being around.

I feel his absence sharply, and my heart drops out of nowhere. Gavril takes my hand, and I look up at him as the others staying in the palace head back, the former Chosen all giggling and talking loudly together.

"Not over yet," he assures me with a soft smile. I look back at him, confused. Then I realize the staff hadn't taken care of the fire yet and quickly realize Gavril planned that on purpose as he leads me back. "Figured a quiet sunset might be more fun." He smiles as he sits and guides me to sit next to him.

"But while we wait for that," he reaches into his pocket, "a gift for you. This one is only half from me," he says as he pulls out a small box. "It's also from your father. He gave it to me, insisting I had to give it to you."

I frown a little as I accept the gift. Upon opening the box, my mouth drops open. I look up at Gavril, mouth hanging open. "M-my father gave you this?" Gavril nods, and I look back at it.

It's our family ring. Father had given it to me to seal my bond to Jake. There's a heart-shaped opal as the main fixture, with a crown on top and two hands reaching to it on either side. The ring has deep meaning.

If Father gave Gavril this with the direction to give it to me, it means far more than Father just giving it back to me. I had taken it off and thrown it at him when I drove him from the palace at the Harvest Ball, rejecting his plan and mission for me. It means he was, no matter how begrudgingly, relenting to consent to my plan, my marriage to Gavril.

Tears flood my eyes, and I bite my lips as I look at it, unsure of what to say or do.

"Did you know this has a history?" Gavril asks me. My shining eyes meet his. "I read about it in a history book. The original designer was from a faraway land where one of their enemies still had slaves. He was taken from his love and became a blacksmith in slavery. During that time, he made this ring for his love. When he finally got his freedom, he returned home, unsure his love stayed faithful, but she had never married, so he gave her the ring, this ring, that he'd made for her in his slavery, and they were married. Perhaps parts are missing as it's an ancient story, but that's why there are different ways to wear it and symbolizes loyalty."

I smile a little. "I think Father told me that when he gave it to me as..."

"As?" Gavril raises a brow.

"Sorry, I just..." I'm overwhelmed. "The fact he wanted you to give it back to me means..." I smile, and a tear slips down my cheek. "He's going to stop fighting it."

"Really?" Gavril sounds surprised.

"It was originally meant to remind me of my loyalty to duty and Jake," I admit, wondering if Gavril will regret giving it to me. "But I threw it at him at the harvest."

"I thought I'd seen this ring before." Gavril nods. He smiles a little. "You're glad to have it back?"

"I'm happy with what it means." I look up at Gavril, eyes shining. "He's accepted my choice."

Gavril smiles gently and takes my hand. "Do you want to see him?"

I hesitate. What if he only makes this lovely day end on a sour note? But he had made sure Gavril gave me this. "When did he give you this?"

"Last night when I checked on how he was doing. He begged to see you, but I told him it was up to you."

"Oh." So maybe he was using this as a means to trick me into seeing him.

"It was after he gave me the ring to give to you." Gavril reads my reaction correctly.

My heart picks up a little. "Alright. Yes. I want to let him try."

Gavril nods. "After we enjoy the sunset?"

"Yes." I nod again, reminded of the quiet moment we'd have in just a few minutes. The sun is going down fast, which is why everyone had to hurry home before dark. Those having to go through town know better than to travel the streets after dark. Father had never let me do that alone, even knowing I was a good fighter.

It is nice to just have a quiet moment to recharge, sitting back with Gavril's arm around me as we enjoy the sunset. Once the sun has vanished behind the sea, Gavril helps me up, and we go to the infirmary.

I wonder how Sage is doing. Still too weak to attend the party, but perhaps better than he'd been last since I'd seen him. I bet Zelda is there wishing him a good night now.

Gavril checks with Stephen that Father is up for a visit. He then goes into the room first. Father sits up quickly, looking at Gavril with a hint of anxiety I don't think I've ever seen on my father's face before.

Gavril pauses a moment, looking at my father with a blank expression before he looks at me to tell me it's time for me to come in, so I do.

Father's face fills with relief to see me, then he smiles widely at me. "Hello cygnet." He greets me the way he has my whole life. "Happy birthday. I didn't think I'd get to see you."

Despite my lingering doubts about completely trusting him, I give him a weak smile and say, "Thank you for your gift. I know what it means."

"I feared you might not." Father relaxes slightly. "Thought you'd think it meant I was trying to remind you of what you should be doing."

"Should?"

"What you'd think I think you should do," he amends.

"What do you think I should do?" I meet his eyes, setting the challenge. How much of his heart was he prepared to permit me? Just enough because he loves me and will support me, or has he seen the error of his ways, even if just a little?

Father let out a deep sigh. "I still don't approve of the royals, but I do think you should be next to rule. And if you have to marry him to do it, and you want to marry him because you choose and love him, I'll support you." It is a lot like what he'd said before, but I think his heart is in it a little more. A bit of him perhaps is thinking the Custod rebellion still won in a way, even if the old royal family isn't gone, he got his Custod on the throne. I can live with that for now.

"Thank you. I hope you'll be there." Even if I don't trust him to take part, I still want him at the wedding.

"I'd not miss it for the world," he promises. I manage a smile. He gives me another small smile and opens his arms, asking for a hug.

I give it to him, nervous and glancing at Gavril as if to make sure I'm still safe. Gavril nods a small promise that I am before I give my father a tighter hug, careful not to hurt the wound I'd given him.

"I love you so much, cygnet," Father says softly, holding me gently. "I've always been proud of you, Kascia. That hasn't changed."

"I love you, Dad." But I'm also scared of him.

He lets go. "To think... all those years ago today." Father sighs and lets me pull back. "Happy birthday, beautiful. Enjoy the rest of it."

I smile and promise him I will, feeling a bit more hope in what my future with my father might be.

Gavril comes closer, and I turn to him, taking his hand to go. I don't miss the shadow that crosses Father's face. I fight not to be hurt or cry. I don't want the two men who should be the most important in my life to be bitter enemies. Gavril let me come here. He's not nearly as hateful to my father, which he could, and many would say should be. My father gave him the scars he is hiding on his back. And yet, he doesn't hold hate in his heart like my father does.

Gavril's plan for the rest of the evening is the cure I needed. We go into the ballroom and listen to various songs to decide which should be our first dance at our wedding. Gavril assures me we can have my mother or someone make a staged piece for us, so we can do something more exciting if we want, but for now, we just play around to pick what song we want. And it's so much fun. I don't want the day to end.

"Thank you," I say to Gavril as we get back to my room for the night. "Been one of my best birthdays, and I expected nothing of it."

"Only the best for my princess." He kisses my hands, then my lips.

I kiss him harder, trying to thank him. He takes it at first, but pulls back, reminding me we should be careful. He kisses my cheek and wishes me goodnight. The final gift of the day is Joy waiting for me to cuddle me to sleep. I seem to sleep better with someone there. I can't wait to see if sharing a bed will further lessen my sleep troubles.

# Chapter 13

The next day, Bella distracts me by getting my staff fully assigned. I know the article has been out for a while, and I'm anxious to see it. But knowing I have my staff all assigned makes it easier to know how to cope with it once I've seen it.

The title feels a tad misleading to me: "How Love and War Unite a Nation". I admit, it's great bait to get someone to read as that's not normally what you see, but it starts with the more cutesy bits of our love story we shared before revealing my background. It's stated with taste and respect, if not a tad biased on how my background with the rebels will give me an advantage in helping quell the fighting.

"You'll get questions back from the people after lunch to review before we get the interview this evening," Penelope informs me, watching me with a hint of nervousness.

"When do I review them with the prince?" I ask as calmly as I can.

"As soon as you're ready after seeing them," Penelope replies.

Bella gives me a smile. "Try not to be too stressed. It shouldn't be too hard."

"Hope so." At least I don't have to repeat the story again.

My staff starts getting used to their new positions as I head to lunch. On the way, someone rushes up to me.

At first, I assume it's a member of staff, but he's not in uniform. Still, he seems familiar somehow. He wears a rather faded olive-green jacket, some kind of faded yellow-colored waistcoat and shirt underneath, dark brown trousers and shoes. He isn't wearing any kind of necktie but wears a proper top hat, which he sweeps off his head as he bows low to me, showing his dark hair pulled into a ponytail and impressive sideburns.

"Your Highness, forgive my hurry." He gives me a charming smile. "I'm Bevill Coppiger. I am with the Purerah Advocate, formerly with the Purerah Union. I wanted to ask a few questions to prepare for tonight."

"Excuse me?" Why wouldn't he wait until tonight? Then I realize how I know him. He was the moderator at the first interviews before Fabian arrived.

"Do you think concerns you accidentally gave a win to the Custod Rebellion by winning the Enthronement are valid, despite rejecting their agenda?" he asks, not even giving me a space to breathe.

"Sir, shouldn't this wai—"

"Are you hopeful this will unite the nation or afraid it will only empower the rebellions, the Custod rebellion at the lead, though it always had been seen as the small yet vocal group?" he presses.

"Mr. Coppiger, was it?"

"Are you afraid that having a Custod rebel on the throne will only further fuel the other rebellions against the royal family?"

I open my mouth to snap, "I am not a Custod rebel", when a voice shoots to the reporter.

"You're being rather presumptuous for a man without an appointment." Damian seems to materialize behind the reporter with his arms crossed and a narrow look in his eyes.

The reporter jumps and whirls around to face Damian. "Ah, hello Sir..." he leads.

"Damian Custod," Damian says straightly, then tilts his head. "Does Fabian know you're trying to steal his exclusive?" He arches a brow.

"I don't report to Fabian," the man chuckles. "Bevill Coppiger." He offers Damian a hand, but I think the name intimidated Mr. Coppige by the plastered on smiles and over exuberance. He's just trying to hide it.

Damian ignores his hand. "Oh, I know who you are. And either way, I doubt he'll be pleased. I'm also aware that not only will your chief editor have words for you about stealing Fabian's beat, but you do not have permission to be here. Do you?"

"I need permission to do my job?" Mr. Coppiger smiles.

"In the palace, yes. And you know it. Now, who gave you a press pass to enter the palace?" Damian says with a firm look in his eyes.

"Ah, I have an appointment pass, right here." Mr. Coppiger reaches into his jacket pocket and pulls out some paperwork.

Damian holds out his hand, waiting. Mr. Coppiger hands it over. Damian takes it and looks it over before looking up at him through the roof of his eyelids. "It says you are here to meet with the grand duke. You are a long way from his office."

"You're sure? Second floor, right-hand side."

"What is this?" It's Gavril's voice. I look look over my shoulder to see him approaching.

"This young man seems to have confused our dear lady for the grand duke," Damian says with a hidden smile at his joke as he meets eyes with Gavril.

"And who might you be?" Gavril questions Mr. Coppiger with an edge to his voice.

"Your Highness. Bevill Coppiger, with the interview team for the Purerah Advocate." He smiles.

"Ah, yes, I remember you." Gavril gives Mr. Coppiger a once over. "And what do you think you're doing here?" He looks at the papers Damian is holding.

"His appointment papers." Damian offers them to Gavril. "Though I found him interrogating Lady Kascia rather rudely a moment ago." He gives the reporter a steely-eyed look.

"Appointment with Her Highness?" Gavril asks, giving Mr. Coppiger a dangerous look before he takes the papers and looks them over.

The second his amber eyes spot the signature, they snap to the reporter, and in the blink of an eye, he's got Mr. Coppiger tightly by the arm. "He sent you to this floor?" he demands dangerously.

"Second floor on the right." the reporter insists, surprised by Gavril's harsh reaction.

"This is the left." Gavril snarls.

"I'm terrible with directions." Mr. Coppiger shrugs.

Gavril doesn't buy it for one second. "Your press pass does not cover someone else's exclusive. You'll have to wait with the guard until your appointment comes to get you. Understood?" The tone Gavril uses is terrifying.

"I have a right to—"

"To do what you were given permission for. The grand duke has no say on you taking any time with Her Highness, and you better have permission to speak to her if you ever try again, or you'll be answering to me. And your position may be in question."

"Threatening me now?"

"I think it's more of a promise," Damian says with a smart smirk.

I hold in a laugh but fail to hide my smile as Gavril smirks his agreement before he gives Mr. Coppiger a warning look once more. "A guard will be escorting you to your *actual* appointment. I see you wandering the palace again, you may not be permitted a pass in the future." Gavril pauses, likely wondering the best way to get a guard.

"I can see him there," Damian offers.

"Thank you. He causes you trouble, you know what to do." Gavril smiles at Damian, then looks at the reporter. "And next time, we won't be so patient. Good day." He pushes the reporter towards Damian.

Mr. Coppiger's expression is scowling offence then glances at me as if I would help him, but I'm not letting this pass again.

Damian takes his arm. "Come along, Mr. Coppiger. We can't have you late for that appointment." He collects the papers from Gavril, nods to us, then leads the reporter away. Mr. Coppiger looks terrified at the idea.

Gavril watches them go before turning to me. "You alright? What did he ask you?"

"Just about my reaction to others, I suppose. I didn't say anything," I promise.

"They shouldn't be doing that. You call for guards if he's trying to attack you next time, understand?" Gavril sounds furious. "They aren't to be allowed to accost you like that in your own home. They'll be hell to pay if I see him or any others doing that again. You sure his questions didn't bother you?"

"No, just... surprised," I confess.

"Should have Damian string him up," Gavril snarls.

"Gavril, really I'm okay." I smile as I assure him, resting my hands on his arms as he holds me.

"They shouldn't... we'll make sure this doesn't happen again. I'll put him on my watch list if I have to."

"Really. I'm fine." I kiss his cheek in thanks, happy at his defense of me.

"Well, let's get to lunch. Then we can properly prepare for them. I'll have to speak to Damian after." Gavril sighs and we go to lunch.

Gavril hardly speaks, looking sour the whole time. I try not to mention why. Before we go to his office to review the questions, Gavril pulls me aside in the main office.

"You're sure you're ready for this?" he asks gently, studying me.

I nod. "I-I'm the right choice. I have to be."

Gavril frowns. "Kascia, this is not about that."

"What?" I frown and look at him.

"This has *nothing* to do with you being the right one. You know that, right?"

I think that over. "You're right." I take a deep breath. "Even if I'm horrible at this, it's still me." It relieves some tension in me, but it also reveals a rather prideful truth I don't want to admit to myself, yet don't feel willing or able to root out.

"That help?" Gavril asks gently.

I wish it did, but it doesn't. Gavril can tell from my expression, and he frowns a little and hugs me gently. "Why doesn't it?"

"I think... I took such pride and joy in being the one they wanted. How stunned I always felt I was so high in the polls. They wanted me, and winning and living up to that meant a lot to me. And I was extra happy to have won as their princess, you know? And... I really don't want to lose that. I took so much confidence and happiness in it and wanted it for them when I didn't want it for me. On days when I was sure you'd never come back, I still wanted to win because I was doing it for them."

"You'd give anything for them, so having them at least support you back meant the world." Gavril nods. "I may not fully get it, but I thought myself silly for being willing to give up the only thing I truly wanted for people who hate and want to kill me. Lead me to realize the right final test."

I smile weakly and nod back. "I can't lose that." But I could. And I'd have to endure if I did, but it hits a vein deeper in me than I knew.

"You won't."

"I might." If I do this wrong, I will. And as ashamed as I am to think it, I'll be no better than the royals already in power as far as the people care. And it means so much to me that I'm not. It is part of why I am going to be good at this even before I knew about the prophecy. And that's what I fear losing. It feels as if I had lost my family all over again, but in a more agonizing way.

Gavril sighs. "I can understand that means a lot to you. I can, but that doesn't change you're the right choice."

I nod and meet his eyes. "I know." Truly, I do. Perhaps I wouldn't without him saying it, but he's completely right. That is not why I fear the crown. I fear losing something else I've held onto and used to empower me long before I felt sure Gavril wanted me. One I hadn't even fully realized I wanted to the depths of my soul, almost as much as I wanted to win to have the man I love.

Gavril studies my face and gives a faint smile. "Nothing shakes that for me or my parents. You're who we need."

"I just *really* wanted to be who they needed and wanted." I didn't realize how much. The thought of losing it makes my heart race, and I already want to cry.

Gavril hugs me and kisses my forehead. "You can only do your best. You don't control them. Just you."

I nod. "It's hard when so much of what you've built relies on other people."

"Yeah, it does." Gavril smiles a little with an almost laugh, nodding his agreement. "Ready?"

"A-as I'm going to be."

He kisses my head one more time before he takes me into his office. Once I settle in, though, he leaves to find Damian and have him join us.

# Chapter 14

I'm nervous, leg bouncing, thinking over the questions that the reporter had thrown at me. Is this what the people want to know and talk about? Is this what the interview today will be: defending myself? How would I not lose my temper at them? How did I not lose what I want so badly?

Bella is there with my press team: Jean and Helena. Godwin and Reinold are waiting too, frowning after Gavril. I hardly do more than glance at them before I look down, trying to take deep, calming breaths as my leg jitters. This is it, the real moment. Talking to Fabian was hard but personal and private. This is different. I am going to be attacked. Any chance Damian or Gavril had to change my mind on that was dashed with that reporter.

This feels like telling Gavril all over again, or when I had to go to him to warn him of the vote of no confidence that the grand duke had attempted. Only this feels much more personal and inescapable. I cannot escape this no matter what happens. I'd have to live with the people turning on me. I blink tears at the mere thought.

Finally, the doors open, and Gavril walks in, followed by Damian. I put on a smile for them, but I doubt I do well hiding my fear, which is alright with me. It is slowly becoming more real as I sit here, terrified of what is coming slowly growing like a gray, fuzzy cloud in my chest.

"Well, if that's everyone, perhaps we should begin?" Bella proffers as Gavril sits next to me and takes my hand, making my leg stop bouncing. I twitch out a bit of a smile.

Gavril looks at me, studying my face before turning to Bella and nodding. Bella smiles slightly and nods at Jean and Helena.

"We went over the questions. We're thinking it would be easier to prepare answers for the... harder ones." She glances at Damian briefly before looking back at me. "Then we can work on the others."

"Whatever works," I say with as much authority as I can while my toes start doing the bouncing in place of my whole leg. At least the toes can hide more easily.

Mentally, I'm prepared for those horrible questions already thrown at me today. *Do you think concerns you accidentally gave a win to the Custod Rebellion are valid, despite rejecting their agenda?*

"These questions were submitted to us, and they collected them from various sources such as the people, of course, — where we wanted — as well as from various members of the press. We're unsure which are which, so don't worry about the audience. Just think of them all as questions from the people," Jean tries to assure me, but I don't know if there's anything they can do to assure me.

I glance at some cards that she's holding. They must have the questions written on them. They are different colors, yellow and blue. For me and for Gavril, perhaps?

"Some are clearly for one or the other of you, but we're going to prepare both of you to answer in case they want a follow up or try to throw you off," Helena says, drawing my eyes to her while Jean prepares the cards to offer us. "Our goal is to give you the tools you'll need to defend yourself as well as send the message you want to send."

"There's a message I want to send?" I have *no* idea what message I'm supposed to send. I'm answering questions, not giving a briefing.

"What message do you want to give them?" Jean asks patiently.

"I don't know." I manage not to snap or yell. I don't have a plan. Unless you count getting out of this without being torn to shreds by the people I've fought so hard to serve and represent. I have no message. This is purely defensive. I have no offense in this. *Don't hate me.* I can't use that.

"And that's alright. But I'm sure you have something. Perhaps, that you were once deceived by rebels, just like many of them, but you can see the truth and want to improve?" Jean offers. "Or perhaps just assuring them that even though you have family rebels, you have no sympathy for their cause. You are telling them for a reason, yes?"

"Yes." I stop myself looking at Damian. The reason is that he told me to, and Gavril agreed. I hate it with all my soul, but I trust them with more than my soul. I know they're right.

"So, use that as your message, and it will make directing your answers easier," Jean assures me. "We don't have to know it. Just you do." She looks down at the cards, moving on.

I am still trying to take deep breaths and not give in to the fight-or-flight response my mind wants to default to.

They get down to the main work. The questions are more emotional than I expected after my first attack, making my heart thud in panic at how I'd keep from tears during the live interview. Questions such as "What changed your mind?", "Are you still close to your family?", "Did you ever plan to do the deed yourself?", "Were you afraid to tell the truth?", and "Are you afraid you'll lose the people's trust after coming out with this?".

*Yes, more than you know.*

But the list doesn't stop there. "What was your purpose in coming out with this information instead of keeping it need-to-know?", "Why did you hide it until now?", "Did you know you'd won before the attack on the presentation?" They all go by rapidly as my team reads them out.

When they finish, they look at me to see my reaction. "So... we just prepare answers for these?" I ask.

"And any questions we may think he'll follow up with." Jean nods. "We are unsure they will ask any of these to the prince, as the main purpose of this interview is to handle your past, and many of these have to do with pressing forward, but we believe we should review them all together."

Gavril's are just as bad as mine. "How did you feel being a prophesied ruler all your life?" "Why did the royals hide the prophecy from everyone?", "How do you plan on uniting the kingdom once more?", "Why are you telling us of the prophecy now?", "How did you not realize she was a rebel sooner?", and "Do you worry your love for her blinded you to who she really is?" The one about not realizing I was a rebel stung hard, and the last is a double whammy, but I blink the tears away before anyone can see them.

"If you'd like to look them over." Jean offers me the yellow stack and hands Gavril the blue.

"O-okay." I look at the cards, but she did a good job reading them all.

"Want to just go down the list one by one?" Bella asks gently.

"Sure." Whatever works, I just want this done. I want this over. I want it over now. If they are going to hate me, then just get to it. But that's not in my power. I hate all of this, so what I want really shouldn't be a factor because all I want is it never to happen.

"Kascia—" Gavril begins.

"Whatever works," I cut Gavril off. I want to talk about how much I don't want to do this even less than actually doing it. I just want it over with. That's the only want I can have.

Gavril stops and doesn't speak, letting the staff press forward.

"Of course, Your Highness. Then first is 'What changed your mind?'"

"Are we sure that wasn't already well covered in the article?" Godwin asks abruptly.

"Fabian might still ask," Reinold reminds his brother calmly.

Godwin sighs and nods resignedly. I swallow as I realize that's my cue to give an example of how I'd reply. I take a deep breath, only to release it before trying again. "As I believe was covered well in the article that was released, when I saw the character of the royal family wasn't at all what I'd been told it should be, I began to have my doubts. I did my research into all the parties which I had never done before and found the truth."

"Which was?" Jean keeps playing the part.

"Perhaps we can answer the hidden question and point out it wasn't just that the prince is charming and handsome." Reinold smiles slightly as we all look at him. "Because really, that's what people are afraid the answer is. That someone who once knew the royal family was no good was so easily taken in by a cute butt."

I think everyone but Gavril and I laugh at least a little at that. Damian doesn't laugh, but he does smile a little. Gavril gives Reinold a look which makes Reinold chuckle while my cheeks turn pink.

"We all know that's not what happened, but that's what the question is really about. So, I propose in our answer, we find a way to make that clear. Perhaps simply adding that you had doubts before you met the prince, unless that isn't true." Reinold looks at me.

"No. It was during the first interview," I murmur.

"Then I'd suggest adding that. Something like, 'When I saw the character of the royal family when I met them in the first interview before even arriving at the palace, I started to have my doubts.' Then the rest of your answer was perfect."

I just nod, willing to do whatever the vell they wanted me to do. Reinold gives me a compassionate smile.

"I agree the answer is good. Add that if you feel it's needed." Jean smiles at me. "It's your moment to get your message across."

*But I don't have one.* I push that thought away as we move on.

"'Are you still close to your family?' is next." Jean smiles tenderly at me.

"With my mother. My father is..." Is what? "Another matter."

"He's going to challenge that and ask for more details." Reinold frowns.

"I sadly have to agree." Godwin is almost wincing.

And it's the question I really don't want to answer. I keep that inside, though, still taking those deep breaths. "So, what can I say to shut him up?"

No one else reacts to what I said, but Gavril's head snaps to look at me.

"More than a vague one-word answer." Godwin is still wearing that near wince.

"Such as?"

They all look at each other. Considering I don't know what my relationship with my father is right now, how could they know how to give an answer that won't get attacked?

"I try to respect him as my father, but our goals and aspirations vary vastly, making much more of a relationship near impossible at the moment?" Helena offers timidly.

"That will take the heat off?" I ask.

Godwin takes a while to reply before making a kind of noncommittal sound. "Likely best that we'll get without letting him lure you into a public therapy session."

"Not happening." I think I'd lose my cool and walk out. No. I can't do that. I'm the true princess, and that's not what a true princess does. I can't walk out. My own goal damns me.

"I agree." Godwin nods firmly. "Perhaps give an answer like that, then rebut with your own question."

"My own question?" I have no questions.

"Turn it on the viewer. 'How would you feel if it was your father?' That should embarrass the viewer, and he'll move on." Reinold smiles a little. "Trust me, that will shut him up."

The others chuckle, but I don't.

We go through the rest of them like this. But then we hit the ones I have no answer for. "Are you afraid you'll lose the people's trust after coming out with this?"

I don't do a mock answer. I just look at them for guidance. None of them expected this turn of events. Jean, Helena, and Bella exchange looks.

"Perhaps we can tie that into the question they had for me that's similar," Gavril suggests.

"They may not even ask it," I remind him, annoyed. I just want this done. I want to have it over, done and move on because this is going to hurt. It's similar to willingly walking up for a public caning, only this is verbal, not physical.

"But it might make it easier to answer if we blend them," Gavril says patiently.

"Whatever." They know better than me anyway, and not fighting it will make it be over faster.

Gavril frowns, but he doesn't seem to have an answer to that.

"Which question?" Jean checks.

"They ask me pretty much the same thing. Why tell us now and why did you hide the prophecy? Mine is about the prophecy and hers about her past. We combine the answers and knock all of them out at once, making it easier to save face and get it over with quickly."

"So, what is the answer?"

"Wanting to be open," Gavril says simply, slipping into the mock interview mode as if it were a role better than I can. "Our intention never was to hide it. In fact, it was given in a public place, but we never made a formal announcement. Those in attendance either chose not to speak of it or repeated their interpretation of it and not the actual words. It was never about hiding it, but we simply did not address it until action could be taken. Not like an infant can honor that yet." Gavril smiles, as if knowing there would be a pause for a reaction. "And before moving forward into this next phase, we want to ensure no one feels we are trying to hide what isn't truly a secret."

"That's not going to work for her question." Jean frowns. "Her situation is completely different."

"Doesn't mean they need to realize that." Gavril counters.

"Fabian isn't stupid." Godwin is wearing that wince again.

"But he has to keep the show going."

"Rebutting that with 'and you' to Kascia is as easy as sneezing." Reinold is looking at Gavril with a bit of concern, saying with his expression "and you know that".

I know what he's really trying to do. He's trying to take the question for me as I have no answer, and it protects me. I don't know how well it would work. But I have no answer. I don't fear losing the people's trust. I know I did. But I can't say that in front of the nation.

"Then what do you propose?" Gavril's tone has an edge to it.

"I think it's safe to allow the princess to be honest." Reinold looks at me in concern.

"No, it's not." I state flatly.

"Your Highness—"

"I'm not that yet, so let's not pretend," I retort. "He is going to turn it on me, so what am I supposed to say?"

"We can't presume to put words in your mouth." Jean is looking at me with a compassionate concern too, but it only annoys me. I know it sucks, no need to pity me over it.

"Kascia, you were honest with us. And that worked," Bella reminds me with a soft smile. "I know it's terrifying to have them rip into you this personally. Really, I do, remember? They did it to me too, but you won for a reason. We all knew, deep down, it was you. If it worked on the other girls enough for them to envy you like Jonquil, then it can work on the people, too."

She doesn't deserve me snapping at her when she just wants to help, so I choose not to reply. At least in this moment, I have that choice.

"Perhaps rephrase the question." Reinold tries. "Instead of 'are you afraid you'll lose the people's trust', we think of it as asking 'are you hopeful it will help?'"

"That's a different question."

"But it has the same intent, My Lady. They want to know if you're afraid that coming out with the truth will make things worse."

"No." *I know it will.* I've already lost them.

"Then assure them you aren't afraid." Reinold smiles gently. "No, I'm not afraid of it. I'm here to try to bring peace, so that's what I'm trying to do.' Simple, easy, and honest."

No, it's a bloody lie, but it will do the trick. I may have to get used to lying to the people. Oh, I hate that so deeply, I fight not to cry here and now, biting my lips so hard it hurts.

Gavril squeezes my hand, but I pull it away. I know he means to help, but I don't want to feel more trapped.

"And an easy trick," Reinold says slowly, pausing until I meet his eyes, "when they ask you what someone else thinks, is to say, 'I don't know, ask them'. The press loves to ask you what someone else thinks, and that is always a trap. Some of these questions ride that line. You can use the default 'don't ask me, ask them' with answers like 'I can't predict how the people will react, but I am doing all of this in the hope of unifying the people not causing further divides.' Don't let him push you into speaking for someone else when you can't."

But these questions are from the public, and that tells me how they feel. They felt betrayed. There is a hint of anger in demanding what I was thinking or how I think they'll react. I'd been right, and the truth of that hurts more than I thought it would.

There's a pause before Damian leans forward in his chair. "Kascia," he says softly, waiting for my attention.

I swallow and meet his eyes, struggling as much as I had with Reinold.

His emerald eyes are soft with care and compassion. "You don't have to lie." He shakes his head softly. "If the answer is yes, you can say so. It is okay to be afraid, to be vulnerable. No, it isn't fun, and no doubt it hurts. But the people love you because they know you understand; they are afraid and vulnerable too. This is about laying down the walls and the weapons between the two sides to encourage trust and open communication. For them, and for you. You don't have to live in secret anymore."

I'm not sure that helps me get where I want to be. I'm still that frightened girl when I first walked into this palace. And she's not who the people fell in love with. I already feel I have to strip down for them. I don't want to do it more than I already have to. Nor do I want the rebels thinking they're winning. I'm speaking to them as much as those who trust me. But if I'm going to hate it anyway...

I nod, but still don't feel any better.

Damian gives me a sad, warm smile and nods, then sits back with a sigh. I may not be as good at reading people as he is, but I can tell he wishes he didn't have to make me do this. But he isn't the one making me. He's just the one who pointed out it had to be done.

They go over all the other questions with me, directing me to be honest, giving me an idea of what to say but not putting words in my mouth.

"You want to practice?" Jean asks gently.

"Sure." Whatever they want.

"Are you hopeful this will unite the nation, or do you think this will only encourage other rebels in seeing one of their own take power?"

"I would hope it brings us together and stops the fighting. As for how the rebellions will react, I wouldn't know. We'll have to see how they behave," I regurgitate.

"Perfect." Jean smiles. But I don't miss Godwin and Reinold exchanging a look.

"What?" I ask them.

They look at me. They seem to want to keep quiet, but when Gavril gives them a warning look, Godwin slowly speaks. "He might follow that up."

"Oh?" Gavril frowns.

"But you were one of them once, right?"

"Not really. I thought I was, but they never admitted the full truth to me. So, I wasn't so much one of them by choice," I snap, annoyed.

"What secrets were they hiding?" Godwin keeps up the game.

I open my mouth even as the rest of the staff in the room look horrified. "That I wasn't a Custod. That my father was disinherited for what he'd done and that the Custods weren't on our side at all. How can I really be one of them when everything I've experienced with them has been deceitful?"

"Perhaps—" Jean begins.

"And so, when you learned the truth, you left?" Godwin ignores her.

"Can you leave what you never were part of? I only did it because I trusted the Custods to keep their oath. Once I learned none of that was real, I just didn't believe a lie anymore." I quickly recall to withhold more emotion. It's so hard. I already feel anger towards the people who almost own my soul for turning on me like this. I loved them, and they turned on me like wolves.

"She's going to be fine," Godwin looks at the overly stressed Jean and Helena.

"No, I'm not!" I almost lost control, already inches from crying. They turned on me. And that is a pain almost as bad as Gavril turning on me. Almost.

"Yes, you are." Gavril rubs my back.

"Stop doing that," I snap and get up. "Do we need to review anything else?" I ask.

"No, but the point is to make it easier for you. You're sure—" Jean begins.

"Thank you, but that was plenty. I need to get dressed for this interview." I turn to leave.

"Kascia—" Gavril tries, but I push my way out anyway.

What I don't expect is to feel someone take my arm once the door shuts behind me. The person pulls me close.

I struggle, trying to push him off, pounding on his chest even, but it's pointless. He just lets me push and beat him until I give up and press my face into his rough shirt.

"Shh, it's okay. You're not alone anymore," Gavril assures me, resting his head on mine. "They're right. You have this."

"No, I don't." I fight to push him away again. I will hate it, and that is unchangeable. Perhaps I have it handled, but I don't "have" it. They hate me, but they can't know how that hurts. I will wear the mask. The one I thought I took off and tossed aside. I hate putting it back on, most of all, for the people I don't have to wear it for. I wore it for the royals on behalf of the people. Now it's reversed. I hate it. I hate them for making me put it back on. I hate them for turning on me.

"You do. You just have to be open."

"No, I don't! Stop saying that!" I try again to push him away, but he's too strong.

"I know you're scared. Stop." Gavril struggles with me, handling me far too easily.

"I'm not scared." I'm furious. I'm angry and tired of this game I thought was over when I won. But it never ends. The rest of my life is a game to be played with all of them. And that's why I'm angry. They lied to me. The hope I'd had was in vain, and I had to share the most personal thing in my life with people who were going to attack it. People I cared for and wanted to trust, but I've learned better. Now, I have to strip and let them throw the stones. I have passed the point of no return.

"Call it something else, but it's alright. You're allowed to feel this way. Stop... fighting me." Gavril has a harder time talking while dealing with my attempts to get away.

I stop. Because I can't win, anyway. I let out a heavy sigh and wait for whatever he wants. He takes me into the hall then into the covere room, locking the door. "Okay. Now you can yell or... do whatever," Gavril says. "No one will notice or try to stop you."

"You just did," I point out.

"You want the staff to see you fighting with me?" Gavril asks.

"No."

"Okay. Now we can talk or fight or whatever it is you want to do."

"I just want this over with," I snap and turn to go.

"That will not make it go faster," he points out.

"I don't care!" At least I am doing something.

Gavril sighs. "It's okay to be scared."

"I'm not scared!" Why won't he accept that? "They hate me! I don't want to do this and don't tell me I have to. I know. Alright? I know. They're going to attack me. I don't want to deal with it, but it's what I signed up for. Alright? So just let me deal with it."

Gavril frowns. "But you're not dealing with it."

I glare at him. "If I wasn't dealing with it, I'd not bother showing up."

"Kascia, it's okay to be scared, to want to run. And normally, I'd be alright with it, but if you don't deal with it, you may have exactly what you fear happen. You can't walk out in the interview, and you know that."

"So let me now when I get a choice!" I snap back.

"We both know that's not helping." Gavril doesn't back down. "Let it out. You don't have to hide from me anymore."

"I don't want to scream at you." I don't want to let it out at him or anyone.

Gavril's jaw tenses. "Then snarl at someone who does deserve it," he says.

"No one does! It's just how it is! It's not anyone's fault. It's just how it is," I remind him. "I know I have to do this. It's no one's fault. I'll figure it out. I always have."

"We'll figure it out. You're not alone anymore. Please, you won. You don't have to be alone anymore. Must you make it worse for yourself by doing so?" Gavril frowns. "Or is there just someone else you'd rather talk to?"

"I don't want to snap at anyone!" I repeat in frustration. He's not listening. "It will only make things worse. Sorry I mind having a reputation of snapping at my staff and those who don't deserve to be snarled at. I can't snap at the people whose faith I need."

"Then pretend to yell at them. Please, just let it out. Bottling it up is driving you crazy. You don't have to suffer like this alone," Gavril begs me, stepping forward to take my hand.

But to me, it's just more confinement, and I can't bear that. The rush of panic rises in my chest and up my throat, making me dizzy, and before I know what I'm doing, I turn to leave.

Part of me expects Gavril to stop me, but no hand yanks me around. No grip closes on mine on the door to yank it away. No arms pull me into a restrictive embrace.

I open the door, step out, and escape without a single obstacle. At first, I'm relieved by it, but as I retreat to my room and let my maids do their work, I long for him.

I ignore the new girl's merry chatter that gets Ro chattering too. I don't care. Sure, it's annoying, but no need to make the new girl scared of me by snapping at her or having Ro talk back, which is what she'll do. Vivian seems to get the hint and tries to quiet them, but Ro isn't listening, and the new girl just follows the flow. I can't say I wouldn't do the same in her shoes.

As they work, a knock comes at the door, but instead of waiting to be answered, the door opens, and Damian steps inside, closing the door behind him. I give him a weak smile. So that's what I felt had been missing. Normally, he would be here to ensure that everything was done correctly.

Damian returns the same smile back to me, then goes and sits on the workbench. He watches silently as my maids work, keeping that gentle smile on his face, but it does waver from time to time, and his brow is slightly pinched.

I try not to stare, but something about it unsettles me. He's afraid. He's unsure how this is going to go too. Perhaps he's regretting asking it of me. I'm letting him down on that as well. But I know it must be done, even as every fiber of my being wishes to flee or shove them away. I don't want to face those that hate me, the ones who turned on me.

When my maids finish, instead of standing back and appraising my look as he normally did, Damian comes forward. His brow tightens, almost forming a hard line. I can see him debate with himself, unsure of what to say. He's never been unsure before. Finally, he takes a breath. "Are you ready?" he asks.

"As I'm going to be." I nod back. I hold back confessing my pure anger because he knows. He might know better than I do.

He nods as his eyes search mine. "You don't *have* to do this. We can find another way to address those questions."

"Yes, I do." It's far too late now. The people expect it and so does Gavril.

Damian sighs and drops his gaze a moment before nodding, and his eyes meet mine again. "Just... tell the truth. You have nothing to fear from the truth, even if it might feel otherwise. The people relate to you. They are afraid too, just... show them you care."

I nod, but I think there's much to fear. Their accusations are plenty to prove I do. If I want their trust back, I have to hide how I hate that I have to do this. How I hate them for betraying me. I can't be honest, or it will be worse than keeping my mouth shut.

Damian looks down again. "I suppose that isn't helpful. I wish I had more to give that was. I'm sorry."

"You have nothing to be sorry for." It is me who isn't handling this like he'd expected or hoped. I feel I'm letting him down.

His eyes meet mine again, and he gives me a weak smile. "I am sorry for you. I'm sorry you have to go through this when it is so hard, and you have already done so many hard things as it is. I'm sorry this feels more like a pressure and a punishment than a liberating experience. I am sorry that there are people who do not and will not understand because they are locked in their own pride and biases. I'm sorry they attack you when you have done nothing wrong. I am sorry for you."

I bow my head. "It's... what I signed up for."

He puts his knuckle under my chin and raises it so he can look into my eyes. "I know. But it doesn't make this any easier. And no matter what happens tonight, even if you end up screaming at Fabian, I love you, and I will still love you. I am proud of you, so very proud." He smiles a real smile, the one he has smiled at me many times before, but this time it is filled with tenderness and compassion. "Nothing you do will ever change how much I care about you."

But I can't afford to scream at him or any of them, or they'll turn on me more than they already have, and I'll lose any hope of turning them around, making the rivalry worse and more personal. "I trust you." It's all I have to get me through this.

He nods. "I know. I just want you to be able to get through tonight and look back and be proud of yourself. What is being asked is a hard thing. And it's alright that it is hard and you don't like it. I don't either. It actually puts Cedrick's struggle to mind after the war with Heklis. What he went through was a lot like this. It's painful, and it's hard, but he made it through those times and so can you. However, you have to get through it. I just want you to be happy with yourself when this is all over, no matter what that looks like."

"I'd like that." If I lose it and yell at them, I know I won't be able to be happy with myself. I have to keep cool. I have to keep calm. I have to be perfect.

Damian smiles a little and gently places a hand to my cheek. "I love you, night angel."

"Love you too." I can't let them down.

Damian nods, then moves as if to pull me into a hug. I return it, trying not to cry because I can't afford it right now.

Then another knock comes to the door. It must be time to head down, even with me getting ready sooner than I had to. I take a deep breath as Flur gets the door, but I move to accept the call without complaint.

Instead of the expected staff, Gavril stands there dressed for the interview, although I can't help but notice a sore or bruise on his left hand. I take a breath to be ready and put on a small, though weak smile.

He returns it with about as much energy as me. "Ready?" he asks gently.

"As I can be." I nod and take his arm. He holds it securely, as if making sure I don't try to run. There's nowhere to run. Why would I bother?

"You look beautiful." Gavril smiles at me as we walk. When my staff designed it, did I ever not? Does it even matter? I'm just as exposed to their attacks, no matter how I dress. Damian quietly follows behind us.

"We'll have dinner after. Then it's over. We can have fun. Nothing between us and the wedding," Gavril assures.

"Of course." I'm sure something else will come up. It always has.

We go to the well-decorated reception room, ready for the show.

Fabian is already there, having his makeup checked and talking to Jean and Reinold. The staff come over and check my makeup in the lights too and do all last-minute preparations, but we're still ready a bit early.

"Want to get into our seats? Be ready?" Gavril asks. "Or do you want to walk around?"

"Whatever gets this over with." I hug myself, honestly still furious with all of them for doing this to me.

Gavril just nods, and we take our place on the loveseat. Part of me wishes I had more distance, the other half fears if I pull back, so will he, and that this will all have been pointless. I can't fail to be what he declared me to be now, even more than when I wanted to prove it to have him.

"You're going to be fine," Gavril promises me, rubbing my hand.

"Conceal, transform," I reply, the old theater adage that means you take your stage nerves and transform that energy into the emotion you are trying to portray.

Gavril frowns, clearly not understanding the term, and opens his mouth to ask when Fabian bounds up. "We're going to get started. Everyone is waiting," he informs us.

I sit up properly and shut my eyes to start the process as I hear them begin the countdown. I feel Gavril give me a quick kiss on the cheek before there's the pause that is the final countdown before Fabian speaks, and I open my eyes.

# Chapter 15

"Good evening, Purerah!" Fabian begins. "Here we are again, with the Enthronement over this time, for our special session. The royal couple is getting ready to marry in just a few short weeks, and their full story has been shared. And what a... a story it is. And today, we get to sit and ask them some questions submitted by many of you. We will likely not get to every one of them today, but hopefully, we can cover everyone's concerns and combine them to get the answers we're all looking for. Now, without further ado."

Fabian turns to us, bows a little, then takes his seat, crossing his legs. Gavril has staged us holding hands well, and he holds mine so tight it's keeping me from moving. It helps me keep the perfectly acted smile on as we settle into this torture.

It is good he did. My heart is thundering a mile a minute, and every bit of me wants to react, move, attack him, flee; I just want to move, get away, lash out. I have to move. It takes all my self-control to stop myself from doing any of those things.

"Thank you for taking the time with us. It cannot be easy," Fabian begins. "Most of all for you, My Lady. We can only imagine how hard it has been for you to open up to us about all of this. These are the kinds of things most people get to hide in their closets as skeletons to dance only in their private nightmares, but you have been willing to open it all up to us, and for that, we cannot be more grateful. What brought you to do what so few of us would have the courage to do?"

*Don't blurt the truth. Don't blurt the truth.* But I want to snap that I don't want to, that I don't trust them with it. Not when they turned on me. That I never wanted to have to expose my most flawed and personal parts of my history to nameless masses.

I look into Fabian's sincere eyes. He really is trying to help. He praises me, acknowledging the difficulty and bravery involved. It's not fair to snap at him. It's not his fault anymore than Gavril's. I want this to be over. I want to let them have at it, attack me, and move on. I want this done. I want this done so badly.

"I don't know." Great, I lead with the three words I didn't want to say. "But I knew I had to. It would only be worse to hide it when I don't want to keep secrets anymore. Secrets have ruined everything."

"Like the lies the rebellion told you?" Fabian asks gently.

I nod. "I don't want to be like them." And keeping my secret would, even if I hate this moment with every fiber of my soul.

"You're hopeful being open about your story will help bring the people together?" Fabian asks a gentle version of one of the harder questions.

"I want it to." But no, I'm not hopeful after the slew of attacking questions I got. They betrayed my care for them.

"So, it's worth the risk?"

"That's the hope." I put on a smile.

"So why come out now and not sooner?" Fabian asks.

I glance at Gavril, sure he hates the honest answer, but at least I could give it in this case. "I feared it would make me guilty of treason, so I'd be executed, or worse." I meet Fabian's eyes. "I'm not exactly proud of the lies that guided my whole life. It's a horrible realization to find out all you believed and were told was a manipulative, twisted lie."

"I can only imagine." Fabian nods his agreement. "So, you were afraid to come forward with the truth?"

"After confessing to the prince... not exactly scared." I really wish they'd stop accusing me of being afraid. I'm not scared; I am angry.

"Then how do you feel?" Fabian's eyes are too full of compassion for me to tell him the truth. It makes me hateful in a way I never wanted to be. I hoped getting over what Jake did to me would fix it. But instead, it just got redirected. To what? Fate, I guess.

"Resigned." I find the kindest way to put it.

"Resigned?" Fabian smiles a little. "I'm not sure I understand what you mean by that."

Why does he have to make me explain? "I've fought my whole life to do what was right. And putting this out now rather than trying to hide it my whole life is best. I don't know how to not do what is needed for my people." *Even if you all hate me for it.* I resist tears.

"Likely being told you were a Custod your whole life has something to do with that." Fabian gives me another understanding smile. I wish he'd stop doing that, so I could at least feel justified in hating his questions. "Were you disappointed you weren't a Custod? Or put a better way, did you like being a Custod and were unhappy to have that taken away?"

"No." I manage a small smile. "As ashamed as I may be to admit it, I never wanted that. I was committed to fulfilling the duty I believed I had, but I'd have been happy in my theater."

"So why not go back to that when you found out the truth?" Fabian asks.

"I could have. Well, I wasn't going to go back to the theater here with my father, but I realized I didn't want to go back to any theater. I... I wanted to win. I wanted him. I wanted to be the right choice for my people." And now they don't want me. I'd fought so hard to be their true princess, their royal, and I revealed I wasn't. I can't stop the tears.

Gavril's grip tightens to try to help support me through it.

"But you didn't have to. That was a choice you could make. Did that never occur to you?" Fabian asks.

"I knew I could. They made sure I did. He wouldn't stop offering." The annoyance slips out in my voice as I nod at Gavril bitterly.

That gets a laugh from the crew. Even Fabian chuckles. "He kept offering? I can see why that was annoying. Made you feel like he didn't want you."

"That wasn't why." Anger comes out in my voice. "He just didn't want to make me do this." Gavril never wanted to force me to have this moment, but here it was anyway. He defended me from it as long as he could, even this morning from the other reporter.

"Because he loves you. It seems like you won him pretty early on," Fabian teases. "I'm sure the secret between you made that harder."

"It made it harder for me to figure out my feelings," I admit.

"Because you never wanted to be princess or queen, even with what you thought your duty was. You were happier just playing one." Fabian smiles.

"Yeah." I manage a small smile. "I never wanted to play the role for real."

"Until?"

"Until?" I repeat with a frown.

"When did that change?" Fabian asks.

I pause. I don't know. It clearly changed at some point, but when? "I just wanted the role. I'm not sure when it went from 'I want this because it's my duty' to 'I want this because I just want it.' I just... did."

"Was it in any part to prove your father wrong? That you were right, and you wanted him to see it?" Fabian asks.

"I have to be right. I'd rejected his way of seeing things, and if I am wrong... I'd have failed everything." This is the biggest thing I don't want to talk about. My worst pains are about to be public gossip. The public who no longer trusts me. I don't want to give them my deepest feelings to play with.

"Did he lead the attack that postponed the announcement of the winner?" Fabian asks. "Was he trying to stop you from being chosen?"

"He never thought they'd pick me."

There's a painful pause. "Your father didn't think you could win?" Fabian sounds horrified.

"No."

There's another pause. "I-I can't imagine how that made you feel." Fabian shakes his head to get back on track. "He expected you to marry some chosen king he hand-picked, but he didn't think real royalty would see you as worthy of the crown. I take it you're not close now, then? Is he staying in the palace?"

"Well... with what he did, he's not really staying in the palace so much as he's under arrest." I shrug a little. "My mother has only ever been supportive, even when she was forced to keep secrets."

"I'm sure that's a comfort." Fabian nods. He hesitates before going on. "How did the royal family take it when they learned the truth?"

"Better than I expected." Gavril takes over for me, and at first, I feel slapped down, like I'd done badly enough that he had to stop me. But then when I'm allowed to be quiet as he answers, a painful tension in my shoulders I hadn't noticed drops, and I'm grateful. "I thought my mother would be afraid of the dangers, but she was understanding and protective of Kascia, realizing the dangers she'd faced to come so far. I am sure that's how many of you felt when you learned the truth." Gavril nods at the impressionor.

*No, they didn't.* I think bitterly. They hate me.

"Certainly, that was my thought," Fabian agrees. "But it wasn't just Her Highness's secrets coming out. Why hadn't you ever made the prophecy public?" Fabian asks Gavril.

"We never meant to hide it, but few people seemed to recall it correctly or they did not recall it at all, so to stop more desperate attacks on the palace when I was still young, we didn't bring it up. There were rumors of it, but no one ever asked us to confirm it, so we left it alone. We decided it was important to remind people of it now, so they could understand the full story. Without understanding that, the rest of the truth may not seem important."

"It must have been intimidating for you to have all that pressure on you." Fabian is not looking at me at all, not even glancing like he normally did in a group interview like this. He's giving me room, but I'm well aware the impressionor is still on me, so I have to keep my face still, but at least, I can let the feelings battling in my stomach scuffle it out. Have I made it through? Is he actually done with me?

"Still is. I'm not done yet." Gavril puts on that perfect smile he uses well with the press and likely the court. "But it's nice not to feel like I'll be in trouble for talking about it. The whole Enthronement was about fulfilling it."

"And you're not worried you failed that? Even with her background?"

I fight so hard not to cry at that attack on me. "No. I'm not worried," Gavril says firmly. "I knew she was hiding something. She had told me enough in her attempts to be as honest as she safely could, and I knew there was more. But I also knew she'd defended us. I knew and still know I can trust her with anything. The hardest part was keeping it quiet. I couldn't tell the girls about the prophecy, so it wouldn't change how they behaved in tests. Although I knew those secrets could create difficulties, they didn't care. She understands both sides of this fight better than anyone.

"The people can react how they will. Rebels feel they won. Those trapped in the middle feel betrayed or confused, but no one knows how bad that feels better than my princess. She's been trapped in all positions, and that background will make her your princess more than we've had in centuries. She makes me a better prince for it. Others may have come with less 'drama', but she's my princess. I knew it long ago, and she's only proved it to me again and again."

I have to look up to keep my eyes as dry as possible and take deep breaths to not to cry in a different way.

"You're not worried that deep love blinds you to the realities of why it may not be her?" Fabian questions.

"I'm not."

"At all?"

"At all," Gavril says slowly.

"Were you the only one who knew about her father?" Fabian looks at me to open it back up to me too. "Or did any of the other candidates know?"

I shake my head. "I only ever spoke to Gavril or my attendant about it."

"And he told no one?"

"I assume not." At least Damian promised he hadn't.

"That must make it all the harder to open up to us about it. That takes real courage." Fabian gives me a small smile again.

"It was my only option," I reply.

"A true princess looks after her people. No doubt you earned winning for that dedication," Fabian assures me before resuming a more official posture. "But that leads to one important question: how was the black cat the key to knowing who chose the winner?" Fabian asks with a bit of playfulness to his voice.

"I have no idea." Gavril plays it up. "I didn't give that quote, and none of my staff did. Maybe Nippers just seemed to like Kascia best."

Of course, Gavril wouldn't reveal Cedrick's disguise to the public. That would be rude without Cedrick's permission.

"Perhaps," Fabian chuckles. "But it certainly confused me. I thought perhaps he belonged to someone important."

"Perhaps he does." Gavril shrugs. Fabian looks at me.

"All I saw and was told was he was a clever stray, and that seems to be true." I put on a smile. "In fact, I named him Nippers for his playfulness and teasing him about wanting catnip."

"Maybe it was that." Fabian chuckles. He then resumes the torment.

"So, when your father interrupted the announcement, did you know he'd chosen you?" Fabian asks, nodding at Gavril.

I shake my head. "No. I didn't know until the formal announcement." Or so I was supposed to tell everyone.

"Did anyone know?" Fabian teases Gavril.

"I think I did a good job surprising everyone." Gavril smiles.

"You do like to surprise people. Such as telling us about all of this now when everyone thought the drama was over. No one questioned your choice of her? Even within your inner circle when she confessed? You said you are certain, but was there anyone else you had to convince? Perhaps you thought other girls might be better suited?"

"Not when I'd made the choice. It was my choice to make at that point, and no one knew but me about her past," Gavril says, not wavering at all, unlike me.

"We all know this has been hard on the princess-to-be, but what about you? Were you afraid to open up about the prophecy? That must have been a lot of pressure."

"Pressure I've felt my whole life. Opening up about it would not change it. I wasn't nervous."

"You didn't worry it would increase attempts on your life?" Fabian tests.

"I'll worry about that as it happens. Worrying beforehand helps nothing. Not when I have more pressing concerns."

"Like ensuring the rebels don't see her being chosen as a win for the rebellions. They got half of what they wanted."

"If they see it as a win, then they're changing their minds about the throne entirely." Gavril smiles. "She's done more to defend me from them than any other woman I know."

"Was choosing her perhaps part of your plan to unify the nation as king?"

"I cannot comment on what I would do as king as I am not that yet," Gavril says casually. "But I certainly am confident in my ability to get all the needed information to handle that when I am."

I'm fighting so hard to keep composed. It's becoming difficult for me to listen to this any longer. I want to run and having nothing to do is not helping. It's taking all my patience and skill to remain poised.

Gavril must have noticed because he says, "But if you have questions about that, perhaps you should wait until we are ready to discuss those things. That's not what today is about."

"No?"

*Not today, Fabian, please. I am not going to be able to stand this much longer.* Why does he have to be so him? I can't take much more of this.

"There will be the normal time to ask questions after the wedding, and you can ask those questions there," Gavril says firmly.

"But they're on the list," Fabian puts on his performance grin. "No comment on your first act as king, your plans, nothing?"

"Not today," Gavril says firmly.

Fabian pauses a bit longer than normal; his eyes are not on us, but I can't see what he's looking at. "Well, if you're that sure, then that covers all the questions sent in this batch. We will look forward to hearing more soon."

"We look forward to going over them with you," Gavril nods his head politely.

"I'll make sure they're all addressed," Fabian promises, and thank heavens, he goes right into the normal wrap up spiel which I mostly ignore, focusing on hiding how much I want to run.

I manage until I see the light go off on the machine, and that tells me it's over. It's finally over!

I leap from my seat without a single thought or realizing I'd done it, and I am racing away before I can even debate if this is a good idea with the press still watching even if the people are not. I find myself bowing my head to Fabian in thanks, though for what I don't know before, I'm already halfway up the corridor.

I go to the only place my mind can think of that no one has ever found me, which is the deepest corner of the library. I just curl up, not caring if the dress wrinkles or anything and just sob out all the terror and pain: how it feels to have all that exposed, how relieved I am it's over, how much I hated it all. And even more how much we're both going to pay for that whole mess.

I've not been there more than a few seconds, half a minute at best when I feel arms around me. I look up, and my shoulders drop to see

Gavril. He doesn't speak, just holds me and I turn into him, bury my face in his chest and just cry. I cry for a long time.

"I know. You did it. It's over. You don't have to do it again. It's out there. They can't hurt you with it anymore. It's okay." Gavril strokes my hair, not caring if it ruined it, and I don't care either.

But it's far from over. "They hate me," I squeak.

"We don't know that. It's alright." He gently hushes me, stroking my hair as I sob.

I know it is going to be bad. I wanted to be their choice. They feel betrayed on all sides. Tomorrow, I am going to face that I am not their chosen princess anymore.

# Chapter 16

I don't remember going to bed, but I wake up feeling slightly groggy in the morning as if from oversleep, but the time looks like a normal morning. Perhaps I had gone to bed early and just it all blurred into the long day yesterday.

I sit up and rub my eyes. It's not long after that my staff come in and start the normal routine. I wonder when they will start giving me a morning schedule run down. Now I have a scheduler.

The staff are happy and efficient. I ask them for the morning paper as soon as I can, but they don't have one. Of course, they knew I'd ask and wanted to delay it. I want to see how bad it is.

"After breakfast, I think they'll start helping you learn the new routines," Vivian says but keeps it vague. I'm ready to go down for breakfast when the door opens again.

"Good morning, ladies." Damian smiles warmly as he enters the room.

"Good morning," they all greet him brightly. I manage a smile and a mumbled a good morning.

Damian turns to me with a kind smile. "How are you feeling?"

"Anxious," I confess, afraid of what would be in the paper that morning.

"Understandable. Did you sleep at all?" He frowns a little.

I nod. "I don't remember going to bed, but yes, I slept." At least I don't remember not sleeping or waking up in the night.

Damian gives me another gentle smile. "Well, hopefully today won't be too bad. I believe Penelope has scheduled time a little later to respond to the letter correspondence about the article."

I swallow hard and nod. "Okay." I'll have to be ready for that.

Damian claps my shoulders with a warm, proud smile. "You'll be alright. I know yesterday was hard, but you did wonderfully. I'm proud of you."

"It could have been pretty bad." I nod a little. It was a mess, but it could have been a worse mess.

"But you got through it," Damian says encouragingly. "Today won't be as hard, but I'm sure Penelope will go over that in more detail with you after breakfast."

I nod feebly. "I just..." I wish I'd done better. "Don't want to make anything worse."

"You won't. Have faith in that." He smiles, then kisses my forehead. I manage a weak smile and nod.

Damian pulls back and gives me another gentle smile. "In time, you shall see. But shall we get you down to breakfast?" He offers his arm.

I manage a slightly more real smile as I accept it. Damian beams and leads me out.

"By the way, you look ravishing today," he praises with a wide smile.

I let out a half chuckle. "Thanks." Not that I have much to do with that.

"You're welcome." Damian smiles again. "I love the way it falls on you," he says as he looks it over.

"What is with the comments?" Damian rarely did this outside of getting ready for something.

"Oh well, Bella did that one." He smiles. "I suppose I'm just saying I approve."

I smile back. "Well, that would make more sense." Honestly, in my mood, I've barely noticed how I look. I'd hardly noticed last night's masterpiece.

He nods. "I'll have to let her know. But do you like it?" he asks honestly.

I have to pause and look. It is a nice piece, a soft purple garment hanging off me nicely, like Damian said, comfortable but carrying a gentle elegance. I smile a little. "I do."

He beams. "Then I shall let her know that as well."

"Thank you." I want her to feel she's doing well.

We reach the dining room where Zelda is only just arriving as well. She smiles at us with a bright "good morning" as she sits down.

Gavril stands as I come in. I scrutinize his face, but he's just watching me with compassionate nervousness. I force a smile. Damian gives him a reassuring smile as he leads me to my seat.

Gavril returns a small smile to Damian as he pulls out my seat for Damian to escort me to before settling me in. I miss the meaningful look Gavril gives Damian as I brace myself for what's coming. Damian bows to us both, promising to see me later, and leaves.

I glance at Gavril as he sits down again. It makes me wonder if he has observed the aftermath of last night's disaster. I look away quickly when he tries to glance at me sideways. But I catch a slight smile out of the corner of my eye, so I look back. He takes my hand under the table, pretending he wasn't looking as he returns to his meal, and I do the same.

When breakfast is done and everyone goes their own ways, Gavril pulls me into the corner he so favors and kisses me intensely, trying to fill some of the empty fear with something else. It helps me relax and smile as he pulls back just enough to embrace me.

"You alright?" he asks quietly.

"As I can be." I'm just so scared of how bad the mess has gotten. I knew Fabian couldn't resist.

"They'll finally help you get the flow of things today. Don't worry, it's not as bad as it seems. I promise," Gavril assures me, stroking my cheek. I offer a faint smile. "Do you need me?"

"No. I'll be alright. I need to get used to this." I can face the mess I've made. I can do this. I chose this life. I can clean up my own broken glass.

"Okay. It's just normal work for me, so if you need anything, don't hesitate to send for me." Gavril makes me promise before he goes about his day.

When I meet with my staff in the Ladies' Chamber, they still are nothing but supportive. Damian is there with Bella. There's also a painfully large assortment of letters organized neatly in rows in a box on the table. I'm afraid of what they are.

Jean is the first one to come up to me to start the day's work. "I am glad to report that the article about the interview was just fine," she says. I give her a look. "No really, it summarizes the situation quite well. It comments on the fact that you seemed to struggle to be open but did well anyway, and how you handled every question with poise. So far, your public response seems positive."

"Which means?" He'd ripped into Gavril, hadn't he? Spared me so Damian wouldn't eat him but went for Gavril.

"No one has rioted," Helena jokes, and that actually makes me laugh. "And of course, it's too early to see much more than the first reactions as reported by the Purerah Advocate. Other papers will follow up, I presume."

"I'd hardly thought of the others," I confess. As the Purerah Advocate was the largest and most respected paper in the nation, it was the one the royal family let provide the interviewers.

"Purerah Union had little else to say either, though it pointed out there were no escalations in attacks anywhere, so it suggests this news was a good thing, but with that first part over, I doubt we'll see too much trouble from it. Most people only pay attention right after an event." Jean is trying to help me feel hopeful. "On the press side of things, it's mostly handling their demands for information about the wedding, but fear not: that is what Helena and I are for. We'll relay the information as needed. I'll give you updates or briefings as needed, or Helena will as we go."

She gives me a warm smile, which I return and nod that she can step aside if that is all.

"We do need to get to hiring your court liaison, but that will be for another day. Damian and I are taking first interviews and reviewing applications. I am hoping we can do that this afternoon," Bella smiles. "I spoke with Hydie and the royal family and staff, and Penelope has worked out what your schedule will look like, so each morning either she or I will come in and give you a rundown of the day each morning. Until Princess Zelda leaves, you'll continue to have breakfast with them and then meet us here. After she leaves, we'll meet and do the briefings over breakfast in your suite. But for this morning, I've given Penelope the full time. She says there's a lot of correspondence to go over."

A knot forms in my stomach as I glance at the box of letters, then look back at Penelope as she stands up. "Don't need to be so full of dread," she assures me.

I simply put on a smile.

She goes over a few requests and meetings we'll need to set up to set my permanent schedule, including teachers and possible teachers I need to approve, including several dance instructors, but I'd rather stick with my mother. We won't start handling the court in more detail until we've hired my court liaison.

But then we get started on the letters, the terrors ready to rip my heart and hopes apart. "There also were some public requests for your time, but I was told that due to security reasons, the guard would rather we didn't accept any of those until after the wedding," she finishes. "But if you strongly feel you want to review any of the requests and try to set them up, we'll do our best."

"Who sent the requests?" I frown a bit.

"I don't think anyone you know. Your cast friends were at your birthday, and none of these letters are from them. It's mostly fan-mail-style requests, which of course you can choose to accept any you like, but it's uncommon and the vetting process is intense by the guard before they'll let them in, and though you can of course overturn the process, it's not recommended."

"I... when did these come in?" I ask with a frown.

"Most came in on the first workday and have poured in since," Penelope says. "In fact, I'm sure I have a new collection of them waiting for me in the correspondence room."

Penelope picks up the first letter in the box. "For an example, this one is from a girl named Sofia Riddle.

"Dear Princess Kascia,

Sorry if I shouldn't call you princess yet, but I think that's the name you should go by. I wanted to write to you and ask for a little more help dealing with this problem I have. I live in an area where all my friends are sympathetic with the rebels. They always have been, and I never felt comfortable with it. I would pretend to agree, but it never sat right with me. After hearing your story, I realized it was okay to disagree and to help others change their mind. So, I defended how I felt about it, but now all my friends are making fun of me, and I don't know how to stand by it. How did you ever find the courage to do it? How can I find more courage? Your story inspired me to realize it's okay to have my own thoughts and feelings that aren't the same as everyone else, but how do you stop yourself wanting to hide away from them and keep standing up for yourself, even when it's hard?

Yours Sincerely, Sofia Riddle."

"What?" I stand up and snatch the letter, unable to believe what I'd just heard, but it reads just as Penelope read it. I note the date. It came in long before last night.

Penelope smiles at me as I drop back into my seat, looking over the letter over and over. "She is one you will either like to write back or perhaps set up a meeting with once the wedding is over. But then there's this one from Lorna Silverling.

"Dear Princess Kascia,

Thank you for sharing your story. If someone like you has had to deal with nasty relationships and get out of them and find better ones, then so can I. I broke it off with my long-standing boyfriend who is always getting into trouble (and me too), and I've never felt freer. Thank you for having the courage to share even those who look the most perfect aren't, and that's okay.

Love Lorna."

My face drops, and I stare at Penelope in pure shock. These aren't real, are they? But the handwriting varies in each of the letters.

"I love this one." Penelope picks up the next one. "Layla writes, 'Princess Kascia, some people are saying you're just trying to get power to get what you want, but I set them right. Don't forget you have friends too. Your prima replacement, Layla.'"

"Give me that." I get up and take that one too. Penelope is just smiling. I look at the letter. This one I know. She was a little girl who'd come to some of my shows before the Enthronement. She had saved all her pennies to buy one of my old pointe shoes at *The Hunchback* and then begged her mom to help her come to the first interview where Gavril and I had signed the shoe. I'd also seen her at the festival, and Damian had arranged for me to give her a backstage tour after we'd done *The Phantom*. She'd sent me this when she worried not everyone would support me?

"Do you know her?" Bella asks.

I nod and mutter the story, not really listening. She wrote me this?

"That one came first after the article." Penelope smiles. "I only just started getting to all your letters."

"They're... a-all like this?" I ask.

"Well, some are a bit more direct." Penelope puts down the letters she'd gone through and reads another one. "How could you wait so long to tell us your story? I thought others might make a better princess, but your story changed my mind. I don't think I could have stood up to my family like that. I admire that courage. I wish I was more like you.

"Danica Locus writes: 'I used to think the rebels were right, but after hearing all your stories, I'm taking a second look. What I learned about how bad it is for some of those people up north made me cry all night. You keep up the fight for us.'

"This is from Lale Hinde: 'I couldn't have been so open about my story if I were you. How did you ever find the courage to tell us? I couldn't have sat through either interview with nearly as much composure as you did. I hope one day I can be as brave as you.'

"Cassa Buttonwood says: 'Thought you girls were all mad to want to join that powderpuff game, but I couldn't have been further from wrong. That was a real struggle, and I'm glad you were rewarded for your humility and willingness to make a difference. I would have run away. I hope I can learn how to be like you one day.'"

"And most of these letters are from girls from age seven to eighteen. I had a few I couldn't even read." Penelope picks up a stack and hands them to me. They're pictures, the kind children draw with badly scribbled names or phrases on them, of what I guess is me and Gavril or... something like that with big crowns.

"Ah," Damian pulls up a letter with a big grin. "Here's one from the Lord Mayor himself. He writes: 'May I extend my heartfelt congratulations upon your winning the Enthronement. There is no doubt in my mind, now the full details have been revealed, you are a perfect choice, even if we will miss seeing you on the stage. I cannot think of a better role model for my grandchildren. I wish I had known how badly you were struggling so we could have been a better support for you. Family rifts are hard enough without the rest of what you have been struggling through. Know we will continue to support you as our princess, and I look forward to working with you more closely. Perhaps one day you will get to see your biggest fans once again. Sending you the highest honors, Lord Yuval, Lord Mayor of Roseple.'"

Damian beams at me as he finishes and offers me the letter. I take it and stare at it, stunned. That is definitely the mayor's seal. It isn't just those young ones who had positive messages for me. He may head only the city court, but it is closer to the court. I shake my head a little. I cannot believe this. These at least are recent. Perhaps I can hope.

"It still amazes me that Ericka is his daughter." Damian shakes his head with an amused smile.

I chuckle. "Me too." I often forget. "I can't believe he dared send this." What if his enemies saw it?

"Well, it might have helped that I offered to deliver it myself." Damian smiles with a slight blush.

"You did?"

Damian nods. "I was out picking up supplies, and I bumped into him, and we started talking. He said he wished he could send you something, so I offered to deliver it."

I smile a little. "He brought it up?" Damian hadn't had to ask. The mayor offered? The mayor hoped Damian would just verbally pass it along.

Damian nods with a smile. "He asked how you were. Then he mentioned the article, and we got to talking for a while before he finally expressed his wish. Of course, when I went to his home later, as soon as his grandchildren knew I was there, they insisted on sending their own letters." He smiles as he pulls a few more from his jacket and offers them to me.

The other staff are smiling as I take them. There are three. The first with the best writing in it must be from his grandson, whose name I didn't know until seeing the letter. I smile a little. He's named after his grandfather. His letter is short but sweet. "We're happy you won. You'll be the best princess ever. You always played a good one. See us soon!"

The elder granddaughter, Clara, writes, "You're my favorite princess ever! And prettiest too, no matter what auntie says." I lose it laughing for a moment, knowing Ericka had to be "auntie". And she drew sweet pictures of me dancing.

The last is from the youngest who wrote her own name, so I'm not sure what it is as it's hard to read. Her drawings depict me as princess with little "I love you"s written on it. I can't repress the smile. I hand the letters back to Damian, unsure where they'll choose to put them all.

Penelope is beaming. "The more stubborn men like those reporters may challenge you, but to these girls, you made a world of difference telling your story," she says. "So, when the court and press are picking on you, remember these women look up to what you did and admire that courage. Just like we do."

I'm blinking back tears for a very different reason.

"Would you like to go through the rest of them until lunch?"

I nod, managing a watery smile. Bella brings over a little basket to put overused handkerchiefs in as I have moist eyes as I go through the impressive piles of letters. Penelope didn't just give me the kind ones, though most of them are.

We come across about four in total that demanded how I could dare give the rebels such a win and that I should be ashamed. One makes my stomach knot, calling me a monster rebel that caused his whole family to die from exposure while fleeing their attacks up north this last winter. I need a moment to compose myself after that one. I can't imagine the pain that man is going through.

Penelope helps me put all the letters into piles, which to ignore, to write back to, and which to arrange meetings with if possible. The hard part for many of them is how far away they are, and we don't really have a budget to pay for their travel, but perhaps they could, and if not, we'd send a proper letter.

But one fear is still nagging. Perhaps this group of people supported me, but those questions were attacks, and last night could have changed minds. How true are these? And does this accurately represent everyone? I can only see a small fraction.

We are running a bit late for lunch with how long it takes to parse through the letters, but I insist on reading all of them. However, it isn't that big a problem that I'm running late because Penelope informs me I am having lunch alone with my fiancé today. Why does that make me a bit nervous too?

# Chapter 17

When Godwin leads me into the private dining room overlooking the ocean, Gavril is waiting near the open bay windows. He turns the second he hears the door as Godwin leads me in with a bow.

"I hope you don't mind some quiet," Gavril says, coming over to me and taking my hands, kissing them. "But I thought you might need the moment to feel no eyes on you."

His eyes are full of concern as he studies me, looking for any trace that indicates how I'm doing.

"I appreciate that," I sigh, mixed emotions swelling in me.

Gavril studies me another second before he lets go of my hands to pull out my chair.

I smile a weak thanks as I sit down, staring at my plate as a mix of emotions swirl inside my chest. I feel certain he's going to tell me off for how I'd handled everything. Now I'm strong enough to handle it all because of the hint of hope in the letters I'd seen.

At least, the next generation doesn't seem hellbent on hating me.

Gavril studies me for a moment before he asks, "Are you doing alright?"

I swallow and nod. "I'm adjusting."

"How did your morning go?"

"We went over all the correspondence I've gotten," I say, mostly still just fiddling with the meal, not paying much attention to it.

"Is that good or bad?" Gavril asks, trying to meet my eyes.

"Um... another surprise." I go with that answer, taking another bite to give myself a second to chew to avoid more questions as I try to figure out my honest answer to that.

Gavril gives me a weak smile. "I think the only way I can respond to that is to repeat the question. Is that good or bad?"

"I don't know," I confess. "After all the attacks from the press, I rather expected a lot of hate mail."

"And?" Gavril smiles a little.

"A lot of letters of support; mostly people who were inspired by my story." I manage a weak smile.

"Yeah? To do what?" Gavril encourages me.

I tell him a few of the stories, daring to mention the Lord Mayor's letter and that of his grandchildren, and Gavril laughs about the auntie comment. "I just never thought... it would make that big of a difference," I finish, still fiddling with my food. And perhaps it hadn't.

"What do you mean a big difference? To them, you mean?"

I nod. "Those girls... It helped them stand up for themselves. With how it almost broke me, I never thought it would affect people like that."

"Why wouldn't it? It made that change for you. It made it for me, too." He takes my free hand. I smile a little, looking up at him through my lashes. "You're going to be great at this. I know it doesn't feel like it, but you are," he assures me. "You're going to be better than I am."

I let out a kind of half laugh and look away. "No, I'm not. You're promised to fix it."

"Only with you." He squeezes my hand. "I hate to see how it's only torn you down. I... but now it's out, it's over. We can move on."

I nod. "Yes, we can move past it." But it is never going to be a blissful happily ever after like everyone says it should be, even for a brief moment. I honestly am braced for the next tragedy.

"Kascia... please, talk to *me*. I feel as if I did something wrong." He frowns a little. "I thought once you got it out, you'd... it would be like the weight lifted. That's not what I see. Please, we're supposed to be in this together. You and me."

"It wasn't exactly a success." I look at him in apology. "They still hate me."

"Of course it was a success. The reception was fine. It takes time to digest it, and that will give you time to win back the few who changed their mind about you, if any even did." He smiles with a slight chuckle.

"But not you." Fabian had forced him to be the villain last night.

"So what? My popularity stays the same. Who cares?"

"You need the people to stop fighting to end this," I remind him, meeting his eyes. "And if they hate you, it stays the same."

"We have time. We have the rest of our lives to worry about that. If all they can do is throw around accusations of my keeping secrets while praising you for having none, I'm alright with that."

My face falls. "Is that what they're saying?"

"I gave a no comment; that's always what they say to no comments." Gavril shrugs. "No big deal."

"I still wouldn't call it a success." My frown deepens. "I'm sorry. He'd have not gotten a shot at you—"

"Don't go there." Gavril shakes his head. "We're not doing that. If that story broke after your father was seen hanging out as we use him to try to stop the fighting, it would be worse. If your press is better than mine, then it's a win. That makes one royal with good press, which hasn't happened in five hundred years."

*But my press isn't better. They still resent me.*

Gavril swallows. "But the fact that isn't comforting you... I still feel like I did something wrong. Why wouldn't you open up to me?"

"I am." I'm not hiding anything.

Gavril pauses, studying me. "I guess you've just... let it all out already."

My face contorts into a frown. "I wouldn't say that. There's no getting this out when it just keeps happening again and again."

Gavril swallows, dropping his head slightly before looking at me again. "You... you don't regret saying yes, do you?"

"What?" I frown.

"You don't regret it... Do you?" Gavril asks, the pain unmistakable in his eyes.

"Regret what, winning?" I frown. He nods, his eyes locked on mine. "Of course not, I chose this."

Something in Gavril relaxes. "It's just... I really thought after you got through it, you'd... brighten back up. To be honest..." He studies me. "It's like I haven't seen you be you since I chose you."

I look down. "It's... not been my finest hours." And I should be shining. I have to be what he declared me to be, and instead, I've failed on most every point. And the people hate me, taking away half the support I'd leaned on.

"And that's okay. It's a rough transition. I wish I'd taken more control. I am so used to being required to be at the mercy of the staff, I left you to have that experience worse than I ever did. I... I wonder if you'd be better off if I hadn't chosen you. I-I know it's you. I know I had to, but... I don't know. It's like winning made everything you struggled with worse, not better."

"You... you don't regret it, do you?" I ask, fear slowly spreading in my chest again as I look at him.

He pauses as he thinks about his answer. "Yes and no. I know it's you, and I want you more than anything. But that doesn't mean what I want should hurt you so much. And I wish I could stop your hurting more than anything."

I look down. "It shouldn't be this hard. If I am the right choice, then I'm good at this," I insist. But I haven't been so far.

"I keep telling you, you don't have to keep trying to prove yourself anymore. You already did that." Gavril frowns. "Though I know nothing *I* say will change that's how you feel."

"I never said—"

"'If,'" he quotes me. "And you're stating you have to qualify for something. That's exactly what proving yourself is. Who do you think you have to prove it to?"

"No one. It's just the truth," I state. "I know it doesn't change it being me, but... I wanted to be the best choice for the people by the people. And... I lost it."

Gavril's shoulders drop. "I see. You passed. There's no getting out of this now, even if you wanted to. You know that, right?"

"Yes. And I don't want out," I insist, not wanting him to go there again.

"You're sure?"

"Gavril," I scold.

"Ah, there it is." He smiles slightly. "The fight. So, you didn't lose it."

"What do you want?" I sigh, annoyed.

"Kascia, it's not what I want. It's what you deserve." Gavril frowns. "You won. You should get to enjoy that, and instead, you're acting more like you're fighting to win more than ever. At least that's what it looks and feels like. And I'm sorry."

"It's not your fault. I know I won. But now I have to live up to it. You should understand that. I am the true princess, so I need to live up to it. Just like you have to live up to being the one who will end the fighting," I remind him.

"But you don't have to live up to it. It's a gift. If I find and marry a true princess, I will end it not because I live up to that promise in more than those two steps. I got step one and step two in two weeks. You don't have to fight to be something you'll be because we kept our end of that promise. Stop trying to be what some unknown someone wants you to be. The Enthronement is over. It's time to be yourself and rule. You will receive the power you need to do it. I'm sure of it. I count on it for me, and you should count on it for you. We do our part; Cedrick owes us."

I laugh at how he says it as he sits back and takes a drink.

"I'm not worried about that part. We'll figure it out when we get there. I did. When they finally let me choose, I took the time to figure it out myself, which I'd already done, and asked for confirmation I got within hours. I'm sure that system will work again and keep working. I'm not afraid of the future. Are you?"

"Petrified." Maybe I wasn't before this transition turned out to be nothing like I'd dreamed.

"Don't be." Gavril gives me a tender smile. "We'll face whatever it is together. You'll be there, remember? I'll be there with you too. It's not just my struggles you will support me through. I'll be there for you. Don't forget that. I know you have amazing staff to rely on, but I'm here too. I'm not locked from you anymore. You're my fiancé. We're getting married in two weeks. There's no reason for you to lock yourself away from me. I'm yours. You won. I don't know how to help you see that."

"I know but…"

"You're scared to do it alone," Gavril sighs in resignation, sitting back in his seat.

"No, I just… I want to live up to it. This week, I… I haven't. And I know I should, but losing the people's support was a worse blow than I thought it would be." It feels like losing.

"I know that's hard, but you live up to it. You are without trying." Gavril takes his turn to insist.

"I was trying really hard when I proved it," I remind him.

Gavril rolls his eyes. "That's not the same thing. This should be when you get to relax, enjoy it. I know Hydie made that hard then… this. But that's over, now. You know that, right?"

"Yes. I know I won. It's just… adjusting." I muster a smile.

Gavril returns the smile to the same level. "I just hate to see it hurt. I know this life isn't easy, but… I thought it would be better than this, and I can't seem to make it any better."

"You do." I take his hand.

"How?" He smiles in amusement. "When have I made this easier?"

"You took the initiative to get the ball rolling with the interviews."

"And you loved that whole experience." Gavril openly laughs in his sarcasm.

"But it was needed."

"But not easier." He meets my eyes. "Or more fun. You—" he stops, frowning. "I just wish I could make it better and not so miserable, that's all."

"I'm sure it will."

Gavril gives me a look. "Don't lie. You don't believe that."

Okay, he has me. I have many doubts it will ever get to be what I'd dreamed and hoped. "It will get better." I'm sure it will be better, just without the bliss or happiness I expected.

"I love you." Gavril is still looking at me with worry and compassion.

A smile forms on my face. "I know," I assure him. "I never questioned that."

"Guess not." Gavril seems to deflate a little as he sits back again, letting go of my hand. "You'll want to make sure to finish. I'm sure you have a long day still."

I realize I'd hardly eaten and instinctively look at his plate. "You should too." He'd not touched his other than the drink of water he'd taken.

"I know." He copies the tone I'd used before, making me giggle as he sits up better to eat. We don't speak much as we quickly eat.

"He's... not leaving until the wedding, right?" Gavril asks.

"Who?" I frown.

Gavril chuckles. "Damian."

"That is what he's said." I nod with a heavy sigh. That will make all this so much harder. "Has he helped with... your transition at all?"

Gavril laughs. "No. He never really has. He takes care of you, and his brother drops hints. That's about it."

"So, they're still unsure how to handle your father not being dead?"

"No." Gavril sighs heavily. "Father wants to abdicate, but Mother won't. So... we're fighting that. I think we all agree, other than Mother, that Father will never be strong enough to resume his full duties."

"Will you make it public that he survived his injuries, though you all thought he'd die?" I ask.

"That's... the fight."

"Don't think you can hide him?"

"We're going to go over options, and then when it's time, we're bringing you into it. This is your life, too. If I take power, so do you," he reminds me. "We're just coming up with strategies for Mother."

"Good luck." I sigh as I finish my meal.

"All anyone can say." He smiles tenderly.

But by now, it is time for us to be about our work again. Gavril kisses my forehead before leaving, going before I do likely because he actually has a time crunch to meet whereas I don't.

But I can't stop the frown. Something is still wrong. Perhaps it's really just me. But there is something going on. Gavril had tried to resolve something, and it hadn't happened. I just don't have a clue what. Which just makes me feel even more of a failure.

I do finally get a look at the article covering yesterday's interview. I have to sneak out of dinner to get away with it, but at least I finally get to see it. It's exactly what I expected. Fabian was perfectly kind to me. His supportive comments carry over, but he rips into Gavril for being hypocritical about wanting to be open about everything but keeping secrets. The rest is a verbatim copy of what we'd said in a transcript, so I don't bother reading it.

But the real disappointment is that Gavril must have misread me slipping off because he doesn't try to see me. I was sure he would, but I finally accept he isn't coming. I try not to be disappointed as I go to bed. Tomorrow will be a new day and hopefully better.

# Chapter 18

In the morning, Bella arrives with Penelope to go over my schedule. It won't be the most enjoyable day ever. At least it's better than it has been, though it's hard to go through it feeling so empty.

I have my physical that morning. It's not as bad as the one I had to do to qualify for the Enthronement, but it still isn't fun. I fight to get my head before I have lunch with Damian.

Damian sets up lunch in the conservatory for us on the loft, which is one of my favorite places. "Sorry if I'm late." I'd tried not to be in a mood after my long appointment.

"Of course not. I doubt this morning was enjoyable." He smiles softly as he pulls out a chair for me.

"Nice to have a quiet moment." I smile again at Damian. The choice for the meal is a bit of a surprise, a nice sandwich tray with nice thick chips to enjoy, which isn't a common treat, but a good filling meal to enjoy. "Oh, lovely." I smile as I select a few chips.

Damian beams. "Oh, good. I actually was worried if you'd like these or not as I know you like fried food, but they get cold quickly, so I leaned a little more on my preference and hoped for the best."

"We mostly have fried food here. I suppose in your homeland that's less common." I take a bite of the unique lunch.

"In a way." He smiles and takes a bite. "Mine sort of took bits from many cultures," he says after a moment. "So, it varies quite a lot."

"With how much travel I'm sure you've done, I'm sure that's true. Perhaps Alalusian food wouldn't be so hard for you," I tease.

"Hard to eat or to cook?" Damian chuckles.

"To eat," I chuckle. "I thought you couldn't cook."

"I don't." He smiles with a nod. "Well, I'm better than I was. I won't burn anything, and it likely won't make your stomach churn, but nothing I make could be called a culinary masterpiece. I leave that to the professionals."

I giggle. "That is helpful," I agree. "So... just looking for a quiet moment?" I was a bit surprised to see he went out of his way to schedule a lunch.

"Well... there is something I need to talk to you about," he says as his eyes go to his plate.

"Oh?" I ask in surprise. Perhaps he'd noticed the mess I made with Gavril and is hoping to help point it out.

"Yes, and... honestly, I... Well, here it is." Damian lifts his eyes to meet mine. "You and I both know that King Aster is never going to return to a full working schedule. Even if he gets strong enough to attend the wedding and coronation as I know he hopes to do, his body will not be able to stand up to the daily pressure of ruling a nation, especially one as badly off as Purerah is."

I frown and nod. "It would be quite the miracle if he could, and we already got that in the fact he survived at all."

"Exactly." Damian nods. "And honestly, I believe he knows and understands that better than anyone. He will need to turn to Gavril, and more so than he already has. It would be unwise for him to travel in his condition. And that presents a problem. The Japcharian summit is only a few months away, and the world summit will immediately follow. Now, the high king will respect Gavril as the crown prince, as he has the authority to speak on behalf of his father, but I doubt others will be as accommodating. Especially not the Japcharian king." He frowns.

I frown a little. "I didn't think of that. They did plan to meet outside of the capital as a middle ground."

"Yes, they did," Damian nods. "But that doesn't mean the Japcharian king will leave his pride at home. You remember the way he acted at the memorial."

I nod. "He was quite angry with me. I don't know how he treated Gavril or the queen."

"He was polite enough for a public event, but at a summit, I doubt he'll be so nice." Damian frowns. "He doesn't see his own daughter as a person with any knowledge or power. He will do the same to Gavril if things remain as they are."

I look down and nod. "That is a problem."

"Thankfully, I believe King Aster also knows this." Damian smiles a little. "And thanks to you, he has seen that Gavril is more than ready. So.... if I'm right, and I usually am, he will make Gavril prince regent soon after your coronation."

"Regent?" I frown a bit. "I've heard of that, but I'm not sure I know what it means."

"It means that unless Aster is physically present, Gavril will be acting king in all matters."

"Oh... why would he do that rather than just... abdicate to him?" I ask.

"Technically, he could, but that would make the current queen Gavril's ruling partner." Damian frowns as he watches me as if to see if I got a hint he'd given me.

"So... how is that different from making him his regent?" I ask with my brows drawing together.

"Physically? Aster retains his power should he be present during a meeting. But emotionally, think about your place if Gavril was made king, and you were not made queen alongside him?" Damian tilts his head as he watches me with concern.

I frown deeply and nod. "Yes, that would make it... awkward." I put it mildly, but it wouldn't be a great feeling. The people who now hate me will laugh. I wonder who they'll whisper should have won behind my back. Is this what Gavril is so uneasy about?

Damian nods understandingly. "And Aster loves you. He would never want to put you in that kind of position, but he must at least give Gavril regency if other nations are to respect him. He cannot force the queen to abdicate. He cannot take away the queen's power or rights to rule. What are hers are hers alone. Similarly, a queen cannot take away the king's rights or powers. So, she cannot stop Aster from giving Gavril power, but honestly, after all I have seen, I very much doubt she will give up hers on her own. At least, not soon. Which... unfortunately... still creates a bit of an awkward situation for you." He winces a little at those words.

"Wait... so even making him regent doesn't really fix it, does it?" But if he abdicates, it would be worse. My husband would leave behind me whereas at least as regent he would be level with me at least a little. Well, he could ask me to work with him whereas, as king, I would literally be a step down from him.

"In many ways, not really. And if this should happen, as I fear it must, there will be many that will not understand. They may doubt and question you. Some may even mock. And this time, I will not be here to protect you," he says sadly. "So, I am giving you this as a warning of what may come, and I beg you: when others doubt, question, and mock you, you *must* stand firm."

I swallow hard. "So, there's a good chance Gavril is going to be given power while I'm not." That is going to be a huge scandal. Well, they already hate me.

Damian sighs and bows his head. There's a pause, then he nods.

My heart drops to my toes. "How... how can I help if I'm stripped of all power or respect by the family that gave me power?"

My mind is racing. I might as well not have won if this is the power that they will give me. No one will take me seriously, assuming the slight from the queen is against me, not Gavril, or perhaps it's the king and queen slighting me together. People may think they regret choosing me. Then again, it was revealed that they didn't regret choosing me. But still, everyone will assume the king and queen disapprove of Gavril's choice. Now even the court will mock.

Damian looks at me, then gets up and comes around the table, crouching beside me as he looks up into my face. "By realizing you have always had power, and it doesn't come from them. You are the one who protected Lilly from that rebel leader. You single-handedly forced a rebel force to retreat. Twice, I might add." He smiles a little. "Once after you slew the leader, then again when you talked your father into leaving the throne room. You were the one who met and befriended the crown princess of Japcharia, and then it was you who was instrumental to the two royal families talking peaceably after Dahlia offended the delegation. And every time Gavril fell or was about to fall, it was you who gave him the confidence in himself to do what was required of him. That, my dear, is power. And it never came from them. It comes from you."

I swallow hard and nod. "Right... I won for a reason." But will I even be useful if no one respects me? I try not to cry or even shed tears.

Damian nods. "And remember, Gavril respects you. He trusts you. He trusts you with things he hasn't told anyone else. Aster loves, respects, and trusts you as well. He placed his life in your hands with his secret. If he could, he would make you queen. No hesitation. And the queen loves and trusts you too, even if her actions may not show it. It is that she still struggles to trust Gavril with power. And if this does happen, it is because she still worries for him and believes she needs to be there for him. It is not meant against you. And perhaps in time, you can help her see it is okay to let go."

"She's the one I can't seem to convince of anything." I try to make light of it, but honestly, I'm afraid I'll just be waiting in the wings until she does.

"She is a *very* slow learner," Damian bemoans. "She has only started to let go of her little boy after the presentation attack. Cedrick saw that as a positive. I, however, am not convinced. After her behavior the night it was believed the king was assassinated, I lost more confidence in her than I'd like to admit." He frowns.

"What do you mean?"

He sighs and stands, walking away from me before turning back to face me. "According to Sage, after leaving your room that night, Gavril went to hers, and she refused to allow him to comfort her or grieve with her. Just assuring him "Mummy is still here for you". Once she learned Gavril had slipped his guard to go on a private date on the roof, she scolded him as if he was a two year old who'd stolen a cookie before dinner."

"She what?" I stare in shock.

Damian sighs and nods. "Yes, you heard that right. Gavril just learned that his father was dead, at least as far as anyone knew at that point, and instead of grieving with the only parent he had left or even being consoled by her, or telling him it wasn't his fault, he got lectured not to sneak up to the roof because it is *dangerous* up there."

I frown deeper. "I can see how that might shake you." Is it sad I'm not surprised?

Damian gives me a weak smile, then sighs again. "Thanks, and while I agree with Cedrick that her allowing Gavril to choose his princess and to comfort her after the attack are positive steps, I believe that they are only the first steps on the long road ahead. But who knows? Perhaps Cedrick is right, and she will surprise us all and agree to abdicate now that Aster can no longer work." He musters another wan smile.

"But unlikely." I bow my head.

"As I see it, sadly so." Damian frowns, then comes to me and kneels next to me again. "But it isn't hopeless." He gives me a small, encouraging smile.

"I suppose not." I sigh heavily, heart sinking again. "Just... it never gets better, does it?" Just one more steep hill after another. It is one thing to think that it was another to have it literally happen the next day, even expecting it.

"Of course it does. You have Gavril now, don't you? And there is no fear of losing him to another girl, right?" Damian smiles at me.

"I suppose."

Damian arches a brow and tilts his head as a small smile comes to his lips. "Just suppose?"

"He doesn't seem to think I act like it," I try to explain.

"How do you mean?" He tilts his head further in curiosity.

"He just... yesterday, when we talked, he seemed unsure I was really happy. Said I was trying too hard to prove something." I sigh. "But it's not to him or anyone," I defend.

"It's to yourself?" Damian guesses with a smile.

"No. I'm just trying to be what I'm supposed to be." The annoyance slips into my voice.

Damian nods and pauses as he thinks about this, then looks at me again. "And what do you think you are supposed to be?"

"The true princess they needed." I smile a bit. "Like prophesied," I remind him.

He nods. "And are you still trying to become the true princess, or that you already are?"

"I... am trying to be that." I try to figure out how to say it. "Trying to... still be that."

"And what makes you think you aren't?" Damian arches a brow with a gentle smile.

"I'm not saying I'm not. I'm just trying not to... not be," I try to explain it. "I almost... royally ruined it."

He gives me a soft smile. "Oh, my dear girl. You did nothing of the sort. This week was hard for you. The interview in particular was stressful and painful for you to have to endure. And I asked you to reveal your past partly in an endeavor to protect you from a worse fate. But there was another part of me that did it because from the moment I met you, I knew you had to be the one, and that day you told me about your past when it was just the two of us, that was the day I knew why. You did not magically become Purerah's true princess the moment Gavril placed that crown on your head. Nor did it happen when he spent half the night praying to know who to choose. No, my dear, you were destined for this before you were born, and your entire life has shaped and molded you into the princess Gavril would need by his side. You are his princess because of who you are. The only way you could possibly 'ruin it' is by trying to be something that you are not."

"I'm pretty sure I already ruined it during that interview." I look down. "But I did my best. It's up to them to hate me or not." And they chose hate.

"People will choose to hate or love whom they will. That is not something you can decide. One bad event, article, statement, or interview will not wholly turn away those who want true change for Purerah's good. You could be the perfect princess, have the perfect family life, do everything right and never tell a single lie, and those with hate in their hearts will still hate you. Jonquil is a perfect example of that. She came here just as you. She saw many of the same things you did and interacted with the royal family every day, and yet she still hates them. And she may hate them for the rest of her life. It is not your job to change her. And it is not your job to change the many rebels just like her who want to hate the royal family. They must choose to change. All you need to remember is there are many Lillys in this world. There are many more Lillys in Purerah than there are Jonquils, and they are the ones who need you."

"I just don't want to let them down." I sigh. But I did, and though it hurts after facing their hatred, it's easier.

"You won't, even when you think you do. We are often our hardest critic. Honestly, I'm one of the worst culprits of that." He smiles slightly. "Even when I succeeded, I felt like a failure. It took me a long time to accept a compliment without issuing a thousand complaints about what I could have done better. It was only when I learned to like myself that I started seeing what others saw in me. Which is something I hope you can do as well someday. Kascia," he leans in and meets my eye more firmly with eyes filled with love, "you are enough. Just as you are." He smiles and gently places his hand under my chin. "My dear girl, you have more in you than you realize. If you understood just how much power you truly have, you'd realize you never needed me. Even if it is nice to be needed." He gives me a beaming smile.

I manage to smile back. "I just don't want to let anyone down. I just... should stop saying just." I am terrible with that word.

Damian chuckles a little. "You'll be *just* fine." He tries to keep a straight face, but he can't help the grin.

I giggle slightly. "I want it to work, is all. I don't want to be disappointed again." I lost my family, my people; I can't lose Gavril next, or worse: disappoint him.

"I understand. No one ever wants to be disappointed, so we prepare ourselves for the worst. Sometimes it helps. And other times, we can take it too far, and we end up building a safety net that causes us to lead timid lives, limiting our growth and our ultimate potential. The sad truth is life is hard and disappointing when we don't reach our goals. But without those hard times, we wouldn't know what happiness was in the first place."

"Like coming here." I smile slightly. "I... I can't let them down."

Damian gives me an amused smile. "Is there something you want to get off your chest? You're repeating that quite a lot."

"That I don't want to let them down again," I say more firmly.

"Them who?" He tilts his head.

"My people, family... Gavril." I frown. "I never seem to know what to do with him." I've always needed Damian's help.

"You realize that is every couple's problem *ever*. Honestly, I wish I had me when I was dealing with my wife," he chuckles.

"Really?" I have a hard time believing that.

"One hundred percent." He smiles warmly. "Closest I got was Cedrick, who admittedly was dealing with his wife and his own issues from time to time. We all have struggles in life, especially in relationships, but it does get better. We all have hills we are trying to climb. The fear of slipping can be frightening and freeze you in place, even more so when you are climbing with a group. Sometimes, it can feel like you are holding the rope to hold everyone up and safe on the cliff. The key is to remember that you are not holding the rope alone. Gavril is holding that rope right along with you, as is everyone around you.

"If you try to be the only one holding the rope, you are likely to fail. That is why Gavril would have failed to fulfill the prophecy without you. You saw what he was like during the Dragian delegation, and again, after his father was attacked. He tried to do everything on his own, and until he allowed you to help him, he was failing. Quite spectacularly, I might add. Only by reaching out and accepting support was he able to succeed. The same is true for you."

"If I can figure out what's wrong," I frown.

"What do you mean?"

"I wish I knew. Gavril just... seemed off when we tried to talk after it all happened. I can't figure out what it is, and he didn't come to see me last night. That's not like him. I just wanted to make sure no one stopped me from finally seeing the article for myself. He's always... Well, since we've been engaged, he's always come after me unless I asked him not to. He didn't. I don't know what's wrong." I sigh heavily, then meet Damian's eyes with my own pained ones. "Do you always have to fight for it? Is that just how it is?" It's always something, another battle to get what I wanted.

Damian frowns and tilts his head. "Fight for what?"

"To... keep a relationship alive."

"Well... you have to put effort into it, if that's what you mean. If you neglect it, your partner may feel unloved or forgotten. But I am going to tell you what a wise young girl once told me." He smiles a little. "Love is not earned or deserved; it is given. It is free. Once given, it is hard to take back. Trust can be broken, and respect can be lost, but love endures. It may take different forms at times, but love is everlasting, pure and simple. Yes, it takes work to keep a relationship alive, but if someone has given you their love, that gift is yours. You merely have to choose to accept it. So no, you don't have to keep *fighting* for it. When someone loves you, when they truly love you, that love is unconditional. And nothing you do can change that. When someone loves you, they always will. No matter what." He says with sincerity in his eyes.

"I just... don't want to disappoint him or be disappointed anymore. What it will be like in our heads is always better, and though people say it will be better than you imagine, that's just wishful thinking, isn't it?" I ask hopelessly. "There's never a happy normal."

"It often feels that way. I can't tell you how many times Cedrick asked that of me and I of others. But it does get better, and the storms do end. I can't say when, but they will. And after they have passed, you and Gavril will both be stronger for it. I only know what I do because I made mistakes and had to learn from them. It is okay to mess up. It is okay to fail sometimes. As long as you don't quit, and keep working at it, things will get better. Yes, the road seems steep at times. And at times, you reach the top only to realize there is another hill just as steep. Those times can be discouraging. And you feel like there's no point because there will always be something new to tackle. And in life, that is often truer than not. But the important thing is to look around you.

"Because the views of your vantage point are beautiful. And you have come so far already," Damian beams as he puts a hand to my cheek. "Sometimes, it is good to look back and see just how far you have come. You aren't that nervous and broken girl you were when we met. You have grown to a woman who is as powerful as she is beautiful, and that is saying a lot." He smiles. "Don't let the idea of another upward trail tear you down. Things are much better than they first appear. But you won't see that if you keep your face to the dirt. Instead, enjoy the views of your vantage point, and these trials will lift you higher to vistas more beautiful than you can possibly imagine now."

"That's been the hope." That hope has been dashed so many times, I'm losing a grip on it. "Guess blissful wishes just painted a better picture of the one thing I thought I'd feel safe in."

He rubs my cheek with his thumb. "I understand. And I hoped you would have some reprieve before dealing with the press and public in telling them about your past, but Hydie ruined that, and I'm sorry." He frowns. "But all that is past now. And more is for you than against you. Hold to that. The bliss will come when the dust settles. And you have so many happy times ahead. I know that may appear hard to believe, but if you can have even an inkling of faith, you'll see it sooner than you realize."

"It's just... not the thing I wanted most." I can't get his affection without a lot of... whatever all this is.

A sad look enters Damian's eyes, and he drops his hand. "I'm sorry you feel that way."

"You're smarter than me. You can see the outcome." I give him a weak smile.

"Give yourself a few thousand years, then we'll see who's smarter." Damian smiles.

"Think still you." I smile a little. "One you'll still have more time than me."

"Perhaps." He returns the smile. "I only hope I helped you, even a little."

"I know. And I'm sure you're right, and it will help." Even if I don't understand.

"I hope so, but for you, not for me." He has longing in his eyes. "All I want is for you to be happy."

"We'll... figure something out." I've just lost hope it could be as good as I dreamed, but that doesn't mean it has to be miserable, and that I'm willing fight for.

Damian nods with a little smile. "I have every confidence in you. Just remember, don't try to do it alone. And I mean that for the long term. You are a brilliant woman, and you have much to offer this kingdom. Gavril would not be able to fulfill the prophecy without you. But you will be hard pressed to find success without him." He says with a half teasing, half serious smile.

"That's what I'm hoping for." I want to do this together. "So... as I said. I'll do my best." I look down. It's just hard when you don't know what you don't know.

"I know you will." He smiles a little. "You'll do wonders. I haven't a doubt."

"I'll try." I manage a weak smile. "I just... wish you didn't have to go." I know he does. It just would be so much easier.

Damian smiles in sympathy and gives my shoulders a little squeeze as he closes his eyes. "Me too, night angel. Me too."

"Well then, why do you have to go?" I joke, trying to fix the gloom I'm so good at making.

"Oh, you know." Damian pulls back and smiles more warmly and playfully at me. "The mentor character always has to die, so the main character of the play can grow."

"But you already died while here." I argue playfully.

He laughs. "You are a cheeky one."

"Well, am I wrong?" I am trying to make him smile and keep it up.

"No, but that wasn't part of the script." He smiles. "The dark woman just improvised it."

"Cedrick does that all the time." I keep up the debate.

"Yes, but he's a phoenix, so he and death aren't friends," Damian jokes.

"But... you go with him," I remind him.

"Yes, well... that was sort of an accident with completely unintentional consequences that I'd rather not talk about," Damian says with an embarrassed smile as he lets go of me and goes back to his seat.

"Maybe you just thought it was an accident." I smile. I see no reality where he wouldn't want to be with his brother on his never-ending mission.

He chuckles. "Maybe so. I suppose we'll never know, but past me with no foreknowledge would have told you it was an accident." His eyes then meet the ceiling in thought. "Maybe. I don't know. I'm not that man anymore; go ask him." He smiles at me teasingly.

A chuckle escapes me. "I suppose not." I pause, looking over the empty plate. "But you'd still not trade it."

Damian pauses as he gives me an understanding smile. "Trade it? No. But I'd be hard pressed to choose between staying here with you and going home with him. I don't think I could ever decide if it was up to me."

"What would he tell you to do?"

"Honestly? Stay." Damian smiles a little.

"Really?"

Damian nods. "He's already told me once. That dark woman accepted my offer for a chance at redemption. I was split on what to do. On the one hand, I was the one who gave her the offer, but that took me away from you. Cedrick told me he'd handle her so I could spend these days with you." He gives me a soft smile.

I blink rapidly. "What? Really?" That's why we've not seen Cedrick around much.

Damian chuckles. "Is it that hard to believe?"

"I guess I just got the impression he was the one who knew you should leave and was reminding you and trying to get you to leave," I explain.

"Oh, no. Unfortunately for me, I have an excellent memory. Cedrick is the one reminding me I have more time. He knows what it feels like not to want to leave. I'm usually the one reminding him. I suppose next time I'll be gentler on him." Damian smiles a little.

"I'm sure he's thankful for that." I force a smile, but my heart only sinks more. Just means later someone else will be the new me to him. But at least I had him while I did. "Would it have been easier to just... go?"

Damian shakes his head almost immediately. "No. No, it would have torn me inside to simply leave and not say goodbye. I don't think you understand, Kascia. You are part of me now. I love you. I love you as real and as deeply as my first-born child. And..." He frowns to himself before looking up at me again. "Part of me wonders how I could ever leave. Still, I know as a parent who must watch their child grow up and move on that it is time for you to experience life on your own. And it hurts not to be able to stay with you through it all. But in time, you will be better for it. I don't leave because anyone is forcing me to go. I am leaving because you need to move on without me."

"I... can understand that." Now is not the time for those tears, so I try to resist them best I can. "Even if I'd just... like to." But he has a point. I really do fear I'll ruin it all on my own.

He smiles sympathetically and puts his hand on mine. "I know, and it will be okay. Know that I will look back and always remember you. But... Now is not the time of parting. So let us put that aside for now and enjoy the moment."

I nod. "I agree." Not that I know what else to talk about.

"Well, as we both are done, how about dessert?" Damian smiles as he gets up and goes to a side table where a covered dish sits.

I giggle. "Oh no, what did you get us into?" I tease.

He grins then brings the dish back to our table and uncovers it to reveal a couple of eclairs. I smile in delight, happy to enjoy my favorite. Damian chuckles. "I knew I'd win with that one." He grins and offers one.

I accept it and leisurely start to enjoy it, mind casting about for a happier topic to speak on.

Damian smiles as he sits and takes the other one. "Wish I could have had you taste one my wife would make. I swear, she did something to make things taste even better."

"You don't mention her much," I admit, honestly having been curious for a while now.

He tilts his head, thinking about that. "I suppose not. Well... what would you like to know?"

"Oh, I don't know." I frown a bit. "What was she like?"

Damian tells me about his wife for a while as we enjoy the treat, helping me feel better about the awkward separation, seeing he won't be completely unhappy he has to leave eventually. Finally, we part so I can go about the rest of my day.

# Chapter 19

A nxiety fills my chest as I join them all for dinner. I realized that though I'd mentioned my fear to Damian, I hadn't actually found any clues on what's going on with my fiancé. I know I have to figure something out tonight, but when I'm clueless, what can I do?

Knowing he may be afraid to bug me after he never showed up yesterday, I go extra slow, so I can catch him. He must know that's what I'm doing because he patiently waits for me.

"Something wrong?" he asks gently when we're finally alone.

"No." Not for me, anyway.

Gavril frowns slightly, watching me. "I thought you were giving hints you wanted me to wait, so we could be alone. Was I wrong?"

"No, I just didn't want you to slip off. It's harder for me to catch you still," I point out.

Gavril smiles softly. "Enthronement rules are over, Kascia," he says gently. "You can come up to my floor and bug me. It will be yours soon enough, anyway."

"I suppose." But when he'd always come for me, it felt stupid as we'd likely meet in the middle.

"So... you can slip off, but not me?" Gavril asks.

"Of course not. I thought you might and was hoping to stop you from doing it." I give him a look.

"You were the one who slipped off last night, not me," he defends simply. "I figured you had been swarmed by people a lot lately, and I realized I'm not really that familiar with your energy levels. When I asked you, you were always excited to go out because you didn't get many chances. I realized perhaps you needed some time alone to recharge, and I hadn't been respecting that, which is why you slipped off hoping for a night to recover with... safer company."

"I suppose that was a logical assumption." I frown. "But you are safe company." I have no idea what he means by that comment.

"Am I though?" Gavril looks at me with the question deeper in his eyes. "Am I just the one you have to impress to get what you want?"

"No. You haven't been just that in a very long time." I frown a bit more.

"But I have been."

"At the beginning of the game, sure. But not anymore. You haven't been that in a long time," I insist. "I promise. I trust you. You know that."

"I do." Gavril nods his assurance, then glances behind him. "But if we want to talk for a while, we best not sit around here."

I agree and stand up. I'll let him lead me wherever he feels more comfortable talking. As we walk the halls, I start up the conversation again. "But.... As for last night, I was j—simply trying to read the article. Everyone was preventing me from seeing it, and I couldn't settle down until I knew for myself what was in it. I thought... you'd follow, eventually. But... you didn't." I look at him.

"I'm sorry if that hurt, but I was simply trying to respect your space. I should have realized you were that private of a person earlier."

"I don't know if I'd say that." I feel so vulnerable and defenseless. He's upset or angry or something but won't let me understand it. He may deny it, and maybe he isn't angry, and I just feel he is. I wish I have a clue what to do.

"Maybe you wouldn't," Gavril smiles at me, "because it doesn't seem that way to you. Maybe you're so used to only sharing what you have to. You think everyone is like that, so it doesn't seem like you're a private person compared to others."

"Maybe so." I can admit that could be true. "But I'm not hiding anything."

"I know you aren't," he comforts me, putting his arm around me for a moment before we keep walking. I wish he'd kept it there, but I get it's hard to walk like that. I could try to take his hand. It feels dangerous, but I try anyway, and he accepts it without any surprise or dislike.

Do I dare just say I feel like he's upset with me? What if he isn't? That would make him annoyed if he isn't already.

I'm quiet for a moment as we finally reach his room, and he opens the door for me. I at once take my normal spot on the two-person sofa like we always did. I miss the flick of a smile that crosses Gavril's face at my level of comfort with the room before he takes his normal spot beside me.

"Were you hoping to talk about what you read?" Gavril asks, his tone still gentle as he studies me.

"What?"

"You said you snuck off to read the article last night."

"Oh. No, I just... worried why you didn't... since the game ended, you have," I point out. "Unless I asked you not to."

"I guess I've heard enough jokes about women complaining that they always have to ask their husbands for things instead of them taking hints. I took that as a good moment to prove I can take a hint." Gavril shrugs. "Like I said, I've not really understood how comfortable you are being around people all the time and realized perhaps you need alone time to recharge."

"You can still spend quiet time alone with someone."

"Perhaps. I just thought maybe you wanted a feeling of normal like it was before it all changed again. Sorry if that hurt. I am trying."

"I know you are. I just... I'm worried about you, is all."

Gavril stops in surprise and looks at me with a new confusion. "What are you talking about?"

"You have... felt, maybe not actually been, but feel stiff," I try to explain. "Not cold," I add quickly, trying not to sound like I am accusing him. "But perhaps formal."

"I haven't meant to be or felt that way," Gavril assures me, moving closer and putting his arm around my shoulders. It seems he really is alright and worried about me, but I am not feeling as sure. "I really believed I was being respectful of your space, is all."

"But I told you and her I don't want my own space. Do you still think I do?" I ask. Could that be it?

"No. Your anger at Hydie over the whole fight proves that."

"Even figuratively?" I check.

"Do you feel like when you're upset you want to be alone?" Gavril asks.

I think that over, trying to figure out how to explain it. "Not exactly. I simply want to stop pretending. To feel like I'm safe to openly feel those feelings with whoever I'm with. And I'll admit that maybe it is different with different people at different times. Because I want to feel safe to feel those feelings without... my feelings making things worse. Does that make sense?" I frown.

"I think so. You want to feel safe to be angry, but you know that being openly angry around certain people — even if you aren't angry with them — will make them feel bad or angry themselves, so your feelings are not allowed to be there at that time. You can safely be open about how you feel without being the bad guy."

I smile and nod. "Yeah. Like you dealing with your parents. And that's okay for most of life, but yeah, when I'm really upset, I don't want to be with people I have to pretend to. I feel better when I don't have to do it alone, but I guess I'm very used to the only way that's possible is to be alone and not express it. But I would prefer to express it safely to someone."

Gavril nods. "I see." But when he doesn't say more, I frown. That fixed nothing.

He must sense that made it worse because he goes on, "I can completely understand that feeling. And that's alright. I suppose there's no one you feel safe with all the time."

"Do you have someone like that?" Perhaps he feels he is very much not on that list. And I want to deny it, but until I know what's wrong, I'm not sure he is that person in this moment.

"I suppose not," Gavril confesses. I smile a bit. His tone and hesitancy tell me he wants to say I am his safe place just like I want to say he is mine, but with how this conversation is going, neither of us is sure we can say that.

"I try to make sure you are. You should be," I test the waters. "And that's all on me getting over that until winning. You couldn't be that person. At least... not until I told you the truth. I know that's why Damian wanted us to tell the world. Then there never would be that horrible secret ready to break me without warning. Why I could do it, even if there was no part of me that didn't hate it."

"I knew it would be hard. I didn't... I knew in my head, but seeing how hard it was was very different." Gavril sighs tiredly. "I never wanted that for you."

"I know. We want it to be easier on those we love," I agree. "But sometimes, what's best is hard. I don't blame you."

"You're sure?"

I nod and meet his amber eyes. They really do look vulnerable, perhaps scared. "Yes. It's not anyone's fault. Well... maybe Father's." I frown.

"Still fighting to let it go?" Gavril asks. "That's what you're trying to process?"

"I'm not trying to process anything right now. I slipped off to read the article that everyone seemed hellbent on stopping me from reading," I confess honestly, slightly relieved to let the anger out. "Why was it so bad I couldn't read it? I had to know, why hide it?"

Gavril smiles with a slight nod. "I can see that being annoying."

"And I thought you might try to stop me too, so I grabbed it as quick as I could and... waited for you."

"Sorry. I just thought you wanted space."

"And you know I don't now, right?" I check.

He smiles and nods. "Yes. I know. You still don't want to talk about it?"

I sigh tiredly. "Not really. I mean, if you want to."

Gavril thinks about it for a moment. "I want to know how you feel about it."

"What I expected before they all hid it from me. Fabian was kinder than I expected, but that partially was so he could lay into you." I bite my lower lip as I look up at my fiancé.

"Well, that would happen no matter what. If I can take the blow to spare you, I really couldn't care less." Gavril shrugs. "We have to try to fix it no matter what, so slightly worse won't do any harm. If it was a pool I'm wading in, it didn't even rise more than a centimeter at best."

I relax a bit. At least he seems to truly believe that.

"Really Kascia, it's like taking the whack of a fan from a baby. It's a hit, sure, but it doesn't hurt. Honestly, a bit funny." Gavril chuckles. "It's nothing."

"I'll make sure I believe that. I believe it right now." I smile at him.

"So... were you really just waiting on me on your own?" Gavril asks.

I sense there is more in his question, but what?

I nod. "Yeah. Until staff came in; I gave up at that point."

Gavril nods. My answer didn't help, but it didn't make it worse either, whatever it is.

"I don't want to be alone." I frown a bit, feeling almost as alone as I did last night waiting for him.

"You're not," Gavril assures, putting his arm around me. I take full advantage and curl into him, resting my head on his chest and shoulder.

I close my eyes for a moment, just enjoying the moment.

After a bit, Gavril adjusts slightly, and I giggle as he reveals a reclining rest that I had no idea was built into this thing. It lets him put his feet up and lean back a bit more, which is more comfortable for me, for sure.

It makes it easier to cuddle into him, yet also not feel like I am crossing a line.

Gavril wraps his arms around me and presses his lips to my head, letting me settle, simply curled into him for a moment, not speaking or making me speak. I really don't deserve him with all I'd put him through.

He seems happy though, quiet a moment as the sound of the fire and rain fills the empty air. I feel guilty breaking a quiet moment, but... I know something is still wrong.

*But he's happy now.* A little voice speaks into my mind. How could I break it over... I don't even know what.

There's a noise at the window. Gavril sighs. "Joy," he explains as I frown in confusion. "I should get her. The staff aren't due for a bit."

I sit up to let him go, a bit surprised she is out in the rain. Poor dog.

"You ready at last?" Gavril teases the dog as she comes in, not dripping wet, but wet enough, she shakes out her coat. "I invited you to come in before dinner when it started raining. You're not allowed to be mad," Gavril tells her, scratching her head, making her pant in happiness before she shakes herself again.

Gavril moves to get a towel, but she instead flops down on the large rug where her water bowl and food bowl rests and rolls on it to get dry. "So that's why that's always wet when it rains," Gavril laughs as Joy takes a minute to get dry.

Letting her take her time, Gavril returns to me, and I can't help smiling as I resume my position from before as he does the same.

A minute later, Joy pants as she comes over to us. She doesn't smell wet. She doesn't smell too bad at all actually, for a dog. Even when she jumps up on Gavril's other side. She really is not a puppy anymore—well, in body. Her legs look a bit too long for her still as she's growing into her size, but she is fine otherwise.

She's panting, tired from playing in the rain and getting herself dry, looking up at Gavril in delight as he scratches her head.

"You nutter dog," Gavril teases lightly as he pets her.

I smile a little and reach across him to scratch her ears. Joy likes that and quiets down, enjoying the pats with little more than a happy, lazy looking smile on her face, tongue slightly sticking out of her happily panting mouth.

It's quiet once more, happily silent, at least it seems to be for Gavril. He seems so happy and relaxed. I hate to ruin it, but I know for our good I have to.

I relax a little as Gavril rubs my arm, still keeping it around me. "It's nice. Isn't it?" he says gently.

I enjoy the purr of his voice in his chest against my ear. I suppose we haven't done anything like this since the rooftop date.

"It is," I agree. Only thing ruining it is the little knot of uncertainty in my heart. It's smaller than it was before, like a sewing thread knotted, but still a knot.

"Can do this more often once the wedding is over." He smiles and kisses my head. "Be much better. Swap out the fluffer for a child or listening to them play together."

"I guess." I fiddle with his shirt nervously. Could I really ruin the moment for him and push when I don't even know what I'm looking for?

"Guess?" Maybe I already did.

I ponder how to respond. "I guess I just can't picture normal being safe and happy." Anxiously, I scratch Joy more, reminding myself to stop playing with his shirt.

Gavril carefully watches, his eyes moving from one hand to the other as I switch actions. "Something wrong?"

"No." I don't want to start this awkward talk like that. And the truth is, I am okay if he is.

Gavril simply nods to himself, watching me with those wonderfully, yet painfully observant eyes. "You're... not nervous, are you?"

"For what?"

"Of this being normal?"

"Not for it to be normal. Just... afraid it won't be?" I try to find the safest way to say it.

"No, I mean..." Gavril hesitates a moment. He studies me tenderly but with a hint of concern. "About the next part."

"Next part?" I really don't know what he's talking about.

"The wedding isn't scary; the wedding night is."

"Oh." I can see how he guessed that. I go a bit pink. "Not exactly."

"You're sure?"

"It's not... doing that," I try to put it delicately. "It's more... not doing that."

"What?" Gavril frowns, still watching me patiently.

"I trust you fully. I'm not scared of that." I debate proving it. There wasn't anyone to stop us, right?

"You sure?"

I can't resist and let the nice moment break for a moment as I push myself up to kiss him deeply. He makes a noise of surprise, not quite a grunt, but he returns my kiss anyway.

I slowly move this kiss into a soft rhythm before I move again, keeping our lips locked as I sit on his lap, still kissing him in that rhythm. *This is fun.* A thrill of excitement runs through me. To share this with the person I actually trust. I thought these moments with Jake were the best part of life. This is so much better.

I move closer to him, still repeating the kisses as he returns them. I get one hand into his shirt and the other tangled in his hair as I keep up this game. The chair drops slightly lower in the recline.

This time, the sound that comes from Gavril is a happy grunt as I do the same, only mine is softer, almost a purr. I keep playing with him, enjoying the feel of him as finally one of his hands finds the back of my neck and the other my hip.

Like I had a million times with Jake, but better as I push the line further with far more trust in Gavril than I ever had in Jake, I almost curl my body around Gavril's, making him turn his head to keep our kisses engaged. I feel safe, unlike any other time I'd played with this line.

I don't know how long we're like this, quite a while before Joy, with a sleepy yawn, makes her dog talking sounds in complaint and puts her paws up on Gavril to try licking at our faces.

"Hey! Joy." I laugh and push her down.

Like the husky she is, she jumps up again with a huff of irritation. I laugh, and it quickly becomes a game. Joy jumps up; I push her down, and she tries again.

I think it takes Gavril a moment to get his head, as I'm still on his lap, to decide what he should do.

"Girls down," Gavril says in the tone he uses to command the dog, but he takes me around the torso and places me down next to him. Joy huffs as if in approval and plops her head on Gavril's lap, huffing at me as if telling me that's her spot.

"No. It's my spot." I taunt the dog, pushing her head off and moving as if to sit on Gavril again.

"I said down." Gavril laughs, holding me in my spot as Joy almost barks, scolding me, and puts her front paws on Gavril's lap and licks at my face as if to assure me it's not my spot but she still loves me.

"Joy!" I laugh, turning my head away.

"Down, girls." Gavril is laughing too as he keeps me from his lap again and tries to get Joy down too.

Joy at least obeys. She carefully places herself on Gavril's other side, having trouble now. She's made a mess of the pillows and curls awkwardly onto them and then puts her head on his lap again, looking at me as if daring me to disobey.

Gavril can tell I'm going to rise to the game again because he laughs as his arms on me grow firmer to keep me from playing more. "We're still not married. We will be in trouble breaking that law," Gavril reminds me. "Royal heirs in question and all."

"I'm not scared of that." I give him a playful, teasing smirk of a smile.

"I can clearly see that now." Gavril laughs, brushing my hair as if petting it like I'm Joy, then kisses my cheek before carefully guiding me into curling up beside him again. "Behave. Both of you. Down girls," Gavril teases, scratching Joy's head and rubbing my back.

I'm smiling though. "I love you more."

Joy huffs but doesn't react further.

"My future wife doesn't need to compete with a dog." Gavril gives me a look.

"Sure?" I give him fake, cute pouty eyes.

"Sure." Gavril smiles and kisses my forehead.

"Then what's wrong?" It pops out before I can think it through.

"What do you mean?" Gavril asks gently. "Nothing is wrong."

"You're sure?" I meet his eyes.

Gavril smiles and nods, kissing my head again. I close my eyes at his touch. "I'm sure." Though that small knot remains, I decide to trust him once more. Perhaps I am just scared of it all falling apart again now I've survived one more blow.

# Chapter 20

"**Y**ou're sure?" Gavril asks Godwin with a frown. I'd been called in for this particular morning security briefing with Gavril, though I'd been told I'd not start attending these meetings until after the wedding. Now I know why.

Godwin frowns with a firm nod. "It was Damian who brought it to the guard's attention, and they have noticed signs that seem to say another Darkman is trying to get into the palace."

"Are you sure it was Damian?" I frown. Damian would have wanted to tell me himself. Something about that seems odd. Maybe it was Cedrick?

"The guard told me Damian told them he thought there was a chance. They started looking into it, and this is the result." Godwin shrugs.

"You doubt it?" Reinold asks me.

"Just... Damian would normally want to tell me himself." I frown. He knows how frightened I am of them. "And it's for sure a different one?"

"I suppose not for sure, but it would be odd for it not to be," Godwin says. "We saw Cedrick himself take her away. I don't imagine he's easy to escape."

"He's still human. He says so himself. He's not perfect," I point out.

"But he won't let anything happen since he's still here," Gavril reminds me. "Neither will Damian."

He pauses to see my relief at that, but it doesn't make me feel better. I'd seen one kill him before.

"And I'm here to ensure it, too." Gavril frowns when I'm not comforted and puts his arm around my shoulders and hugs me close. That gets a smile. Gavril relaxes a little, glad to see me comforted by something. "I doubt we're really in any danger," he continues to assure me.

"I hope so." We're so close. Not another attack. "Why would they try again? Father can't pay them."

"Captain Sonia believes it's likely they're looking for their lost member. They hate it when their own betray them to the light," Reinold explains. "So, you should be safe. They just want her."

"Unless they think it's her fault their own betrayed them," Godwin points out.

"Fair," Reinold agrees with a slight frown.

"We handled the last one. We can handle this one," Bella assures, giving Godwin a look.

"Exactly," Gavril agrees. "I'm not worried."

But I can't help but be worried. It's been one thing after another with no break in between. And another Darkman attempt on Gavril's life is more than my heart can bear. The last attempt almost succeeded...

I think my nervousness nudges Gavril to try to be close. Damian tries too, but I feel better with Gavril there. After all, it's him I'm afraid of them taking from me. And Damian couldn't always be there as he works on other things to prepare for the wedding.

I know he is making some unique changes to the princess's suite to fit what I'd like. Although I had been teased with some of it, I still haven't been given the full details. I imagine Damian, as the original designer of the castle, would know what to do.

In Gavril's office, we're going over RSVPs for the wedding, checking them and marking seating arrangements and the like when a sound I haven't heard in a while strikes the air.

Gavril jumps up instantly. He'd grown up reacting to that sound often, I'd imagine. I wonder if he can help but jump to react to the alarm. It means rebels have broken into the palace, or perhaps just the grounds. Before the Enthronement, they hadn't managed to break into the palace itself. Is it even possible without inside help?

I stand up and look at Gavril. Godwin hastily gathers some papers. I don't know where the nearest safe room is. Gavril takes my hand and leads me to the door. It's a quick trip up the hall where he twists the head of a random bust to open one of the nicest safe rooms I'd seen in the palace.

Gavril hurries me inside and looks around to be sure there is no one else who should jump in. When he's sure it's just the three of us, he comes in and lets the door slide shut.

"Do they all release with a latch at the bottom?" I ask.

Gavril nods, frowning as he likely wonders how I knew that. Then his eyes light up as he recalls someone had to show us when we escaped the safe room after he'd been stabbed. He smiles softly at me but doesn't comment. I doubt he recalls much of that event.

This safe room has a few beds. More cabinets line the walls here too, and it has a second door.

I open my mouth to ask.

"This saferoom and a few others have passages to an escape tunnel," Gavril explains. "It leads to the underground docks for a sea escape if needed."

"Has anyone ever needed it?"

"Not in my lifetime."

"Is it locked?"

Gavril frowns, watching me as I go over to it. "The key is beside the door in a little hidden latch. Run your hand over the left side, and you'll feel it.

"No need to play with it." Godwin looks over the paperwork he'd brought into the room with him. "No good in losing it."

"So, you couldn't get in from the other side."

"No, why?" Gavril asks, worry still in his eyes.

I give him a half smile. "Just thought..."

Gavril's eyes light once more with understanding. "You're worried about that Darkman report."

I nod.

Gavril smiles gently and comes over, putting his arms around my shoulders. "We're safe here. That thing isn't getting in here."

"The last one got into some of them," I point out.

"She tormented the answers out of a guard and didn't get the chance to share those secrets with any other of her kind." Gavril rocks me slightly. "It's perfectly safe."

I try to take in his words and find comfort, forcing myself to nod. Gavril kisses my head and lures me away from the back door.

He looks around for something to do, but there isn't exactly much in these safe rooms.

"Good thing I'm here or who knows what you two would get up to," Godwin teases, leaning on the wall while continuing to flip through the paperwork he'd gathered. Perhaps we could keep working while we waited.

"Like what?" Gavril gives him a look.

An idea strikes me to make me forget the tension.

I smirk. "Like this."

As Gavril turns to look at me, I almost knock him over as I practically tackle him with an intense kiss.

Godwin huffs. "Exactly that. I think we can just resume our work if you don't mind."

I giggle as I pull away. The look of pleasant surprise on Gavril's face makes it clear we won't get much work done.

Godwin at least tries. It is twenty minutes at most before the loud click sounds that tell us the door has unlocked itself and the alert is over. They'd driven off or captured all the rebels.

When we step into the hallway, the captain of the guard greets us.

"They didn't breach the palace," she informs us. "Seems without help, they're back to their old ways."

Perhaps that means there is no Darkman around to be afraid of. I can only hope so. I'm not sure I am ready to have to fear another one of those monsters.

# Chapter 21

I t finally feels like it's all coming together. Wedding planning and decorating are well underway. I'm getting used to my staff in their roles, and they are adjusting to them well. The sudden panic of having to plan such a massive event on my own is ebbing away. Excitement is taking root over anxiety and I'm finally looking forward to the event.

After all, shouldn't a girl who fought so hard to marry a prince look forward to her royal wedding? It's supposed to be that way. It's taking some time to adapt to this concept after envisioning a wedding that was extremely underground and inexpensive. I find myself enjoying actually daydreaming about all I can do, within limits, of course.

Perhaps Gavril had picked up that I'm still more anxious than excited because he steals me away one afternoon, insisting no one bother us. The only person who seems to mind is Godwin. Perhaps he simply doesn't trust us. No one else is worried, though. I'd not crossed the line before, even if I flirted with it.

"So, what am I in trouble for?" I tease Gavril as he leads me out of the castle by the hand, through the normal side passage through the gym.

"Who said you were in trouble?" Gavril smirks with a playful grin.

I give him a play pout. "Well, I'm being pulled out of my normal duties for this, you know."

"That's supposed to be a reward, not a punishment." Gavril smirks as we enjoy the weak sunlight.

I'd expect to be doing something a little more interesting, but I am in a simple day dress. Gavril can't have anything too crazy planned in that case. Or so I presume.

Perhaps we're off to explore one of the navy ships as we had so long ago, or maybe he just wants to get to the beach without being seen.

It's neither.

He takes me to the north side of the grounds, which I had rarely explored. The west side leads down to the beach. On the south side are the rose gardens, while on the east side, there are gardens: open fields for display at the entrance. The north side has more fruit and vegetable gardens, but I don't know what else.

We pass through the various plants: some tall, some short, but all flying by as Gavril leads me along at a rather playful pace.

"Where are we going?" I finally ask with a little laugh.

"The centerpiece," Gavril replies.

I am about to ask the centerpiece of what, but we arrive before I do.

There's a large open circle in the center of all the gardens. It has a beautiful motif of the Purerahian emblem done into the slabs in a gray-scale design. I don't know what it's there for, though.

"A long time ago, this was a hedge maze," Gavril explains as I try to figure out what it's for. "This was the center reward. But as supporting ourselves by growing food was a more pressing matter, they took down the labyrinth and replaced it with the gardens."

I had completely missed how the plants weren't in the rows most gardens used. They were in circle patterns. It was a circular maze rather than a square. I imagine from the palace windows it would have looked amazing. The gardens probably have a pleasant view. I'd only seen it once or twice out of Lilly's Chosen bedroom window, but I wasn't paying much attention to that when I was there.

"This is an odd—" I begin to comment on the strange reward when out of one of the small holes I hadn't noticed in the pattern on the ground, two little beads of water shoot up and over the circle before splatting on the opposite side of the circle.

I gasp in surprise.

Gavril laughs, and four more appear, hitting each other in the center before splattering against each other.

I laugh as four more appear from different corners and do the same.

"What do you think?" Gavril asks.

"It's... a royal splash pad," I tease.

"What?" Gavril frowns.

I laugh at his confusion, unable to help it. "You know, the little places where children play in the water coming out of... well, the pad at the bottom. It's this. It's exactly this."

"Oh. We call it the Leap Fountain, but I suppose 'splash pad' makes sense if you plan to play in it." He looks at the water again as its little dance gets more intricate. It's like watching water droplets dance.

Instead of just the beads of water spitting out of the holes, gentle jets bend into arches into intricate water designs as the pad at the center gets more wet. The wetter it gets, the more color appears in the stone.

My eyes widen as the traditional Purerahian blue of the rose appears with green stems, and the shark and dolphin get whiter bellies and the proper shades of gray for their backs.

"Wow..." I breathe at how detailed the colors become the more wet it gets. What kind of artistry could make that happen?

Gavril smiles to watch my surprise. "I thought you'd enjoy it."

"It's like a water ballet and water painting at the same time," I say as I watch the magic. It was almost as good as Cedrick's New Year's firework display.

But, it's not very long. The jets of water impress me with how high they can get, how they seem to spin around the circle, and how precise the water droplets can be: dancing to the music it makes as the water flows, splatters, and splashes against each other and the stones. But after five minutes, all the water stops all at once in a sudden swoosh, as if by the wave of a conductor's wand. And as one, the rest of the water falls to the ground with a great splash.

I laugh as the droplets get everywhere, even on us. Out of excitement and habit, I clap at their performance. Gavril laughs heartily.

"What? It's simply polite," I defend with a warm smile.

"Not like the water can hear you."

"I think it appreciates it," I insist.

I start as a droplet of water zooms out of one of the holes up to my face. It looks vaguely like a little fairy. It bows to me before it melts and drops to the floor at my feet.

I give Gavril an amused look.

"What?"

"Water magic, Gavril. I know that was you."

"You simply proved me wrong. There must be a water fairy or something that runs this thing," Gavril insists.

"If you think I'll fall for that, you're as deluded as your mother is about how young we are." I can't stop myself from smiling.

"How dare you?" Gavril feigns over the top offense and puts a hand to his chest as if mortally wounded. "I certainly do not think of you as a child."

"You do if you think I'd fall for that trick." I shake my head.

To prove he did not think me a simple child, Gavril crosses the minuscule gap between us and kisses me the way no man kisses a girl he thinks of as too young and innocent.

I can't help but almost purr in pleasure at the surprise as I return it, wrapping my arms around his neck as his encircle my waist.

"I believe we are quite grown up," Gavril almost growls into my ear, making me giggle.

"And still just engaged," I remind him.

Godwin would never let us alone again if we flirted too close to the line. And this is not a maze anymore. The garden is open to anyone to see us.

"Just engaged? You say it like that means as little as seriously dating." He gives me another play pout that reminds me of his father so much I can't help but laugh.

"Well, when it comes to pushing this line, it doesn't mean that much more," I point out, playing with his collar and waistcoat below it. "So perhaps we should look at it like that."

"To me, that still means other girls are still an option."

"Well, I'm not just a girl, am I?" I tease, giving him a look Godwin would throw a pillow at me for.

"No. Not in any sense." Gavril kisses me again. I gasp when he slips his lips from mine to the round of my jaw.

"Stop it," I giggle, hitting his chest playfully. I love it, but I will not let him get us into trouble, so the next time we're alone will be the wedding night.

"You stop it. You started it."

"I did not!" I laugh, but I don't break free from his arms.

"You did too. I had to prove I don't think you a child because I believe there is a water fairy in this fountain."

I gasp in mock offense like he had. "You still think I don't know it was all you?"

"Me? I don't do magic."

I hit his chest again, laughing at his silliness. Someone might see us, but there was no way anyone can hear us. There is no possibility of letting out his secret, and it doesn't matter. The world had seen him using his water magic to protect me from the darkwoman when the rebels sabotaged the announcement of the winner. He's just enjoying taunting me.

"There are no fairies in Purerah. They're all down south in the Unknown Forest." I know this as well as anyone.

"There are plenty in Hyvil. Maybe one stowed away with Zelda and decided this fountain was a great place to live," Gavril defends, but his stupid grin gives him away.

"If it's that small, then it's a pixie," I point out.

If one uses the wrong term when speaking to a real fairy, they get offended. Pixies are the small, winged people. Fairies are the same size as humans.

"Not in Hyvil. I don't think they have the taller fairies there anymore, so they're just all fairies." Gavril shrugs. "Zelda thought all the human-sized ones died out."

"Either way, there is no water pixie down there." I give him a look. The excuse to stay in his arms is fine with me. "That was you."

"I wouldn't mock you like that."

"Yes, you would. You little sneak. You are your father's child."

"Are you sure? Most people don't think we look alike at all."

I smile softly. I had seen it more and more since my father's failed attempt to assassinate the king, but no, Gavril looks a lot like his father. Yes, Gavril is darker skinned: a blend of his parents like a rich chocolate milk or hot chocolate. But they have a similar face shape. Gavril certainly got that mischievous smile from his father, even if the other smiles are uniquely his own.

I smile as I recall how I used to memorize, collect, and categorize every smile Gavril gave me. It was when there was no doubt in my mind that we could not be together. A little way my heart pleaded to have something of his no matter what when this moment felt too impossible.

"You're far more alike than people think. Most of all in looks." I meet Gavril's eyes.

"Oh great, so you think I look old and goofy?"

I lose it laughing. I know he's kidding because his tone and expression make that painfully obvious, but he perfectly placed the comment.

"No!" I'm still laughing. "I think your father must have been quite the looker when he was younger. And the goofy is a choice. Do you want to look goofy?"

"If it makes you laugh like that." I giggle as he rubs his nose on mine before holding me. I settle into it like a child settling to sleep. "That's a treasure worth collecting."

"You are easily the most handsome prince I know."

My smile slides as Gavril pauses. "How many princes do you know?"

I laugh again. This time I know Gavril is trying to see if I am making a joke or mean it as a true compliment.

"That's not what I meant," I assure, still laughing as I pull back to see him better. "You are the most handsome man I've ever dated."

"That's one of two."

I roll my eyes. "I'd say I ever kissed, but with the theater, that number gets awkward."

"So you wouldn't say I'm the most handsome man you've ever kissed?"

I shake my head. "It just sounds like I'm stretching the truth. Certainly, off the top of my head, you're the best-looking man in my opinion. But to say you're the most handsome man I've ever seen sounds like too much of an exaggeration to be honest."

"I don't know. We're having a good time being overly dramatic."

"You want dramatic?" I tease.

I then jump in surprise as water from the fountain suddenly hits my check.

"Gavril!" I laugh.

"That... wasn't me." Gavril frowns then jumps as he gets a hit too.

He turns around as if he knows exactly what he'll find. I peek around him and see a giggling Zelda with a very embarrassed Sage leaning on a cane for support.

"She does it too?" I ask.

"Not very well. She turned on the... ah!" He jumps as we're both caught by some of the jets.

In our teasing, we'd wandered onto the fountain pad. We undeniably got carried away in our kisses to have tripped this far back. We're almost in the center.

"She just turned it on," Gavril says as we're hit by two more.

I laugh and twirl in the water. It gives Gavril an idea. He pulls me into a proper hold, and we start to dance across the pad, even as it soaks us.

Zelda laughs heartily at us. Sage is still shaking his head. "Did you have to tell them we were here like that?"

"I think they liked how it turned out." Zelda is smiling.

"You should join us," I tease them as they walk over.

"Uh..." Sage does not look sure.

Zelda pouts teasingly. "Not with your cane then?" She grins. "We could just skip."

"Skip? Ah!"

Zelda shoves him into the water.

Gavril laughs as he catches his friend to make sure he doesn't fall. "You're going to have your hands full, you know. We're a playful lot, us royals."

"Oh, shut up," Sage snarls. Then winces as some water hits his face.

Zelda, on the other hand, is more than happy to skip into the water. "See, stiff one? It's fun!"

She pulls him up.

"Dancing in the rain, natural or fake, is quite the romantic pass time," Gavril agrees, suddenly twirling me before kissing me full on.

"I am *not* doing that," Sage insists, watching us with a mix of amusement and disgust.

"You're too weak right now to hold me up anyway," Zelda excuses, kissing his cheek. She laughs when they're both hit with one of the jets.

The jets are too much for most of us, and we step out of the way. Gavril and I are more soaked than the other two.

"Doc is going to kill you," Sage says to Zelda.

"He told me to get you outside to lighten your mood, get some boost in mood and sunlight. I have done that. You do have more color in your face." She kisses his cheek again, making that color go pink. She giggles in glee.

"Can walk you back if you want," Gavril offers.

The look Sage gives Gavril was clearly a "yes please, save me" plea.

"Sounds like a nice walk," I agree and take Gavril's arm.

Dr. Stephen sees us as we enter the medical ward and laughs to see how wet we all are.

"Thank you for not soaking my patient at least." He smiles at all of us. "What did you do? Shove the royal couple in the ocean?"

"Splash pad," I say.

"Splash... oh, the leap fountain." Dr. Stephen nods. "What did you do, spin in it?"

"Dancing actually," Gavril corrects.

"Ah, but of course." He smiles in amusement, rolling his eyes. "Let's get you all cleaned up then. I think that trip did our Sir Sage some good."

Sage looks displeased at this conclusion but lets the doctor and his staff do their work.

"I should get cleaned up as well," Zelda sighs.

"If Sage is up to it, we could do dinner — just the four of us — in my suite if that's easier," Gavril offers.

"He'll be good!" Dr. Stephen calls over even though he'd left our group to look after Sage.

We all laugh.

"Sounds great. I'll see you then." Zelda beams at us and leaves.

"I should get cleaned up too. My poor maids are going to be too used to having to dry me up to make me presentable," I sigh.

"You bet they are." Gavril kisses my neck, making me giggle. "We could clean up together, you know."

"No, we can't." I laugh as I shove him away. "I'll see you for our double date."

"Double date? Oh yes, I suppose that is what you'd call that." Gavril is grinning as if realizing he's mistakenly won a massive prize. "Most excellent, I'll see you then."

He almost knocks me off my feet with how he kisses me. I can't stop smiling. If I had any thoughts of no longer being excited for the wedding itself, today did a grand job fixing it.

# Chapter 22

The next day, we're hard at work planning the wedding. Gavril stays close. He stays close because he is worried that his hard work helping me yesterday will be ruined if he strays too far. At least, that's the impression his behavior gives me.

Damian makes sure to be there as well; he and Bella hint at the themes they have been using for my dress as we make plans for the bridesmaids' dresses.

Gavril stands on the other end of the table, looking over the suggestions and lists. I keep looking at him for some reason. Damian spots my anxious glances and catches my eye, giving me a little smile to try to assure me. I return it best I can. I feel bad for being so anxious when no one else seems to be, but I'm sure it will be fine.

"It's okay," I say more to myself than Damian.

He nods and smiles a little more. "It will be." There is a mixture of emotions in his eyes, but the only one I can pick out is his desperation to help me.

"Thanks." I feel guilty for making them nervous too. "Shouldn't be so jumpy," I try to joke. Gavril just watches with sadness in his eyes.

"It's quite understandable, My Lady." Damian smiles softly. "I'm sure every bride gets those pre-wedding jitters," he jokes, though he knows that is not it.

Gavril and I both laugh at that.

"Can make one nervous," Gavril teases back. The smile he gives me tells me he wants to joke that I am more comfortable with the aftermath of the wedding because of how I'd teased him before.

"Does that indicate that you are?" Damian smiles at him.

"No. I'm used to having to do such fancy ceremonies," he jokes with a playful shrug.

Damian chuckles. "Then you're faring better than I did."

"Really?" Gavril's face drops slightly in shock.

"Oh yes. I was bloody petrified," Damian chuckles. "The day of, I spent the whole day pacing my room. Cedrick had to point out that if I spent much longer fretting about it, I was going to be late."

"Why is it that bad?" Gavril asks, suddenly making me worried we'd now make Gavril scared.

"It isn't, but one shouldn't be late to their own wedding." Damian smiles amusedly.

"But you were pacing all day. And you're comfortable with fancy," Gavril points out.

"I was worried I'd muck it up." Damian shrugs. "Forget a line or what to do. Believe it or not, but I was extremely insecure, especially back then. Sometimes, I still am; I simply hide it well."

"Right. Still. That's like... your thing. Theater and all that," Gavril replies.

Damian gives him a soft smile. "You didn't know me then. I was a different man. As I have said to Kascia several times now, I doubt you'd have recognized me. Sure, I could still put on a front, but to the woman who saw right through me, I could hide nothing. And let's just say, I'd been enough of a cocky twit to her during our courtship, I feared she may reconsider."

"Still. Just a ceremony, isn't it?" Gavril is still frowning.

Damian continues to smile that same soft smile, but the corners of his mouth turn in amusement. "Sure. If you want to think of it that way. Just your average life changing, one-in-a-lifetime ceremony."

"Yes... but what's so frightening about the event itself?" I think he's actually making Gavril nervous.

"I suppose you'll have to find out when you get there, because I'm not sure I can explain it to you," Damian chuckles.

"Alright." Damian has clearly done the opposite of what he meant to do, but I decide to ignore that, as I really don't want something else to be anxious about.

Damian watches him another moment. "Do you think there is something to be frightened of?" He arches a brow.

"I guess so." Gavril shrugs a bit.

"Why? Simply because I suggested there was?"

"I'd... not say that." Gavril tilts his head noncommittally.

"Then what would you say?" Damian leans back and knits his hands together in front of his mouth.

"Apparently, I simply don't know what I don't know." Gavril smiles back. "I'll get nervous sooner or later, it sounds like."

"Not necessarily. But many do. I was simply saying you're better than me, and my every explanation only served to confuse you, so I stopped trying. But I'll try once more if you like." Damian smiles gently, still amused but also trying to comfort Gavril. "The ceremony is only as thrilling or frightening as you make it. I was anxious to be married, but I feared I wasn't ready, so I threw myself into a whirlwind of worry, trying to think of everything I could do to make it perfect. But I failed to realize in that moment, I had it wrong. It wasn't up to me. Marriage is a partnership, just like the ceremony itself. You meet her eyes and take her hand, and everything else falls into place because you do it together."

"I just thought the ceremony was the easy part." Gavril shrugs.

Damian grins with a chuckle. "Trust me, it is. But you're wiser than most men, Gavril. Most don't figure that out until later."

"I've had way too long to think about it," Gavril chuckles.

Damian laughs. "That is fair."

"I think the planning is the worst," I complain, looking at the papers in front of me.

Damian gives me a smile. "That is also fair. That's why you have help."

I smile a weak thanks. "It's... something."

"You have this better than you think," Gavril assures me, but stays where he is, looking over his list.

"Thanks." It still feels like it's all spinning out of control. I want to ask if it ever gets easier, but I suppose I don't want to hear a no, and I know Gavril won't feel great when I ask that question.

I shudder at a sudden chill and look over at the windows, but none of them are open. With a slight frown, I shift my gaze from Gavril to Damian, checking to see if they noticed it. Gavril has looked to the windows too.

But Damian tenses as if going on alert, and his eyes become steely as they narrow and look to the shadows of the room, not bothering with the window. He finally settles on one shadowy corner closer to the door with a dark look on his face.

That makes me tense. It couldn't be. How could they get in again so easily? I had almost forgotten about the darkman sightings.

A deep chuckle fills the room. "You noticed me faster than normal." The voice taunts. This one is male, but just as chilling as the last one.

I let out a little squeak and back up towards Gavril without thought. The second laugh makes me jump almost literally into Gavril's arms, making him jump too as he catches me.

Damian stands and draws his sword from his cane, pointing it at the shadowed corner. "I know your kind well enough to know your stench when I smell it," he snarls.

"You're sure about that?" I jump again as the voice comes from right behind us.

Gavril's grip loosens, but I only grab onto him harder, even as he lets me stand on my own. I miss his look of surprise at the fact I don't run.

"Pretty--- Ow!" The Darkman had appeared right behind us, and Gavril elbowed him right in the face instantly.

Damian chuckles and gives Gavril a nod of approval. "Careful. You'll find this prince is no pushover, and you are not welcome here. Leave while you still have a chance." He glares at the shadows.

"Why? I enjoy being back." The Darkman appears near the door, crouched for a fight. He's darker and ashier than the woman had been, with eyes almost glowing against the dark. I let out another squeak and back closer to Gavril, feeling safest with him.

"Hm, she looks like she keeps a good tight hold." The look in the Darkman's eyes makes me shudder worse. Gavril snarls, tensing as if to jump him himself.

"Please don't," I almost whisper, not wanting to lose him.

"Too scared?" The Darkman taunts.

Gavril's eyes harden.

"Are you?" Damian lights his sword with green fire and leaps and swings at the Darkman in one blinding moment.

The Darkman leaps aside with impressive speed. I'm stunned he got out of the way in time. He gives Damian a rather reproachful look.

"I haven't feared you in a long time," the Darkman snarls back. Shadows of some kind, or perhaps just magic that looks like shadows, form in his hand. I'd not seen that yet. The Darkwoman from before made nothing quite like that.

"Then perhaps it's time you learned." Damian gives him a dark smirk. "You know you can't hurt me. Why are you here?"

"You took the shadow from me. I want revenge." The Darkman's eyes flick to me. He is upset we took the girl who was here before. I shudder, and Gavril tightens his grip on me.

"I simply gave her a choice, and she chose the better road. Want to join her?" Damian says with a cocky smirk.

"What do you think?" The Darkman smirks back.

"I think you're going to leave them out of this. They had nothing to do with what happened." Damian watches him carefully, his sword still drawn.

"Where is Cedrick?" I ask, looking at Gavril who shrugs, tensing for a fight too.

"On the contrary, they're why I'm here," the Darkman sneers and makes the lunge at Damian.

Damian steps back into the shadows behind him and disappears, avoiding the Darkman's attack who falls on his face, and Damian steps out of the shadow behind him. "Oh, you missed." He mocks a pout.

The Darkman mutters under his breath for a moment as he gets up and turns to Damian again.

I jump as a flash of flame erupts in the far corner. Cedrick appears in the center as they fade. "How many bloody times do I have to chase you away?" he snarls at the Darkman.

But not too surprisingly, the Darkman takes one look at Cedrick in all his phoenix glory and golden light and lets out a kind of squeak of fright and a, "no thanks." And in a streak of darkness, shoots for the window.

Cedrick dives after him. It's kind of pretty to watch the bright golden light as it follows. I'm suddenly reminded of Zelda's magic.

Damian relaxes and extinguishes his sword as he smiles. "About time he turned up."

"About time?" I cry, heart in my throat.

Damian arches a brow with a frown. "Weren't you just asking where Cedrick was?"

"Oh... I thought you meant you were waiting for the Darkman to show up." I relax a bit. And I flush. He didn't exactly ask for Cedrick's help last time.

"I know." Damian smiles understandingly. "But that one is a bit trickier to deal with. He worked hard to become one of the higher leaders of the Darkman's order. I'm surprised he made the effort to come here, but they *really* don't like it when Cedrick and I 'steal' their followers."

"That... happens often?" I ask.

"At times, yes." Damian smiles. "They once started a whole war over it, but that was before Cedrick truly accepted his role as the Merlin. Now they don't bother with such an extreme measure as it's hard for them to be around him."

"I imagine." I lean back into Gavril, who holds me tighter. "So... that's just going to keep happening, isn't it?"

Damian smiles softly. "Not if Cedrick has anything to say about it. He'll chase them all the way back to Dark Mountain if he has to," he says, watching the window, then meets my eye. "I promise you, Kascia, they won't come near you again."

"But if he goes back to the mountain and tells them he failed again, they'll keep trying," I point out.

"No, they won't. Because Cedrick will remind them what happened the last time they messed with the light. They are more afraid of losing what they have than they want to nurse their pettiness for revenge. Just trust me on this." He smiles. "We know what to do."

I nod. If they'll go to those lengths before leaving, there is no reason to think they'd return. "Thanks Damian."

Gavril nods too. "Thanks."

"Welcome, both of you." Damian bows his head to us. "And thank you for your quick thinking," he adds to Gavril. "How did you know he was there?"

"His voice may echo, but you can tell where it's coming from when it's right behind you." Gavril admits with a small shrug. I frown. Something's off.

Then it clicks. "I guess you could have handled him on your own, couldn't you?" I give Gavril a smile.

"I-I don't know about that." He rubs the back of his head, making me giggle. I don't know if I've ever seen him do that.

"I don't know. You protected her without me saying or doing anything." Damian smiles. "I doubt I was really needed here."

"Of course, you didn't have to tell me to protect her." Gavril sounds a little annoyed. "But against that magic, I doubt it. I can be fair and say you were needed. I wouldn't know what to do with him."

"You have magic of your own and skill that is hard to match. Don't sell yourself short." Damian gives him an approving smile. "And I'm sorry. I meant no offense with the way I said that. I simply meant that you picked out where the Darkman was without warning or needing to see him like I did. You surprised him and left me thoroughly impressed once again. Which is why I agree with Kascia that you likely could have held your own against him in a fight."

"Because I can hear?"

"Well... you were listening for it. I wasn't," I point out.

"Well... as a fighter... well..." Gavril's ears turn a bit pink. Sure, my father had trained me, but perhaps he's right, most warriors in the fight mentality may have noticed the Darkman.

"Still. Not everyone would have caught him that quickly." Damian is still smiling. "It is okay to accept the compliment," he half-jokes.

"I would, but I don't think it's that impressive. Anyone paying attention could have done it. I still couldn't have defeated him, anyway." Gavril shrugs.

"Just because you haven't, doesn't mean you couldn't. You didn't have to defeat him. I'll grant you the humility if you like, but don't count yourself out simply because you have never done it before. You'll be doing many things you've never done from this point forward, but that doesn't mean you can't." Damian smiles at Gavril the way he often has at me during our talks.

He chuckles. "I suppose not. Still. Thanks."

Damian smiles and bows his head to him both in respect and that parental pride I've often felt from him. "You're most welcome."

I bite my lower lip, trying to hold in a smile. I think Gavril finally saw how Damian actually feels about him, and he's still unsure he believes it, but he clearly sees it, even if he looks surprised.

He tries to brush it off by kissing the side of my head. "We should finish up unless you need a break."

"Oh... sure." I don't know what I need. Other than to not have to do this anymore.

"Well, I don't know about you, but I think it is time for tea." Damian smiles and slips his sword back into his cane.

"I think that's a good idea," Gavril agrees. "Let's have some tea to calm down."

I smile a bit as Gavril kisses my head before going to request a staff member bring tea.

Bella is in a bit of a state, asking if I'm alright after what happened. Thankfully, she doesn't take too long to calm down before we settle down to working on today's project: arranging interviews for my court liaison. I keep wondering why I get the "luxury" of picking someone, when Gavril had always had his assigned. I remind myself I should see it as a privilege, but with all else I have to do, I don't feel so lucky.

"There are some... hang-ups," Bella admits.

"Hang-ups?" I frown.

"A few chosen have applied, but we don't know that the king and queen will give them high enough rank for the job," Bella explains.

I sigh. "Let me see the list, so I can at least say if I'd even pick them before we go over that with their majesties."

Bella hands me the list. I snort the moment I see the first name. Ayesha? Hadn't she left early on? She was one of those who ran away out of fear of the rebels, I think. She isn't even applying for the court job. Her application is for a maid position. Oh, right, I can see from her papers she was a maid before becoming a chosen. To my surprise, so had Jaine, who had been so rude to me during that same attack. *No way.*

I ignore those and keep looking. Pamia applied to handle my books. I barely remember her, and I have my own staff to choose from for that. Payge applied to be my correspondence manager (her papers showed her experience as a scribe), and Florence applied for the actual job I'm looking for.

It's difficult for me to remember Payge at all. I have to double check she even was a Chosen. I have a record that she got eliminated during the first date test. No wonder I don't remember her.

Florence, though... She was a lawyer with her own practice, even at her young age, before she was chosen. She might have the background for it. Though I'll admit, the image of her scrambling through her presentation makes me a bit nervous, but since she runs a law practice herself, she can't be that bad. She almost hit the top ten.

But is that enough that the king and queen would give her the rank of at least earlaness to be my court liaison? Or did she have to hit countess as it's a royal job? I'm not sure.

"Florence is the only one I'd bother taking to the king and queen," I tell Bella. "But I agree. I don't know if she'd get the needed rank."

"I was personally given the impression your number has a lot to do with it. I think the top ten were set for countess, but that could also have been personal as... Damian chose me." Bella frowns.

"Take her name to them, and we'll see. I think she'd at least earn an interview." The corners of my mouth turn up in a smile. I could see her doing well at the job, but again... what made her fail makes me uncertain. I'll have to ask her about it, even if I feel bad doing so.

"While I do that, look over our notes and the papers for the people we already interviewed, including Florence," Bella offers me the stack of papers. "Then we can decide who to call back."

While Bella leaves to take Florence's name to the queen, I nod and begin reviewing them.

I review the papers until it's time to meet some other new staff members before Gavril joins me, as does our new Custod guard. I can't imagine Sage is happy they've sent us one already.

"So... is he for you or both of us?" I ask in confusion. After all, I have Lila.

"I'm guessing both, as they only sent one. Unless they are just giving me a specific Custod they promised, but in that case, I personally would make him both." Gavril winks at me. I roll my eyes.

Our new Custod guard is younger than I expected. He's likely about my age. His red hair is surprisingly bright but not too bright, swept back to tease the nape of his neck. He has a gentle yet warm smile though I can't help but notice a small scar on his jaw that's easier to see as he smiles at us, his hazel eyes are warm yet sharp, carrying a look almost like Sage does when he's working. There's a slight crease between his brows, which are low to his round, hooded eyes. There's a warmth yet seriousness about him that fits what I feel a guard should be.

He wears a typical Custod guard outfit. I can see the chainmail hidden under his waistcoat and cloak. His pants, boots, and jacket are all a basic brown to match most anything; his cloak is a tad brighter of a color and the waistcoat is a teal blue, almost Purerahian blue.

He bows to us, and his warm smile isn't as pulled up on the side of his face with the scar, making a kind of warm half-smile, not quite a smirk, but close.

"Your Highnesses," he greets us, "I'm Cedar Custod, an honor to serve you." He then meets eyes with Gavril. "I am a newly promoted high guard, proven in my ability to stop attempts on a life by how I defended the queen of Aborgalia on a risky journey back to her homeland through Dragia and your rebel forces. I am fully devoted and able to protect her."

I look at Gavril, a bit surprised by Sir Cedar's immediate assurance of his skill. But it seems to have helped Gavril because a tension in his shoulders drops, making him look less formal.

He handles Gavril's questioning well. Gavril clearly sees him as my guard, if anything, and wants to be sure Cedar can handle filling in Sage's and Damian's shoes. I'm not sure *anyone* could do that, but Sir Cedar certainly seems up to the job. I feel comfortable with him. Besides, I'd still have my cousin.

It gets better when they bring Joy in, and Sir Cedar declares her his "co-worker" and happily pets and tests her obedience. Joy, as always, impresses everyone with her skill, even if she's mouthy about it.

Sir Cedar explains his mother raised guard huskies, which is why he is so comfortable with her. I think he's a great choice, even if Gavril is still giving him a side eye.

But at least we have the rest days between now and when we'll start interviews for the new staff. I have that happy thought in mind as I work.

The first rest day is, thankfully, not too exciting. Gavril sneaks us out onto a boat to enjoy the ocean for a while, even letting me meet some of the trained dolphins our navy uses. We have had little sea warfare to use them in, but they technically are not tame. They just learned we'll pay them for their help and have learned to understand our commands.

It is fun to enjoy some of the things Gavril truly enjoys before we have a quiet second rest day after services (which is still a bit odd. I'm still getting used to sitting with the queen in the royal section). But then we have a lovely lunch and play games with the queen, Zelda, my mother, and my grandparents for a few hours before Zelda, Gavril, and I visit with Sage for about an hour before the doctor insists we need to let him rest. Gavril then leads us to tea with just my grandparents to visit, though he makes sure I'm between him and my grandmother.

Even after spending the rest of the afternoon with them until dinner, I'm still unsure how to handle my grandmother. Perhaps it's because I had so many women friends and influences over the past year and so few male ones that made it so much easier for me to bond with my grandfather. My grandmother is fun, bright, and makes me wonder how she could have given birth to my father. There are times I can see hints of my father in grandfather, his dry humor at times, and how he patiently waits for his beloved wife to stop twittering away like a happy sea bird.

We end up discussing wedding plans for a while. Grandmother likes to bake and decorate treats, so we discuss letting her help with the cake. Grandfather will act as the main Custod in all the events from the wedding to the coronation, so he'll be busy enough fulfilling a duty for the whole affair. I'd almost forgotten what it was like to just have a quiet family afternoon like this.

But then the first workday rolls around. I'm set to be in interviews for my court liaison all day. Sir Cedar insists on being there for security, which I don't really mind.

Bella has an answer about Florence as well. The king and queen planned to give her earlaness at least, but said if I wanted someone with a higher rank, they'd make her a countess for me. I would prefer her to be the highest rank I can get away with to help with the court's respect.

As much as I hate to admit it, that is part of what helps me make judgments on which people I put on my short list for the job. The court is far more likely to respect a higher ranked official, and I cannot ignore this even if I wish I could.

Gavril also wants to be there for these interviews, which I allow. It is going to be a crowded room, but I think that will help us tell what kind of negotiator we'll be dealing with. Are they intimidated by so many? That may prove they aren't the best man or woman for the job.

Bella comes over with the papers for each candidate, organized by which interview is first. We scheduled an hour for each, but whether we'll need the full hour for all of them remains to be seen. We squeezed Florence in last because she had to travel for this second interview.

Damian arrives about twenty minutes before the first candidate's interview and reviews suggestions and gives us his thoughts, reminding us it is our choice, but he advises us to use our heads yet to trust our instincts on the candidates.

As he'd already interviewed them with Bella, he (like Gavril) will just observe, only speaking if he sees a red flag he's sure we'll miss.

But finally, we begin the process.

The first thing I notice about our first candidate is she appears intimidated by Sir Cedar standing there silently. Perhaps it's because she'd spoken with Damian before that he didn't seem to frighten her. Nor did Gavril, for some strange reason. I'll confess, that makes me nervous. It also makes it hard to have a solid conversation with her as she keeps glancing at Sir Cedar as she speaks. Her interview takes the full hour.

I have only a few minutes to add my notes to those from Bella and Damian's first round of interviews before we bring in the next candidate.

This one doesn't seem to have anything wrong with him. He looks right at us as he answers our questions and asks his own questions, and sure, he asked more than the last candidate, but there was just something about him that didn't quite click for me. But I can't put my finger on it, so I don't voice it, feeling it unfair to judge just on a feeling.

We break for lunch before resuming interviews again. I'm not sure how needed the break was, other than that we were hungry for lunch. I don't know if the break makes me more anxious or if it clears my head.

The third is lovely and bubbly and answers smoothly with many smiles. She seems capable, and I don't find fault with her, but I'm not quite sure what to make of her as I'm still not sure exactly what I'm looking for.

The fourth impresses me in that she doesn't seem to fight for us to like her, unlike the others. It's like she's seeing if she's a good match for us as much as we are. It's like she would enjoy the position, but she wants to make sure she'll be happy in it and good at it as much as we want to find someone who will be good at it, and that makes me more comfortable and makes it easier to dig deeper. She, like the second candidate, also has experience with the dwarven language as well as a little bit of sign. At least... I think they do. Gavril tested them both, but as I don't sign, I don't know how good it is.

The first definite "no" is right before Florence's interview. He is cocky and rather arrogant with me. I can tell from Bella and Damian's expressions he had not behaved like this in their interview with him.

As I'm still trying to get my grip on how to do this job, he's shoving his arrogance at me with the way he seems so sure he can teach me how to do my job better than the others. He doesn't act this way with Gavril or Damian, but he does when speaking to me. I have enough people talking down to me without hiring someone to do it.

But then it is time for Florence's interview. I expect her to be a bit shy or ashamed when she comes in, but she is neither. She smiles warmly, curtsies properly, is perfectly friendly but professional, as this is an official interview.

As she handled her delegation perfectly, it is clear that she has the skills. She knows some of the court already and, of course, is fluent in the law.

"I hate to have to ask, but I'll admit it keeps coming to mind," I finally lead into the question I don't want to ask after a while. "You were disqualified because you struggled with your presentation. How did you manage to run your own firm alone with that struggle?"

"A few things." Florence smiles understandingly at me. "I had amazing staff who helped with the visuals. I feel blessed to have found good people for that. I can present fine, but I'll admit that was my first time having to manage my disorganized notes into something visible. On top of... I was so nervous, so sure I'd be out with that test that I made it true."

"And why aren't you going back to law, then?" I ask.

Florence frowns slightly. "Honestly, Your Highness, hopelessness."

I frown in confusion, but she goes on to explain.

"I was one of the few defense lawyers in the city. Most are just law students who handle the clients unable to afford their own defense. I thought if we could give them proper defense so they could find some shred of mercy... it might help overall relations with the public and royal family.

"Sadly, even with the scarcity of people who are able to afford their own firm and afford great staff, like me, I still wasn't getting nearly enough cases with fair trials. Panels are not effective in detecting which rebel group they align with because people lie on their jury panels. They want to be paid and saying they are allied with any would disqualify them.

"It's why I joined the Enthronement. As princess, I could do something, right? I could try to rebuild the firm, I suppose. But now, I don't see it making much more of a difference. I'll likely try to do just that if I don't get this position or something better out of my time here. Using my law skills for the princess would do more good than all my won and lost cases have."

I nod a bit. "So, what would you do if you had to present like that again?"

"Know I won't get fired over it and relax," Florence laughs. "I was far too scared to do well in that, even if I had been organized. I also would seek out more help. Feeling unsure if it was allowed, I didn't even ask our teachers for help. I shouldn't have been so prideful."

I nod. "Few are willing to admit that."

"Wish more would. Make our justice system work again." Florence smiles sadly.

I think over her answers as we cover a few more questions before ending the interview.

By then it's dinnertime, but I'm not ready to end the day. I need to talk out my thoughts, so Bella arranges a group dinner with all those involved with the interviews to talk it all over.

Gavril doesn't like the first candidate. She scared too easily, and he feels she'll get bullied by the court if they go with strong arm techniques. Reinold agrees. Sir Cedar wasn't even doing anything.

Reinold also doesn't think the third is a great choice. "If you clicked with her, then by all means, but I've not found the bubbly ones to handle the court well," he explains.

Bella disagrees, and they have a brief debate over it before we move on, reminding me it's up to me. But I can see their points of view, and after the bubbly Hydie freaked me out, I am happy not to have another toxic bubble in my staff.

That leaves the second and fourth candidates as well as Florence after I say a hard no to the fifth. I do admit I found the woman more comfortable, and Gavril seems to prefer my court liaison be female, but he too doesn't have any other complaint about the second candidate, and he feels it unfair to choose on that alone.

"But who you feel more comfortable with does matter," Gavril reminds me. "And in the case of Lady Florence, I think that is the biggest reason to not pursue her further at this point. Would it be too hard to work with someone you were competing against?"

I give Gavril a look and wave a hand at Bella. Gavril laughs. "One who didn't click into your gang of sisters at the end."

I laugh at that too. "No. That doesn't make it uncomfortable. It might be easier with someone I at least know instead of a stranger."

"So, she makes it to the final round?" Gavril checks. I think it over and nod.

She has more law experience than anyone else who applied. It's just her failure that makes me unsure. She is the most qualified. Though the others have maybe a tad more experience with the high court, no one comes close to her law experience.

As I leave the dining hall, I feel someone touch my shoulder. I look over and smile at Damian.

He returns it softly. "May I speak to you a moment, privately?"

"Of course." I nod and let him lead the way.

He takes me into a side room and closes the door, then turns to me with a smile. "You did well today. I'm proud of you."

"Oh, thanks." I smile. "Not something I'm used to."

"You're welcome. And honestly, it felt like it was something you've done every day." He smiles warmly.

"Thanks." I brush my hair back. "But... you have concerns?" Why else would he pull me aside?

"Only one, but it has little to do with today," Damian says. "I just feel it would be wrong if I left and didn't say something about this particular topic."

"Oh." Another one. How bad could it be this time? "I understand."

He nods, then glances at the floor, then back up at me. "Well... for starters, I believe you mentioned you noticed something has been off with Gavril lately." His brows pinch together, watching me with concern in his eyes.

"Yes." I sigh and fold my arms. I never seem able to figure him out.

"Well, I believe you are right, and it likely has been going on longer than either of us realize. It's simply been more... subtle until now, but in the past two weeks, I have taken to watching more for evidence, and I believe I have finally figured it out." He smiles just a little as he pauses a brief moment. "He's jealous."

"Jealous?" I frown. "There's... no one here." I avoid Jake like the plague these days.

Damian gives me a sympathetic look. "Kascia, he's jealous of me."

"Of... you?" I manage to get out.

"Well, you do always contribute everything — your look, your ability to win — to me. Admittedly, my own pride likely added to this. That may be why he challenged me to do *The Phantom* in a month. He wanted to prove there was something I couldn't do, that I'm not perfect, so he didn't have to worry about trying to compete with me. And I tried to let him have it, but I couldn't help myself." He grimaces.

"I thought he just kept teasing because he wanted to see me perform," I almost mutter, fiddling with my dress.

"That is part of it, too. I simply have been looking back and seeing how it all could have built into this issue. Though a large part came from the rules of the Enthronement itself. Because you couldn't go to him, you confided in me. But recently, I heard him say something that made me realize he may believe if given the choice, you'd rather me than him. And he likely still believes that. At least, until a few days ago." He smiles a little.

"A few days ago?" I frown. "But... nothing changed."

Damian's smile changes to one of assurance. "It didn't have to." He rests his knuckle under my chin. "When the Darkman attacked, who did you go to?"

"Gavril."

"Exactly. Even though I was closer to you, it was Gavril who you wanted. He made you feel safe. And don't worry, I'm not offended." He grins slightly.

"Well... that is how it's supposed to be," I mumble. Perhaps it also was a desire to protect him. I don't really know. It was just my instinct.

"It is. And I'm glad for it. And you know what? I think he knows that now. Or at least, he may have started to believe it. I'll warn you, it may not go away overnight. In fact, I'd be dumbstruck if it did, but your instinct to go to him proves he has nothing to fear. And the only reason I am bringing it up is if he hints at it again, I want you to be able to talk to him about it."

I look down. "I see. It is... complicated." At least now I knew what it was. He's been angry with me for it.

Damian uses his knuckle to lift my chin and meet my eyes. "Not as complicated as you might think." He smiles softly. "You have already proven where your heart lies. All you need now is to assure him."

"I hope so. I couldn't see it. I knew it was there, but..." I sigh. "Been struggling to solve it for days."

Damian's face fills with compassion, and he pulls me into a hug. "I understand. And it is alright to struggle. It is okay to need help to solve the problems we each face. That's why we were put in this world together, to help each other."

"You'd think I could do it better on my own before they took you away." I manage a small laugh.

He smiles. "Perhaps. But honestly, you sound like my daughter. Five years into her marriage, and she was still 'struggling' to be the 'perfect wife'. But you don't have to be perfect; you just have to love him enough to try. The rest will work itself out."

"I don't need to be perfect; I just... thought I'd know him more by now. I suppose Enthronement walls made that near impossible." I smile a bit. "Just... need to accept that."

Damian pulls back to look at me. "Kascia, I pray you never stop learning new things to love and appreciate about each other. Your marriage will never be dull if you do. And... that includes things like this. It just means you have more excuses to show him love."

"I suppose so. I get what you're saying. I just... guess feeling the letdown he had when I pushed him away." A sigh escapes me. Do I know who I am marrying?

"And that can happen, but I didn't tell you this so you could burden yourself with it," he says with eyes full of concern. "I only wish for your happiness and for you to have the strongest relationship possible."

"I know." I smile. "And it will be, I'm sure. I'm just... understanding why he felt disappointed that night." I meet Damian's eyes. "He had the same kind of... feeling when I was stressed and pushed him away without meaning to. Only fair, I guess."

"I'm not sure about that." He gives me a little smile. "But will you be alright?"

"Yes, I'll be fine." I honestly laugh. "It's not that bad."

"Good." He relaxes a little and smiles more. "Well... you should go. I'm sure he's waiting for you."

"Likely." I smile a bit again. I open my mouth to speak, change my mind, and give him a hug.

He hugs me back tightly. "I love you so much," he says softly, "my dearest daughter."

"I love you too." Not that it should make Gavril envious, though. "I'm still sorry you have to go."

"Me too." He sighs. "But my time is not yet." He pulls back and smiles. "Go on." He nods to the door. "I'll see you later."

"Okay." I manage another smile then go. Perhaps it was just what I'd learned that left a knot in my stomach still. Damian doesn't think Gavril still feels that way, so it will be fine. I'll get used to it. Whatever it is.

# Chapter 23

The next day, I go over resumes and suggested classes I should take in the morning to help me grow into my new position. It's not easy to decide with so many suggestions on lessons: more than I could ever do, yet I do not want to fire anyone; I want to provide people with jobs. But I only have so much I can do. Let alone how many job applications I was getting, also more hopeful applicants than I could ever interview.

I set up to do interviews with those possible teachers and lessons tomorrow afternoon as I'll spend the morning interviewing the final candidates for my court liaison.

But this afternoon, I have real work to do. After lunch, Gavril brings me up to the second-born royal's suite where they have hidden his father for recovery.

"So, this is it, uh?" I ask, feeling my stomach tighten.

Gavril gives me a half smile and nods. "Father and I have even been practicing how this might go. Mother won't be there yet. We thought we'd talk to you together to see what you think. Trust me, we both regret we haven't had the chance sooner."

We step into the room, ignoring Jake on guard, and step into the room. The king smiles and greets us, inviting us to sit. He greets me more excitedly than normal, taking my hand as I sit down. He's happy and excited to see me, almost too much so as if to make up for how miserable this is going to be.

"To put it neatly, we need to figure out a way to tell the people the truth without them turning on us for it." He smiles at me.

"You're not to stay in hiding, then?" I assumed as much.

"I could be content with that, but it likely is not possible for many reasons." The king gives me a gentle smile. "The biggest being the doctor says with support I should have no trouble performing your coronation."

"What?" But then he has to show himself in full.

"It would mean much to me to have that honor." The king holds my hand as tenderly as if I were his own child. "And it is my right to do so."

"The queen will never allow it."

"She also fears giving Gavril power so soon," the king reminds me. "And that is our advantage. If they know I'm alive, they no longer are pressuring for you to move to majesty status. And that could be our bribe."

"And what of the public's reaction?" I frown. Many would hate it, rebels most of all. "And the fear of another attempt?"

"We have the main perpetrator in custody. And I'm not as high of a risk as I was. It's not as much of a fear, plus I have more of a say now. I'm still king, and more are being made aware. What needs to be decided is the best way to handle the whole affair and talk Her Majesty into it."

I swallow and nod. That can't be easy. "Do you intend to rule again?"

The king gives me a sad smile. "No. Sometimes, the entire afternoon in planning and debriefing is too much. I doubt that will improve, and this kingdom deserves better. You're ready." He nods to both of us. "The queen, however, may not be. We can stress more about that after the wedding. I doubt we can win both duels simultaneously."

I nod my understanding as the door opens, and the queen joins us. She greets us all warmly, giving her husband a kiss on the cheek. She sits beside him on the bed as she always does, though Gavril and I sit in chairs by the bedside. Though now I think on it, the king looks stronger than he did even when I first saw him looking so sickly. He's not so pale, and he sits up on his own better.

I take a breath, preparing myself for whatever this might turn into. "I believe we have coronation arrangements to work on?" The queen almost beams at me.

I give my fiancé a sideways look. He looped her into this by saying it was about coronation plans? Gavril raises his brows, clearly telling me "It is". I suppose it is because the king plans to run it.

"Actually, the wedding plans are all they pressured me to work on. No one asked me much about the coronation," I confess.

"The coronation will be more political and less fun. We've tried to keep that off your already busy schedule," the queen explains. "The most personal touches are the guests you wish to invite and your attire, but I believe your attendants are handling that well for you."

I smile and nod my agreement.

"It's a simple ceremony. We'll run rehearsals the day before the wedding," the king says. "Easy as pie."

"Now who can run the ceremony..." the queen goes on.

"Do... I get a say?" I ask, taking the opening that might make her more readily accept the king as a suggestion.

"Of course." The queen turns to me.

"If... it's possible, I would be honored if the king would do it." I look at him. He smiles softly, seeing the opening I took.

"I'm not sure that is wise." The queen frowns. "We still haven't found a way to announce his surprise survival."

"Could not the coronation be a good chance as there is so much other big news to cover? Help bury it under the rest of the day's massive events?" I offer tentatively.

"I'm unsure we should even make the truth public," the queen confesses.

"If he's going to resume his duties, we have to," Gavril says with a hint of concern in his voice. Our practice has paid off. The queen is clueless as she frowns.

"He's right. Give him power, or I'll have to step back into the spotlight," the king agrees with a graveness to his voice I know is an act, but the queen is none the wiser. I mentally swat the anxiety in my stomach as I hope it works.

"So why not let him perform the ceremony?" I ask with a hint of begging in my tone, showing how badly I want him to do it. I can almost feel Gavril's pride in my ability to so neatly fit into this plan.

"The people could riot, and that would make the whole day's efforts fruitless." The queen frowns.

"Perhaps if the news was already out then?" Gavril says. "Fabian did well with Kascia's uncomfortable announcement. He can handle this."

"But..." The queen frowns. "That brings so much attention. We hoped the coronation would overshadow it."

"What if we don't make a formal announcement?" I offer. They all look at me, even Gavril and the king seem unsure of what I'm going to say. "We have to publish the itinerary for the event, correct?" The queen nods.

I smile softly. "Then why not simply write that the king is presiding in the itinerary. Let the press do with it what they will. We can answer questions when they come, but that may just soften the blow."

"We never did formally announce he was dead. And people often hold memorials for royals stepping out of office before they actually do," Gavril says. "They will presume it's that."

"That sounds like a safe way to manage the press." The king nods, clearly impressed.

"But no one said you were stepping out of office," the queen reminds him. "Gavril and Kascia will just be married."

"We'll worry about that later," the king says.

"We cannot let them think he's taking power if he's not, or they'll think we are taking the opportunity away from him," the queen insists.

"Showing the king is alive will make that more of a question and not an assumption. I doubt they'll see it as stealing anything," I assure the queen.

"It's far too soon," the queen says. "And that is the bridge we will cross after the wedding if it comes up."

"Your Majesty, if you trust him, you'd see the best choice for him and your people would be to—"

"Trust that people will take hope in the prophecy," Gavril cuts me off. "Most of all, those who are not fully opposed to us." I stop and look at him, mouth slightly open. I was defending him. "I agree with Kascia's idea. I think it's a wonderful idea. We can announce it safely that way. We give them the plan, saying Father will run the event and let it go as it will from there."

"I agree." The king nods. "It's safe and allows a smoother transition, and perhaps the wedding news will help drown out my being there as well as soften their reactions. That will help manage those expectations."

"But..." The queen frowns.

"Dalilly, we have to tell the people I'm alive or pass power to them," the king reminds her tenderly. "And you are not keeping me from our only son's wedding and hiding in plain sight will be difficult. It allows us the safest path of both worlds. I say we do it. Let the press do what they will with that announcement, and we keep silent on it until after the coronation. No comment on it until after the event."

"Fair." Gavril nods as if that was his sacrifice for the compromise, though I highly doubt it is.

"But..." The queen is running out of excuses. "Well... alright. You're right; if he is to rule, the people must know it. I just pray it will not be our regret."

"It won't." Gavril puts a hand on her shoulder. "We're going to be fine, Mother. This is when things start improving. We made it this far. If we keep our end, the rest will be provided."

She manages a weak smile and looks at Gavril with pride. I see hope there. She's starting to see him as older and capable, but she's not there yet. Perhaps it will not be as bad as Damian feared. Or perhaps if this goes badly enough, it won't matter. If there's another attempt on the king's life or a serious riot with casualties, she may sing a different tune.

Her anxiety is really hard to manage. It makes sense she was the one born to this life, or she'd never have been chosen for it.

But I still think it's worth pointing out to her how disrespectful it will be to Gavril not to formally give him power when, to everyone else outside this room, he's king in all but name. Though I suppose the second call of the king's death cry hadn't been performed, perhaps on purpose to avoid offending the queen. "The king is dead, long live the king." Only the first cry had gone out, perhaps because all knew the queen may not give up power to a new king so soon when she had a legal right to hold on to her position for another two years without a king beside her.

I open my mouth to try to point some of this out to her, but I feel a kick from Gavril. It didn't hurt at all, but it was just enough to warn me to stop speaking outside the queen's line of vision. I give him a look. We should try to talk her into it. Why does Gavril keep stopping me? I might be the only one able to change her mind in time.

Gavril gives me a warning look as the queen then starts on other points of preparation about the coronation to make sure it's all to my liking. I just nod, steaming under the collar at Gavril's actions.

He can tell. When we wrap up as the king looks more worn, Gavril addresses it the moment we get privacy, pulling me into his suite before we go down to dinner. "I'm sorry, but you can't just start telling her she's a bad ruler and mother because she doesn't want to give me power."

"Someone needs to point it out, or she'll never give up power. That will land us in more years of this misery. It says you'll bring peace, not them," I remind him.

"It doesn't say I'll be king when I do it." Gavril shrugs. "And maybe after the wedding, it will be easier to talk her into it, but trying now will not end well."

"She likes me, and I'm outside of this issue, and I know how the people feel. If anyone can talk sense into her, I can," I argue.

"Or make her wish she could take back her decision to let me choose my wife," Gavril points out. "She has no power to send you away now, but do you want to make her debate that? You don't want to make her your enemy."

"She wouldn't hate me."

"You have far more faith in her than I do. I don't want you to have to endure what it's like to be the princess-heir when the queen dislikes you. It's a miserable state to be in, and I don't wish it on anyone, most of all you, who holds my heart." Gavril gives me a tender smile and cups my chin.

I speak before he goes on, though. "So, why don't you let me try? I could help her at least think about it."

"Kascia, standing up to her like that never works. I've tried it a million times." Gavril frowns a little as I pull back. "If I had any hope *she* would listen, I'd let you. It's not against you. It's her I do not trust."

"But what if I could?"

"Is it worth the risk of her hating you?" Gavril asks, still looking at me in tenderness and not in any anger. "You don't want her seeing you as taking me away or taking her power. Could you imagine what her anxiety will lead her to think and do?"

"Take her out of power, and she doesn't have to worry."

"That's not how anxiety works." Gavril chuckles a little. "She'll stress either way, Kascia. I promise it was not against you. I am only trying to protect you against another hard blow before the wedding."

"You think I can't handle more?"

"I'm sure you are that strong, but I've already put you through enough. I know I can't stop it all, but what I can, I will." He gives me a half smile. "I love you. I know this is hard. I only want to make it easier and not make more drama."

"You can't protect me from the pains of royal life," I point out. "Unless you take it away from me."

"And I'd never do that," Gavril says evenly. "Trust me to know what I'm doing."

"I do, but..." I sigh. I am getting angry at the lack of power on the larger stage.

"Want to fix it?" Gavril guesses with a compassionate smile. "Not yet. We will. We'll figure it out, but before we can override her or make a move, we have to get married."

I sigh tiredly, feeling dejected. Gavril wraps me in an embrace. "I'd do anything to spare you this pain."

"But you knew what this life came with when you chose me," I remind him. I wish he'd stop trying to protect me from the life I chose when I let him declare me his bride.

"What?" Gavril pulls back enough to see my face.

I sigh. "I... you keep trying to shield me from the pains of this life when there is no way to do that. You tried to make the interview easier when that wasn't going to happen. You want to stop the pain? You shouldn't have chosen me."

Gavril's brows draw together in confusion with a slight frown. Then I see understanding come into his eyes. "Ah, I see. You're probably right. I can't stop it. In the Enthronement, you had to prove you wanted this life. You had to open up, which is why I pushed you to do so. I'm sorry if my attempts offend you. It's not that you can't handle it; I just..." He sighs and cups my chin again to help my eyes meet his amber ones. "I love you. I hate to see you hurt. It breaks my heart to see you hurt, especially when it's because of me."

"It's our life." I frown.

"Soon it will be," he agrees warmly with a smile. "Let's just not have old married couple spats until then, at the very least, shall we?"

I laugh and wrap my arms around his chest, letting him embrace me and rest his head on mine. "This is going to be one battle at a time, then?"

"Get the news about Father out there, get through the political rehearsal dinner, get married, get your crown, take a break, then we can handle Mother's insanity." Gavril nods, still resting his head on mine.

"I want to do it all," I complain.

"That's my princess." He pulls back and leads my lips to his. "I know you want to fix it all. You want to fix it now. I'd hate to see how strong of a rebel you were before."

I gasp in offense and push him only half playfully. "Hey!"

"What? You sacrificed the life you wanted for the people at least twice. What if my family and I were on the wrong end? I'd hate to have you as an enemy. You're stronger than you realize, my love." He smiles. I can tell he's resisting something. "You could stop this single-handedly on the throne."

"No, I can't."

"Yes, you can. Maybe my parents were right, and you are the one who fixes it."

"Don't say that." I hate that idea, and I hate how it makes him put himself down again. "Not even joking."

"You're that powerful, my princess. You always have been, dear Esther." Gavril turns to me and kisses me gently, still holding back slightly. "Sometimes, you're just so tempting." He smiles.

"What?" I grin. I had never truly felt I was tempting to him. Not since the date when he was forced to see how far I'd go, and that was just a test.

"You are. I know you'll be mine, and you're so... beautiful, strong. I'd love to call you mine." He gives me a mischievous smile. "But I have to wait."

"You're getting better at flirting." But I don't know if I believe him. I had seen Jake lose it, but not Gavril.

"Hey!" His tone makes me laugh. "I'm not *just* flirting. I mean it."

"Do you?"

Gavril kisses me, hard. "Every breath," he breathes in that low tone that makes me shudder in pleasure, and my heart beats in joy.

I can't resist. "You sure?" And I catch him by surprise and shove him onto the sofa behind him.

Before he can figure out what to do, I get onto his lap like I had Jake and kiss him deeply. I resist going for some tongue.

Gavril is caught off guard, and I feel him hesitate, but then he puts a hand to my neck and the other to my waist. I love this position. I kiss him smoothly again and again. I love flirting with this line. I hadn't realized how much until I stopped and now get it with who I love most.

There's a knock and then the door opens. I turn to look and see Damian had come in. He's making a face. "Good grace, Kascia. You're just like Piper," he complains. "Why do I always walk in on these things?"

But I beam in happiness. Being compared to his beloved eldest daughter is likely the best compliment I could ever have received.

# Chapter 24

My days turn into a whirlwind of wedding preparations. The next day, I select my teachers, and after careful interviews and pondering, I feel it's safe to have Florence as my court liaison. She's humbled and honored, and eager to prove herself.

The days rush by. I have tea with Damian often to plan and spend time before he's gone, and I have many a meeting with various members of staff including the wedding planner. I hire my teachers, and I make guest plans and arrangements for those guests who will stay in the palace. It's a busy whirlwind that is stressful, but exciting. Most of all, I love taunting Gavril with each chance I get.

It's all too soon before my first official event as princess arrives. (Unless you count the interview.) It can't be too bad, right? It's just a formal meet-and-greet style party with all the members of court and rulers of Purerah.

Bella is stressed about her first solo design on an official event, but it looks amazing: midnight blue with silver star patterns with actual constellations hidden in it. Gavril's suit matches as well, making a pleasant effect.

Having met most of the high court at the Christmas Court Dinner, it isn't too hard handling them. The hardest part is dealing with the grand duke. When he reaches us in the reception line, he smiles that grand smile of his that always made me uncomfortable, though it is warm. His coiled hair and beard look perfect, as do his maroon-colored clothes. What makes everything worse is who is on his arm. I've never seen the grand duke with a woman before, but he has his plus one tonight.

My stomach drops as Forsythia's snake-like smirk greets my eyes. She matches the grand duke in a maroon dress of her own with no sleeves other than black beads around her shoulders. The dress hangs off her, as limp as her straight black hair, making her look like the snake-like seductress I knew her to be.

She'd been my only real threat during the Enthronement and now she's hanging off the arm of the grand duke!? The man who assaulted me in view of the prince, hoping he'd think I wanted the attention and eliminate me.

Gavril's arm tightens angrily, holding mine protectively, though his smile and demeanor otherwise seems perfectly relaxed and friendly as he greets the grand duke. He's had to pretend to be nice to him plenty of times. It's the queen's anxiety that protects the grand duke from Gavril and even made it pointless for me to accuse him of assaulting me. The queen would side with him, even now; I'm sure of it. The man is annoyingly protected by the careful anxieties he's weaved into the queen about how much she needs him. The king being alive doesn't help that at all.

I pull myself from that thought to make sure to behave right in this moment. There are impression lights flashing already.

"What a surprise." Gavril puts on a smile. "Lady Forsythia."

"Hopefully more soon." She winks at Gavril, teasing she doesn't have her position yet. Not that anyone does other than Bella, and hers is unique. Forsythia looks at me. "You know how lucky you are." I can feel the hidden hatred in that statement.

I put on a smile, too. "What do you mean? You have a man well suited for you right now." Perfectly honest, and it sounds like praise for both of them when it isn't.

"I suppose I do." She smiles a sickly fake loving smile at the grand duke, who returns it with less good acting, making it look fake to me. This news might be the biggest tomorrow if they don't catch on to the king running tomorrow's event. "It will be an honor to serve you, princess." The bitterness is veiled, but I hear it in Forsythia's voice.

"I'll make sure you're not forgotten." *And sent far, far away.* I wish. Now the press sees her with the grand duke, if I do that, they'll all say I'm scared of her, and that I want even less than her hanging around.

"I look forward to seeing my role." She is playing the part perfectly. Thankfully, I'm better at it than her, and we make it through.

I glance at Gavril, who gives me a brief glance back. That combination is dangerous. If it goes through, they would be the ruling couple next in line after us unless we have an heir fast. I'd not put it past Forsythia to try to off us to get power. The grand duke already has, and that was without that twisted snake's help.

But we have no time to talk or think about it as we greet the rest of the guests. And then it's a painful set of smiling and playing happy for the guests. The queen and grand duke are talking too happily for my tastes as Forsythia plays the perfect silent lady, seen but not heard. I wonder if anyone else will comment on how suggestive her outfit is.

After enduring the meal, there are toasts and lots of them are placed randomly through the courses, the grand duke's featuring as the "biggest" of the night to help him feel a part of the royal fanfare. It's how we are avoiding giving him any part of the wedding and reception other than as a guest. We do the same with most every governor in Purerah, several important committee heads, and the like. They all speak as if they know us and compliment us and how they hoped or knew it would be me.

The grand duke does similarly but spends a bit more time also praising those who had lost and highlighting how this union will not fail to help unite the kingdom, setting us up to take the fall if it does fail. And those are only the bigger traps he set for us.

After it's over, Reinold and Florence want to give us a summary of what they noticed during the event on the court dynamic. I'm bored and tired of sitting, and very sleepy, but I agree. I understand it's Florence's first official task, so I endure it.

Gavril somehow notices my struggle to pay attention, as this meeting isn't any news to me. "You can go change," he offers. "I'll let you know if you miss anything." He rubs my back. "You should go up to bed."

"But—" This is my duty, after all. And I don't want to disappoint Florence on her first job. But she doesn't seem to mind at all. I hope she's not good at faking.

"It's alright. I'm sure you'll do it for me sooner or later." Gavril kisses my head and lures me on. Grandfather comes to take me to my room.

"Are you doing alright?" he checks.

I nod. "Just a long night." I frown. "And that girl with the grand duke... she was a Chosen."

"Yes, people were whispering. Did she seem to like the duke before?" Grandfather asks.

"No." I frown angrily and explain my relationship with her and Gavril's as far as I knew.

Grandfather's frown deepens as I talk. "Hm. I'll make sure she's watched. She sounds like a danger, and if she manages to get the ring from the grand duke... her hopes of queenship might be in sight if she plays her cards right, and the grand duke has already been playing that game for some time."

Exhausted, I let out a sigh. "I didn't think I'd be dealing with her again."

"I'll protect you as well as your prince," Grandfather assures me, kissing my head as we reach my room. "This is yours, right?"

I laugh. "Yes."

"Good. It will be much easier when you're in your suite." He kisses my forehead. "Goodnight, my dear."

"Good night, grandpa." I smile at using the name before I slip into my room.

I groan to see the mess of articles that are published the next day. The front page, at least, is what we expected, talking of the king being alive. Fabian extensively researched various sources to verify the truthfulness of the information, but unfortunately for him, no quotes were obtained from us or any of our officials.

What really makes me mad is the article by Mr. Coppiger that talked about Forsythia's big stunt on the grand duke's arm. But rather than question what she was doing, he wonders if it only made me look bad by not looking princess enough in comparison. But he didn't have the guts to post a picture of the two of us to let readers decide for themselves. He just claimed she rivaled me.

I almost roar in frustration and throw the article. Now she has a leg to stand on to steal our good press and try to set herself up as the "should have" when I get any bad press. I had half hoped that someone would expose her as the opportunist she is, attempting to hijack my press. Then she would not be a problem in the press from here on out. I was wrong.

Florence is surprisingly patient with my frustration. "Too bad we can't get some kind of legal angle on that. I'll look into it," she assures me, picking up the paper and fixing it for me.

Grandfather is angrier than me. He's muttering about how he'd like to take her out of the picture with Grandmother scolding him.

Zelda too is furious. "I should send Sage after her," she says at breakfast.

"He'd better jump on the ship right after," I say dully.

"I'm sure she's not the last Chosen who will try to set themselves up that way," the queen assures us. "Just brush it off. The press will get bored with the nobodies in no time."

Gavril and I exchange a look. We both highly doubt that. Forsythia will make sure of it unless she and the Grand Duke have a big dramatic break up where she seems the bad guy. Otherwise, she's charming her way into the spotlight. She will be a problem for who knows how long.

And as expected, there is so much speculation on the formal plans with the king leading the coronation. But as we refused to comment, all Fabian could do was guess. Do we mean someone filling in for him? Had we only declared him dead to fool the rebels? What does that mean for the line of succession? But without confirmation, it is mostly bickering reporters.

The real problems are the courtiers who were not informed. And we stand by the "no comment" even with them. Reinold and Florence are proving their worth by handling and deflecting the court with perfect poise. Grandfather had to firmly put himself between the grand duke and me a few times.

The grand duke is seething and furious that he was not let in on the secret and demands answers I refuse to give. He can't affront me and expect me to cave to his anger. Gavril is even more firm. I even hear a rumor he or his new guard got into a fistfight with the grand duke or one of his officials.

However, not all of it is bad. A surprising number of letters come in, addressed to myself or Gavril from hopeful governors, city rulers, and even common citizens asking if the news is true with a tone of nervous hope. Perhaps it wouldn't be as dangerous as we feared. The reality is, until the event happens, there is no way to be sure.

There's only one distraction left.

The next day is my bachelorette party planned by Alsmeria who did not know that being princess didn't make me rich, so she had gone for the most jam-packed day we could get, feeling I deserved it. All my closest friends are there from the theater as well as Lilly, Bella, Azalea, Zelda, Rose, Isla, Florence, and of course Vivian, Flur, and Ro are there and ready to enjoy a day of fun.

Alsmeria takes us onto a boat for a cruise day, and we play on a small island in the bay to enjoy the warm weather, attempt and fail at surfing, play in the sand, and the like. After, we have a luxury lunch on the boat before the fullest spa day most of us had ever had in the royal spa.

We wrap up the evening with a nice buffet-style dinner to make it easier for us all to enjoy one amazingly beautiful karaoke night, if I do say so myself.

It helps that half of my friends are actresses like me. I think Alsmeria figured out why I used to not drink and had drinks for everyone, but I'm worried about it making tomorrow harder when I want nothing to ruin my wedding. It didn't stop a few of my theater friends from getting tipsy, though.

But in the end, we all had a wonderful time. I don't have one gloomy thought in my head when I drop off to sleep that night.

# Chapter 25

It is finally here. After all the blood, sweat, and tears, all the sacrifices, we'd made it.

I awake on my wedding day unsure it's real. I'm instantly very thankful that royal weddings are done differently than normal weddings (held at sunset), so I don't have all day to pace in anxiety over it.

I'm reeling at the idea, this really is my last day in this bedroom when the door opens, and my maids enter to get preparations started, all beaming and happy with excitement, even my new personal maid, Briana, who is fitting in better than I hoped.

My maids have just gotten the whole process underway when Bella comes in, looking slightly harassed, already dressed for the wedding. Her dress is stunning, as always. She only ever was outshined by Damian's work, and that gap is closing with Damian's tutorage.

My wedding dress must be one of the most lavish yet, as Flur is meticulously adjusting my corset and petticoats as the doors open again, and my mother, grandmother, and Alsmeria come in.

I beam at them, and they're already beaming back at me. Grandmother already has tears of joy in her eyes. Their happiness is infectious, as it makes me realize this is all real. It's really happening. I am finally getting to marry the love of my life in a few short hours. I'm excited yet scared at finally making this enormous change.

"I'm so proud of you." Mother gushes and hugs me, stepping onto the little platform my maids have me standing on to make their jobs easier. "Part of me can't believe we're really here." Mother laughs, wiping her eyes to stop tears forming just yet. "I knew you had to get into this to get free, but I don't know if I ever thought it would really happen like this. I knew you could; I just... these endings aren't real."

"Don't jinx it." I laugh, but inside, I am admittedly slightly nervous something will go wrong. It always has.

"You got to the happily ever after. Enjoy it," Alsmeria insists. "I hope you all know how to work this." She's looking at the stunning dress draped across my bed.

"Wait until you see yours." I smile. Briana, my new personal maid, goes to get her dress.

More maids are then brought in to help my guests don their dresses as well. My former bedroom is now filled with privacy screens and stands for the women being dressed to perch on and bustling with maids.

I'm almost done at last when Alsmeria hands me a few garters to choose from.

"You're kidding." That doesn't seem princess-y, does it? I suppose the lace piece with white roses and pearls is fancy enough. But is such a tradition really going to pass at a royal wedding?

"What? Princes don't have fun?" Alsmeria asks.

"I just don't see them planning that," I admit. "Kind of... scandalous for a royal, isn't it?"

Grandmother chuckles. "Maybe we should ask the expert. I'm sure Damian will be along soon now you're fully dressed."

Now she says it, I'm surprised he isn't already here. Perhaps he's nervous about privacy.

Grandmother proves correct when Damian comes in just a few minutes later. He looks as perfect as he always does, wearing the teal colors that we'd decided the bride's side would wear. The teal suit has patterns to it that are hard for me to define but give the suit the right amount of texture to pop. In contrast to the rest, his necktie and flower in his breast pocket have a pinkish peach color. The ribbon he wears in his ponytail is the same. It makes his emerald green eyes pop attractively. I wonder how Emily would react to the look.

Alsmeria immediately asks him about the garter, which makes me blush. Mother chuckles and hugs my shoulders as Flur and Vivian work on the veil, pinning it into my hair and the tiara carefully. I try to keep still and not roll my eyes for their sake.

Damian chuckles warmly. "Whichever she likes. That is why I made them."

"She's not really going to allow that, is she?" I ask with a slight frown.

"She is if she's afraid of offending the Merlin." Damian can't help but grin.

I giggle without restraint. "Seriously?" I should have known. Mother laughs too.

"Let's put it this way. If you're not wearing one at the start of the wedding, Cedrick will put it there magically," Damian says straight-faced with a warmth that tells me he was serious.

I giggle. "In that case." I pick the one with a rose and stars made of pearls. I refuse to let Alsmeria help me get it on, despite her desire to do so. I don't need to know how high she'd try to get me to put it. She just giggles and helps work with the jewelry.

But finally, after my longest preparation ever, I'm done. Mother helps me slip the shoes on, and once I'm on my feet, they lead me over to the mirror to admire the surprise.

I'm sure it will be stunning, but I'm still nervous to see it as if it couldn't ever match what I'd imagined.

I am right. It is better. The top is stunning. It's a sweetheart neckline yet it looks like a wrap sleeve at the same time with soft lace at the edges and it covers my shoulders. Stunning diamond and silver bead work, reminding me almost of snow and ice in the best way, makes its way up the wrap style around my arms in a simultaneous cap-wrap sleeve.

The necklace rests perfectly in the line of the sweetheart neckline. The long full skirt is simple, long and beautiful, mostly satin with a soft, transparent, white top that has little hints of stars sewn into it, so subtle I have to look closely to see it. The overskirt has a folded flap design at my sides portraying amazing lace roses: again, so subtle the light has to catch them just right for me to see them.

The veil is just as stunning, pinned perfectly so it drapes down my arms, before it naturally flows back. I see diamond stars hidden in it as I look down at them on my arms with a delicate rose here and there. It looks so elegant and simple and yet so grand at the same time. A delicate balance only Damian could master.

The final stunning detail is the tiara, which Damian must have made, with pearl and diamond stars and flowers that aren't too flashy. The tiara isn't too big but stands out just the right amount to blend into the veil. My makeup makes me shine and makes my blue eyes pop naturally. The only reason I can tell I am wearing makeup is that I know what I look like without it, and the lipstick is too perfect to be natural.

I take my own breath away. Finally, I release a soft breath. I wish I could find words. They did a spectacular job. I don't know how to thank them, thank Damian, or find words adequate to praise their work.

Mother beams and hugs me, still holding my arms and resting her head on my shoulder. "Like it?"

I nod.

She smiles. "You look stunning."

I nod my agreement, still unable to find words.

I think my speechlessness pleases my maids just fine. They look happy enough to burst.

But it's Damian's eyes that I want to find. I wish I had words to thank him for this. He's always been far too good to me.

He has a warm, teary expression in his eyes as he looks on me with his soft smile. "Do you see what I see?" he asks.

"I hope so," I reply.

"As do I." He smiles tenderly. "You are..." He takes me in with a delicate breath. "Simply gorgeous." His smile grows a little with pride. "I couldn't be prouder of you, night angel."

I swallow tears and give him a watery smile. "Thanks Damian." My voice is thick with emotion. I couldn't have done this without him. I'm a bit scared to move in the dress and ruin it.

He smiles as he gently takes my hand and kisses the back of it then smiles up at me. "It was my pleasure, My Lady," he says and bows his head to me.

I can't help it, and I don't let him stay that distance and hug him tightly. Damian accepts it and holds me close. He says nothing for a moment, just holding me in his warm embrace. I hold it a long time before I finally pull back, blinking away the tears, so I don't ruin my maids' work. I suppose there will be time for that later. He isn't gone yet.

"Maybe Sage had a reason to fear you. You'll take the prince's breath away," Alsmeria teases to break the mood. I laugh as I blink back the last of the tears.

Damian laughs too. "All too true. Well, we best move down there soon. Don't want to keep him waiting." He beams, then goes over to his workbench and slips on a pair of gloves, followed by his wedding ring and one I'd never seen him wear before. It is gold and has the mark of a bird on it.

Bella checks the time. "They should be ready soon. It's about time. In fact, we may be behind. Let's go!"

Mother chuckles as the girls gently pull me along, seeming more excited than me.

"Flur, is her bouquet ready?" Damian asks.

Flur nods and goes over to get it. I take a deep breath as she brings it over. It's beautiful with the Purerahian roses, white roses, a dark green colored flower that looks a little like a rose and soft peach and gold flowers. I take it with a nod of thanks.

They take me down to the main floor and to the capitol sanctuary, which is attached to the castle grounds. I can see the bustle already. Press swarms the area as well as people desperate for a glimpse of the activities. Guards hurry about keeping them in line. My mother ignores them and just guides me to where they want me to wait.

That's when all of this finally sets in. This is actually happening. The others leave to find their seats or to make sure all else is ready. They all wish me good luck or congratulations as they go, finally leaving me alone as I wait.

Taking deep breaths, I fight the butterflies. I would think "I wonder if I should go through with this", but I know it is far too late for that. I'm currently processing the sudden reality of how real this is. I'm about to get married. This is it, no turning back. Can I really do this job? Can I really handle this?

I pace a little, which helps. I hear a slight sound around the corner and walk over to see what it is, only to laugh as a voice I know well calls out, "Don't!" The urgency in Gavril's cry of warning makes me laugh. "I can't see you yet."

"What are you doing?" I ask, smiling as I lean my back against the corner so he can't see me, but I'm as close to him as possible. It sounds like he's doing the same just on the other side, out of sight.

The warmth of his hand teases mine. He'd slipped it around the corner without looking. I smile and take it firmly.

"Having all of them stare at me is making me nervous. You?" he says conversationally.

"Nervous?"

"I was fine until Damian made me think there was something to be scared of."

I laugh again, the tension in me dropping. "It's nothing. It's marriage he feared and his bride running away."

"The latter is a good reason."

I roll my eyes. "Gavril."

"What? Part of me worries you're just going to decide you aren't the one and vanish."

"Now why would I do that?" I ask, shaking my head. "Are you trying to make me nervous?"

"Are you nervous?"

"I was anxious but I feel better now," I reply honestly. "It's all this hurry up and wait."

"No take backs?"

"No." I laugh. "You're a goof."

"Be fair. Every time it starts to seem like we made it, what has happened?"

"What has happened? We're here, aren't we?" I can't stop smiling.

"I told you. You'll decide you were wrong; it can't be you and vanish."

"I haven't done that."

"Thankfully, you've not run, true, but that's what you've tried to do every time we finally got close. Don't deny it. When I first kissed you, when I told you I'd choose you, it didn't take you long to build a defense. Maybe it's paranoia, but I at least had to hear you say it once." I can hear the smile in his voice, and I enjoy feeling him play with my fingers.

"I'm not going anywhere," I promise. "You?"

"Only if you're there." Gavril squeezes my hand. I smile slightly, and we share a quiet moment of pondering together.

We keep hold of each other a minute longer before Gavril has to go. "I'll see you in there."

"Not until then," I tease.

How did he know exactly what I needed? His visit helped my nerves quite a bit, but it didn't completely alleviate them. The butterflies had settled to the gentle ones that came before a performance. But this is no performance. This is the most real thing I'd ever done.

It isn't much longer to wait before Damian and my mother return. Grandfather is with them this time. His proud beam at me makes the first tears of the day start in my eyes. It's the pride and joy I had hoped would light my father's face on this big day. But no matter where my father is, I'm sure he's wearing a scowl either way.

"You are beautiful," Grandfather says, kissing each of my cheeks before stepping back to admire me. "My sweet princess." I hear my father calling me his "sweet cygnet" in my mind and instantly long to hear him say it and look at me with the same pride my grandfather does. But I know it's not possible.

"Thank you." I do smile, and I mean it, but there's still a little sore on my heart. At least my grandfather fills that at least a little.

"Couldn't be prouder," Grandfather assures me. "I'll see you in there." He links arms with my grandmother to walk out in their assigned place in the procession.

"We're ready." Mother beams and kisses my cheek. "You'll come out after me. Ready?"

Nodding, I swallow. I smile, and the tension relaxes again. "I'm ready."

Mother smiles, tears in her eyes again, and gives me a last hug. "I'm so proud of you." She sighs. "I love you, Kassie."

"Love you too, Mama," I assure her before she goes to let them know we're ready.

I sigh and look at Damian. "This is it," I say. "I'm ready for this, right?" I tease.

"So long as you believe it." He smiles back. "My Lady." He offers his arm.

I smile and take it. "Sir Damian." I take a deep breath. "Thank you." He didn't have to stick around even this long.

"The pleasure is mine. I assure you." He beams. "I'm glad I got the chance to be a part of your journey," he says, squeezing my hand.

"Me too." I'd have a very hard time without him.

Mother returns and smiles at us. "We're starting." I let out a last nervous sigh and nod. The excitement is finally kicking in. It's real. This is about to happen!

The music rolls on, and soon, Mother is taking the walk. I smile and squeeze Damian's arm. I'm extremely excited with nerves. I'm glad that even though he's leaving, Damian is still there for these last moments.

Soon it's our turn, and Damian guides me down the aisle. The collective gasp that rings out as I step into view makes me flush pleasantly and smile.

I see all my friends, Isla, Azalea, and Lilly, sitting towards the center. Closer to the front are Rose and Zelda sitting with the other royals that were invited. Sage, dressed up for the occasion, is sitting on Zelda's other side. He gives me a crooked smile as if saying "well done, sister".

I beam at Princess Tsikyria, who bows her head approvingly at me with a smile. Her red and gold dress makes her look like a princess. I beam and nod at all of them, remembering Lady Keva will have my head if I wave.

But then I look up and finally meet eyes with Gavril.

I beam.

He looks better than he did at the funeral, and I have to admit I liked that suit far too much. This white suit is similar, with a white sash marking him as prince as well as a silver marriage crown, which looks a lot like the king's crown, if I recall right. The suit fits him well, unlike the countless ones he'd worn before. I'm sure Damian did this one, too. There are hints of silver throughout it as well. I wonder if they are stars like mine, but I can't tell from here.

But it's his beaming smile that mesmerizes me. I tense with excitement again, hoping my face doesn't split with how big my smile is.

We finally reach Gavril, and Damian takes my hand to offer it to Gavril. Damian gives Gavril a soft yet serious smile.

I smile too. I know that look.

Gavril seems to understand it too and nods his promise to Damian before taking my hand.

The moment his hand touches mine, I'm instantly filled with electricity. I beam as he pulls me up to stand with him. If he doubted I'd pick him over Damian, that brief exchange should be proof enough.

I start slightly when the officiator's voice begins. I expected a Keeper, but instead it's Cedrick. This shouldn't surprise me. I wonder how many people will talk as so many now correctly guess he's the Merlin. But even with that, it's hard to listen as I look into Gavril's eyes and can't stop smiling at the joy of this finally being real. He's going to be mine, and no one can take it or win it out from under me.

Even with my heart so lost in its flutter of joy, we get through all the steps, kneeling, taking hands, all the traditional things. Mostly, it's just locking eyes with Gavril's stunning gold eyes. I'm never not going to love that unique amber color.

It feels like far too long before we're finally pronounced husband and wife, and Gavril pulls me in for the kiss. I melt into it and kiss him back hard. I just kissed my husband for the first time, and the thought fills me with pure excitement and joy. I kiss him deeper. He returns it, filling me with excitement and desire.

It's as if we're back on the rain covered rooftop, dancing in the air on the raindrops. The world is gone, and it's nothing but us: filled with our passion, love, devotion, that allows us to fly. I'm filled with electricity that lifts us into a world so much better and stronger than we'd ever been.

When we break apart, it feels like coming up out of a warm, glorious sea. My eyes meet his magnificent amber ones, and my heart soars at his adoring, joyful smile. Mad cheering bursts into my ears, and I realize it has been ongoing for some time.

I laugh and turn to nod and finally to wave at the onlookers. Gavril keeps an arm around me, and I keep one around him as we cordially greet the guests.

"Kiss her again!" Cedrick's voice drowns out the others. It sounds like it came from the back of the room, even though he's right there.

I laugh once more, but Gavril is quick to obey.

He grabs me, spins me around, and kisses me deeply, intently, setting off an ecstatic fire in the depths of my being, suddenly full of passion and desire as I return the kiss, absorbing him into me. Gavril's deep intention lures me closer, and he almost knocks me off my feet as he dips me back in the kiss, making my heart race in an electric kind of joy.

I like this new bold side of him. I am excited to see more. But eventually, I think I hear the queen or perhaps the king or someone else telling Gavril to let us up.

Gavril pulls me up, and I kiss him on the cheek in thanks.

Then I hear the king's voice. "Let them at it," he complains.

I laugh harder; Gavril is hugging me as if to hold me up. I'd never been so happy in my life as I settle my face into Gavril's shoulder as he holds me, so happy to be enfolded in him with him, my husband, my eternal ruling partner and companion in all: my prince.

The cheering from the guests is no less than it had been when I first heard it. I look over them, wondering where the king and others are seated.

The queen looks stunning in a peach dress, almost like a peach sunrise. The king's matching suit is deeper in color but suits him well. They're on the far side of the front row to avoid too much attention. It also lets the king's cane rest without tripping someone. The king smiles and gives me a small salute. I'm so happy to see him looking normal and gleeful there with his wife. She's clearly been crying.

I scan the bride's side as I wonder where in the crowd my family vanished. They hide on the far side of the front row, with my father tucked furthest away, a shackle on his ankle to keep him in place. Mother sits beside him to ensure it. Grandmother is beside her with Grandfather on her other side, clapping and beaming in joy.

The only face not beaming in joy is Father's. He is smiling, though. His eyes shine a little and not in the sadness I'd expect, but more like he's deep in the forlornity of knowing his baby girl has grown. Do I dare hope?

Gavril doesn't see where my eyes go, though. He's still laughing and happy. He kisses my cheek and proves me wrong.

"You see him?" he asks gently.

I nod, smiling to cover it up.

"We can let him stay or send him to his room. Up to you." Gavril kisses my jaw to keep up appearances.

"As long as he behaves." I giggle and wrap my arms around his neck.

"What about me?" Gavril kisses my neck, and the whole crowd goes crazy. I laugh, but then sigh, as it feels fantastic. That is new.

"We have a reception to get through," I remind him.

"Fine." He sounds just like his father complaining about following his wife's orders. I grin. That is me. I am his wife. And that feels wonderful.

# Chapter 26

Once we're out of the hall, they have to make a few adjustments to my dress to make it easier to dance in. It also gives Gavril and me an excuse to slip off for a moment to ourselves after they finish.

The moment we finally soak in what had finally happened and that we are alone for a moment, Gavril embraces me tightly, pressing his lips against mine as I happily absorb myself into his arms.

"We're here." He sighs, his hand cradling my cheek still as he beams, eyes still closed.

I smile and return the kiss. "We made it."

"I can't believe it's real." Gavril laughs a little before kissing me again, his other hand wrapping around my waist. I smile slightly as I kiss him back. I can't believe it's real either.

We enjoy a moment like that, just soaking in the joy of the moment. "Thank you." Gavril kisses me deeply.

"For what?" I giggle.

"Well, you just married me. You can't get out," he jokes.

"I wouldn't for the world." I tangle my fingers in his hair as I kiss him intensely. "We may have a long way to go, but I wouldn't have it any other way."

Gavril smiles and takes my hand. "Me either." He kisses me once more. "Just a minute," he begs of me.

We spend a few minutes just standing there together, wrapped in each other, enjoying the truth of our official marriage before Gavril takes my hand, and we step into the party.

A round of applause greets us. We spend far too much time thanking guests for coming and for their gifts, which we will open later. (When? I don't know with my coronation tomorrow, but I'm sure we'll find time.)

After we get through everyone, by some miracle, we are called out for our first dance. That must be why the people I actually want to talk to, like Princess Tsikyria and Lilly, tried to keep their meet and greet brief.

Gavril leads me onto the floor, and we step into a smooth waltz. I smile at the song they play. Too perfect. It's magical. Gavril was always my best dance partner, but this is a whole new level of magic.

It's so nice to be close to him, feeling perfectly in tune with him and admiring how good he looks and enjoying how beautiful I feel in my dress. I love it. I love him. As long as there are moments like this, we can take on whatever struggles lie ahead. Even if one is the longest civil war in history.

Gavril finishes with a twirl and dip before he kisses me deeply. I get my fingers tangled in his hair again, almost knocking his crown off as he pulls me up. It gets a good chuckle from those watching. We do our best to get through as many dances as we can, as that's one of our favorite things together, but soon we have to play host and hostess again.

We don't have to endure too long, though, before Cedrick, the little traitor, tells me to throw the bouquet. I know what he's leading up to. I'm so glad Damian warned me.

I turn, and Gavril jokingly indicates which way I should throw. In a gesture of annoyance, I roll my eyes and push him away before I close my eyes and toss it.

Gavril fist pumps and beams at me. "Now I just have to get Sage," he teases.

I hit Zelda with the bouquet.

I giggle and take Gavril's hand as they then have us cut the cake. I'm guessing they asked to cut the cake now so the guests can eat while they enjoy Gavril dealing with all the petticoats I've got on. Though I get some pre-payback by getting him covered in cake, which he responds by kissing me and getting it all over me. I should have thought that one through. His father is quite the trickster, after all.

But when Cedrick tells Gavril to go for the garter, I burst out laughing as Gavril pales slightly with nerves. "We're married," I remind him.

"I feel like if I do this, I fail the Enthronement," he admits. I laugh so hard I have to hold on to him to keep upright. He laughs and kisses my head. "I'm glad you find it funny."

"Cedrick likes this part; you can just get it over with," I tell him. "It's on my left leg."

"Shh, you aren't supposed to tell me." Gavril chuckles. "But thanks for the pity."

Gavril makes kind of a show of it before he genuinely has some trouble finding it. I guess I am wearing a lot of skirts. I don't even really feel his skin on mine until he finds the garter. It makes me shudder. I am used to being touched on the leg. A lot of dances and lifts require that. I'm pretty sure Gavril and I have even done some of them, but I guess the unfamiliar situation and lack of tights I normally wear when I'm touched that way makes it quite different.

"Sage is in the back hiding," I tell Gavril when he finally pulls it off.

"My right or left." Gavril grins.

I think. "Stage left."

Gavril blinks. "What?"

"Your right." I giggle. Gavril nods and gives it his best.

I swear Cedrick used magic to help because it literally bounces off Sage's head, making him jump, as he'd been ignoring the situation, before it falls into his hands. He takes a moment to realize what it is.

I laugh.

Sage has never been so red. He drops it with disgust, making Zelda laugh even harder. I detail it all for Gavril, who loses it laughing.

I glance around for Damian, curious about how he's been passing the time. The night is getting late, and soon Gavril and I will finally get to slip away. I don't know if I'll see Damian again.

I spot him sitting towards the back, enjoying watching us. He's close to my father, who's a bit grumpy, sitting at a table. Damian smiles and gives me a small nod. I let out a sigh of relief. I'll see him tomorrow.

Then I notice the king going over to my parents. My mother is sitting with my father still, looking happy enough for both of them. I glance at Gavril, who's trying to get the grand duke off him. Gavril feels my gaze and looks at me. I nod at the table.

"Oh yes please," he says as he sees the interaction about to happen.

I smile, and we hook arms. I come up with an excuse. "Should have the mother/son, daddy/daughter dance before we go."

"Perfect," Gavril agrees.

As we walk over, the king actually tries to give my father a hug. Father flinches back, not only as my father tried to kill the king, but I slashed him across the chest just weeks before. Any hug would hurt. I try not to laugh at how my father lets out a funny kind of noise that clearly conveys "don't touch me".

"Aw, come on. We're co-dads now," King Aster complains. "Just one. I'm not a scary in-law, promise." He moves for the hug again.

"No, no, no." Father pulls back. Gavril chuckles as I hide my laugh behind my hand.

"Alright, we'll warm up to it," Aster claps Father hard on the back. My father's gasp of pain is oddly amusing to me. Gavril nudges me as I laugh, as he's fighting not to laugh himself.

"Aster, play nice," Queen Dalilly finally manages to say, hiding her own smile.

"I am. We're family. We can be nice. Right?" The king claps Father on the back again. "Good thing you stabbed where you did, or we'd not be here."

"Goodie." Father mutters sarcastically.

Mother is losing it laughing. She's laughing so hard she's not making a sound.

"I've been taking lung steroids for years for a lung condition. Likely how I pulled out. So let's be glad it was a lung this time," Aster goes on.

Father's face... his face! I hold on to Gavril to not fall over laughing. He looks incensed, confused, angry, and bewildered all at once. I think he's wondering what was his bad luck that the one time you went for a normally fail-proof plan like getting a man in the lungs would fail this one time. Mother is still laughing too hard to make a sound or help.

"Guess the Creator has his ways. And now we get to be friends. Though you have to keep your guard," Aster reminds him. "Just one hug?" He tries again.

"No thank you," Father says in a tight voice, pulling away like an angsty teenager shying away from an embarrassing parent's hug.

"Just one."

"No."

I laugh as Father tries his best to resist the king's hug. "Fine, then at least say hi to the rest of the family." Aster whistles, and Joy trots up to my surprise.

"Hi Joy." I beam at her.

She says "hello", but she must know better than to jump at us dressed nicely.

"Joy," the king says carefully. "This is Dad Two."

Joy tenses and declares my father a "squirrel".

"No, Dad Two." Aster tries.

Joy insists he's a squirrel, her hair standing up a little.

"No, this is Kascia's dad," Aster corrects.

"Oh, wow," Joy complains her "oh no" sound.

"Yes, so be nice, but also make sure he behaves." Aster nods.

Joy insists he's a squirrel. I laugh.

"How about Squirrel dad." Aster tries.

Joy tilts her head, thinking before she says okay.

"Good." Aster smiles.

"Squirrel?" Father frowns.

"She calls you 'squirrel' because you are trouble coming through the window," Gavril explains, drawing attention to us. "It's okay. Sage is 'Weirdo', and she likes him."

Joy repeats "Weirdo" and looks around.

"Be nice. I'm sure he's still in pain," Gavril tells her.

"But him you can love." The king points at my father.

Joy likes that and jumps up on my father, making him gasp.

"I'm in pain!" he declares, but Joy does not seem to care, panting happily before jumping down.

"Okay, that's enough." Mother finally gets herself together.

"We're getting ready to head out," Gavril says, "But we need to give you your dances." Gavril offers his mother a dance. She flushes in pleasure and takes it.

"And as you can't dance." With a look, I communicate to my father that he doesn't deserve to have this. "I was hoping you would." I smile at King Aster.

"I'd love to. However, I'm not quite up for that." He gives me a warm smile and leads my eyes elsewhere. I look over at Damian first, but then realize he's looking at my grandfather. Of course, I should have thought of him.

I beam at him, getting him to look at me. It hadn't even crossed his mind, apparently. "Would you?" I ask, holding out my hand to him.

The tender smile that crosses his face as he accepts my offer makes me beam in happiness. I'm sad to admit the annoyance that crosses my father's face only makes it better. Yes, deep down, I'd love my own father to be part of this special moment with me, but he did all he could to stop this. So, to me, it's satisfying to have a good substitute and one that annoys my father.

"I'm not very good," Grandfather warns me as we get into position.

"That's okay. It's not about the dance." I smile as I let him lead, but I'll admit, when he's unsure I take over leading once or twice. But I really don't care. I love dancing with him, anyway. I feel safe and loved here in the way I should with my father.

"I couldn't be prouder of you," Grandfather says to me as we come back into a closed hold. "You know how much I love you, don't you?"

I smile and nod. "I can't understand how you loved me so much when you hardly knew me or that I was real, but I do know that you do."

Grandfather smiles and kisses my forehead as the song ends. "I love you, grandpa," I say, and it feels wonderful to say, to call him that.

"And you sweet Esther." He smiles, cupping my chin.

I laugh and hug him. He had no idea that was Gavril's name for me. He saw the connection, though. The name means "hidden" as well as "queen of the night sky". And of course, her story is one I relate to. He saw that and picked the name for me. It's much better than cygnet because my parents met performing Swan Lake, anyway.

Gavril makes sure I don't mind when he asks his mother for a second dance. I expect to wait for him, but Cedrick is standing there, smirking at me and looking at Damian as if daring him not to dance with me.

Damian rolls his eyes at his brother, then smiles at me. He bows, then lifts his head and extends his hand toward me. "Would you do me the honor of gracing me with a dance?"

"I would be honored." I smile and take his hand.

Warm pride floods me as he straightens up and leads me onto the dance floor. I sigh with contentment as we slide into position. It is a truly special experience to share this moment with him, as I am absolutely certain that I would not have reached this point without him. It's a sweet dance.

When Damian returns me, the king says he got cleared for a brief dance, if I'm willing. I'm more than willing and accept it with a smile.

"I'm spoiled by all of you," I joke.

The king laughs.

We are quiet for a moment. "I'm really glad you're here."

"Don't worry, if your father doesn't shape up, you have me," he promises. We dance simply to avoid agitating the king's weakened state. "I'm just glad I can. Took good care, so I'd get through today."

"Thank you." I kiss his cheek. "For everything."

"You're welcome." He smiles and kisses my head. "I couldn't have asked for a better princess." I glow with pleasure. "Until you give me a granddaughter, anyway." I lose it laughing.

I make sure the king doesn't overdo it as we return to where we were. Gavril is kissing his mother's cheek before he helps her sit back down.

As I get settled, Damian comes over with a gentle smile and his hands clasped behind him. "Well, normally this is when I'd say I have a gift for you two, but you're already wearing them."

"What?" I smile and look down at my dress. Gavril chuckles and holds up his left hand. I take a second to catch on to what he means. My heart melts a little more. Damian made them.

Damian smiles as his eyes go to my wedding band, then back to my face. "Kascia, Gavril," he looks at him, "these rings are very special. They are made with metallic gold."

"Why is that special?" I ask. I know it's rare and expensive, but Damian makes wonderful works that are priceless all the time.

"Because outside of the dwarves and gargoyles, there is only one man to have been able to manipulate metals such as metallic gold, silver, and steel. The metals bear magical properties, and it is said that when two lovers wear emblems forged from the same piece of metallic gold, no matter where they are or how far they are apart, they will find each other again. The life ahead is full of love and joy but also trial, but no matter what may separate you physically or otherwise, remember you will always have one another to get you through it."

My mouth falls open a little. My eyes had sparkled in tears many times today, but nothing like this. I smile with a trembling lip and jump up and hug Damian tightly. There was no greater thing he could have given me.

Damian pulls me in and holds me tight. "You're welcome, my dearest lady."

"I can't even say how much it means." I hug him just a little more tightly before I pull back to look up at him.

Damian beams with glassy eyes. "I'm glad I could give them to you. Both of you." He smiles at Gavril. "Of course, I did need Cedrick's help to make them," he says, as his eyes land on Gavril's ring.

"We can't even begin to thank you." Gavril smiles and goes to shake Damian's hand. I give Gavril a look. Gavril represses a smile.

Damian smiles as he takes Gavril's hand only to use it to pull him into a hug. Gavril is caught off guard but laughs with a soft chuckle as he accepts it.

"Thank you," Gavril says. I can hear how much this all means to him in his voice, even if he won't admit it.

"You're welcome," Damian says meaningfully. After a moment, he pulls back and claps Gavril's shoulder. "You will do great things," he says with confidence.

Gavril smiles and meets eyes with Damian. I don't think anyone but me had ever said anything like that to him, and from someone like Damian, it meant the world. I think it's just Gavril's foolish male pride that stops him from saying any of that with more than in his eyes, though.

Damian smiles and nods a "you're welcome" as though he understands. I smile, holding in my reaction, taking Gavril's arm, which only makes him smile in greater happiness as he holds me more securely.

"Not sure you could have done anything else to give us a greater gift." Gavril looks back at Damian. "We could never thank you either—" Gavril stops to realize Cedrick had vanished. Gavril sighs in a kind of unsurprised yet annoyed way.

Damian half smiles. "Sorry. He's never really liked parties, unless there were children he could play with."

"I think he's more embarrassed to get a heartfelt thanks." Gavril chuckles a little. "But that means he knows."

"Indeed, it does." Damian nods with a smile. Then he pulls out his gold pocket watch and checks the time. "But it is getting late." His eyes lift to meet ours as a soft smile lingers on his lips. "Shouldn't you two be off soon?"

"One person you've got to see first." We turn to look over to see Cedrick has brought over a very embarrassed looking Sage.

I smile though and go over to hug him. He's surprised but accepts it with a happy smile.

"Ah, of course." Damian chuckles as he snaps his watch shut and slips it back into his pocket.

"What? He was being stupid. And if he could stand that long, he'd have been the best man."

"Was," Gavril insists with a chuckle and embraces Sage like a brother. "I hope you'll return it." Sage gives Gavril a warning look, which Gavril ignores.

"It was more than enough to be here," Sage says.

"You're free to move forward when you're ready. We'll both make sure." Cedar, who'd been hovering out of sight the whole day, steps in to join us. He wasn't as good at vanishing as Sage was but good enough. "Pleasure to finally meet you."

The look Sage gives him makes it hard for most of us not to laugh. He really is unhappy about being replaced. I can't see why. It let him be free to have what he came here to have, to finally marry like he'd fought for.

"Oh, don't be sour, Sage." Damian gives him a playful but meaningful smile. "No one likes a brooding vampire."

"I'm sour," Sage insists.

"We both won. Nothing wrong with that," Gavril chuckles.

"It's because he isn't *supposed* to get what he wants." Damian smiles as he folds his arms.

"I didn't say that," Sage defends, taking a seat. Zelda leans on the table instead, looking exasperated.

Damian chuckles. "You didn't have to. Your expression says it all. Though that gold may not be helping."

"Gold?" Sage frowns.

"Yes, gold, as in the color you are wearing. It's bright and happy, and you're just sad," Damian says, amused, then looks at Cedrick. "Aleph would have complaints."

Cedrick chuckles. "He would. And I'd agree with him. It might be a frightening change, but if this day should teach us anything, it's that it's worth it." Cedrick looks up at the stunningly decorated ballroom, exactly like the sketch the planner made, before looking down at Sage with a meaningful, tender look Sage can't meet. Cedrick is good at that.

"But I believe you have a moment to slip away." Cedrick turns to Gavril and me.

Gavril smiles almost shyly, and his neck may have gotten a bit red, but I ignore it, smiling as I wish everyone farewell and thank them for the most perfect day. I still can hardly believe it's real, and it's only going to get better. It was worth the wait.

# Chapter 27

We get to lie in the next morning, and I'm far too comfortable to move. My sleep problems clearly are on hold.

Having Gavril so close helps. It makes sense, as having Joy sleep in my bed had helped too. I soak in his gentle breathing that settles something inside of me, bringing a feeling of safety in sleep I'd never known before.

I sigh contentedly as I settle into his shoulder.

His sleepy grunt fills my ear, making me smile as I feel him slowly wake up. I listen to the deep sigh rumble in his chest as he stirs awake and looks down at me, running his free hand through my hair.

"I'm still always pleasantly surprised to find you weren't just a dream," he says conversationally, a hint of sleep making his voice a bit deeper than normal.

I beam, holding in the giggle. "I never want to step out of the dream." I nuzzle him again, making Gavril smile and hold me tighter. "Or let it end."

"One more day, then I'm all yours," Gavril reminds me, kissing me deeply.

"You already are," I purr back and wrap my arms around him as I turn my body fully to his and kiss him back, already feeling drawn to him like a magnet.

"You're being crowned today," he reminds me between kisses but doesn't pull back.

"And who thought that was a good idea?" I complain through my open-mouthed kisses as I wrap myself ever closer to him. He's so firm, yet soft, in my grip.

"Every political expert we've got," Gavril replies as his lips move from mine to my jaw to just below my ear to my neck.

"Experts? Don't think so." I half giggle, half purr.

We might have been stuck there a long time if there wasn't a knock on the door. I groan in frustration, not wanting to be interrupted.

"You'll want lunch before you get ready," Vivian's voice reminds us.

"She's right. I could eat a horse." Gavril teases me by pretending to eat my neck, making me laugh.

"I am not a horse."

"Much better than a horse." Gavril grins and wraps his arms around my waist.

"Kascia! I know it's hard but come on." Vivian isn't letting up.

"I wish I had something to throw." Gavril sighs sadly. "However, they're right. We can get this over with, then it's just us the whole week," he teases, kissing my throat before pulling away.

"Where did you get that much self-control?" I complain with a longing moan. I couldn't have pulled away so easily.

"Years having to put up with parents' wishes and respecting you no matter how tempting you were." Gavril grins and kisses me deeply before getting up to dress.

I sigh and do the same. It takes me a moment to recall which dresser is mine, but Gavril goes right to his as it has always been his, letting me cheat.

Once presentable enough, I go to the door Vivian knocked on that leads to what would technically be my room, but it is more like my dressing chamber. My four maids beam at me as I step in.

They had brought up a mix of breakfast and lunch foods as it's about lunchtime now, and they didn't know what I'd be in the mood for having only just woken up.

It does take me a bit to get myself to eat as they get me ready.

Once I finish eating, I look around. I'd not taken the time to admire the rooms yet. Damian had done a brilliant job. The colors of the rooms are perfect, and the mix of the royal colors are my favorite. The dressing room that was supposed to be the bedroom is calming and perfect.

I smile, unable to help myself, and rush into the main suite to take a look. It's just as perfect. Welcoming, yet as hopeful and fresh as the sea itself. The white, Purerah yellow and blue curtains flutter in the breeze of the open window.

The happiness bubbles up into a smile, content with the room I'd use to welcome many guests as princess. It's perfect with the right decorations. There is a mix of theater memorabilia, both mine and from other shows I love, beautiful views of the sea, ballet themes: all the things I adore perfectly displayed.

The last room I check is my studio and study blend. Though, the dressing room could also be used as study as it has a work desk in there as well. But this room I have great plans for.

I gasp in surprise and delight.

They transformed the room. There are still bookshelves and the like, but mirrors now run along one long wall for dance and dance barres on either side both in front of the mirror and on the other side.

The floor is a lovely wood with the springiness for dance. It's a beautiful soft red brown wood color that matches the room. The desk rolls across the floor as smooth as anything in the center. It has the same design as the king's desk with the blue stone and stunning blue and gold wood.

But the real spectacular view is the oval, stained glass skylight Damian had added. It is a depiction of a Purerahian rose with the dolphin and shark swimming nearby and a stunning night sky behind it. It takes my breath away. I love it.

I giggle and twirl in the dim colored lights on the floor. It will be so perfect when I use it in the late mornings and afternoons. I wonder if it would catch the moonlight too. It is perfect.

I then recall the time and skip back into the changing room. My maids set right to work. Bella comes in to help as well. They work on the finishing touches as Damian arrives.

"Good morning, ladies." Damian bows his head to all of us.

"Can we call it morning?" Ro jokes.

Damian chuckles warmly. "I suppose not, so good afternoon then."

"I'm sure you've been busy." I smile at him. He was probably working hard on whatever he has to do before leaving, though perhaps he doesn't have much to do now.

"I had one last thing to see to, but it's all finished now." Damian smiles back. "How are you feeling?"

I take a deep breath. "Bit nervous, I suppose." The wedding was fun. This is business. I officially will be taking the oath that will make me a legal Potentate, though yesterday had effectively made me a member of the royal family.

"You'll do wonderfully," he assures with a confident smile.

"I suppose I don't have to do much. Just say yes." I smile as they wrap yet another petticoat around me. There are a lot.

He chuckles. "Indeed. But I meant more than just today."

"I'm not sure what you mean," I say as I eye what looks like the next layer.

He sighs and gives me a gentle smile. "You're really going to make me explain it?"

I smile a little. "You mean it's over?" He means he's about to leave, doesn't he?

"I mean it has just begun, and you, my dear," he says, putting his fingers gently under my chin, "are going to make an excellent princess." He smiles proudly.

I smile back. "Thanks to you." I don't see all my maids roll their eyes.

"Perhaps a little," Damian admits with a bit of a smile. "But you did the real work." His smile grows a little with pride. His eyes appear glossy before he closes them and shakes it off. He then draws in a breath and lets out a sigh. "But we can save the mushy stuff for later. We should focus on getting you ready."

I nod. "Right."

And there are quite a few layers to go. The final part of the skirt is amazing: dozens of gold-colored layers that are long on the inside and shorter on the outside, making them look almost like a rose. Then another layer goes over the top of the skirt, embroidered with gold and a stunning Purerahian blue. This part also goes over my top, clipping in the middle but opening up around my chest with stunning designs along the edges, making a closed-then-open look.

The high collar also adds some amazing, bejeweled beading work and gold leafing that turns into a long cape that's also blue and embroidered with stunning golden patterns. Flur then puts my hair up into a splendid bun with golden roses pinned into it. They'll put the official tiara on during the ceremony, so Flur is careful to make sure my hair will shape it perfectly.

Once they finish, I turn to the mirror. I look like a princess even without the tiara. I look ready to be queen with how powerful I look. A smile appears on my face.

"As always, you're all too perfect at this," I praise, giving them a turn. This dress also has the same tricks to have it ready to dance in after as a celebration ball is, of course, scheduled, which will be open to more people than the wedding.

"You think of everything," I laugh. Damian smiles and gives me a slight bow in thanks.

"He does." Bella sighs. "Sorry, it's going to take me a while to catch up to him."

"No, you did quite well," Damian says. "Don't sell yourself short. This is as much your creation as mine. She designed the cape as well as giving me some helpful tips," he adds to me.

"Then you'll have no trouble with this," I assure her.

"I hope so." Bella sighs and adjusts how my cape flows down my back just a little. "As long as I'm half as good at my job as you're going to be."

A knot forms at the center of my chest. "I hope so too." I smile.

I won for a reason. Damian didn't help me pass the final test. He even suggested not to back out, or at least, he had in the past. That last win was me, and I need to remember it. Damian helped me become who I needed to be. But I am the one who became her.

Damian smiles at the pair of us, then turns to Bella.

"Here." He takes his leather-bound notebook from his inside jacket pocket and presents it to her. "My notebook, as promised." He smiles. "There are a few pages left, if you wish to add to it."

Bella accepts it, barely holding in her excitement. She's biting her lower lip to keep her emotions in as she accepts it and holds it to her chest. A little excited squeak slips out anyway.

"Congratulations," I chuckle. Apparently, she thinks that is a big deal.

Damian smiles and nods. "Indeed. She's all yours now. Take care of her," he says to Bella with a caring earnest in his voice.

Bella smiles and nods, still hugging the book. "I promise," she assures him with the same sincere air.

"Thank you." Damian beams then turns to me. "Now then." He touches my arm and turns me to the mirror. "Tell me, what do you see?"

I look into the mirror and can't help but smile. The first thing I see is how many people I have supporting me, but that's not what he's talking about. I look at myself, at the stunning work they did, like I normally do. But then I meet my own eyes. I see what I've been blind to for so long that Damian and my maids weren't.

"A true princess," I reply.

Damian beams, knowing I am not just saying that. I knew. "Then you're ready."

I nod. "I'm ready." I have what I need. It's just time to set to work. "Shall we?" I turn to Damian.

He nods and offers his arm. I accept it, and he escorts me out.

Gavril is just stepping into the hall with Joy on a lead. She's wearing a cute little royal cape in the royal colors. She yips, happy to see me. I laugh.

"Stunning," Gavril praises and bows his head to Damian. "Ready?" he asks him.

"She is, indeed, Your Highness," Damian says, offering to let Gavril take my arm.

"She is, are you?" Gavril asks him but takes my arm. "Want the dog?" he jokes.

Joy barks happily, tail wagging. There's something in Gavril's eyes. I guess he knows it must be hard for Damian to go.

Damian chuckles. "Sure, I can handle a troublesome husky."

"She likes you. She'll be nice." Gavril smiles and hands over the leash.

"I'm going to miss the suits he makes you." I find this suit fits Gavril well.

Gavril glances around, but only Bella and Damian are there, so he quietly says, "It's just what happens when they actually tailor the suits." I laugh.

Damian chuckles too. "Perhaps Bella can do better."

"If only that were the biggest problem." Gavril rolls his eyes. I'm sure budget is the issue.

"Don't worry, I taught her how to haggle a price." Damian smiles.

Gavril chuckles. "We'll see on that." He smiles at Bella.

"Perhaps so. But come along, or they'll start the coronation without us," Damian teases.

"Can't without her," Gavril jokes, pointing at me, but we start making our way to the throne room.

"Could try," Bella says.

"Well, then they have no one to crown. Unless they want to crown Joy." Gavril looks at her. Joy wags her tail and makes her "yeah" sound.

Damian chuckles. "You think you would be a good princess?"

Joy tilts her head with a concerned sound. I laugh. I guess I'm not the only one who isn't sure.

"Isn't she a princess dog?" Bella asks. Gavril laughs hard.

"Now there's a thought." Damian chuckles.

"So... that's a no," Bella guesses.

"That's a no," I agree.

Joy pants happily. "She's happy hunting you-know-whats." Gavril smiles.

"What?" Bella frowns.

"S-q-u-i-r-r-e-l-s'es," Damian says.

"Oh." Bella nods. "And princess dogs don't do that?"

"Why you lost," Gavril teases. The glare Bella gives him makes me laugh.

"If you ask Lady Keva, no they don't. But if you ask Cedrick, that may be a different story." Damian smiles.

Bella smirks. "I'm sure he does."

"It's Cedrick, of course he does." Damian grins.

Gavril smiles his agreement, but we're getting close to the throne room now.

"Remember what we practiced?" Gavril asks me.

Nervously, I swallow but nod. I remember. I am ready. This is it.

"Hey, you got this," Gavril assures me, tilting my chin up to meet his eyes. "Today is easy. We're just making it official."

Nodding in agreement, I hide a swallow. "I just want it over. I have more important things to do." With a small smile, I grip him tightly.

Gavril chuckles. "Let's just get you officially blessed and crowned, shall we?"

"Let's."

Gavril beams at my playful tone. He looks at Damian. "Feel free to pass Joy off to whichever servant or other noble you want to pass her off to."

I don't see Damian's reaction though, as Gavril leads me to the right and up the curving flight of stairs until we reach a golden door. He takes a deep breath and looks at me. "Are you ready?"

My head bobs a quick yes. "As I'm going to be. You?"

Gavril smiles and nods. "I'm ready." He holds his arm out, palm down and at an angle level to the floor. I smile and put my hand on his arm, matching.

"You learned quick," he jokes.

"Some things a princess just knows." I beam.

Gavril returns it with the brightest smile I've seen yet. He kisses my lips tenderly, which I return for the brief moment. "You're more than ready."

It's a simple yet elegant entrance. There's elegant ceremonial music playing that directs the entire event. It's odd how I'd performed a version of this for plays dozens of times, but this is different.

For one, the "stage" was far grander. All my hopes to help my people are about to become real, in a far better way than I ever dreamed.

The doors open, and Gavril and I step out. I follow Gavril's lead in pivoting to the left and descending down the steps. On the opposite side, the queen and king mirror us. I smile at them.

The queen bows her head properly, tiara glittering in the light. The king gives me a cheeky wink. I think he's glad his wife didn't see it. I look out over the many people there.

The throne room transformed into a presentation room. The polished wooden surfaces were made more elegant with Purerahian blue and yellow banners and signs. The light from the grand dome shines golden light across the room with the occasional golden shaft.

The guests are much the same as yesterday, except that there are a few more court officials than the ones who were invited to the wedding. They are scattered throughout the court seating, and the additional seating placed on the throne room floor. The room is filled with the shimmer and sparkle of fine gowns and suits.

Though the room is crowded, it doesn't feel stuffy. To me at least, it feels open, airy, and bright. Perhaps it's the delight and smiles on most every face. The hope that this event brings to court and citizen alike.

I spot Fabian frantically trying to take notes. He's also hiding a smirk and keeps glancing at Mr. Coppiger, who has Joy on his arm as he tries to take notes. Joy is not making it easy. She tugs at her lead as if to get to us, making it harder for the reporter to hold pen and pad steady. I try not to laugh. She isn't being too crazy, but keeps moving, tail wagging, to see Gavril and I, even if she doesn't know what's happening. Adam is taking impressions from the back with the rest of the press team.

Alsmeria and most of my friends from the troupe are sitting together. I notice Isla has someone who looks like a male version of Rose sitting beside her. I smile and grip Gavril's hand with mine.

We finally meet the king and queen in front of the four thrones that sit there now. Gavril leads me to his father's right side, where I kneel for the oath. The happiness in the room mounts.

Next to the king is the keeper, who keeps and records all official history, and they both stand over me. The king offers his hand to hoist me up so I can accept the two coronation objects: the first, a special sphere with the Potentate bear and shield crest on it. I hold that in my left hand, cupping it delicately. It weighs more than I thought it would, even made of gold as it is. I guess it is heavy like the weight of this new responsibility. The second is a golden scepter with Purerah's emblem with our signature blue jewel cradled by four pearls at the top, which I take in my right hand with my palm facing down as I hold it.

My heart races like a happy, nervous skip in my chest, but I am prepared for this. I have a hard time not beaming through the whole thing, and my smile keeps slipping out.

As the king begins, the keeper stands beside him, ensuring that all is done properly. "Princess Kascia." The king's voice is stronger than it has been.

"Will you solemnly promise and swear to uphold the oath of a Potentate as a princess of Purerah and all the promises and oaths associated with it?"

I nod once. "I solemnly promise so to do."

The king gives me a warm, loving, comforting smile. "Will you so swear to upload justice as well as the laws and traditions of Purerah as set by the Potentate law and code given by the Creator in all your governing?"

I smile one more time. "I solemnly promise so to do."

"Then by the authority of the Creator given to me to stand in His stead, I hereby name you crown princess of Purerah."

The excitement of the silent crowd is palpable, as I curtsy low, and the keeper takes the scepter so I can cup the seal in both hands to make sure I keep it steady as I lower myself down and offer the ball in both hands to the king. He takes it from me, handing it to the keeper before turning to his right where the queen is holding the cushion with the princess's tiara on it. The king picks up the tiara, and I bow my head, lowering myself slightly in respect, as well as making it easier for him to put the tiara onto my head.

I bite my lips to hold in the smile, closing my eyes as I feel the king crown me.

"And I accept you as my heir and princess," the king says, then offers me his hand to help me stand.

I'm overwhelmed with a new feeling bubbling up from my stomach and blossoming in my chest, a power, humbling and ennobling at once as tears make my eyes shine as I accept the king's offered hand. My smile is so wide it might be the biggest smile I've ever worn. The king beams at me, then offers my hand back to Gavril, who takes it. I beam at him, and Gavril beams back.

I turn to face the delighted crowd like we're supposed to, but before I can, Gavril catches my cheek and kisses me, getting an approving whoop from the onlookers before we turn to face the crowd.

"May I present to you," the king calls in the loudest voice he can, "Your crown prince and princess, the true heirs of Purerah, for your approval..."

The king goes to go on but stops at the look someone in the crowd gives him. He stops dead and bows, stepping back. The whole room goes silence in surprise.

I frown. This was not in the rehearsal. I glance at Gavril, noticing his slightly lifted brows in surprise before we look to see where the king had been looking and freeze.

Cedrick is handsome and charming, annoyingly so sometimes, but I'd never seen him look quite like this. I'd never seen a suit like that on him before. The main thing that catches my eye is the fiery cape he wears, the edges of which shine with a dazzling light as if the thread itself were made of crystals and genuine gold. It hangs off him beautifully as he strides forward with a power I'd rarely felt before. If no one knew who he was before, they couldn't mistake him now. Cedrick Custod, The Phoenix, Merlin of the Creator.

He steps up with a youthful bouncing skip and bows to the king.

Fear locks my lips. What is Cedrick up to?

Normally, I'd be worried he's about to do something stupid, but not now. The change of demeanor from him was undeniable. There's a power and grace and... love about him that makes me certain he has nothing in mind but to help and care for us. I'd never felt that so strongly before. Gavril squeezes my hand comfortingly. But I'm not afraid, just... speechless.

"Not to usurp you, Your Majesty," Cedrick says to the king. "But please, allow me to present them in my authority."

Aster would not say no to that. He nods to Cedrick and steps back. I lift a hand to my chest to handle the rush of feelings that rise up inside me. What is he about to do? The wonder and tension I feel is amplified by the nervous anticipation from the crowd.

"May I present for your approval," Cedrick's voice is so much more powerful, beautiful, comforting than it ever has been before, like the rush of the sea itself: powerful, soothing, yet too strong, it is frightening, "your future sovereigns, Prince Gavril the Anointed," I feel Gavril tense at the unique title, "and Princess Kascia the Valiant."

I squeeze Gavril's hands. I think I just found out what it's like to hear and know you're part of a promise he's making. What do these titles mean?

"Do you so accept them?" I swear Cedrick's declaration is half a dare for the people to reject us.

I'm overwhelmed with humility, feeling honored and humbled by the roaring reception we receive. Looking at Gavril, I blink back tears and see him give me a watery smile. I see in his eyes the same quiet humility, but he also has a twinkle of determination in his eyes. He will not let them down.

We turn back to our people, and without needing to be directed, bow to them. Well, I curtsy as a bow in this skirt wouldn't get far. Cedrick smiles and takes my free hand, kissing it. "Well done, his true princess."

I open my mouth, unsure what I'm going to say: thank you? You're welcome? The endless outpour of power and joy overflowing in my chest has no words. But Cedrick gives me a slight smirk over my hand and vanishes in a flare of fire.

I start in surprise and the crowd cries out. I back into Gavril who takes my arms as if to protect me, but there's nothing to fear. Just a feather left on the ground where he'd stood. I'm too overwhelmed to react at first, just staring at the fading flame.

"Again." The queen sighs tiredly, too quiet for anyone but us on the throne platform to hear. The king and keeper chuckle, though.

"People of Purerah," the keeper addresses them to break the silent moment. "You have yourselves, your new princess." He waves a hand to invite us to bow to the crowd again as they shake themselves from the moment and applaud.

It helps us get back to the moment, and Gavril and I bow once again to the crowd before the music plays once more, marking the end of the ceremony.

The crowd erupts into cheers, many getting onto their feet to applaud and express their support.

Staff escort the guests from the throne room to the ballroom, as Gavril and I stand there digesting what just happened.

Gavril smiles at me and kisses me. I hear an impressionor snap. "You made it." He smiles, stroking my cheek with his thumb.

I smile. "We did." But what does all that mean?

Once the throne room is clear, my staff does their work on my skirts to prepare it for the party. Though admittedly, we're all quiet as we think over what just happened.

The party is full of people talking about what happened. The Merlin's appearance caused quite the stir, but we try to ignore that best we can for the moment.

Per tradition, we start with a dance between Gavril and I after which I dance with the king. Before long, it is time for the formal meet-and-greets... again. How many more of these do we have to do?

Gavril can see the exhaustion in my eyes because he leans over and whispers, "Last one for a while. It's just so they can boast that they spoke to the princess as a princess."

"Stupid," I mutter as the line begins.

"We can do whatever we want after," Gavril assures me.

"Anything?" I give him a seductive eye.

"Not in public."

I hide my snort as the line starts.

I'll confess, it's hard to focus on the people I'd spoken to already recently in similar line ups. I find myself watching in slight envy as my maids, dressed in stunning gowns that I'm sure Damian made due to their gorgeous designs in silver and blue, enjoy the dance floor and party behind those meeting me.

There are a few new people this time. Many of them nobility, such as the high king, who we had to invite for fear of offending him. Most of them are not that engaging, different officials who didn't come to say hello at the wedding. However, one in particular grabs my attention. The Head Custod, Sir Cedre.

I think I see how he looks like Cedrick, only because I'm looking. It has been more generations than I can count between Cedrick and Sir Cedre, but his eyes are like Cedrick's but not as vivid electric blue, more of an aquamarine color, and his hair might be the same texture, but it's more of a dark brown than Cedrick's black.

"Honor to finally meet you." Sir Cedre kisses my hand. "I did not give you my felicitations yesterday as I thought I'd let the family enjoy the wedding more. Truly beautiful ceremonies."

"Thank you." It's odd not to be afraid of him when most of my life, my father has made me nervous about the head custod.

"Only disappointment is all my ignored invitations," Sir Cedre teases me.

I turn pink. "To be completely honest, Sir, my father hid them from me. Trust me, if I'd seen them, I'd have accepted it all in a heartbeat."

"Ah! That explains it." He chuckles warmly. "It turned out for the best, however. How else would he have ever met you?" Sir. Cedre smiles at Gavril. "Lucky man stole her from me."

"With pride." Gavril smiles back.

Sir. Cedre laughs. He's not nearly as formal as I thought he'd be. Of course, my father's description of him is vastly different. He is much more like Cedrick than not.

"Not that you seem without talent as I watched you dance. And a little birdy told me your voice isn't a disappointment either." Sir. Cedre smirks.

Gavril gives me a look as the head custod moves on.

"I didn't tell him," I insist, offended. "I just met him too."

Gavril is frowning a bit, but our next person greets us too soon to discuss it further.

But we finally get to disperse the reception line after over an hour, and are able to enjoy the party freely. I am more than happy to use it to forget that real life is coming up again, fast. The real work will begin soon, and even more on my heart is that soon Damian will leave. I know he'd not leave without saying goodbye, but part of me fears it with how Cedrick just vanished.

Just as I think this, someone appears at my side. "Might I bother the new princess for a moment?" he asks, tilting his head toward me.

I beam at him and nod. My heart still aches a little, though. I know it's goodbye.

Gavril smiles a bit and kisses my head. "It'll be okay," he assures me before letting me turn to him.

Damian smiles warmly. "It is near my time. But I wonder if I could trouble you for one last dance." He extends his hand toward me.

I smile and take it. "I'd love that," I admit.

Damian beams, glassy eyed, as he leads me to the dance floor and gives a nod to the orchestra conductor. He then guides me into position as the orchestra starts up.

I have to bite my lip to stop myself from tearing up, and even then, I think a few got in anyway. I know that song. It is the same one he'd helped me prepare for the talent show when he was first assigned to me. It feels so long ago. Simultaneously, my heart is warmed and hurt by it. I smile through my tears, though. Damian is too good at this. He's too good at everything.

"I thought we'd end where we began." He smiles as he leads me into a turn.

"I agree," I say as I turn back into him. "It's perfect." I swallow the emotion. So happy yet sad simultaneously. It is like losing my father, but worse because somehow Damian's come to be far more of my father than my birth father ever was.

He nods and swallows. I think he's holding back tears. "Perfect," he agrees, as he brings me back into hold. "I'm so proud of you, of how far you've come, Kascia. I really couldn't be happier for you."

I manage a smile. "Thank you. That means more than..." My throat catches. "Anything." I take a deep breath to hold in the rush of emotion.

Damian gives me a warm, sad smile. "And here I thought coming here with Cedrick would be boring," he jokes.

I laugh through my borderline tears. "Well, guess you're wrong sometimes."

He smiles with a half shrug. "That happens now and again." He smiles, then twirls me.

I enjoy the movement, enjoying and trying to treasure and memorize how it feels, so I can remember whenever I really want to feel the moment again. Damian is an excellent dancer, and dancing with him is different than others. Everyone is different as a dance partner. And though Gavril is my favorite, Damian is a very close second. I'm going to miss feeling it. His smile, his advice, his work, that little smile he gives as he admires his work on me. I'm going to deeply miss him.

Damian is quiet for the remainder of the dance, letting me live in the moment as he guides me around the dance floor. As the song comes to an end, Damian slows with it, then drops hold and just looks into my face, his eyes riddled with a warm sadness. Then he pulls me in and hugs me.

I hug him tightly, trying to blink back tears. "Thank you," I manage to get out.

He takes in a slow, careful breath and returns the pressure. "Any time," he says with a smile in his voice, "My Lady."

I bite my lips to try to retain the tears, but I can't stop them now. "Will I ever see you again?" I ask.

"One day. One day, you will," he promises, then pulls back, his hands on my arms. There are tears on his face. "And I told myself I wouldn't cry." He chuckles and wipes away a tear with his thumb.

Despite my tears, I still manage to smile. "I couldn't even dare to try." I hope otherwise, but it really feels like saying goodbye to my true father. Damian is the one person who has truly taken care of me like that, protected me, and provided for my needs. I hoped it wouldn't feel this awful. But it does.

He smiles, then takes my hand. "Come on. I have one last thing for you." I smile and nod back, letting him lead me wherever he wanted.

He leads me back to Gavril, then collects something off one of the tables, then turns to Gavril with a smile. "Is there somewhere private where I can say goodbye?"

Gavril nods and leads us into the same room where he'd told us about the prophecy. The room seems so much lighter now as Gavril turns on the lights.

Damian thanks him, then sighs deeply and turns to me, fiddling with the small thin box in his hands. "I made this for you. Sort of a wedding and coronation present," he says and offers me the box.

I blink and accept it, tilting my head in curiosity. I delicately open the box and gasp.

It's a stunning golden dagger. It's beautiful with detailing in the hilt and even in the blade. I see the Custod mark done into the blade and recognize the unique traits that make this a Custod dagger. I take a deep breath and look up at Damian, unsure of what to say. Finally, it comes out. "But... I never was a Custod."

"But you are." Damian smiles. "I saw it in the way you defended Lilly, not only from the rebels, but from those who wanted to break her spirit. I saw it every day in the way you treated and loved your maids. And it was clear in your desire to protect your people, to do what is right, no matter the cost. You may not have the magic of a Custod, but you have their spirit, their passion, and their fire." His smile grows warmly as his eyes sparkle. "I saw it in you every day. You're like my own daughter, Kascia, and I want you to remember that." He swallows back the emotion in his voice and looks at the dagger again. "It is a tradition that once a young Custod has passed their Test that they are presented with a special dagger in honor of their oath." He looks up and meets my eyes. "You have passed your Test, Kascia. And while you are a Potentate now in name, blood, and duty, I hope you remember the Custod at heart."

I can't stop the tears rolling down my cheeks, most of all when he says my name. In an attempt to control my reactions, I bite my lips to try to hold it in. I finally get my head enough to put the box down, so I can embrace Damian. I don't want to say goodbye.

"Thank you." It means more to me than anything.

"You're quite welcome." Damian takes in a sharp breath as tears leak from his eyes and he holds me tight. "I love you, Kascia, so much. Someday, I will see you again."

"I love you, Damian." The tears won't stop now. "Thank you for..." I swallow the emotions, "being the father I needed."

He beams as tears still come. He doesn't even bother wiping them away. "It was my pleasure, My Princess, My Lady." He sniffles a little. "It has been an honor to serve you."

"Thank you." I try to wipe tears. "I love you."

"I love you too." He smiles, then pulls back and uses his handkerchief to wipe his tears away and offers me a clean one.

I smile a little and take it and do my best to dry my face. "I'll miss you." I don't know what else there is left to say.

"As I will you, my dear lady." He smiles, then makes his face a little more serious. "Now, I have a mission for you," he says to me while indicating to the dagger.

I smile. "What would you have me do?" I ask, sniffling a little.

"Keep an eye on him for me." Damian nods to Gavril, grinning a little. "I hear he's a tricky one."

I smile and laugh through the tears. "I'll do my best," I promise.

"That's what I like to hear." He claps my hand, then takes a breath and sighs as he brings his hand up and rests it against my cheek.

I swallow to stop the fresh tears. "Well..." It's so hard to say. "I guess this is it, then." As I breathe in deeply, I brace myself. "I love you. I won't forget anything you did for me. Thank you." I hug myself to keep myself together.

He smiles. "You're quite welcome. I..." He takes a breath to steady himself. "I have loved every moment. I wish it could have lasted longer, but my time has reached its end, and I have done all that I can for you. I am really going to miss you, but you will work wonders. I know it." He beams proudly and rubs my cheek with his thumb. "Goodbye, Kascia."

"Goodbye, Damian." I bite my lip to hold in tears again. Although I'll miss him a lot, I'm worried about becoming annoying by repeating myself. "I-I'll see you." It didn't have to feel so final, right? I'd see him; I just... will never know for sure when.

Warm tears sparkle in Damian's deep green eyes as he smiles back. "Yes, you will." He finally pulls back his hand and looks past me to Gavril. "Goodbye, Gavril."

Gavril smiles and bows to him. "Goodbye, Damian. Thank you. And don't worry. I'll take care of her for you," he promises.

I swallow hard, as that means more to me. It was the promise Gavril should have made to my father, but he didn't care. I hug myself tighter.

I love these two men so much it overwhelms me. How did I ever get so lucky?

"I'll hold you to that." Damian smiles, then sighs and reaches back and picks something up. "Can't forget this." He smiles, making sure I see he has the scrapbook I made for him in hand.

I smile and nod. I'd made sure to update it as best I could. Though part of me wonders how he'll ever keep it as he jumps in time, but I'm sure he will.

Damian takes another deep breath, then nods to himself. "Until next time, night angel," he says, and with his head bowed, bows deeply, showing me respect as a princess.

I smile through the almost blinding tears and bow my head back. "Until then." I wish I had a sweet name for him, but I don't.

He lifts his head and smiles at me for the last time. His eyes never look away from mine as darkness gathers around him. It quickly envelops him. And just like that, he's gone.

"Goodbye." I whisper, then bite my lips to stop myself from sobbing.

I hear Gavril sigh and come over to me. He hugs me tight. "Shh, it's okay. We're alone," he promises. "We have time. It's okay. I'm sorry. I know..." He swallows hard. "It's okay. Take your time."

I didn't expect that. I don't know why, but I didn't expect Gavril to just... invite me to go ahead and cry. But it helps so much. I feel so much better as I take even just a few minutes to cry it out. I'm surprised it doesn't take longer, but perhaps it's because I know it's silly. He's like his brother. They're invisible but really always there if needed. So, it isn't really forever, even though it feels like it. I smile a bit, picturing Cedrick doing the same for Damian right now. I'm glad they have each other.

Gavril holds me tightly, letting me do as I need until I finally get control over myself. I nod as I pull away from his chest. "I'm alright," I say, my voice a bit thick.

Gavril offers me his handkerchief to let me wipe away the tears and clear my nose. "Um... to me, your makeup looks fine, but will other girls notice and ask?" Gavril frowns, watching me. "And more importantly, do you care?"

I shake my head. "I'm fine." I take a few deep breaths. "I'm really going to miss him."

Gavril offers a sad smile. "Me too, but you'll always have this." He smiles and picks up the blade and offers it to me. "He included a leg sheath. I can help you get it on."

That is the perfect way to get a real laugh out of me. Gavril smiles and helps me do just that, so I can have it with me. He then kisses my head and hugs me tightly one more time.

"You're better at this than you think," he says. "You're more ready for whatever is next than me."

"I guess we'll find out." I swallow and take a last deep breath. "Let's go back." I take Gavril's hand. "I could do with a few dances."

# Chapter 28

Gavril had wisely used his one week of mourning that was denied him when he thought his father was killed to make sure no one bothers us for our honeymoon. Sure, we can't afford to go anywhere, but that excuse and our own sneaky ways allow us the freedom to do as we wish, anyway.

The extra space with our adjoined suites helps with that as well. We even sneak out to the same spot by the river where Jake and I used to meet. I can't explain it even to myself, but I want nothing more than to share those intimate moments with Gavril there, letting ourselves cross the line Jake and I never dared. I'm more grateful than ever we didn't, as doing this with a man who truly loves me is a million times better. It is like erasing the heartache those former moments caused.

The whole week is blissful, magical. We'd never been closer in any sense of the word. We dance, we snuggle, and explore all these new feelings and experiences. We talk and laugh a lot. I've never been happier or felt safer or closer to anyone. Even when I start to form a love-hate relationship with how he likes to fiddle with my feet using his own when we snuggle at night or when I get quiet, and he worries I am nervous to say something. It is cute on the one hand but annoying on the other.

And alright, there are other things that annoy me. If he scrunches up his shirt and tosses it aside like it is a ball again, I am going to pick it up and throw it at him. But those little things really don't seem to matter when it normally ends with us teasing and snuggling all night away.

We've done a pretty good job of finding all the unique places to slip away, even sneaking into my old room and a safe room just for the pleasure of being outside our rooms, and it is fun knowing we ducked the staff and guards.

My sleep disorder seems to have vanished. I'd forgotten my sleep tea the first few nights but slept better than I ever had, so I don't even bother anymore. Gavril's soft breath with the sound of the ocean outside, his warmth and security beside me as we sleep in each other's arms or snuggled is the real cure I needed.

Gavril never passes up a chance to pamper me, treating me better than a queen. I try to do the same back, but he is so eager to treat me, it is difficult. And I find he truly finds real joy in spoiling me. I'm not sure I understand it, but he finds genuine joy in how I relax at his touch or how I feel so adored in his affections, no matter what we are doing.

How could I have ever wanted someone else when this man was ready to love me with all my flaws and quirks better than anyone else in the world? I later feel guilty, realizing that Gavril had done such a good job, not once in that week does it cross my mind how much I miss Damian.

All in all, it results in a lot of complaining and throwing of pillows at poor Godwin when the magical week finally draws to a close, and we're back at our royal duties.

My first day as a working member of the royal family begins. It turns out to be a rather bittersweet day. As they had informed us, the staff brings up breakfast, ready for us once we were dressed for the day. I step into my section of the washroom and the bedroom/changing room to let my maids get me ready for the first time since the coronation.

"You sure you're ready for today?" Flur asks anxiously, reminding me of my mother.

"I'll be fine. I've had this long to get ready. I'm a prophesied princess, remember?" That was the line Gavril had inspired me to use. Anytime I felt unsure or anxious about my ability, I'd remind myself of that.

The door opens, and Bella walks in. Suddenly, my heart sinks to my toes. I half expected Damian like it used to be. But he'd never walk in like that again. I fight not to let it ruin my mood. I like having Bella. It's not against her. I just will miss Damian sorely.

"Good morning," Bella wishes us. "We have the rundown of the day. We were lucky we didn't have to change much. You have the security briefing over breakfast; Godwin and I coordinated what briefings you both should attend in the morning. Then after breakfast, we'll get started in your office with the court summary planning, then lessons, lunch, and after that, the rest of your day is finally meeting with all the court members you approved."

I nod. It's the same routine I'd approved before the honeymoon. It's now time to face it.

When I sit down in the main suite with Gavril to eat and attend our briefing, he kisses me on the cheek as I sit down. He's already scanning the day's newspaper and sipping at something.

"I thought you hate coffee." I eye his glass.

"I do. It's just hot water, lemon, and ginger," Gavril says.

I should have known. It sounds like the kind of thing he'd like in the morning. I decide to give it a try myself. He laughs as I steal his cup to try it. I'd rather have a little honey in it.

"There's plenty in the pot." Gavril gives me a playful look as I return his cup to him.

Flur quickly pours me a cup and asks if I want anything added. I tell her to put in half a teaspoon of honey, and after letting that stew a moment, it's perfect with my potato cakes and bits of spinach, complemented with fruit-sweetened oatmeal and fresh fruit.

Gavril barely pays attention to what he's eating as he scans the paper. His expression doesn't give me much clue to what he's finding inside. I smile, admiring his handsome jawline and focused eyes as he slowly sips at the tea and reads.

"Good morning, Highnesses," Sir Cedar greets us as he walks into the room. Good thing he did. Part of me was debating jumping my husband, looking far too attractive at his work. "And before we start, good news: no one but me knows you slipped out that one night, so let's keep it that way."

I lose it laugh as Gavril spits out a bit of his tea and looks up at Cedar. I suppose we should have known he'd have realized what we'd done.

"What? I said no one else knows," Cedar defends with a warm laugh. "Would you rather I not mention what I know next time?"

"I think I'd rather have known that you were hanging around in the forest all night," Gavril mutters.

"It wasn't all night." Cedar rolls his eyes. "Besides, I only found you as you were just leaving, giggling and all that." Cedar shrugs. "And I do not need to know what else you did. But we can cover security."

He goes on to brief us on the updates for the week. It had been mostly quiet. There had been one or two attempts from more unregulated press trying to get pictures or gossip on the honeymooning couple, but other than that, it was mostly quiet. "The rebellions seem to be deciding how to handle the new princess, as she's still quite popular. We'll see how that pans out, but for the moment, it seems we get a break as they assemble themselves."

"Nothing from Marque Kitsune up north?" Gavril asks.

"No, as of the moment, he seems to be doing what he was asked and is keeping in line. However, I do know he's coming in the hope of getting an audience with the new princess shortly. I will request an update of happenings after he leaves," Cedar replies.

"One false move, and I'm putting in a substitute until proper elections can be run." Gavril shakes his head in annoyance, smoothing out the paper as he puts it on the table. I glance at it, but nothing stands out to me.

Reinold comes in with Florence to give us a report on the happenings in court. There were some minor trials to report on; nothing that was going to be passed up.

"However, they are champing at the bit to start trying the rebels who broke in when the Enthronement winner was announced," Reinold frowns.

"I think the court's reaction is a mix of them wanting to see how our new princess reacts as she has personal attachments to the rebels as well as their desire for vengeance for the rebels ruining the moment," Florence explains. "Lady Jonquil, who is in custody, is high on the list of those they most want to go after. Because she was Chosen, her case is high profile. I'll confess, in their shoes, I'd likely be anxious to get her too."

"I'll coordinate plans with the king to decide how to proceed with those trials as soon as possible. Inform any pushy members of court that the king is still king for the moment, and though I'm acting on his behalf, it is up to him. And if you feel the need, warn Jack that more people may try to seek an audience with my father. As always, send them to me," Gavril orders smoothly.

He's so firm, confident, and it comes so easily to him. My heart beats a little faster as I admire his confidence, the small almost-smile playing at his lips, the soft but confident lines of his jaw, the observant yet gentle focus of those stunning amber eyes. They are all setting my heart on fire and leaving me hungry for him.

"Do you have an exact line you'd like us to use for that?" Florence asks. "For me or Her Highness, if they ask her? She is meeting with some members of court this afternoon."

"No line unless you have a suggestion." Gavril looks from me to our staff.

"No. I'll use what I said before. No trouble." Florence bows her head to him. "And there is a full legal backup for that answer. Your father is head of judgment still, and we will respect that. Easy answer. I will get started preparing for those meetings unless you have anything else?" Florence looks from me to Gavril.

I shake my head and look at my more experienced husband. Gavril dismisses her with a small wave of his hand once he is sure I am alright. She steps out, Reinold following.

Then it's time for us to part ways. I'd been with Gavril the whole time since the wedding. I dread having to go it alone again. Gavril appears less torn about it than I am. I don't know if that should sting, but I shouldn't be so bitter about it, I know. We'd get sick of each other without a break to do our own work.

He kisses me deeply before we part, wishes me luck and asks me to call on him if I need anything before he steps into his study, and I go into mine to begin the day.

At least my first lesson of the day is law, which I had asked Florence to teach. She had admitted a tad of nervousness, but other than messy notes, she is amazingly comfortable teaching me. After that, I have history and political science with Lady Hydrengia. As it's the first day of the week, I have my first lesson in the Dwarven language as well. Gavril and I meet up for lunch to talk about our day and enjoy the company. I had sincerely missed him.

"So hard to keep my mind on work and not with you," Gavril agrees. We end up having to hurry to finish eating, so we're done on time and ready for the rest of our day.

I could have taken the meetings in my study, but I decide its time we get used to my new office.

The front section is Bella's office. It's much like the one Godwin has for Gavril. It's not as small as I thought. It's not as large as mine, but in a pinch, she could have a meeting with three other people in there. And there's space for those who would be waiting to come in to meet with me.

Bella had already decorated it with her own personal touch. She likes the white and gold with hints of roses here and there. I know her favorite color is red, so the use of roses and other flowers is a nice personal touch.

My office was another surprise prepared by Damian. I beam in delight to see he'd known what I'd like as well as he had with my suite. It has a slightly more calming feel to it. It's like the ocean at night. There are stunning stars, even shooting stars, done into the wallpaper and carpet. I suppose playing Asteria, goddess of the night sky, made this a fitting domain for me. Upon closer inspection, many of the stars are actually yellow cassia flowers, the root of my name.

Though the flower is said kaw-shee-uh and my name is said Kas-se-ah, but it has the same meaning and root. The cinnamon flower, the nest of a phoenix. I pause as I think about that meaning for a moment, now knowing I am a prophesied princess does that name have more meaning?

Then I notice some of the flowers aren't cassia or stars... it's edelweiss. I beam at the reminder of our time on stage together. It means the world to me. It is associated with Damian's wife Emily and the character I played in *The Phantom* of course, but it makes me feel closer to Damian and his family. Like I am a part of them. I hope I'd get to meet them one day.

I sit at my desk and admire the decorations. The king's birthday gift to me is on the desk, as well as my mask from the harvest ball. I smile as I pick up the mermaid themed mask. Under that detailing, it's a simple light blue mask with yellow waves, but it's a perfect treasure. The pink and purple one from my time on the stage with Damian is also there.

The last thing is a beautiful small statue of a tiger with clear green eyes in a defensive pose, as if about to attack anyone who upsets me. There's another on the left side of the desk, opposite the first. This one my eyes land on more often and is in a more relaxed position, as if to comfort me. I smile and run a finger over it as if petting it. Damian will always look out for me. The sparkle of their eyes makes me smile.

But now I've enjoyed the small view of my new workspace, it is time to get to actual work.

It's... interesting. Most of the members of court I meet with have a cause of some kind they want to bring to me to help with. Some make sense, like the district that is struggling with child homelessness, or the need to spread awareness about the prejudice and misunderstandings wounded soldiers face that make it hard to meet their needs (and of course, all of these causes ended up circling around to the problem of us royals being secretly broke).

It's certainly got my mind going on what type of work and aid the court expects from their princess, helping me brainstorm my first move as well as inspiring some ideas on how to handle the inequality within the royal household.

We're wrapping up for the day with Florence and Bella, trying to organize and prioritize the notes from the day which Penelope is a master at taking with impressive speed yet legibility.

"Is it normal for courtiers to come to their princess with this first?" I ask as we're almost done.

"Pardon?" Florence frowns.

"These look like the kinds of things you look for charities to aid with," I explain. "Is that normally done through a sitting princess when there are international as well as national aid organizations?"

Bella and Florence stare at me for a moment, blinking before Florence says, "There hasn't been a successful charity or aid organization on a national level in Purerah in over fifty years."

"I figured. But even international aid?" I ask.

Florence frowns and glances at Bella, who is also frowning. "I'll admit I didn't know about this either until I was working on it after your coronation," Bella says, "but there hasn't been a trace of international aid organizations giving assistants to Purerahians in a long time."

"How long?"

"I can't find a record of it," Bella confesses.

I look at Florence in confusion. "Is that because there was a lack in princesses who handled those things?"

"Not... exactly," Florence says carefully.

"Those organizations exist internationally, don't they?" I check. "I'm almost certain there are programs for homeless children and wounded soldiers in other nations." I recall many of the born princesses talking about charities like that which they had worked with. "And they were international." I know for sure Princess Rose and Princess Amapola had worked with the same group to help children in Athadina and Alalusia. I'd heard them talk about it often.

"Yes, they do, but... they don't deal with a hopeless ghetto like us." Florence winces to see my reaction to that.

"Are you serious?" I demand.

"I have sought their aid in cases where the only living parent is locked up for repeatedly stealing food, so my client's children didn't end up on the street. They repeatedly ignored me or told me they had no Purerahian branch with no plan to set one up." Florence is still wincing as she waits for my explosion.

"So, what have our people been doing?" I demand in horror as well as anger.

"Trying to turn to their royal family or the rebels who often will take in children with nothing." Florence winces harder.

I recall Father doing that dozens of times. I'd even helped him at the last Restoration Day celebration. A sickly, angry snake writhes in my stomach.

"How can they just ignore one of the neediest groups in the world?" I demand. "If they're following their proclaimed mission statement, how can they just ignore those who need it the most?"

Florence shrugs. "They seem alright with it."

"I'm not," I snap. "What needs to be done to get them to set up branches here?"

"I wouldn't know, Your Highness. I'd have to research it." Florence glances at Bella, who nods that she didn't know either.

"Kindly find out. I want that as our first priority, and if we need court support, we'll find what we need to get it." I nod firmly. "That, and we need to get our own household in order. I noticed that some positions here are being looked down upon in ways that do not set a good example, as we're trying to teach our people to treat each other as equals."

"I know what you mean." Bella nods. "I can get to work on plans for that."

"Let's start with a well-worded statement to give them at the start of the meeting to set up new protocols to allow this to be dealt with." I give a firm nod. "I know you're already working on that." I glance at Penelope, who also handles my schedule.

"I am working with Lady Bella on it." Penelope smiles at me.

"Good." I nod firmly. "Those two things should be our first order of business on my agenda. Then, of course, we'll start meeting with Lady Lilly and preparing for the summit with the prince's teams as well."

"And giving the Chosen their titles," Penelope points out.

I look at her. She's smiling at the other two, and I look at them. I realize they were too embarrassed to bring it up as it involves them.

"They got their jobs without their official titles, Your Highness." Penelope is still smiling.

"That is completely up to the king and queen as well. And you're right; we need to get the other girls their jobs. Get with Godwin on that. I know he's been working with the king and queen on it," I order Bella, who nods with a sheepish smile.

"You deserve your official titles." I smile at both of them. "It's just not me who gets that ball going. Between us, I'm pretty sure you're both getting countess. I know I want that as I don't know if I could win duchess."

"Of course," Bella laughs. "We know what you'd want to give us."

But Florence is blushing at the idea I wanted to give her the rank just below royalty. Many in the line of royalty were even in the duchess category if they weren't direct grandchildren of the ruling head.

"Meanwhile, it's about time for your special dinner," Penelope points out.

We quickly finish the last-minute notes and touches before I hurry to get ready for dinner.

It is a rather special dinner. I'm delighted to see Sage, his mother Alliea, his father Gentian, and Zelda joining us for dinner: all dress up a bit. Sage looks nervous as he accepts my hug of friendship, glad to see him doing better. Zelda is almost glowing beside him, taking his hand when she can.

The king even joined us. I was happy for the fun get together until I find out the reason.

"I've accepted the offer," Sage says like he's finally accepting a grim yet honorable task. "I'm moving to Hyvil with my family. We'll return with Zelda's ship."

I can tell Sage is still uneasy about the choice, but the rest of our happiness for them hopefully helps. Gavril claps him on the back with a knowing look in his eye, but there's also a look I know well. The same bitter sadness of parting I'd had with Damian. The two men are like brothers. It will be hard to see Sage go.

"Only the final farewell party before we head out." Zelda smiles at me.

"I am getting it all arranged tomorrow," I assure her. "By week's end, perhaps?"

"Excellent!" Zelda beams.

I work with my team to prepare the boat party for those of us who'd agreed to the fun event; it feels like a lifetime ago. That as well as my own personal list of what jobs I'd like for each girl (if I have an idea for them) to help the king and queen decide what ranks to give the Chosen girls.

We're halfway through the work part of my day when Jean rushes into Bella's office, the entryway to mine, saying she had to talk to me urgently.

I tell Bella to let her in.

"We have a major press fight going on," Jean informs me with an anxious grimness. She puts down, not a newspaper like I expected, but a magazine or newsletter or some kind that I've never seen before.

I pick it up and scan the featured article: the girls who'd lost the Enthronement are angry and bitter about not being given their royal positions yet. Lines like "I guess it was all a lie" and "she just doesn't want to award those she beat out" stick out as I scan the article.

"Tomorrow, the major newspapers will cover this," Jean says. "I know you've already begun making plans."

"You literally interrupted my work on it," I sigh in frustration. "We only just got married, and it's not even up to us." I groan in annoyance. "They have to be placated, or they'll start a fit."

"And a lot of them are saying it's you holding it up because you don't want to reward your husband's exes." Jean frowns.

"I thought we might set up a formal event in the palace to give them their titles and jobs in person. It might be the only way to go now." I look at Briana, who is my runner. "Would you go inform my husband and his staff of the event? We quickly need to plan and ensure he gets his list of job requests or title requests for the Chosen to the king and queen by this evening. Thank you," I add as she nods and quickly leaves.

I sigh in frustration once more.

"Shall we prepare a statement?" Jean asks.

"No," I shake my head, "not to the press. Work with Penelope to overnight statements to the Chosen girls, though. They can leak it to the press if they wish. Let the ladies know their positions and jobs are in the works, and they haven't been forgotten. Tell them we've been working on this since day one."

"Which is true," Bella adds.

"And they will get invites to the formal event for the awarding of their titles, and for many of them, their jobs, but we cannot promise that they will all receive a position as we do not pick their rank, so we may not have jobs already planned for all of them. At the event, we'll check to make sure if they still want a job or not. I suspect a few plan to run for office, and a formal job may not be what they want right now."

"Most will expect one anyway," Florence points out.

"And I agree, but maybe we'll get lucky, and a few will be honest. And some, we can promise to back." I nod, exhausted by the idea already. "Get those messages out as soon as possible."

The two bow their heads and hurry out of the room to get started. I do pause a moment though.

I came up with that and gave the order so easily. Perhaps what Damian said about an enchanted blessing coming with a crown is true, or perhaps I'd always had it in me.

"We should get started on what's needed for the charities tomorrow. We may want to hire some Chosen girls to help us with that." I look at Bella. "If we need to change the lesson schedule for a while to make enough time, we'll do that. We'll just have to apologize to our teachers."

Florence snorts in amusement.

"You'll still work, that fair?" I laugh.

"No. It's... they're your teachers, Kascia. I-I mean Highness." Florence bows her head to me. "Not ours anymore."

"Oh..." I go a bit pink. "Right." It isn't like she is in lessons with me.

"We'll get it done," Florence promises. "Shall I have Lady Bella stay with you while you get through the rest of the appointments?"

"Unless you feel it's better for you to stay and her to make arrangements." I look between them.

The ladies look at each other. "I'll go," Bella offers.

Florence nods. "I am the court expert, I suppose," she chuckles.

I smile and invite Florence to sit in the spot nearest me as Bella goes out to get started and send in the next person I have to meet with.

That night, Gavril and I, rather than doing our normal relaxing after dinner, go over our lists — even though we both submitted them — just so we can be sure we're on the same page.

I'm discouraged and a bit tired. Not even a full week, and it feels like I've been working for a month with no headway and mostly exhausted and discouraged.

"Hey, you're doing fine." Gavril can see the discouragement in my eyes and kisses my temple.

"I guess... I understand how your father isn't healthy enough for this job. I'm already feeling worn thin," I confess.

"It gets easier, and you get used to it," Gavril promises. "We did just have a lot of time off."

"I guess." I sigh once more. "Likely we'll have to give up our first and second rest day to give these girls their demands."

"Aw, come on," Gavril pouts.

"When else can we do it? We don't have time to put it off." I point out. "And we did *just* have our honeymoon, Gavril."

Gavril grunts his displeasure with a drawn-out grunt. "My mind is still there."

I laugh. "We have time now that we're done with this. And you already knew I had my party with the top girls this rest day."

"What?" Gavril pouts.

I laugh. "We told you this already."

Gavril grunts unhappily again.

I chuckle and rest my head on his shoulder. "You goof head."

"And they're stealing our evenings. I'm not mentally ready for this yet." He keeps up the play pouting, resting his head on mine.

That reminds me of my other problem.

"And what do you know about international charities?" I ask him as he pulls away to let me slip out of my dressing gown and into bed.

"Like in general?" Gavril asks, and I nod. "Um... they normally have chapters for each nation and then subchapters for each city. They're run like a tight business that lobby us like anyone else, but that's about it. We don't deal with them much here."

"Has it always been like that?" I ask as I slip into the sheets, sitting up on my elbows as I watch Gavril get the lights and get in on the other side.

"As far as I know. Recall I also was kept out of most official work until recently," Gavril says as he settles into bed. I settle beside him so we're facing one another, a slight frown on my face. "Why? Something wrong with them?" he asks me, resting his head on his arm to look down at me.

"They don't seem to be here," I explain my thoughts after meeting with all the couriers lobbying for charitable causes.

"A princess is often the one who spearheads a lot of that on the government side." Gavril nods a little. "And princes who aren't already part of the running government. But they often are more like... pet charities, if you know what I mean. Causes they decide they want to be behind. I can't think of any examples. If you ask her, Zelda would definitely do it. I'm sure she does them at home."

I nod a little, still frowning. "I just don't understand how they aren't here."

"Well, no princess to handle them."

"No, I mean, even without that, wouldn't Purerah, with its high poverty level, draw in lots of services like that? So why aren't there any charities running openly and regularly here?" I look up at Gavril. "They don't normally rely on government support, do they?"

"No, for legal reasons they normally are separate from the crown, save for our public support or manual labor. Like when we went and helped that farmer. Rebels burned part of his land, so we came to help. If a non-government charity had organized it and not us, we could attend and promote it, but we can't give financial contributions as it would be seen as putting non-approved public funds into a private entity, possibly making it an unregulated government institution. It's against the law to help prevent them from being unelected government officials." Gavril is watching me with a slight smile. "That really bothers you, doesn't it?"

"Well, yes. They have lots of work to do, and sure, the people here can't donate much, but that's why they are international. They fundraise more in well-to-do nations. We helped with one during our tour when I was at the theater. So, I thought they were here, just like anywhere else. They should be here. And I want to know why they aren't."

"I'm sure you'll figure it out. Sounds like you found work to do all on your own." Gavril lies down on his side, his normal position, and I naturally settle into him, still frowning as I contemplate how many lives could have been saved, how many children wouldn't have been dragged into fighting for rebellions, and how much less suffering there would be if there was proper support.

"We would do more if we could." I frown deeper. "But you can only do so much broke."

"I know. Trust me, I've often daydreamed about what we'd do if we had the money they think we do." Gavril sighs heavily.

I smile slightly. "Like your Christmas plans," I giggle. "I was so mad at you for not trying to push for what you wanted for Christmas." It feels like a lifetime ago, another world.

Gavril chuckles. "It was so hard not to explain. I knew before, but that moment proved you'd be the first girl to push and ask. Athadina was more than generous with their help."

"I still can't believe they paid for the whole wedding." I frown a little.

"Their gift. It was an expensive one, but they were more than happy to give it. I think I told you one of the loans they gave us had some tricky math, so it actually had a negative interest, and the interest ended up paying it off. It was a smaller loan they thought we'd miss. We would have if I wasn't bored and desperate to think of a plan so I could fulfill the prophecy before the Enthronement began. I never told my parents, but the king laughed at me."

I chuckle. "I can see that. They really are like family."

"Only kind of extended family I've ever known. The one year they came for Christmas was a madhouse. They stayed extra time because, of course, traveling in the snow is hard and, being further north, they get a lot more than we do. It was an excuse for an extended winter vacation for them. A lot of royals have two palaces: the summer palace where they spend most of their time, then the winter palace where they get away for the winter when travel is too hard to really do much governing."

"Did your family have one?"

"*Our* family owned one a long time ago, but we sold it in an attempt to pay off the dragon. No idea where it was."

"If you could have one, where would it be?" I ask him.

Gavril has to think. "Winter? I'd put it on an island out in our seas somewhere. Less snow sure, but I'd love the privacy and places to study the animals."

"Not up by Mer Lake?"

"Never been, but I'd be happy to try it. That's a *lot* of snow." He smiles and kisses my head.

I groan as he starts teasing my feet with his again.

"Don't say you don't like it," Gavril laughs at my reaction.

"I don't know if I do," I admit. He does it all the time, and some-times it fits the mood and is great, but it seems like every other time all I can feel is "again?".

"Sure you do," he chuckles and kisses my forehead, then my cheek. I know where he's going and kiss him deeply and wrap my leg around his, and we forget all about what we were talking about.

# Chapter 29

At least, I have a fun end of the work week to look forward to. The rest of the week is making plans for the Chosen girls, trying to figure out how to work with the charities, and the like. Before I know it, it's finally here!

I don't take any meetings during the last workday. The whole afternoon and evening are for this party.

I shouldn't be surprised that gathering all of us is not difficult. Rose, Azalea, and Isla are all staying at the embassy. Bella and I, of course, both live in the palace with Zelda staying with us. We greet the others excitedly.

The whole evening is a blast on the water, enjoying the sunset, talking, laughing, enjoying the dinner and treats that we'd brought along. We laugh and snack and tease each other and reminisce about the good times, the girls that drove us crazy, and how much we've missed each other.

Rose and Zelda will return home early the next week. Rose, at least I know I'll see again, but Hyvil is a month away by sea. And with our broke kingdom, who knows if I'll get to visit or if she'll get to come see us again?

But that night, none of these sad thoughts surface. We laugh like sisters, and it's as grand as my surprise party, if not better to enjoy with these fellow survivors of the Enthronement and royal sisters. Three of us are royal; the rest are the highest of court. Well, Azalea doesn't have her job yet, but I have a job well in mind.

It feels like the longest party we've ever enjoyed, yet all too short as it feels like now it's done; the solo work truly begins.

With Gavril's complaining, we get the pressure on his parents to set up the event for the Chosen girls on the first rest day, which we had originally planned for the party.

Gavril, still a bit miffed to be left out of the festivities, is watching me as I get ready. But his staff and mine all agree having "the ex" there wouldn't be good for anyone.

"You're wearing your tiara, right?" Gavril asks.

"What?" I frown. "Why would I do that? These girls are going to hate me for beating them. I don't think flaunting it in their face is a good idea."

"Last time you dealt with these girls, you were equals," Gavril reminds me. "And now you're not, and many of them will need to be reminded of it. I know them better than you do in many cases. These are girls ranging from Forsythia to the girls dismissed on the first day. You need to ensure they remember your position now. You are the princess. And though you were equal once, you aren't now, and they cannot push you around or make you feel guilty for it. And they shouldn't even try. Your tiara serves as a reminder of the power you possess, and they should not dare to challenge you.

"Gavril, they're a bunch of girls. They were trying to win a powder-puff game in their minds. The later girls like Dahlia, yes, will be like that, but they will already recall the power I have. They don't need the reminder."

"I think you underestimate how hateful some of those lower girls will be." Gavril gives me a warning look, almost a glare. "I will avoid using names, but you might recall Jaine may have a grudge. She blames you for getting her eliminated."

"The guards told your parents about her fight with me, not me."

"Truth doesn't matter in vengeance. You'll wear your tiara."

"The crown princess tiara will be too over the top, and it's the only one I have," I remind him.

"I'm sure Damian made you like a dozen or so." Gavril waves off. "It will match whatever Bella planned for today. You'll wear a tiara. You don't have to dress all grand, but you need to wear it. Trust me."

I sigh, but it doesn't seem like a fight worth having. It isn't that big of a deal. I think they'll warm up to me more if I don't lord my status over them. I won't act that way, so it's possible the tiara won't make that big of a difference. More importantly, it will comfort Gavril.

"Alright, if I have one, not the crown princess one, I'll wear it," I agree, but I still think it silly.

"You have the name guide?" Gavril checks, glancing at Bella.

"Yes, Your Highness, I got your list," Bella comforts my husband. "But she's not going to need to reference names often."

"Some will be offended if you don't remember their names. In many of their minds, they were bigger competition than they were. You don't want to put them down, even if they're the only ones who see it that way."

"It's not a battle, Gavril," I chuckle. "I won. They know that."

"They can and will still cause trouble," Gavril insists. "Don't give them the motive or excuse to."

"Alright, alright." I still think he's being paranoid.

Thankfully, Gavril was right. Damian had made around ten extra tiaras for me, and two more Bella designed and learned to create, making the dozen Gavril had guessed.

The dress Bella had chosen is emerald green with soft butterfly sleeves, bodice bedecked in emerald beads fading down to the long fluttering skirt that hovers just above the floor once I have the shoes on.

The tiara is what Bella calls a felicity tiara. Gold and pearls twist in flower designs with five points, with the center bloom being the largest, fading the emeralds out to the ends of the flower. The two top points of the center flower are soft set with pearls. It's just under two inches, since anything above two inches reaches into queen territory, as I'd learned in my lessons.

The final touch is a set of emerald earrings that dangle teardrop emeralds from two stones and a matching necklace with a pendant version of the tiara at the center, finishing off the V-neck of the dress that outlines me well but doesn't show cleavage as a princess never shows cleavage in public. The idea that is only for my beloved is something I rather like.

"Are we sure it's not too over the top?" I fret to Bella.

"The dress is much more like what you wore during the Enthronement, not as grand as a princess normally wears, and the jewelry isn't flashy. Our prima lady, yes, the princess, but you don't look like you're trying to outdo them anymore."

"You already did," Gavril smirks.

He'd sat at the desk to work; he'd even been reading. He betrays that he'd been paying attention though as he smirks, stands up and kisses my cheek.

"You'll do fine. They can't bully you unless you let them. You have this." He smiles gently at me. "I'll see you when it's over." He kisses me on the lips this time, taking me away from this stress to a moment of bliss, just for a second, before he leaves.

"It may not be fun, but this will be easy," Bella assures me with a wave of her hand. "You've already handled them before. Let's get down there so we can greet them as they arrive."

They start arriving before I've had a chance to review the arrangements in the dining hall with my staff.

I recognize the first to arrive immediately: Emmalina. She was the number one non-born royal at the start, but Gavril dismissed her during the interview phase, shocking many of us.

She is smiling and has a clear air of grace about her befitting royalty, but there's also a bit of annoyance in her eyes as she looks me over, likely wondering what I have that she doesn't. She looks royal: dark skin, coils pinned perfectly at the back of her head, accented by the dangling earrings she wears, matching her soft pink lips and dress.

"So glad to finally be back," she says brightly, but I don't miss the hint of envy or perhaps annoyance with my taking my sweet time.

"There is much to manage. I've only had a week as a working royal, and Ga—the prince and I wanted to assure we picked the right positions for each of you. As stated in your invitation, we'll take time one-on-one to discuss the positions we've decided, and we'll get you into your ranks as soon as possible."

I hold back snapping, *I'm sorry planning the biggest wedding in Purerah ever took so long, so you had to wait.*

Most girls behave the same. At least they aren't too hostile. Though I'll confess, a few do seem to have murder in their eyes. I cannot blame the girls whose names I can't remember. I quickly learn all the girls assume they were more memorable than they were.

Bella whispers their names to me before they step up to me. Veronica, Violet, Payge, and Daisy give me glares when they think I'm not looking that honestly frightens me. With Bella's help, they couldn't have known I couldn't recall their names, could they? I'm not sure if I'd ever personally interacted with them.

But not all the girls are so rude and stick to formality. Rachel clearly finds my being proper an annoyance. She had failed the obedience test, so perhaps she found my obedience an act.

"We're all friends here, aren't we, Princess?" She smiles at me brightly.

I have a suspicion I know exactly what she is up to. She was one of the girls Fabian had mentioned to me as already gaining a following in Nerine. Was she trying to win favor to make a bid for their court rep or mayor or whatever she had her eyes on easier? Lucky for her, that is my hope for her too.

"I certainly hope so," I reply. "I also hope we can respect our new titles and positions."

Thankfully, that makes her stop pressing, but there is a tad bit of resentment from her, I think.

I'm happier to greet Elice. She is more casual; that is for certain. If she is going to do a good job at the position I have in mind for her, we somehow have to get it through to her why etiquette is important. I am fine with her preference to bow rather than curtsy, but she should have some royal demeanor about her if she is to represent us.

Ericka is a whole different level of "buddy, buddy". She plays up that we'd been friends during the whole Enthronement. I don't miss the dirty looks many of the girls give her when they know full well that's a load of dung.

"Always going to be the best of friends, as true princesses are," she twitters at me. I wonder if she has any relation to Hydie.

Sadly, it creates a more competitive and hostile environment around the room. Perhaps as others arrive, that will die down.

The tension becomes so bad that I glance at Bella before I invite them all to enjoy the refreshments that have been laid out and relax as we wait for the main event to begin.

I am slightly humbled as I tense myself.

Forsythia has arrived.

She walks in with that coy smile of hers. She greets me just fine, though, much like she had at the rehearsal dinner. I don't trust her but treat her as kindly as anyone else.

I notice Cedar keeping an extra close eye on her as he patrols the edges of the room. There is no need for him, but he and Gavril felt it imperative that he be there. Perhaps it is just to make us all feel safer. Lila is there patrolling too. I don't need both of them.

Cedar is eyeing several girls with more suspicion than others. Forsythia, of course, Ericka doesn't surprise me, but the fact he's wary of Jaine, Heather, and Violet does.

Violet is a girl I hardly remember, but she gushes over me, insisting I make the perfect princess. But I don't miss her snide remark that her red hair would go better with my attire.

Jaine perhaps I could understand. She insisted it was my fault she was eliminated after she'd argued with me in the safe room during one of the rebel attacks.

Heather... She has a cocky personality, sure, but dangerous?

Perhaps Cedar forgets we already weeded out the rebel plants and sympathizers. I confess a frown drops my face as I think of Jonquil. I thought of her as my friend, and honestly, I wish I could have that version of her back. But that was just the character she played to get our trust, nothing more. I was the fool for falling for it.

It's a breath of fresh air to greet Azalea when she arrives. She's beaming as she curtsies to me, as if that was always our relationship before she asks what her job will be. Unlike everyone else, she is not interested in asking about titles. She's eager to work. It melts my heart in gratitude. I also have big plans for her. Very big plans.

Lilly is a relief as well. Though she'd already started her job and had to step away from it to be here, everyone thinks it important she be honored at this event as well. No one wants the press making it look like she was slighted. Most of all, if the Japcharians caught wind of that and looked down on their new ambassador because of it.

When Dahlia arrives, there is a none too subtle collective groan across the room. I am not overly pleased to see her either, but at least I have the decency to be subtle about it.

Dahlia doesn't seem to mind at all. She smirks at anyone who looks at her. She's not at all dimmed in her smugness.

Thankfully, all the girls have arrived by the official start time.

I forgot how loud Kamala's voice is. That was one thing from the Enthronement I am happy is going to stay in the past.

When they've all arrived, Bella gives me the nod to assure me everyone is here.

I clear my throat. I've been dreading this moment. I'm not sure how my defeated competition, as they saw it, will react to me using my authority. I know I have to, and it's rightfully mine. But will they see it that way? And will that help me use their skills or make it worse?

"Thank you all for coming," I manage to sound perfectly calm and collected. "It's so good to see you all again. We have much work to do, and I want to make sure you all have time to ask all the questions you have about your positions. We have tentative plans for all of you, but I want to discuss them with you. I'll remind you, you are free to reject the jobs we give you, but if you do, that's the only position we offer you. You keep your title, but we will not go through jobs until we find one you'll say yes to. It's the job we offer, or you're on your own. Perhaps if you have a request, we can take it into consideration. But the terms of the contract do not require us to find a job for you. Just that you are offered one. Understood?"

There's a murmur of agreement. *Not very ladylike,* I think. Lady Keva would be scandalized at how the girls she'd trained behaved. Though I suppose she only taught half of them.

I glance at the back of the room. Perhaps it's the impressionors and reporters in the room. Mr. Coppiger is here with Adam for their paper, and a few others I don't know are here representing the other papers, I suppose. Fabian must have thought this assignment beneath him. The main reason I'd allowed them is so they could publish the titles given to each girl today. Perhaps I should have done this live. Then the girls would have behaved better.

"Your ranks, however, are not negotiable. And therefore, we'd like to start with those first." I turn to Bella who hands me the Purerahian scepter the king had given me to use to give each of the girls their titles.

I have the girls who already know their jobs and titles go first. To make it easy on me, I give Bella hers first. She got the highest rank possible as a duchess. She only needed to have countess for her job, but she was in the top five and in a job where duchess was perfectly reasonable.

The countess position pleasantly surprises Lilly. She too was given a rank one step higher than was required for her job, but she had been a gem who deserved the extra reward, and the Japcharians will respect her more the higher rank.

Florence also is made a countess. High for her, not quite making it into the top ten, but I wanted her to have the best rank I could manage with her working in the court on my behalf.

With those already working in their jobs out of the way, we go alphabetically. Many look unhappy with their position, even though few got higher than their number in elimination.

That is, apart from Azalea. She is made a duchess (the only other one apart from Bella). She is flabbergasted. She stammers, "thank you" with surprise and joy in her eyes. She has no idea how much I want to use her rank, and again, she is one of the three girls in the top five who isn't born royalty. The top five reward is the highest rank possible. Isla, having been one of the three to pass all the tests, was made princess ward, but to avoid the press discussing if perhaps she or Zelda should have won, they don't want to make a show of it. So, we just hope the press will not notice.

Bellatrix follows her, who was eliminated early on. Her eyes go wide in surprise at being made a baroness, but she is the only one from her city we trust. Most of the lower-ranked girls are being given jobs as the royal representative to their cities. And Bellatrix will need the boost in rank to be taken seriously in her city court.

But otherwise, most girls either get exactly what they want or lower than their pride had assumed. None say this, of course, but I can see it in their eyes or the set of their jaws at the annoyance at what they see as an insult.

Dahlia doesn't surprise me at all with her glare at me after I proclaim her Marquises Dahlia. She'd been expecting countess, I know it. But she hadn't shown us enough faith to want to reward her with more. It isn't like she'd accept any job we give her anyway. We have one for her, but we all know she'd go back to playing ball, not regulating the taxes on its profit.

Elice gives me a look of surprise at her viscountess status. It is exactly what she'd earned. Perhaps at least one of these girls is humble enough to see perhaps it is better to expect less in order to be pleased with more.

Emmalina is smug about her viscountess-ship by the end. No one else who had left that early got that rank. The queen was sure she'd be good as our representative to the capital's city court, so she needed a step up.

The bitter look from Ericka when she's only an earlaness doesn't surprise me either. She expected to be a countess or duchess. She didn't make the top five. She was in the top ten, but we also don't want to offer her a job that keeps her nearby. Honestly, Gavril and I wish we could have her working for her father again. Gavril had worked hard to make up a new job for her that kept her away from us as much as possible.

Forsythia gives me a hidden smirk as she kneels before me for her title. I wish I could knock her over the head with the Purerahian scepter instead, but I don't.

I declare her an earlaness. She doesn't give me much of a stink eye. Instead, she gives me another little smirk as she stands up. "I'll be a duchess soon anyway," she whispers to me before bowing and stepping back.

Not if I can help it, but I know full well there's nothing I can do about it. It is the only reason she hooked up with the Grand Duke, I'm sure of it.

With Cedar eyeing her, I am worried Jaine may glare, but she takes her baroness rank with perfect grace. Cedar was too anxious.

The girls given the rank of dame (most of those who failed the first two or three tests other than Emmalina and a few others) all give me glares when given the lowest rank possible. Perhaps we should have just left them as Ladies (the title all the Chosen got when they were brought to the palace) and been done with it.

Violet almost lets out a huff of amusement when she's made a viscountess. It was exactly what she'd earned. Maybe she found the alliteration of her new name appealing.

She gives me a huge smile, her lips as red as her hair as she bows her head in thanks and backs up. She is the last one to get her title.

Now the really icky part.

"Thank you all for the service you have given and will give. I'm proud to make you nobility of our realm. Please enjoy your time during the rest of the festivities. Duchess Bella will come and collect you when it's your turn for your one-on-one with me to offer you your position."

We'd set up a nearby meeting room to make it quick and easy. My office isn't that close, and we don't want to drag the girls through the court offices.

I go in reverse order. I call Violet to follow me.

"I hope you are happy with your title," I say as I invite her to sit. Bella and Florence sit in chairs on my left while I sit in an armchair across from the Chosen girl.

Viscountess Violet drops down into her chair with a huge smile. I wonder if it's painted on. Is she hiding something?

"Of course I do." But then she sees something in my expression and giggles nervously. "Well, alright. I was expecting a little higher."

"Why is that?" I ask pleasantly, hoping if I understand I can help them see their position is exactly where they want to be.

"Well, with how the prince felt about me, I thought he'd at least say a proper 'thank you' with earlaness," Violet confesses.

I have to pause to contain my annoyance. I highly doubt that is true. Gavril has no reaction or comment to her anymore than anyone else. She must be wearing rose-colored glasses looking back. Perhaps many girls are. Heaven knows I'd force myself to seek positivity in order to survive the heartbreak if I'd lost.

"What job were you hoping to get with that title?"

"In the royal court, of course." Violet laughs. "Viscountess... that limits me to the city level. I belong in the royal courts."

"Really? Why do you feel you'd be a good fit there?" She is a stable hand by trade. How could she be a great fit for the royal courts?

Violet smiles in a way that makes me uneasy. I can't think of another way to describe it other than unhinged. "Oh, I've had a way with the court for quite some time. I thought you'd want to put those skills to use, is all."

I'm starting to wish we didn't choose her as the royal representative to her local court. "Well, prove you're good with your local court, and perhaps one of the royal courtiers will hire you. That can help you get a higher rank if they want you and no one else." That is rare, but former Chosen are more likely to manage it. If some royal court member really wants her, I have no doubt the king and queen, or even Gavril will approve the title boost without a second thought.

"Royal rep to the Gaillardia's court?" Viscountess Violet asks.

I smile and nod. "Yes. You'd represent the royal family in their court. You'd speak what you'd think we'd speak if we were there and report to us on events happening in the local court you believe we need to be apprised of."

"So, it's not like I'll never come back here?" she asks.

"Not at all." I smile. "You'll report to our court liaison with what you've found. You'll have plenty of chances to get to know those who work in the royal court to improve your position."

"Hm," Viscountess Violet nods, "alright. Not a bad position then. Where do I start?"

"The king's court liaison will have basic guides for you and those who will have positions like yours. He will contact you all later today when we know everyone who has accepted the position and arrange meetings to get you up to speed before helping you settle into your new positions at home."

"Excellent. This is a fair arrangement then, Princess." She bows her head to me. That deranged smile is back. I force myself to ignore it.

"Thank you, Viscountess Violet. We are deeply thankful for the sacrifices you have made for your kingdom so far. And I will thank you in advance for those you'll make in the future."

"Oh, don't thank me yet." She smiles.

Why are her smiles so creepy? How had I forgotten that? Perhaps I just never saw her around. She can't be that crazy. Gavril would have said something.

I smile and stand to mark our session is over. "Thank you again, Viscountess. Until we meet again."

"Until then, Princess." She stands, bowing her head with a curtsy, and Bella sees her out.

"I don't recall her being such a creep," Florence says.

"I guess neither of us hung out with her much." I smile back. "Hopefully, we don't have too much of that."

Thankfully, there aren't many that are that unpleasant. Those made dames, like Veronica and Prisa, are a bit stiff, but when both are offered their jobs as Union Head Representatives for their respecting trade skills, they perk right up.

(Not that I have a clue what they'll do in those jobs. The lack of funds and other problems have pretty much made the unions little more than an empty symbol. But perhaps setting many of these lower ranked ladies as Royal Union Representatives would help bring them back. Though if that is a good thing... I'm not sure. Won't they demand things we can't give because we're broke?)

They all go well in similar ways until I get to Payge. I don't remember Payge well either. The baroness almost falls into her chair with impressive power for a girl who was a scribe her whole life.

She gives me a death glare. "So, what fake job are you giving me, Princess?" She spits the title at me.

"The royal family," I correct her gently, "worked hard to find the right jobs for everyone. And I am particularly pleased with what His Highness suggested for you. Your skills as a scribe are well known. We'd like to offer you the position of court scribe in Wellasyth. We tried to keep everyone close to home if we could. Keeping records at the border is extremely important. And we think you'd be perfect.

"In time, perhaps, if you are interested in working here in the royal court in the same position, we'd be interested in taking your application and petition at the time the position opens up. Sadly, the king and queen wouldn't want to force the current scribe out of his job, but there are rumors he is preparing to retire soon. I will ensure that you receive a message to apply as soon as possible if you would like to make an attempt to secure the position.

"So, an empty promise of better?" Payge looks me over skeptically.

"If I could promise it, I would, but as I'm only crown princess and not yet queen, I can't promise it. If I am in power at that point, I will be happy to promise you the position. There is no one else I'd rather have." I give her an honest smile. I'd rather it be someone I knew, even vaguely, then a total stranger. And she does come highly recommended by those she'd worked for.

"Really?"

"Really." I smile again.

"Fine. I'll take it," Baroness Payge says. "But I'll make it public if you deny me that job if it pops up."

"And we'll respond as we must." I don't want to threaten her, but it likely isn't going to be my call, anyway.

Baroness Payge nods stiffly. "Alright then, Princess." She stands up and bows her head to me. "I'll serve at your pleasure."

"She is your crown princess; you curtsy or bow," Bella suddenly interrupts.

"Bella..." I whisper. I didn't need to intimidate them.

Baroness Payge does as asked before stalking out.

"Hey!" Bella snaps.

"Bella, it's fine," I attempt to calm her.

"No, it's not. You wait for the royal to dismiss you before you leave," Bella says. "The way she glared at you..." She pauses. "I'll be back with the next girl." Bella bows her head to me and steps out.

I sigh and look at Florence. I expect her to return my exasperated look, but she looks strained and widens her eyes at me. "Princess Kascia, you really can't see how she looked ready to murder you, can you?"

"Many of them have been glaring at me. It means nothing." I shake my head, rather amused.

"You're too trusting, My Lady." Florence smiles. "Too good for some parts of this job, I think."

I open my mouth to ask what that is supposed to mean when Bella returns, but she doesn't have the next girl. She has Cedar with her.

"Oh Bella," I sigh. "You and Florence are here. I'm fine."

"I'd like to get a gauge on them, anyway." Cedar disagrees. "I'll hardly be noticed."

I sigh but allow it. "I used to spend days with these girls in a room. They're not that dangerous to me." I try to help him at least not look so grim.

"You hadn't taken their coveted crown then," Cedar replies coolly. "I agree with Lady — pardon me — Duchess Bella. I will keep watch. At least give us that comfort, Princess Kascia."

I sigh once more, but as I'd already allowed it, I will permit this silliness.

No one else has comments or glares anymore dangerous than the others. The death glares are as common as thankful smiles. Marigold has a rather deeper hatred behind hers, but it isn't much more than anyone else's.

The most striking thing to me is how few girls question the "royal representative to so-and-so union". None seem to think it "fake", and all of them, even Latana who receives the Toymakers Union Representative offer, is delighted at the job.

Many others are appointed as the royal representative to their local city, like Viscountess Violet. None of them turn down that job.

Rachel is a sticky one.

"I can do more," she insists the moment she drops into the armchair across from me.

"I know you can." I smile back. "I've heard how well you're doing, supporting your refugees and garnering support for the royal family. If it was up to me, we'd make you mayor or head of the Nerine court, or even Nerine's representative in the royal court. But those are all elected offices. Offices we've ensured your rank is high enough to get."

Rachel tries to frown as if in confusion, but a hint of a smile betrays her. Fabian's guess was right. She does have those ambitions.

"And I won't tell you which one to run for." I give her a smile of understanding. "But I will tell you no matter what you pick, unless you're up against another Chosen, my husband and I will be endorsing you."

"Really?" Rachel's eyes light up.

I nod. "For obvious reasons, if you run against another Chosen girl, we won't be able to take sides unless there are some seriously huge extenuating circumstances, but we do plan to endorse you against any other candidate."

"Thank you, Your Highness." Rachel is beaming. "I couldn't have asked for better."

"I truly look forward to working more closely with you. I've heard good things, and your people need it most." I stand to mark the end of our discussion. "In the meanwhile, we can offer you Royal Representative to the Nerine court."

Rachel frowns. "Will that make it harder to run?"

"Honestly, we don't know. I will tell you if you don't take it, we have another girl here in mind," I admit honestly.

Rachel bites her lip. "Why do I get it first?"

"Luck. You got to meet with me first."

Rachel nods. "So, I don't get long to think on it."

I debate breaking our plan. "We have another job in mind for the other girl, if you accept this. If you promise me you won't tell anyone, I'll let you choose between them."

"Not a soul," Rachel promises.

"We want a royal representative to the refugees themselves."

Rachel winces. We knew the two girls would struggle to pick one. They are about equal in status. The two had failed the same test and so we couldn't even use that as our deciding factor. Both would be good for their campaigns.

"Will you offer the other girl both choices?" Rachel asks.

"I won't tell her someone else turned it down, but I might offer depending on her reaction," I confirm.

After another moment, Rachel says, "I'll take the refugees' representative."

I smile. Personally, I had thought her a better fit for it than our second option. I had just tricked my way into getting what I wanted.

"Excellent." I tell her what to expect next, and she's seen out.

The rest are easier, though a few more death glares and rude language make Cedar and Bella nervous. Bella taps her foot, and Cedar makes himself more obvious to intimidate the threatening girl. I wish they'd stop. I am safe in the palace with these girls. They got into the Enthronement, after all.

Jaine's meeting is one of the worst, but why wouldn't it be? She blames me for being kicked out so soon. She is not happy with baroness, and being made representative for a union doesn't please her either. At least her union is an active one. She used to be a maid, perfect for the serving staff union, which covers royal, court, and entertainment and hospitality staff.

She takes the job though, even if her language is a bit crude for a baroness.

Cedar looks ready to follow her out.

Hanna is the next interesting meeting. She is the other Nerine girl we knew was running for an office. I give her the same offer I gave Rachel, only I don't tell her about the other job we have planned.

She has the same hesitation and questions. I just pray the fact they know we won't endorse either of them if they run against each other will help them not run for the same role. We want both of them in positions of power in Nerine.

Forsythia is next. We both play the game, do the dance, and pretend we're friendly and all is well. She has the nerve to play coy.

"I don't need a job," she assures me. "I know you promised us one, but I don't want to move."

Of course she doesn't. She wants to keep the grand duke on her finger so she can marry him and become the grand duchess. Then she'd see him dead followed by me, so she could either wiggle her way to marrying Gavril or try to kill both of us, so she could just take it for herself.

"But we picked a position of honor for you," I insist. "Ambassador to Alalusia. It's a comfortable job, as they are our closest allies. It's a beautiful country. They will be excited to have you." I keep up the game.

But Gavril and I were right. She refused it with all the fake graciousness of a queen.

She leaves with a wicked little smirk at me. Cedar has the nerve to double check she didn't touch my drink.

"Stop being paranoid. You'd have seen her touch it," I point out.

"Still... if someone wants you dead in that group, it's her, and she's evil enough to try it," Cedar says.

"And cocky enough to think she'd get away with it." Bella is glaring at the door where she left.

"Can we please stop worrying about an assassination attempt that won't happen so we can get this done? I was hoping not to be at this all day." After Gavril was so disappointed to have another rest day together stolen from us, I was hoping to give him a treat for his patience.

"Don't be so sure," Cedar says.

"None of them are dumb enough. It would be so easy to catch them. They got into the Enthronement for a reason. None are that dumb, and you're watching," I protest.

"Still. Better to be careful." Cedar shrugs.

"Bring in the next girl, please," I beg Bella. She nods and does as I ask. Why does Florence look nervous too?

Ericka is next. Really? At least it is easy to fake kindness with her. She accepts her fake job as Court Correspondent Manager with all her bubbly happiness and leaves as if she's skipping on a cloud.

"She's too dumb to try anything," Cedar jokes.

I give him a look as Bella and Florence laugh.

But the laughter dies with how Emmalina almost cross-examines me as if trying to figure out how in creation I outdid her. She brightens at being the royal rep to the city court, though. Cedar is obviously worried about her too as she leaves.

"No one wants me dead," I repeat. "At least, no one that is dumb enough to try anything here."

Elice is a hard one, but a relief as I don't have to worry she'll gouge my eyes out anymore. Her job is... odd.

"You are so talented. You've gained such a following, and the rebels want you dead for how well you speak out against them," I say to her. "I want you to be the royal representative. In a nutshell, you keep doing what you're doing, but we'll work with you on where to go to give your messages of support or speaking out against the rebels. And of course, we'll pay you and help manage your travel."

"That's the only catch?"

"If you call it a catch, Viscountess Elice."

Elice beams. She loves it and accepts it eagerly. I'm relieved. I knew I needed someone like her to help support us. Another voice, not a royal one, speaking those words of peace, may help us actually bring peace at last.

Her happiness stays with me until Dahlia walks in.

She speaks as little as possible. She, of course, turns down her job, then stomps out with little fanfare. At least she wanted it over quickly, just like me.

The rest pass smoothy, well, for me. My staff still are afraid one will try to stab me in the middle of these meetings, apparently.

The most exciting one is Azalea.

I knew exactly what I wanted for her early on. She was the 'mom' of our group. She was a perfect second mother to her siblings, and I know how she loves children.

"Head Orphanage Coordinator for the royal family," I say.

"What!?" Azalea stands up in excitement. "Really?"

I smile and nod. "Really. You'll report directly to me. Our children are the ones suffering most in this war. From my own experience, I'd guess seventy percent of our homeless are children. We need to fix that. And I think you're the perfect person to help me with it."

"Oh yes, yes, yes, yes!" Azalea beams and hugs me. "But then... Why the high rank?" she asks as she pulls away.

I laugh. "You made it into the top five. The lowest rank you'd get is countess, and I wasn't going to stand for that. You come out a duchess or princess."

Azalea laughs, hugs me again and starts rattling off what she'd like to do.

I chuckle. "How about you write down your plans and let me finish my work?" With an excited nod, Azalea gives me proper respect before leaving.

She was the last interesting one. Apart from my staff still expecting every one of them to be an attempted assassin at any moment.

Thankfully though, that means I get a short break before I give them their final address, toast them, and then call it a day— at least work wise.

I pull myself together and stand up, nodding at my staff that I'm ready to step out.

The staff that are manning the party had anticipated the final toast I planned to give, and most of the girls have their drinks in their hands.

A servant offers me mine. I nod a thanks to her as Bella picks up her drink and uses a soft bell to get the room's attention.

I smile graciously at all of them.

"I wanted to end this special moment by offering a toast to you all. Thank you. Thank you for your sacrifices, your willingness to continue to serve your people, and for all your time spent at the palace." I raise my glass toward them.

"A toast to your futures. May they hold all your dreams and joy beyond what you can dream."

The toast seems well received, and I smile slightly as I drink to them.

I know I'm not a huge fan of most alcoholic drinks, but why does champagne either have no taste or taste far too acidy?

I contain my disgust though, making sure to drink as little as I can get away with. Some of the girls down their glasses, possibly to help them deal with their anger or disappointment. Others sip more carefully. Forsythia is smirking over her glass.

"You're all going to be powerful assets to the kingdom and its people. We seek to bring peace, not just to end the conflict, but between the hearts of our people, and you fine ladies will be key in all of it from the least ranked to the highest," I assure them.

That got a happier reply, and most drink to the idea. I smile a little, glad to see them finally feeling satisfied. I have big plans for them, even the ones I want to shove out of the way are big plans.

I put down my glass and wish them all a safe trip home. "If there are any last-minute things, I'll wait a bit longer for you."

They all curtsy to me to officially mark the end, most muttering something like "Thank you, Princess" or "Pleasure, Your Highness".

It feels so odd to be addressed this way. I thought I was used to it by now, but it leaves me a tad lightheaded and feeling disoriented, like it isn't real. What's even stranger is it doesn't go away like it had every other time. Why did I feel so... strange?

I blink as the world seems to swim for a moment. My heart is beating faster than it should, making my head lighter. I know I'm not great at holding my liquor, but seriously?

Elice, Violet, Forsythia, and Florence pause, watching me.

"Your Highness?" Elice frowns.

"Kascia, Princess Kascia, are you alright?" Violet asks me in concern.

"You look oddly pale, Princess," Elice agrees.

"Kascia." Bella's tone of concern is the last thing I remember as the world suddenly bucks from side to side like the deck of a ship. Dizzy, I stumble, trying to grab hold of something to steady myself. And that's the last thing I remember.

# Chapter 30

"I don't care if you have to run blood tests on the whole cursed lot of them!"

Each syllable rises a fresh throb in my head as I awaken gradually.

"They tried to kill her. That's attempted murder, an assassination of a royal, no matter how petty the motive!"

I groan as I peel my eyes open and struggle to push myself up. The feel of sheets against my arms tells me I'm in my own bed.

Gavril is standing near the door with a group of guards, snapping at them with Cedar standing between them, yet off to the side, watching with anger and grim agreement set on his face.

I've never seen Gavril look more angry: red in the face, teeth clenched in fury, and his eyes alight in rage. "None of them are to be let out until we can prove beyond a shadow of a doubt they are innocent."

"Are you sure—"

"This is treason, damn it! Yes."

"Are you sure you're not being too harsh?" Rose's voice comes from the armchair not too far away.

"No, if they don't stamp this out, it grows," Zelda's voice adds, wobbling as she shakes her head. "We still deal with this in Hyvil. If you are too soft, they keep trying."

"W-what happened?" I ask, pushing myself up. I'm still in the emerald green dress. As I reach up to soothe my pounding head, I notice the tiara is no longer there, although everything else remains.

"Kascia," Gavril sighs in love and relief and comes over to me, enfolding me in his arms.

"One of the girls slipped something into your drink," Zelda says grimly. "Sadly for her, the royal family is prepared with most every kind of antidote on hand, and Dr. Stephen was hired for his expertise on such things. He was able to find the correct antidote so fast, even I'm impressed."

"Thank heavens." Gavril sighs and pulls back, looking into my face with deep concern. "You feel alright?"

I nod. "I feel ill, like after that long night in the storm, but I'm alright."

Gavril nods and holds me tightly. I wish everyone else would go away so I could hide with him. I drop my head onto his shoulder, trembling as I take in the reality of what had just happened.

I'm shaken by the idea one of the girls I'd chosen to trust and planned to bring into my circle had done this to me. They hate me beating them that much, or perhaps it was just their hope they'd redo the whole thing, and they'd win the second time around.

"It's going to be okay," Gavril promises. "We have them all locked in the Ladies' Chamber, and they won't be leaving until we figure out who did it."

"But those that are innocent." I frown. They'll make a mess of this. Bile rises to my throat, making me want to retch. The press likely snapped impressions of the whole thing. Fabian is going to wish he'd come.

"We have taken all the impressionors that were there. We're hoping someone caught the culprit on film without realizing it," Gavril says. "If it lasts longer than a day, we'll find other arrangements."

"They must have done it after they met with you, so those you interviewed first had the most time, those at the end the least," Rose says.

"Not if they did it before meeting with her," Zelda disagrees.

"We'll worry about that later." Gavril spots how I pale at the thought.

My heart aches for Damian right now. He is so good at reading into people to figure out their motives. Even without magic, he could look them over and tell us at least the three most likely.

"For now, you should rest." Gavril's voice breaks through my longing. He turns to the guard and dismisses them to fulfill his orders. "Cedar, are you going to assist?"

"Sage and his family said they'll handle that for us. I'm making sure there's not another attempt. They could be rebel sympathizers who will go for either of you, or even if it is as silly as a girl fight, they may try again," Cedar replies.

The door bursts open, and Grandfather steps into the room. A wave of relief washes over me to see him.

"Thank Phoenix, you're alright!" he cries in relief as he comes over to me. Gavril lets go of me to let me hug my grandfather. "Who did this?" He looks at Gavril while holding me, eyes full of fury.

"We're working on it. It was one of the girls in the room for sure." Gavril's voice is edged with hatred.

"Envious little brix," Grandfather snarls and holds me tighter. "We'll catch them."

"Sage is helping investigate," Cedar assures Grandfather.

"I can assist him." Grandfather looks at me to make sure I'll be okay.

"W-whatever helps." I really don't know where anyone should be. This is all so new to me, and I know I can't be selfish.

Grandfather frowns and looks at Gavril. I don't see what expression he makes in reply, but Grandfather nods and holds me tighter. "We won't let them hurt you again."

"I never thought they'd do this now." Tears fill my eyes, making my headache worse.

The mattress under me rises slightly. Gavril had gotten up. I realize he's going to leave.

"Gavril!" I call out before I can stop it, but I close my mouth the second it's out. I can't be selfish. He must have work to do to catch who tried to kill me.

Gavril stops and turns to me. My lips shake, and I turn my eyes to the bedspread. I shouldn't have called him back.

The next moment, arms wrap around me. I fight not to cry in front of everyone, biting my lip with a sniff. A princess must be strong in the limelight.

"We'll see you later," Zelda promises, and she and Rose leave; making me realize with them and the guard gone, it's just Gavril, Grandfather, and me.

"Do you know who it was?" Grandfather asks gently.

My lip quivers again, and I shake my head, blinded by tears, and bury my face in Gavril's chest. An overwhelming yet mixed gratitude rises like a gentle tide over me.

The gratitude that he's mine and I can feel safe to huddle in his arms. In my chest, fear dances that they almost stripped my life from me out of envy. In swirls the gratitude that my grandfather is here, more loyal than my father ever had been, and finally, I'm filled with the pain that the girls I opened up to betrayed me.

I might have melted into tears then, but the door opens again, and my mother comes into the room. I immediately square my shoulders without conscious thought.

"Oh Kascia, I'm so glad you're alright," Mother sighs and comes over to me. "You feel alright?" I swallow and shake my head slightly. "Do you feel ill?" Mother checks, running her fingers over my cheek.

"A-a little," I confess.

Mother's pause and softened expression tells me she read me correctly and knows I mean I don't feel alright in ways other than physical.

"I would be petrified in your shoes," she admits with a soft smile.

Trying to avoid crying, all I can manage is a weak smile. I'm the crown princess; I have to be strong.

"If you don't need me, I'll check in and make sure your father isn't giving his guards grief trying to get to you." Mother kisses my forehead and gets up to leave.

"You don't have to go." I don't mind if she does, but she shouldn't feel like she doesn't belong in my world anymore because it's a royal one now.

"I don't want to make it harder. You have many people trying to care for you." Mother gives me another gentle smile. "And that alone is overwhelming, I'm sure."

I nod a little, admitting that to be completely true. It isn't my small intimate world anymore. It isn't just my mother, Damian, and my maids. It's not just Gavril being completely safe around, either. I have a larger staff, the girls that are still here, grandparents, parents, in-laws, and, of course, Gavril, not to mention the hundreds of guards.

I tremble, and Gavril holds me tighter. I close my eyes and attempt to hold back tears. It would only make my headache worse, anyway. Grandfather frowns deeper.

I didn't expect such a blow this soon into my royal life. Attempts sure, but nothing like this and not so personal. It isn't just "the princess" they are after; it is Princess Kascia they want to hurt. Me, not just a figurehead, but me. They know me. But it didn't matter.

Gavril sighs and rubs my back. "I'm sorry. I should have realized someone would try something and been more careful with security."

"I should have been on watch. I've been too hands off, not wanting to crowd you like the queen does," Grandfather apologizes. "It was not fair to expect Cedar to handle everything on his own. I won't make that mistake again."

Before I can reply, the door opens once more. Gavril scowls a little, perhaps wondering why no one knocked.

Grandmother comes into the room. She sighs in relief like everyone else and comes over, caressing my cheek.

"My dear girl, thank heavens you're alright. Your father is livid."

"I'll handle him." Mother sighs and gets up to leave.

"I think it might help to let him see for himself." Grandmother frowns, then looks at Gavril. Of course, it's up to Gavril.

Gavril hesitates, then looks down at me. My face contorts into a frown. I don't know. I want to give him a chance to be in my life again;

I truly do, but I am so afraid to have that trust broken. What if he just causes more trouble in his own twisted way of helping? But to see he really does care for me could be comforting. I'm too confused and honestly slightly in shock at what had happened to have an answer for him.

"Perhaps it might help him trust us more," Grandmother hints. "But if you're not feeling up for it."

I don't know. I frown, perhaps deeper, and look up at Gavril as if for an answer. I really don't have a clue what I want and even less what I should do.

Gavril hesitates again, looking to everyone else in the room with just his eyes before meeting Grandmother's. "Alright. With his usual entourage, it should be alright."

Grandmother nods and bows, leaving.

I steal my courage and bow my head to get it on straight. Mother frowns and rubs my back. "It's alright now, Kascia. We'll have this all figured out in no time. It's alright."

"I just... didn't think the first attempt would get so close or be so personal," I confess, "or that the attacks would be against me. I thought I'd been the people's champion princess."

"This has *nothing* to do with that," Gavril says firmly. "This was jealous girlfriends fighting, as much as I loathe it. I doubt there was a second rebel who managed to join the Enthronement ranks. I think I may have guessed who it may be if I'm right about the motive."

"We'll find out who. Sage will do all he can, and he's a horror when he wants to be." Grandfather smiles. "This will not go unpunished."

There's a noise at the door once more, but this time, we're prepared for it. Father barges into the room, looking harassed and disheveled. Grandmother comes in after him.

"Kascia." He rushes to me. My honest reaction with how fast he moves is to pull away. "Are you hurt?" Father asks, taking my hand.

I shake my head. "A-a little out of sorts, but I'm okay," I say in a tight voice.

"Thank Phoenix." He sighs and ignores that I'm currently quite happy in my husband's arms and hugs me tightly.

I hate it, but it makes tears rise to my eyes as I'd missed this and feeling safe too. But I'm also frighteningly aware that he'd fully ignored Gavril was right there.

Gavril, for his credit, doesn't complain or comment, letting us have the moment. Father holds me for what feels like too long to me, but it likely was short. He then pulls back, studying my face with a hand on my cheek. I'm ashamed. I'm scared of what he might do.

I wish he'd kept his hand there the next moment when he stands upright and rounds on Gavril.

"How could you let this happen!?" he demands. "You're supposed to protect her from this."

Gavril blinks in shock at the unexpected assault. "I was supposed to know a jealous girl was going to try to poison her with a dozen guards in the room, including one of your own?" Gavril's voice has an edge to it that doesn't surprise me.

"You should have been there."

"If it was a failure on any part, it was your own Custods who were in the room! I'm not the one who threw her into a world she wanted nothing to do with."

"You're the reason she couldn't climb out."

Gavril gets to his feet. The way it jostles me makes my head hurt. "I offered her the choice more times than she'd even have liked. I've been the one defending her while you pushed your agenda."

"I trusted you to protect her. Not even a week, and she hardly survives an assassination attempt," Father snarls back.

"You act like you gave your permission," Gavril scoffs. "We all know what you'd like to do if you could."

"You're supposed to protect her. You failed."

I can't take it. My head is throbbing. I'm still so confused. And I hate watching them go at it like this. Father just can't accept my choice. Gavril, understandably, is wary of my father, and Father has to go and blame Gavril for this. I can't fight the tears anymore. The tears blind me, and I struggle against the sobs I'm locking tight in my chest.

"It was the girl you spurned that caused this," Father goes on.

Gavril had either seen or somehow heard or perhaps sensed the tears that I couldn't stop from rolling down my cheeks because he turns to me, ignoring my father's jibe. It lures Father's eyes to me too.

Gavril reaches out to embrace me, but Father moves to do the same and glares at Gavril for getting in his way.

I pull away from him as Grandfather takes Father's arm and pulls him back. "Regain her trust then maybe that will be a fair fight," Grandfather warns my father.

"She's my child!" Father rages at Grandfather.

"Whose trust you broke, and like it or not, that boy has done a far better job looking after her than you have lately. He's her husband, and after all you've done, he is the first to try to comfort her unless she says otherwise."

"You can't just take her from me." Father can't escape Grandfather's grip, though.

"We gave you a chance, and all you've done is stress her more. You're of better help assisting us in finding out which of the brats did it." Grandfather's tone is firm, harsh, and commanding. It reminds me of Father's in my training as a child, which is comforting. "Come on."

"She is my child."

"And her husband and Mother have her well in hand," Grandfather warns.

"Come on." Grandmother nods to the door. "We can better help her by finding who did it, as your father said. Let's go."

Father is tense in anger with them but can't really deny the pressure the guards are putting on him to leave. But to my surprise, Grandfather hands Father off to them before looking at me as they and Grandmother leave. "Do you need me?"

I swallow and shake my head. The fact he stayed as long as he did is enough. Mother looks at me as if asking if it's alright if she goes too.

I force a weak smile and nod. For the moment, I am safer and better comforted by my husband.

Mother kisses my cheek before following my cursing father. Grandfather kisses my forehead, brushes a few tears away with a sad smile and tender compassion in his eyes before he leaves.

Once we're alone, Gavril kisses me gently to comfort me. I hold on to it as if breathing the air I need to live as long as I can before I start to cry again and latch onto him.

"I'm sorry. I didn't mean to let him pull me into a fight like that. It's hard for me not defend myself when he attacks like that," Gavril apologizes.

"It was him, not you," I manage to get out, fighting to hide in the embrace I love and trust above all others.

"Shh, I'm here. You can cry or scream or kick or whatever you need." He strokes my hair. He frowns a bit, realizing my tiara is gone. But then he stiffens.

"Ian!" he calls after him in an impressively loud voice.

Grandfather rushes back into the room.

"Whoever grabbed her tiara. Rose and Zelda didn't get it, and it wasn't on the floor. Whoever took it is likely your jealous girl."

Grandfather beams in understanding, nods, racing from the room.

"We'll have her." Gavril smiles and kisses my head and holds me close. "I won't let them hurt you again. Until *I* approve them, you aren't to be alone with any of the Chosen Ladies. Your grandfather and Cedar should be in the meetings as well as your lady, alright?"

I nod. It doesn't matter to me. I don't know how to know who to trust even now. I thought I did. I was wrong again. Gavril cradles me as I sob into him, just like Damian used to, patiently comforting me. I couldn't have asked for better.

"I-I love you," I stammer out between sobs.

The smile that crosses Gavril's face could light up seven galaxies.

"I love you more than life," he assures with a tight embrace to prove it. "You're my very soul, Kascia. I didn't know I could grow to love you more than I did, but you're all of existence to me. I am here for you, no matter what that means. I'm right here. What do you need?"

"I just need you." I shake my head a little as I keep crying until the headache is too much on top of the sobbing, so I just let him hold me until I slip into a healing sleep.

I'm not left alone over the rest days. If I am not with Gavril, Grandfather is with me, and if they both are busy, Cedar is with me, though personally, I think Gavril needs the guard more than I do. Lila takes rotation too.

The ill feeling lasts the rest of the day, but by the next morning, I am physically okay though my heart still aches with a slight tremor of fear.

When work resumes the first work day, they try to get me back to a normal schedule before telling me the results of the investigation. My teachers are extra gentle with me, though it's not really needed.

After lunch, I'll have the meeting to go over what they've found. I am anxious about it all day.

Gavril's trick with the tiara and Sage's intense intimidation to get a confession worked like a charm.

It was Viscountess Violet who had done it. She was still convinced she and Gavril were meant to be and when I'd told her she would not be assigned to the palace, taking away any chance to woo him away from me, she decided to take more drastic measures. Sage used the fact she'd taken the tiara as proof, and she gave a heartfelt confession.

As it's treason, a member of the royal family needs to officiate the judgment. The king should be the person to do it, but apparently, Violet is requesting Gavril do it. I'll have to testify as the victim, so I'm not an option, making it harder to reject her request.

"Why would she want you? Normally, even if you wanted to, you wouldn't be allowed with the personal connection. Not that your father doesn't as well, but it's still different." The queen is frowning in concern and confusion.

"I don't know. She's mad to think I'll go easy on her." Gavril shakes his head.

"Does she think she can make the magic spark between you flare up in time to save her?" I ask.

"She could be that deluded." Gavril nods.

"Can you really keep someone that dangerous locked up for life?" The queen frowns.

"Can I justify executing her when I'd like to wring her neck with my bare hands?" Gavril retorts. "And how would that look to the people? First big judgment, and I execute her."

"But she's far too dangerous to be left in jail, even under the highest guard, if she is convinced she can charm and wiggle her way into the fairytale she's dreaming of." The queen pales slightly.

"If it comes down to it, once a jury finds her guilty, and it's sent to me to confirm, I'd banish her," Gavril says. "Harsh enough to not be called weak, but not so harsh to be pegged as cold-hearted."

"Where could you safely send her?" The queen's brow furrows.

"She could stir up other nations against us," the king agrees.

"Sir Ian suggested Hyvil. Sage thinks it a brilliant idea. If she acts up over there, Zelda's father is known to be harsh on uprisings with the high level of unrest in his kingdom. So, either he does the dirty work, or she starts over, too far to hope to return. And if she does somehow get a boat to bring her, and she lands in Purerah, the punishment is death for going against the banishment. I see less risk in that action, but that's only up to me *if* I judge."

"But you can't. It's too personal," the queen urgently reminds him.

"But the law says the accused can request a different member of the royal family." The king shakes his head. "I think the law is on her side on this."

"It's stupid!"

"The law was made to help an accused avoid being judged by someone who would be biased without being forced to incriminate oneself. However, she is using it backwards." The king shakes his head again. "Legally, if she wants it, she gets it, unless the person is unavailable."

"We could postpone the trial until he's unavailable," the queen suggests half-heartedly.

"We need to act quickly to make sure this is handled. They think I'm soft, the rebels go mad," Gavril vehemently disagrees.

"He's right. The rebels are testing to see where we are weak." I look at the queen. "And no offense meant, but now that I've seen the whole picture, I believe perhaps fear of being too harsh in the eyes of the people has extended some of this tension. They already dislike you and being too soft won't fix that."

"Plus, if she is as dangerous as you fear, we shouldn't leave her waiting," the king says, taking his wife's hand.

The longing I always feel when I saw their bond rises in me, stemming from the first time I saw it. It was just after Jake had shattered my heart.

I start slightly as Gavril takes my hand, giving me a soft, assuring smile. I beam, and it takes all my self-control not to jump at him that instant. I don't deserve him. My heart is brimming with love and gratitude for what I finally have. I have exactly what I longed for, only better than I thought it would be. I force myself to focus, though. We're still working.

"So immediate action would be wise." The king nods grimly. "I'm afraid we will probably have to give the accused what she wishes. And you have a plan of action going in, making it easier to handle whatever she does."

I nod my agreement. Gavril squeezes my hand. "We'll make it swift. I already have counties working to make a fair jury. It won't be easy with so many biases. The people have become more enamored with their new princess. Viscountess Violet did not pick a wise time to attack her. The last riot wasn't even against the royal family but demanding Violet's head."

"What?" I gape at Gavril.

"Yes, I thought your staff would keep it quiet so as not to upset you," he says with a half smirk. "The rioters want her head and demand it now. I've never seen this type of protest before. I admit, it made me happier with my people than I've been in quite some time."

With that in mind, the trial takes place as soon as possible, taking up my afternoons as a required witness. I wish it was a short case, but it isn't.

The first day is just about selecting jurors, which is a painfully long process. Even with the volunteer system in Purerah, it is hard to weed out people who could be honest jurors. In fact, some argue it's harder than random selection. But it is fast. I can't imagine a random selection for a case like this being done in a day.

The second day collects statements from the defense and prosecution, judge's reminders, and the like.

I finally get my testimony over with on the third day. I am the first witness up. The other witnesses called are Bella, Sage, Cedar, Heather, Payge, a few of the palace staff who were there, and a few castle guards.

The hope had been to end the trial that day, but it is getting late. The judge agrees to wrap it up the following day.

The next day starts with a review of the evidence placed so far, allowing both parties to reexamine any witnesses they had or call forth any new ones before the final statements.

Thankfully, there aren't any new witnesses. Violet's defense struggles to explain her "not-guilty" plea when she confessed to Sage that she'd done it. It is likely the main reason we are able to do this as quickly. I feel sorry for her as she finishes her remarks.

The prosecution has a much easier time. As he stands, he almost smirks to himself as he addresses the jury.

"Ladies and gentlemen of the jury, you have seen all the evidence. The defendant had motive, means, and opportunity. She confessed to Sir Sage Custod she poisoned Princess Kascia as stated in his testimony. She was found holding the princess's tiara. Witnesses noted she was the only one not frightened by the incident, and she herself has confessed she'd do anything to make what was 'wronged' right.

"If you are honest with yourselves, you will see there is no other option but to charge her guilty as there is no reasonable doubt she would, could, and did commit the crime. I trust you all will make the right judgment call. And I will remind you, you are not accountable for whatever punishment is affixed to her crime. You are merely here to give a verdict of guilty or not guilty, and that it is the judge's duty to exact justice or extend mercy. Thank you."

The jury does not take long to deliberate. They return only twenty minutes later and unanimously declare her guilty, passing up her sentencing to the sitting judge.

The sitting judge swiftly passes the sentencing over to Prince Gavril as the defendant requested.

At this point, a formal review of the evidence is summarized by the court scribe to Gavril (even though he'd been there the whole time. Standard procedure and all that). Then the prosecution says their piece. The victim is traditionally given a chance to speak, but I don't want to speak in my own defense to my husband in court, and it is perfectly legal for me to pass on my chance to plead my case to the judge.

Finally, the condemned is allowed to speak. I thought Violet might trust her lawyer to do it or at least have her lawyer at her ear to help walk her through what to say.

Instead, her lawyer frowns, holding in her reaction as Violet almost pushes her aside to stand up and make her case.

She looks up at Gavril with eyes full of a devoted obsession that might be mistaken for love. It certainly is an obsessive adoration.

I tense defensively to see it. I know I had to let many girls admire him like that when we were vying for his hand. But it still makes me miserable and angry to see.

"This court has found me guilty," Violet begins. "But if I am guilty of anything, it's of being deeply lost in true love and a passion to correct the wrongs that will condemn this kingdom. In your heart, Gavril, you know I'm the one you should be with. It's fate. Even if I was the one to poison her, it wouldn't be wrong."

I miss Gavril tensing in the kind of anger that normally means he's about to hit something as my own eyes flood with a red-hot anger. *How dare she!?*

"I was eliminated only over a misunderstanding. Perhaps I was too blinded by the true love that binds us and has always bound us, but fate has a power greater than ours, my prince. I should not be punished for the crime of loving too purely for this world. We are meant to be.

"You were promised you'd end this war if you married your true princess. Even if I was the one who tried to kill the imposter, it wouldn't be a true crime or a cause for guilt because it must be done. We have been bound by fate and prophecy. I am a perfect princess, and you and I are perfect together. Mercy must be extended, and the imposter removed, so the true love and passion you've lacked from this marriage are righted, so this kingdom can flourish. Please, Gavril, you feel it. I know you do."

The way she leans towards him in admiration and devotion, letting her sleeves slide to look more pathetic and alluring, how her eyes fill with tears of devotion as she looks up at Gavril. It makes an angry bubble rise in my stomach, threatening to burst. He's not hers to look at like that!

Several people jerk into movement. Sage steps forward as if to attack her, but Zelda stops him. Grandfather moves as if to attack her too, but instead stops and takes my hand, helping me stay on my throne. He squeezes my hand to help me stay composed. I give him a slight smile of thanks before turning my eyes to Gavril.

The last person to move is Gavril. I glance at him, afraid he might lunge at her himself. But when I see his face, a wave of fear strikes my heart. Will that stiff expression melt into regret? I don't know if I could bear it if that's what happens.

Instead, the stiff expression melts into disgust. His jaw set in annoyance. His eyes burn with loathing for the woman who grovels at his feet, trying to be as sexually appealing and alluring as possible, and yet, innocent and devoted to him as a saint. It is sickening to me, but to Gavril, it looks like there is no greater sin.

"You assume much, Violet." Gavril almost spits her name at her like an insult.

Violet flinches and starts to cry. I think she expects it to help. That somehow it will melt his heart, make him realize he was madly in love with her, and change his mind.

It doesn't.

Gavril's eyes sharpen, and his nostrils flare as his arms clench in hatred. The anger in his eyes expresses how deeply her words offend him. And that isn't taking in the fact that Violet had the nerve to try to kill me, the heart and soul of his very existence.

"Gavril, please, you know it's me you've wanted. Always."

The whole room makes a noise of either disgust or protest as she throws herself to be as close to Gavril as the barrier between the floor of the throne room and the throne area allowed. Her dress is almost falling off her as she looks at him, begging, trying to look as attractive and yet pathetic as possible. How does she think this will work?

I tremble in tense anger. My face is hot with pain and anger at this woman trying to throw herself onto my husband.

Gavril ignores her extra pleading. "You loved nothing more than a dream you made up for yourself. And that has pushed you to a life you never wanted. I have seen the evidence and know you and how you behaved with me during the Enthronement and find you guilty. I have no doubt you're capable with your reaction to being dismissed. I hereby sentence you to banishment to the kingdom of Hyvil: never to return, on pain of death."

Violet's face turns almost the same shade as her namesake.

"How dare you!?" she shrieks. "Your tests were wrong! It's me you're meant to be with. I am the perfect princess, and your parents saw it before that witch entranced you all. You'll pay for this mistake and beg for forgiveness from me; bet your souls on it! You will be where you belong, Prince Gavril. Don't you forget it!"

These screams go on as the guards grab her. Then Violet rounds on me.

"You're dead!" she shrieks at me as they struggle to drag her away. "You're dooming us all! The prophecy meant me, you brix! You hear me! It was me!"

Her screams are finally drowned out as the doors shut. The court starts to mutter and discuss as they stand up. Court officials assist the jury as they exit.

Everyone has no problem moving on but me. I sit there. The old fear of what if Gavril chose wrong returns like a sickly bubble swelling in my chest.

It's a painfully odd feeling. The icy dread as the fear she could be right swirling in my chest, painfully mixing with the red-hot anger I felt at her desperate attempt to seduce my husband from me.

I *know* it isn't Violet the prophecy meant, but the way she'd screamed at me... I am still growing used to how to handle people hating me that deeply, and this is personal. I don't think Dahlia or Ericka or even Forsythia hated me that much.

"You alright?" Gavril asks quietly, making me jump.

"Fine," I say quickly.

"She's just a jealous little brix; you know that, right?" Grandfather had been watching me. His face carries a soft concern that reminds me of Damian.

"I do." I nod with more assurance than I feel.

"Still not used to them screaming like that," Gavril guesses, taking my hand to help me stand so we're level.

I wish he'd knelt down to make it easier for me to process this painful hot/cold feeling, but he's right. If he knelt beside me, the court would notice. I shouldn't show how much that little brat had shaken me.

"No." I shake my head. "I'm still getting used to this part of royalty."

"You're doing better than you think." Gavril smiles, tilting my chin to meet his eyes. "You're perfect, my Asteria. Come. We have the rest of the afternoon free. We can talk it out, or I might just end up tossing her in the ocean myself."

I giggle and take his arm. My beloved husband is happy and takes pleasure in whatever it takes to protect me. Between him and my grandfather, I couldn't be safer or more loved.

# Chapter 31

I think we all breathe easier once she's locked up, so we can officially give the other girls their jobs. But another more depressing event is happening first.

Rose leaves the day after it all settles down, but I know I'll see her when I get my turn to attend the World Summit either this year or another year, so it's not as bitter as the other parting: Zelda and Sage.

I wonder if that means Isla will come to stay, as we'd had the court management position saved for her just in case, but she is more comfortable living in her own space away from us. I understand how hard it would be to be the third wheel in the family if she stayed with us again. I suspect she'll still be getting palace support, living in her own area of the castle or elsewhere.

Sage's parents are also going to Hyvil, but no one is sure if they'll be staying in Hyvil with them long or not. I can't help but wonder how the king of Hyvil is going to react to Zelda losing the Enthronement but still coming home with her king-in-waiting on her arm.

I'll miss Alliea's humor. She jokes she'll miss Joy, who comes along for the farewell, but Gavril has ensured it's not too bitter. He presents her with a little husky puppy: a little boy with red patterns on his head that are almost like little horns down his face. He's calmer than Joy was at his age but is so happy to lick and love all over Alliea.

"You hate me that much, don't you?" Sage sighs as Gavril beams at Alliea, cooing at the puppy.

Gentian, her husband, chuckles, not at all minding. Now the mystery of who I am is out, he's been much less intense, and surprisingly, he actually is quite a laid-back guy.

"No. She was just so happy to play with Joy, and I thought you all could use a pick-me-up during the anxious ride over," Gavril defends with a smile before he and Sage embrace like brothers.

"I can't believe it's over." I turn to Zelda as I already hear tears in her voice as she comes up to me. She hugs me tightly. "I can't really believe we may never see each other again."

I fight my own tears as I hug her back. "Maybe if we get this mess figured out, we can come visit Hyvil sometime."

"Gavril would love all of it," Zelda half laughs, half sobs. "I'd love to show you my world. Gavril's water magic would really help him fit right in, and you'd love the music and the people." She sighs. She's fighting not to cry harder than me. "And of course, we can try to come visit again for sure. I'm determined to make it work."

"So, it's not goodbye forever," I try to comfort her. "I couldn't have made it so far without you."

"At least it wasn't just us left at any point, like we feared." Poor Zelda manages a weak smile. "Write all the time."

"I'll need to get one of those birds," I laugh.

"You'll just send mine back every time. I'm getting one just for you," Zelda insists. "Promise."

"Promise," I assure her. "I'm going to really need your help still. But you can at least be happy to be going home. It will be your wedding soon, right?"

"Takes over a year to process that, knowing my father. Oh, good grace, please say you'll come." The sudden horror of realizing we may not be at her wedding is devastating.

"I'll drag Gavril along no matter what," I say, hoping we can pull it off, but if Gavril gets power soon... the kingdom can handle two months without us, right?

"If I have to rent you all a dragon to make it faster, I will," Zelda insists. "I'll pay for it. You tell me what they'll charge, and you'll have it."

I laugh at that. She may not know we're broke, but she knows how to bribe. "Not sure he'll like that, but we'll do our best."

"Hurry it up; can't miss the tide," the ship captain calls to us.

Zelda's eyes swim in tears as she hugs me one more time. "Until then?"

"Until then." I manage a smile. I don't think I'm going to realize how much I'll miss her until she's gone. Unlike with Damian, this just doesn't feel real.

I notice Gavril and Sage seem to be quickly wrapping up their rather awkward farewells. Men are so stupid about these kinds of feelings.

Sage comes over to Zelda to help her pull away. She has to give me one more last quick hug before he gently leads her away.

"You be good, little threat," Sage teases me.

That makes me laugh and cry at the same time. "Told you I wasn't dangerous."

"Still a little secret. You're worthy of it. Don't forget it, sister." Sage then shows a surprising level of emotion in hugging me like a little sister. "Take care of him for me, and if he doesn't look after you, I'll shadow over and beat him up."

I laugh as I return his hug. "Thank you, Prince Sage."

His mouth twitches in discomfort at the name, but it's going to be true soon enough. I smile and pull away to let them go as the captain calls out again.

Gavril puts an arm around my shoulders as we watch them hurry onto the ship. My heart drops like a rock when the plank is pulled up and the sails drop.

Sage gives Zelda a tight, comforting hug before she races to the edge to wave to us as long as she can: calling out she'll miss us, write soon, love you, and all that stuff. Gavril laughs as he waves back. She doesn't stop waving until she's too far away to see us, and we stay until that moment. I think I see Sage pull her into a tight hug again, but they're too far to see.

"She'll be okay. She's stronger than she's acting," Gavril assures me.

"I don't think I'll really feel she's gone for a while, then I'll cry like her," I half joke with a sad smile.

"You've had so many goodbyes lately; I can fully believe that." Gavril smiles and kisses my head. "Come on, let's get to riding lessons; that will be fun."

# Chapter 32

It's crunch time. Time to get in all my meetings with the court, representatives, and my staff to get work moving. First up, getting the household staff in order.

It is rather intimidating to call the entire castle staff together to go over how things are going to change. I miss Zelda in this moment. She would have known how to handle this. Some guidance on how other princesses do it would have been nice. But it is up to me now. Damian left to let me stand on my own. Zelda has to do the same.

Hydie is happy I'm taking the initiative at first. But... she also doesn't know what I'm going to do.

I know I'll need Hydie's help to arrange it, but I'm nervous of what she'll say if she finds out what I plan to say. If I am in charge, then I am making some changes. I first want to get rid of the class system the staff seem to have implanted into themselves.

The kitchen is the highest nobility of the staff. Those that directly serve the royal family, direct maids, delivery staff, and the like are the next level. The grounds workers, the cleaning staff, and the laundry staff finish the hierarchy.

This has to end. Every one of them is needed to run this palace, and this attitude is causing discomfort among the staff, not to mention how it makes me feel being shoved around and dictated to by these rules.

The scary part... I learned I am fully in charge of their wages. I have a set budget, and of course, and I must obey the rules about the base pay, but otherwise, their salaries are my responsibility. I have certain slots to fill that must be filled. I can't make new positions unless it fits the budget. But it gives me power to control so much, I feel too powerful. But I can use this.

"You want all the staff?" Hydie frowns as I tell her what I need and how long we'll need. "Pausing all work for an hour and a half?"

"I know it might disrupt things, but..." But I am going to disrupt things, anyway. *You're Princess now. This is your job. It's alright,* I remind myself. "But I need to address them all at once. I apologize that it may delay things. That's why I tried to choose a quieter time."

"Why do you need the whole staff at once? You can meet with the heads, and they can work it on down," Hydie suggests.

"No. I need them all to hear it from me," I insist.

Hydie pulls a worried face. "Alright, but I don't see any reason you need to address them all at once. They'll be working double time or overtime to get it all done."

"I know. And I am sorry for that, but this has to happen. There are changes that must happen, and I want to do it all at once."

"Perhaps I can help you with those choices." I see the fear in Hydie's eyes. She thinks this is about firing people. And it isn't. Not yet.

"No, thank you. I know what I want to say. Please, just arrange it as soon as possible at the quietest hour. I presume that's after lunch clean up, correct?"

"Yes." Hydie nods. "That would be correct."

"Good. Then set it up. And if you feel it needed, you can apologize for the delay in work it will cause." But I have a bad feeling, the only group it really bothers is the kitchen, and of course to them, that is the most important thing. Well, that thinking will change soon enough.

"What do you have to say to them all at once?" Hydie asks.

I can't avoid this question. "I'm changing how things are done," I state simply. "Starting with how we prioritize workers."

"Prioritize workers?" Hydie frowns. "With all due respect, Princess, you haven't seen the running of such a household as this. I would suggest you take more time to learn about such work before making such a drastic change."

"Isn't that why you dragged me around the palace, getting to see them all?" I smile, putting down the work schedules I'd been review-ing. "I think you trained me well enough, don't you?"

Hydie stammers. She doesn't want to say she did a bad job, but she also is afraid of whatever mad choice I'm about to make.

"You did a fine job. I'll see you just before the meeting, then." I give her a bright smile before leaving.

I doubt they'll like the changes to their work shifts I'm making, but they are quite skewed. Those with the "lesser" jobs have absolutely painful schedules. I think the arrangement can be a bit fairer for every-one.

My next painful lesson in royal politics, even among their staff, is stories get out. Rumors circulate, and someone must have seen what I was working on, and the rumor of my changing schedules gets out.

Just before the meeting, Hydie finds me.

"You will disrupt the whole morale of the staff," Hydie frets. "They are used to their system and they like it."

"Some do," I correct. "But the kitchen staff are given far too many privileges and reliefs others are not. I think there should be fairer coverage for other jobs, too."

"Coverage? You mean you're changing the system for when someone is out ill?" Hydie's voice gets a bit shrill towards the end.

"I think the laundry staff should have backup, too," I state simply.

"But... th-that's not as timely as other jobs," Hydie insists.

"Cleaning staff get backup assigned from the laundry and other places." I point out. "So why do they back people up but not get backups?"

"It... it isn't... Your Highness, that's not how the system works. And it's worked so well for—"

"And I understand it has worked. But I doubt those on the bottom appreciate how it's run. I'm making it fair. I know people don't like change. Most of all, forced change, but we can't run our staff like this and expect our people to see each other as friends and equals when my own staff don't. This is a change I can make. Unless you're suggesting as *my* head of staff you can override me?"

"Of course not! I simply—"

"Then let me do my job as I see fit. It will be fine. You'll see." I smile gently at her.

The staff are impressively on time. They're better than the nobility I'd called to a meeting.

The tension in the room is thick. The only two rooms in the palace large enough for everyone to fit in are the dining hall and ballroom. Most of the staff work in the dining hall, so that's where we arranged it. They bring in that same portable stage they'd used for announcements done out of the dining hall or reception hall, which is slightly smaller and closer to the front doors. It is the only way to ensure they all could see me.

They bring in chairs and most sit staggered so they can see, while others stand around the edges.

There are so many of them. I'm one girl, and there are over a hundred of them. If they truly don't like this, they could ignore me. What else could I do?

No. I have power. I had to use it. I have to make it more even.

"Is everyone here?" I check.

There's an awkward pause. I look at Hydie. "Is everyone here?"

"Well... a few had to be on shift to ensure—"

"I wanted everyone." My face flushes. They already are undermining me. What could I do?

"Well, some have to look after the children, and the other royals may need—"

"The prince knows I called this, and his personal staff are attending. The same with the king and queen." I had told them this would happen, and none of them minded. The king joked about firing the ugly ones.

"But the children—"

"Then have them here. I don't care." I try not to snap, but she's undermining me again. My ability to actually be in charge is starting to feel like an illusion. "I want them all here. We'll wait. If it takes longer, it takes longer."

I don't miss how the heads of the kitchen staff fidget, but they are getting the lion's share of everything, so I don't care.

"But Your Highness—"

"The sooner they are here, the sooner they are back," I reply as coolly as I can.

Hydie finally accepts I won't pull back, so she rushes off with another girl I think is her unofficial assistant to hurry and bring the others. I knew this may take a while. It's possible that they have scattered in random places around the palace.

What I want to do is sit down and bury my face in my hands. I may have won that, but I am humiliated by how she didn't do exactly as I asked and how I almost lost the fight to get it.

Instead, I have to look calm and in control. The others might take advantage of me if I don't. I look at the crowd and decide to ask them to help me see which job team is where.

My heart drops like a rock.

The laundry team is completely missing. They must be the ones handling the work while others attend this meeting. Of course they are. I want to scream, but I don't. I make sure they save space for them when they arrive at the front.

When they all finally arrive, I smile at the sounds of the children. I understand why they are at least sent to the back, though. They would be distracting, so I allow that.

One little boy sees me. His eyes widen big. He either knows my face or maybe figured it out from the bejeweled headband my staff had chosen for the day because he tries to run up to me.

I am flattered and beam to see his excitement. I'm just about to stoop to greet him. The boy knows it. But then Hydie stops him.

"You don't just run up to a princess, sweetheart. You need to behave," she says gently to him.

The boy takes a moment to realize he is being told "no" when he saw I was about to say "yes". He is too young to handle that disappointment without tears.

"I know. It's okay to be—" Hydie begins.

"I can make my own choice on this, Hydie," I interrupt her.

If every eye in the room wasn't already on me, it is now. Hydie stares at me, scandalized.

The boy senses Hydie's weakness and pushes out of her arms and runs to me.

My smile is the biggest I'd worn without Gavril nearby in ages as I bend down and catch him in a hug. I couldn't bear his tears of disappointment. Most of all when that's how I feel. I need this hug far more than he does.

Wait... this is an excellent chance to show an example.

"Want to help me talk to all the workers?" I ask him.

He gasps in surprise and nods big. I smile and pick him up, standing and setting him on my hip.

His squeals of happy laughter echo around the surprisingly quiet room. I giggle and tickle his neck slightly, to more happy child giggles, before I go to the center again to address the room.

The only regret about that move is not realizing that holding a child on your hip that long isn't as easy as it looks. I haven't had to hold something like this for so long in at least over a year, if not longer. I have to work on my arms before I have my own.

"Thank you all for waiting. I know it's stressful to have timely work delayed," I start out. "But as I've learned more about how this palace operates and my role in maintaining its order, I knew I had to make changes."

The tension is right back. Many people fidget uneasily. I swallow hard. I can do this. I can handle them. The little boy drops his head on my shoulder. I smile slightly. Terrible two, uh?

"For the moment, I am not eliminating any positions or removing anyone from their current positions," I start out to try to drop the tension.

It works. I sigh in a bit of relief too.

"Rather, it's the structure I wish to change." I gain a little more courage. "I have observed an... unofficial hierarchy among the staff. This is evident not only in attitudes towards the best jobs, but also in how tasks are shared across teams and even in wages. Though it's fair to say the system scales for the experience needed to each position and the work they do, there also is a disconnect that the more favorable jobs are rewarded with more than they're due and the worse jobs compensated less.

"This is backwards. The harder jobs that are less enjoyable should be compensated for this fact to make it fair. I have worked hard with royal accountants to ensure the adjustments will be small and bearable for each position so that your standard of living will not be seriously changed."

I then go into more details about the adjustments. And at first, this doesn't appear to win me many favors. They all must assume they'll be paid less.

"And going forward, I will be taking reports on how each individual and team is doing in their tasks. This will determine if we need to make staffing changes. And that is true for all positions, no matter how lofty or lowly they may be viewed."

I take a deep breath. Now I have to explain why. The frustration and resentment in my changes are clear. I have to do my best to rebut this. And if any staff member is too bad... I can still fire them. I just hate sending anyone away knowing how hard it is out there. But they are getting the rules now. They all are. And so, if they fail to meet them, it is on them. I have to remember that.

"I can no longer stand by and watch any member of my staff be treated as any less than another. You may try to deny it happens, but I have seen it for myself.

"When I was shown around to each of your departments, the 'lowliest' of the staff were the only ones humble enough to treat me kindly *without* an agenda," I point out bluntly. "And I find it rather disappointing that the castle staff, who should exemplify what their princess wants in her people, are so judgmental towards their fellow workers. I don't care what station you work in; you're all equal to me. You all may think the laundry is the worst, but it was the only place I felt safe to go when I wanted a quiet moment with staff I could trust."

I hope I'm not being too harsh.

"And there will be punishments for not seeing and treating each other as equals on the same staff. Yes, there are managers who give orders and the like, but to me, you're all the same. No one is too low to work with me and my family directly, and I hope you all learn that quickly. I don't want to see any more elitist nonsense among my staff. Is that clear?"

Of course, no one objects; they fear for their jobs. But I hope it can become more than that in time.

There is certainly less tension in the room. I wrap up by telling them their managers would have their adjusted schedules, back up assignments, and pay scale tomorrow morning. I don't want them to lose more time.

The staff are happy about that, at least. They break the moment I dismiss them and hurry to work.

A woman comes over to take the little boy. He's sleepy but beaming at me as she takes him, waving "bye-bye" sleepily. I beam and wave back, although I feel relief in my right arm when she takes his weight off of it.

I'm worried I wasn't clear enough or compassionate enough as the staff leave. My staff assure me my speech was just fine, and they'll do their best to help make sure the changes I want to see will happen.

I see signs that perhaps my speech had worked when I see more variants of staff coming to bring things to me and my direct staff from all the different departments. I notice the Chosen girls I meet with to set up their new jobs notice it too and are impressed.

Next, I have to get the Chosen girls who had accepted jobs into their positions. I work with Florence, Godwin, and the king's court liaison to ensure all our court representatives are ready. I also assign Florence to help the union representatives figure out how to start their work.

The only girl left is Isla. She is our princess ward after all, and her assignment doesn't have her work with me as directly. I feel bad about that, but Isla assures me that she prefers it this way. It gives her more time with her "target members of court", whatever that meant.

But once I have all the girls settled into the jobs we've given them, I also have to ensure the girls who will not be working for the crown sign their acknowledgement that they rejected the offer we'd given them. That should have happened the day before, but with Violet's surprise, we didn't have time to make them sign it as they left. Dahlia is the hardest signature to get because she doesn't want to stop playing Sparkleball. I suspect she hoped we'd give up, and when she was too old to play ball anymore, she could demand a job from us. I know the verbal agreement was legally binding alone, but to protect us from time-consuming lawsuits, I want it in writing.

When that all is finally done, taking far longer than I'd like, it is time to turn my full attention to the Japcharian summit and pre-plans for the world summit shortly after.

Lilly had left to keep working with the Japcharians after the ceremony. She returns shortly after I get my staff and the other Chosen girls settled. It was perfect timing!

I'm hopeful this won't be too bad. It's not like planning their first visit or even Dragia back in the Enthronement days. I had made fast friends with Princess Tsikyria, and Lilly had managed similarly.

Lilly seems confident and helps paint a hopeful picture as she discusses how she was able to secure the location and get it all set up for our arrival and that of our guests. The best part is, unlike last time, the communication between the two nations is smooth. I recall how the courtiers working on the delegation meetings during the Enthronement complained about Japcharia being difficult. Lilly had no such problems; she is doing great!

However, we do keep hitting one snag.

King Di and those who represent him will only accept requests that come directly from the king or queen. It slows things down, and the strain of the stress makes Gavril look paler and tenser by the day.

After meeting King Di, I'm not surprised. He had been harsh with me for having no authority. In his mind, a king deals with other kings, not baby underlings. Not that Gavril is a baby underling by any means, but I fear that is how King Di will see us as only the crown prince and princess.

I don't dare mention any of this to Gavril, though. If he knew how King Di had treated me before I was princess, he'd be harsher toward the king than we can afford. Besides, it's not a big deal. I'm crown princess now, and King Di has to respect that, or he'll disrespect the current rulers and our nation as a whole. And as he needs our help, he wouldn't dare.

Though I admit, I'm a tad nervous when no one else is worried he might keep up his hatred. At least the royal family will run the main event.

"That includes you," Bella scolds when I accidentally let that feeling slip into one of our wrap up meetings at the end of the day. "You are Princess Kascia now. You are a member of the royal family."

"I know. I just mean the real ones, you know?" I say.

"No, Kascia, and you shouldn't either. You have the same magic, same oath, and are part of their family now. You shouldn't feel so separate." Bella frowns. "No matter what anyone, including yourself, says."

I sigh heavily. "I suppose, but that's how King Di will see it. And that's what matters. I'll help as best I can, but I'm glad I will not be the point."

"You did well with their delegations and the others. You'll be fine," Bella insists.

"But he hates me," I remind her.

"Kascia, you are much more powerful than you think." Bella frowns. "And we all knew it even early on. There's a reason the other girls were always after you or envious of you. It wasn't just after the moment in the safe room, either." She reads my face correctly. "You fulfilled the prophecy for a reason. If we all knew about the prophecy, most of us would have dropped out long before with no hope of winning."

"Including me," I point out.

"Doesn't matter. Most of us would have thought it was you. You were the one prepared for this. You can't keep thinking you're separate from them. You're just as worthy to be a part of all of this. You *and* the prince will save this kingdom. You are a key part of that. I wouldn't be surprised if Japcharia is somehow part of it. You'll figure it all out. I have every confidence in you." She smiles at me.

"How do I get someone to play nice when they won't just because it's me asking?" I ask dully.

"We'll find out," Bella insists. "But apart from that, we have good news from girls who are tracking down the charities. Well, good and bad. They are at least getting answers. Truth is, no one seems to think it's worth sending aid when it will just be squandered. Other places will take the aid and build from it."

I scowl. "So, they won't try?"

"Don't shoot the messenger. That's what the reports are saying. They are trying to see if they can get those charities to start one with their help, but it sounds like it's an uphill battle. They will ask for your help if they need it. The charities are aware you are the one sending them."

"Good." I get up and pace. I feel so scared I'll be unable to make any difference. "What else can we try?"

"You're doing all you can for the moment. Trust your people," Bella insists. "They are fully committed to helping you."

"Rachel?" I ask. She makes me nervous; they all do. They were in equal competition with me not that long ago. Not even a year has passed yet.

"Kascia, they all respect that you won. You picked the right girls to be on your team. And not just Azalea or Isla. Even those you don't know that well. You're doing great."

"Thanks, but I'm not sure that's true." I muster a smile. "Nothing has changed."

"Yet. At least on the grand scale, but on the smaller scales, it has," Bella insists. "The people have never been more pro-royal."

"But what have I *done* to make that happen?" I ask.

"You told them the truth."

I sigh in frustration. That wasn't my choice. I feel so unsure. I have power and nothing I can do with it.

"Give it time," Bella says slowly.

"Right. Time." Time to do what?

"Kascia, what's wrong?" Gavril asks as soon as our staff left the room that night. He can tell I'm antsy.

"Nothing." I giggle at his instant worry.

"You're tense." He rubs my arms and kisses my neck. "What is it?"

I sigh tiredly. "Just thought... hoped... I'd feel more confident in fulfilling my duties at this point, is all."

"You've only been royal for a few weeks. Besides, you've had the worst part already." He kisses my temple, still behind me. "What makes you nervous?"

"I just... am getting no help from the organizations I reached out to. I'm unsure how to help the whole mess with Japcharia be easier. It's just been... a lot of work and no results yet."

"Be patient. It takes time. Some staff forget to call you princess sometimes, and I get cross with them for it." He smiles in satisfaction.

"Gavril, don't." He doesn't have to snap at them. "I'm already trying to get them not to be so judgmental of others in different jobs from them."

"Irrelevant. They need to recall who you are," Gavril says firmly. "And so do you sometimes. You're my princess, and you are the future queen. You command that respect. I doubt they mean any harm, but if they continue this irreverence, I'm sure those who need to be whipped into shape will do it too."

"Maybe." The charity organizations treat my representatives as little more than a pest.

"Maybe? Kascia, have you noticed them disrespecting you?" Gavril sounds cross already.

"No. Not to my face," I hedge.

Gavril sighs with frustration. "I see. Perhaps we need to enforce some things."

"Don't. You don't want to be known as harsh," I insist.

"Kascia." Gavril gently turns me around. My eyes meet his amazing amber ones before he kisses me deeply. "My Esther, my Asteria, my goddess of the night and queen, you are all those things and just as powerful." He breathes softly, lips millimeters from my own still. "And they need to treat you that way. Anything less is pure disrespect."

"I was nothing more than a lady not that long ago," I point out. "They forget."

"You were always more than that," Gavril insists and kisses me again, deep, long and tender.

I'm lost in for a moment, letting Gavril guide me back until he's pushing me back onto our bed, lips still locked. "And I knew it but couldn't choose you yet. I knew it was you early on, remember?"

"Doesn't mean they all do," I say, enjoying wrapping my arms around his neck and how his fingers play at my waist.

"Then we need to remind them every time you walk into a room," Gavril insists, kissing me over and over. I groan in pleasure and play with his hair with my fingers. "You should wear a tiara to any official event, including meetings. At least until they are used to it."

"Gavril," I sigh in complaint, "I don't need to. You don't."

"No, I wear crowns," Gavril disagrees and kisses me again.

"No, you're not using that." I put my hands on his chest. "I don't want to wear one. Remember what happened before? She poisoned me?"

"She would have anyway." Gavril brushes it off with a shrug and kisses me again, getting closer to me.

"I was right that day. I didn't need it, and I don't now," I argue, pulling away slightly and sitting up a bit.

"They need to respect you. The tiara reminds them if they slip it's on them, and we will act on it. Otherwise yes, they might forget. It just is a gentle reminder, so we only punish those who need it." Gavril doesn't give up and keeps kissing me.

"Gavril Potentate, you stop that." I pull away.

"What? Royal duties." Gavril once more brushes it off.

This is one thing I'm learning to find really annoying about him. He sometimes is more flippant about things than he ought to be, and these kinds of things are high on the list. He isn't going to charm me into agreeing just because I adore how he kisses me with his hands teasing at my waist and his strong arms enwrapping me.

"Take something seriously for a moment," I complain, sitting up all the way so he's not over me anymore. "I shouldn't wear one all the time."

"The others will agree with me. You need to command respect, and if they need a reminder of your true royal nature, what's the harm in it? If they don't change, then we can punish them fairly." Gavril sighs in annoyance at my slipping away, but he doesn't keep chasing me. I do love that he respects me enough for that. Jake used to chase me. "It's to help and protect you. It's a simple thing, and don't you enjoy wearing them?"

"Well, yes, I do," I defend. "But they are important. They shouldn't be used carelessly."

"They're not. You wear them to remind people who you are. I'm not saying you should wear the official one. Damian made you plenty. And we can make more with shells if needed. My princess deserves her crown. My queen should shine as the star she is."

I'm already annoyed with his playfulness as he sneaks in a kiss on my cheek, then ear and neck.

"Gavril," I say warningly.

"Fine." He pulls back, still annoyed. "Kascia, it really isn't a big deal. You wear a tiara during the day. So what? Mom used to wear one every day until the Enthronement. I'm sure she doesn't now because she doesn't want to make you feel out of place. I'll let her know our plan, and she'll wear them too."

"But you and the king don't," I point out.

"Good luck getting my father to wear one regularly. I'd need more than the one I have to get away with that. Besides, we're guys; we would rather wear as little jewelry as possible," Gavril points out, giving up and lying on his side of the bed. "It's not against you, Kascia. It's against them. Besides, wouldn't you like to?"

"I..." I know I can't say what I thought.

"Kascia," Gavril says warningly, "Be open with me, or I'll wiggle it out of you."

"You really need to stop playing that card." I give him an annoyed look.

"But it's my favorite," he pouts. "And royal duties and all."

"Uh-ah." I roll my eyes but get into bed too.

Gavril snaps the light off like he normally does and wiggles closer to me, so we're facing one another, lying on our sides. "But in all seriousness, my Asteria, you should. It will help you command the power they should know you have, and if they aren't, you know they are disrespecting you. It will give you the chance to show you will use the power you have. When have you been able to do that?"

I frown, thinking about it. "Just with the staff."

"And they aren't the ones I'm worried about. They will adjust either way. I'm worried about the court who have looked at you as a means of getting into my pocket," Gavril says, studying my face as he leans on the pillows. "They need to see that you are a figure of power now too. If a tiara doesn't do it, you can punish them and stop wearing it and just choose to act without it. That a fair enough deal?"

I hate that he's good at getting compromises. Most of all, when it's mostly a win for him. Then again, getting to say "I told you so" is appealing. I don't get those often.

"Two months?" I ask.

"Two months wearing it and if it doesn't work, you can stop right then. If it works, you only have to do it for a year," Gavril says. "Then we can reevaluate. Fair?"

I sigh. "Fair." He can have this one. Then I can actually win it in two months and say so.

"Close the deal?" He wiggles closer.

I laugh and wrap my arms around his neck and kiss him as he comes closer to me and puts his hands on my waist.

"Sure." I cave in.

I burst into giggles as he abruptly pulls me against him and starts kissing my neck and shoulder. I adore him even when I hate him.

"I live for every second I get with you." He kisses my lips.

I teasingly entwine my right leg with his. "I love how you make me better."

"You already were. You just needed help to see it, my Esther." Gavril kisses my lips deeply, then my jaw. "You are the most beautiful thing that's ever graced this earth, sea, or sky."

"Only in your eyes." I sigh at how he caresses my skin.

"No. To all who behold my Asteria, goddess of the night sky, queen of the sea, and ruler of my soul." He kisses me deeper, and I surrender to the man I trust with every fiber of my being, trusting and loving him deeper than I knew was possible.

# Chapter 33

Two weeks until the Japcharian summit, and I'm full of anxiety over it. Gavril notices and takes every chance to soothe me by any means, which leads to some awkward complaints from our staff about how to handle coming into our offices. The bedroom was well understood to knock and never enter without permission, but our main suite and offices... Well, if the queen heard what was happening, she'd be annoyed.

Or maybe not, as I come to painfully learn.

I'm going from my room to my office when I hear some courtiers talking in front of the door to the throne room.

"If the staff are to be trusted, it won't be long," one is saying. I fight hard to place the voice. It's one of the governors, I think.

"What a relief it will be. Having just the one link in the line of succession has been a strain for so long. I hate the grand duke so close to the throne," says another voice.

"I'm sure that's why he claimed his favorite of the Chosen girls at court after it was over," the first voice huffs.

"She is a pretty one. Quite charming," says the second voice. I don't know who it is. I'm sure of that, so I'm guessing it's the governor's assistant.

"Indeed, not a bad choice for any one single man seeking more of an office," agrees the governor. "But I'll still breathe easier once there is more security on the throne. Perhaps then the prince can finally take power."

"Still leaves only one link," points out the second voice.

"I suppose, but a younger one, and with the king's health in question... That article in the paper certainly shook people."

I know the one he means. The one Fabian's little friend wrote, questioning if the king was healthy enough to rule.

"So, an heir is just what they need. I'm glad to hear there seems to be good news on the horizon to that end," the governor says. "Staff can be helpful with their rumors among themselves if you learn to listen at the halls."

Just like I am doing. I've learned much by doing the same thing.

But a sick feeling had entered my stomach. I know we are expected to produce an heir, but we've not even been married a month yet, and people are happy and expecting it any day now? I knew pressure would come fast, but this fast?

"Your Highness," I suddenly hear the two men say.

I jump a mile and go to back up, forgetting I am not the only one with that title in the palace.

"Oh, Kascia, I didn't expect to see you there." Gavril turns the corner I'd been hiding behind. "I was just coming to see you."

"O-oh?" I say.

Gavril frowns. "Are you alright?"

"Fine," I say quickly. "Who were you talking to?"

"No one. Well, I passed Anthurium's governor. We're working with him to make sure the summit is secure there." He frowns. "Are you sure you're alright?"

"Just him and his staff?"

"Yeeeees. Kascia, did you hear something?" he asks more quietly. "Don't worry, they stepped out when I passed."

"No, no, just them talking gossip." I wave it off. "Are we meeting with him this afternoon?"

"Yes, just you and I. Mother and Father have other things to discuss. Then I have a meeting with Father afterwards."

"Good." I nod, feeling that knot still in my stomach.

"Hey, are you still nervous?" he asks me warmly, stepping closer and putting his hand into my hair as he kisses me. "You don't have to be scared of them."

"I know." I look down. "I just... Well, it's odd to be the main gossip topic."

"They'll get bored. Did they say something bad?" Gavril asks.

"No, no, not at all. I'm just used to overhearing horrible things when I do that," I joke.

Gavril laughs and kisses my forehead. "I completely understand. It saved me in a pinch, my Esther. Shall we?" He opens his office door for me.

I smile and step inside. I will admit, though, I'm hardly listening as the staff outline the current plans for what we need in Anthurium for the summit. I should be paying the most attention. I am the hostess and will handle all of this end of it. I'm just so distracted.

When Father expected me to steal the throne with Jake, the expectation I would produce an heir as soon as possible was a scary part of the deal, but one I'd accepted. But I also knew full well Jake would do most of the ruling, as I had never thought myself good enough for all that. Now I am a huge part of the political landscape *and* also expected to have an heir as soon as possible. Am I ready? Does it matter? My people need and expect it.

So soon though?

It's not like we don't mention it in a joking manner. Gavril delights in snapping at the staff that we're about our "royal duties" when they want us to hurry and get up or focus on our work. But realizing that is even more accurate than I'd realized is terrifying.

It's even worse for me when we meet with the governor. I recognize his voice, and he's delighted to meet me more properly than a lineup, complimenting my lovely lavender outfit.

"Goes well with your tiara," he says.

"Thank you." I manage a smile. It's still bitter.

Gavril had been right. Most courtiers suddenly recall to call me "highness" or "princess" instead of "lady". Some still mess up, and Bella is faster than me to correct them, and instead of laughing it off, they all had become nervous and apologized. Gavril had been right. Not only do I not get to say "I told you so", but I also have to wear a tiara to all official meetings for a year.

"You are positively glowing," the governor tells me.

I recall how people often say that about expecting mothers. After that comment, I have a hard time following the meeting. Gavril notices but can't ask until after he meets with his father before dinner.

I don't mind.

I follow the schedule done up by my staff, but I am noticing I'm getting more gaps in my meeting slots.

The court wasn't excited to meet me and see how I could be a helpful tool in their political belt. I was losing significance already. Or perhaps they hope to be kind to the soon-to-be mother princess.

The thought makes me want to scream and cry. I thought with Gavril I'd be more than an arm decoration and heir producer. It seems I was wrong. My schedule is quickly all about the summit prep. No one cares for my time anymore.

I am dismally wondering how long it will take for Gavril to notice my horrid mood. I give him a wan smile when I join him for our last meeting of the day. Vivian is the only other person in the room. Others are due to show up later, but honestly, I am early with so little else to do.

Gavril returns the smile.

*Oh great,* I think he can see something is wrong already with the look in his eyes.

He opens his mouth to ask when that dreaded alarm goes off.

"Again?" Gavril sighs. He nods at Vivian to follow us as he takes my hand.

We are heading to the nearest safe room when something hits the window beside us and shatters it. Gavril quickly shields me with his own body and pushes Vivian forward, away from the glass.

I don't know whose scream is louder: mine of worry about what just came through that window and hurt Gavril or Vivian's scream of shock that Gavril had taken the initiative.

Before I can gather my wits and check if he's okay, Vivian grabs us both and pulls us along. We run to make sure they don't see us through any of the windows and throw something else.

I half expect to hear the pop of another one of those gas things that had made so many of us sick before. I don't hear anything though when we finally reach the end of the hall.

Gavril looks around to make sure we're all unharmed before he pushes me in the saferoom first. He almost does the same to Vivian, but she swiftly sees what he's about to do and ducks in on her own.

He follows last, panting from our sudden run, but I also see the hint of a wince about his face.

"Are you okay?" I ask, fear in my eyes as I take his arms.

"I-I think so." But there's pain in his voice.

I turn him around to look at his back. There are glass shards all over his jacket. I brush them off as carefully as I can. He winces.

None got through, did they? I quickly yank his jacket off.

"Ow, careful," Gavril grunts as he lets me help him. I don't see more shards in his waistcoat.

At first, I believe it's fine since he wasn't cut. However, I start to wonder... Whatever broke the window? Did that hit him?

I gently touch his back. He tenses from head to toe with a grunt of pain.

Filled with fear, I quickly get his shirt off. There aren't any cuts. I have to feel to make sure with all his scars, but the glass didn't cut him.

A sharp wince cuts the quiet when I touch his left side, though. Something big must have hit him there. I don't feel anything odd about it at first. He winces less harshly as I touch it more gently. It might be a bit swollen.

Vivian appears next to me and hands me a cold compress. "Hopefully it is just a deep bruise," she says in worry.

I nod a thanks and take it. I rub it a bit to make sure the cold feature is activated. The chill infects my fingertips. Gently, I press it to the spot.

The wince is softer this time, and he relaxes slightly. "Thanks. That helps."

Vivian hands me some medical wrap to help secure it in place for now. I nod a thanks as she walks away, likely to keep looking for supplies, I guess.

I tenderly feel Gavril's side, but he doesn't react. A sigh of relief escapes from me. "I don't think it broke a rib or anything. Could you tell what it was?"

Gavril shakes his head. "No. It was round. Kind of felt like an extra heavy ball for kickball or something."

"Maybe they just launched one of those with a slingshot." That was doable. And it would break a window and hurt a lot for sure, but it couldn't break a rib or do serious damage without something stronger than anything the rebels could bring onto the grounds.

"Hopefully. It hurts a lot, but I don't think it's serious. It feels like an extra nasty bruise. Just in a spot hard to avoid irritating."

"This compress should help. And that should heal fast." I smile a bit, relieved it isn't worse.

I turn to say thanks to Vivian, then stop. I'd become so used to Gavril's scars, I didn't think twice about it. But there are only a handful of people who know about them. Now Vivian has seen them.

Guilt riddles my face as I look up at Gavril in apology.

He catches my expression and frowns, trying to turn more to see me. "What?"

"I... I forgot you don't like... people seeing your scars," I whisper. It's not like Vivian... wait.

I look at Vivian, but she's not even phased. She's checking the supplies in the room for anything else that could help.

Gavril looks at her too, frowning. "She's the first not to react to them at all."

"Hm?" Vivian heard his not-so-much of a whisper and turns. She clearly hadn't been listening.

"I..." I don't know how to address it. Maybe she didn't notice.

"I'm trying to find something to just tape it in place for a while, but I can't find anything," Vivian explains. "Do you need something?" She looks from Gavril to me. There's no way she misses his scars, but she doesn't react at all.

"Vivian, you amaze me," I confess. I couldn't have covered up my shock and questions in her shoes. Not even close. Even as a maid who knows to keep quiet and private. And she certainly is the queen of it, but... this is impressive.

Gavril, on the other hand, is studying her. "You knew."

How? How could my maid know about Gavril's scars?

"About?" Vivian frowns in confusion.

"You know what."

"I don't..." But then she looks at his back. "Oh... that." She looks away, blushing. She didn't notice them. It suddenly occurred to her that we found it odd she didn't react.

"How... did you know?" I ask, stunned. "I didn't tell you."

"No, My Lady, you didn't. I..."

"That's how you knew." Gavril snaps his fingers and points at her. "When you served that second date, you didn't have to ask how my tea was done. You've made it so many times, you remembered."

Vivian flushes. "Y-yes, sir."

"You used to work for him." I put it together. Gavril had said the staff that was there that night would know. She'd once been on his personal team? Why wasn't she working for him anymore?

Vivian nods. "For about three years, My Lady."

"And why did you stop?"

Vivian looks at Gavril in apology. He looks more ashamed than her. "Most staff didn't even last that long working for me before the Enthronement."

I recall the rumors that he was short-tempered and harsh on his staff, so no one wanted to be on his team.

"I'm... sorry for whatever I did that was the final straw and all before," Gavril mutters.

"We shouldn't have treated you like we did," Vivian accepts it without question. "You were nicer when I didn't treat you like an arrogant brat."

"I thought I was an arrogant brat."

I repress the smile, but Vivian isn't smiling, not looking at us.

"No. You just were a grown man tired of being treated like a child by everyone in your life. I didn't realize it until after they reassigned me—"

"You didn't request the transfer?" Gavril's tone is pure shock.

Vivian shakes her head. "There just came a point where they felt your staff shouldn't be girls close to your age."

That makes sense. If Gavril flirted or get close to any of his female staff, that would ruin his call to marry a true princess. At the time, they assumed that meant a born princess. I briefly wonder if that was supposed to be what happened, and it was supposed to be Vivian. She'd be even better at the job than me. If she'd accept that fact... so maybe not.

"Oh. That makes sense. Staff changes so much I never noticed." Gavril is still watching Vivian. "Why didn't you request a transfer?"

Vivian blushes. "I... stupidly thought I could get you to stop being such a problem. But then I... was there that night. I finally saw you as a person. They took me away not long after, but... I regret treating you like that or thinking about you like that."

That explains a lot.

I suddenly recall all the times Vivian assured me I really was the best match for him. It wasn't just her saying it as my staff member trying to cheer me up or because she had faith in me, though she did. She actually knew him well enough to look at the girls and know I was the best match for him.

She had even often said things that made it sound like she knew him well. She may have said she worked for him. Vivian may have even realized what I'd seen when I was shaken about his scars, and that's why she knew to give me space and how to help Damian assure me. It answered questions I didn't even know I had. She really is the perfect maid. She didn't even mention it.

"So... I guess I'm the one who should be sorry," Vivian admits. "My hope was that you would... forget."

"I almost did. I thought you seemed familiar on that date, but I had so much else on my mind until now," Gavril admits, watching her. "You really are the best maid in this whole place."

Vivian blushes in pure pleasure at his compliment. I smile too. I already knew that. There's no way I could ever let her go.

"It looks like it is just a nasty bruise." Vivian breaks the moment when none of us know what else to say. "I can see it forming. I'll see if there is treatment for that in here."

"She really is too good," Gavril mutters, watching her in surprise.

"We have the best head maid ever." I smile, giving him a look.

He smiles at me. "And someone who I don't care sees me shirtless." Vivian and I both stop with how hard we're laughing.

The bruise does look rather nasty by the time they sound the all clear. We help Gavril put his shirt and waistcoat back on, wincing.

First, we have the doctor check he's not more seriously hurt, but he can't detect anything worse than the nasty bruise. So, once he's given a clear bill of heath and a salve to rub on it before bed to help with the pain and to help it heal faster, we meet up with the king and queen to get a recap of what happened.

The rebels hadn't gotten inside once again, but they had broken several windows tossing balls filled with sawdust to make them heavier. There weren't any deaths, but a few injury casualties. It wasn't a serious attack. It seemed like without an inside person they were well stuck on getting into the palace. We really do have some impressive staff.

# Chapter 34

T he attack doesn't make the next day any easier. It's painfully meetings-free. I work on lessons, but the afternoons were supposed to be for working with courtiers. No one had requested to see me.

Instead, I work on plans to figure out who I can reach out to so I can start trying to push my incentives. It doesn't make me feel any more hopeful, though.

I wonder how I'll hide my mood from Gavril, but it turns out I don't have to. He's already in his own mood. I forget all my problems in worry.

He's quiet, and not in a good way. It is how he is around his parents when he disagrees, but knows they'll not take him seriously. What had his father said to him? Or is his bruise really paining him?

That night, I can't even get him to be playful with me. That deeply worries me. Since we'd been married, he always started it, and I fought it (most of the time playfully, not seriously). It's the first time I initiate it, and he barely seems to notice.

Honestly, I am a bit crushed. Can't I excite him like he does me?

"Are you in pain?" I ask.

"Hm? No. Why?" he asks.

My cheeks flush. "No reason. You just seem... off."

"Off?"

"Am I boring already?" I tease him as he finally sits on the bed, and I get up behind him and wrap my arms around him. "You won't even look."

Maybe I should have asked for a more exciting night dress. I really am starting to fear for the one power I thought I had over him: to get him to open up and soften when he gets tense and dark.

"Boring?" He frowns in confusion. "No one would ever call you that," he assures me, but there's not a hint of the teasing husband I'd found so annoying. I'm deeply missing it.

I just blink, not sure how to answer.

"Are you sure you're not hurt?"

"No. That salve you put on it at lunch worked wonders."

I frown deeper. Then what could be so wrong?

He frowns a bit. "Did I... say the wrong thing?"

"No. No. I just..." I try to make it playful and not serious. He hates that, right? "Thought I'd be able to excite you more, is all. I thought you were the one pushing—"

I don't even get to finish my sentence. He turns to me, puts a hand at my waist and kisses me so hard it knocks me back. I'm too stunned to react as he kisses me deeper, more. His little teasing hint of tongue makes me smile and wrap my arms around his neck.

But then I get my head and lay my head back to break the rhythm.

"Wow, what was that?" I smile.

"I love you," he breathes and kisses me more then kisses beside my ear and my neck, the way he loves to do. He holds me tightly, almost desperately. "I adore you. You're my everything." He kisses me and does the same pattern on the other side, holding me like he fears I'll go away. There's a fear and desperation in his actions that frightens me.

"Hey, Gavril." I try to calm him down, putting my hands on his chest before meeting his sad eyes. As I stroke his cheek, my hand lingers, and I look into his pained eyes with a mix of love and concern. "I'm all yours. I'm right here, and I'm not leaving. What's going on? You've been off all night."

"Nothing, nothing," he insists and kisses me again, lifting me and settling me into the center of the bed.

"Gavril." I put my hands on his arms. "You don't have to do this right now. What's going on? Don't lie to me, darling." It's fun to call him that. I never have before. I run my hand over his cheek and into his hair, still studying him with that concern.

He takes my hand on his cheek with one of his and holds it there as if treasuring it like he fears it will be gone. He shuts his eyes as he soaks in my touch.

"Gallant Star, you're scaring me," I say gently. "What's going on?"

Gavril doesn't answer. He just pulls the blankets over us and cuddles up to me on his side. I nuzzle into his chest, lying chest to chest, letting him hold and protect me.

"My prince, what's wrong?" I ask, letting him hold me like this. "I'm still all yours. I haven't left you or done anything to leave you."

"You're mine. You're enough. You aren't boring," Gavril insists and clutches me tighter. I swear I hear tears in his voice, even if there aren't any in his eyes or on his face.

If I wasn't so afraid of why he is acting like this, I'd likely adore how tender and loving he is with me, but I know something is wrong.

"Gavril, I was just trying to cheer you up. Normally, you'd have been teasing me, but you weren't. Something is stressing you. I thought we were trying to be open with each other. No more secrets," I remind him, stroking his hair at the back of his head as he holds me. I'd love this if I wasn't scared for him.

"You know you're my fire, my heart, soul; I'd do anything for you."

"I didn't doubt it," I promise him. "You're scaring me. No one is taking me from you," I say it half as a statement to assure him I'd not let anyone take me and half a question wondering if someone is trying. Is this about me not being pregnant yet? For heaven's sake, we'd not been married for hardly a month!

"Never." He is promising me. I can hear it in his tone as I feel him shake his head with a hint of desperation. "You're perfect. Mine, and they should all know it."

"I've been wearing the tiara. You were right," I speak the bitter truth. "Did someone say something?"

"Not yet," Gavril says quietly.

I pause. "Yet?" Why would he expect someone to say something? "Gavril, what's going on?"

"It's not fair. You earned it; I... I can't accept it." He shakes his head.

"Accept what? Gavril..." I pull back and take his face in my hands to make him meet my eyes. "I will be there. No matter what floods, hurricanes, rebels, or whatever else arises. I will be there. I promised, and I'm not breaking it. I will be there beside you, no matter what darkness falls. You don't doubt that, do you?"

"No, no." Gavril shakes his head wildly and holds me tightly. He almost picks me up. I feel as if I have no control to stop him, but I don't want to. I am concerned by his behavior. I've never seen anything like this from him. I curl into him, trying to think what to say or do.

"Then there's nothing to fear." I smile tenderly. "We're together. One. We're a ruling couple that nothing will break, not even each other when we try, right?"

But he just grips me tighter.

"Gavril, you have to talk to me. What is it?" I ask, unable to keep the fear out of my voice now.

"I love you. More than life, worlds, kingdoms, powers, anything, everything." He shakes his head.

"I don't doubt it." I frown. "Please, my love, talk to me."

"You don't deserve this. I don't want to take it." He shakes his head.

"Take what?" I ask.

He quivers in my grip. "Father can't handle the travel."

"We expected that," I remind him gently.

"And Mother will only make it harder."

"I know that too."

"And she will not give up her throne to give it to me."

"Well, to me," I tease. "You don't become queen, I do. Don't take that from me."

I said the wrong thing. Gavril grip tightens, and his tears wet my cheek and neck as he clutches me to him ever closer. I frown, unsure what that means.

"Hey, I'm here. I was just trying to make you smile. You know what I mean." I stroke the hair at the back of his head. I'd never felt him so scared or sad. It makes me sad, yet a small part of me finds joy in that I get to be here with him to help him when he's this defenseless.

"I want to give it to you. I want to give it to you more than anything," Gavril insists. "You earned it. It's yours. You deserve it and will be far better than my mother, Queen Airabelle, or any before or after you. You... you should..."

"I know. Gavril, I'm not turning it down. What are you talking about?" My chest tightens.

Gavril takes several deep breaths, almost gasping, so I hold him tighter. I wish I could hold him tighter, but I'm not that strong. His shaking worries me. What in all creation could they do to us? We're married; they can't force us to be separated now. It isn't possible. What is he so worried about?

"Father needs to give me power, but he cannot force Mother to abdicate," Gavril finally says.

"I am aware," I say slowly. *What is going on!?*

"If he abdicates, and she doesn't, she's my ruling partner, not you."

My heart drops to the floor. "So that's what he has to do." I fight tears. I knew this might happen. Damian warned me.

Gavril shakes his head. "No. He wants to save face as much as possible. He's crowning me regent in two days."

"Oh."

That is a good thing. Then I recall what Damian said when it came to what it means for me. When he said it, I was scared and sad, but now it's real. Most of all with my struggles to get people to respect me, it feels like the king slapped me in the face with spiked iron gloves.

"I-I can't take it. It will make you look like they don't think you were the right choice. They'll all laugh at you, and the people will be angry or mock you. I love you. I can't do this to you."

"Oh Gavril."

That's why when I teased him about being boring, he immediately fought to make me feel I wasn't. He fought to help me feel wanted and valued. I mean everything to Gavril, and he has to let them tear me down after they shoved me up into the spotlight.

"I can't take it. He said I have to, but I can't. I hate her!" Gavril snaps suddenly, making me jump. "She hates me so much she is going to tear you down for it. She's so obsessed with keeping me young and is sure I'm too young for it. She doesn't hurt me; she hurts you. I hate her."

"Gavril." I should know what to say. I remember how I hated my father for what he'd done. I know what it is like to loathe a parent so deeply for what they'd done to you or those you love, but... I don't know what to say. I don't want to be between him and his mother.

"I love you. You deserve it. You will be a million times better than she ever was, and she won't let you because of me. And I hate her. I hate her. I hate what they've made our lives. It's not fair. I can't take it."

That's when I finally realize what he's saying. He will not accept the regency. It would make him acting king, making Gavril the highest ruler in everything except for when the king actually came into the event itself. It puts full trust and power in Gavril. Damian had made that clear. If he says no...

"You have to take it," I say in shock. "Gavril, you have earned this too. If the Japcharian king is to accept you, you have to take it. That is why your father is doing it, right?"

Gavril nods. "I don't care."

"You should care. We have to stop them from attacking us," I remind him. "And if he only listens to you as king or regent, then you must be king or regent."

"I won't take it. Not when it makes you less than a princess. They'll scorn at you, the people, and other nations. You might as well have become my wife by breaking oath. I can't do that to you."

"You have to take it." I put my hands on Gavril's face to make him look into my eyes. "I know what it does to me, but you can't turn it down. You have to accept it or we might as well call off the summit. He will not listen to us. But he will to you once you're regent."

"I can't."

"You must." I fight tears that sparkle in my eyes. "I respect that you want to defend me, but we won't be able to save our people this way. You have to accept what you can get."

"I won't." Gavril shakes his head.

"What if he then resorts to abdicating?" I ask. "Then what? You have to reject the throne if you say no."

"He won't do that."

"He will if he must!" I emphasize.

"I don't want her," Gavril snarls. "I am not ruling with her."

"As regent, you don't have to. If he has to abdicate to force you to accept it, he will. I know it's bad. I really do, but I'll take it. We have to, or all we've worked for to save our home is for nothing. My fight to share this bed with you will be pointless. The whole Enthronement will have been pointless. You have to do it. Please, if you love me, do it," I beg him.

Gavril's hands tremble as he takes my hands still on his face. He holds them in both of his and presses them to his lips. "I can't do this to you," he says with a trembling voice.

"I know. I do, but you must. Please, if you love me, don't make all of what we've done pointless. If I have to b-be n-nothing more than your pretty princess and bearer of your h-heir, so be it."

It's what I hated and had just determined I didn't want to be, but if I have to, for him and my people, I would. I still have him. I may not have power, but with Jake, I never expected it. I knew Gavril longs to give it to me with his whole soul.

"It won't be forever. She has to step down or pass away eventually," I point out. "I-it's not forever." I just have to wait, yet again. "Please, Gavril, you have to accept it."

"I am not me without you. I can't have it when you don't." Gavril shakes his head.

"Did you already tell your father no?"

"No... I told him it wasn't fair to you, and he understands, but it's all he can do." Gavril shakes his head again. "I can't. He might be able to, but I can't."

"Yes, you can. Because *I'm* asking you to," I insist.

Gavril shakes his head, tears showing between his shut lids as he shakes his head, holding my hands to his chest, then he pulls me in to clutch me to his heart.

I settle there, wishing I had any other answer for this man I love and adore. "Gavril, please, take the regency. Ignore what it means for me."

"I can't."

"Then accept that I accept it and will still be right beside you. I'll be there as you take power, even if I don't. I will be there as the strong woman behind you." That is bitter. I was meant to be his help and equal.

Instead, I'd be the woman behind the great man throughout my life and history, and little more. They'll all forget about me. But that doesn't matter. I'd love some honor, some understanding of all I'd been through, respect for the power I am still accepting I have inside me. Now I learned it, it was gone. So be it.

"I'd give anything," he says, holding me tenderly.

"I know. And I'd take another way, but there isn't."

"If I say…"

"Then all we've done is for nothing. Please, Gavril, take it. I still can help you."

"You're the true princess, so much better than me." I can't tell if he's laughing or crying with how his chest bounces. "I love you. You are more of me than I am."

"I know. I love you with all I am, but you have to do this. I'll help you do it. I'll be right there."

"What?" Gavril pulls back. "No, no, you shouldn't be there."

"If it helps you accept it, fine." I put a hand to his cheek.

I know how it would look. I'd look so powerless, so small: the little wife walking behind her husband, doing whatever he asked. But if he needed me there to prove it to him, I'd do it. Part of me wants to. Yes, I'll look weak to them, but I know I'm stronger than all of them. It doesn't matter what they think.

"You have to accept it. I sold all I dreamed of to get this far for my people. Please, don't make it all for nothing."

"You're too good." Gavril shakes his head. "I don't deserve you. My family doesn't deserve you. My people don't deserve you."

I smile sadly. "I still make the choice. Please, if you love me, take it."

Gavril nods, not able to meet my eyes. "I can't do this to you."

"You aren't. You're doing what your people need. They are doing this to me," I try helping him see it differently. "You cannot turn it down. It's not your fault. It's the only choice." It's theirs. It's the queen's. Damian was right that it would come to this. And I would simply have to accept it.

I have the main prize, anyway: a man so devoted to me that he's broken at the thought of making me into less than I am. A man so in love with me, he'd throw away his duty and what he'd wanted all his life to prevent me from being made to feel small. A man who is so desperate to make sure I know how worthy I am, he throws his feelings aside to give me whatever I want to feel loved. A man who trusts me enough to be this vulnerable and broken with me without reservation. He didn't struggle to tell me what was wrong for his sake. He was afraid to see the pain in my eyes. I have the truest prize there ever could be. This man bound to me for all of time.

"I love you," he says, kissing me. I accept the much-needed stress relief. "With all my heart and soul."

"And I love you. You're the best prize I could win. I can accept not having the rest if I have you." I stroke his cheek.

He kisses me again, and again, and again. I smile and wrap my arms around his neck.

I whisper into his ear, "I'm yours. And I couldn't love it more." I smile with joy. Such a bitter moment, yet there is such joy too. I really could never ask for better.

# Chapter 35

But dealing with the event itself is even worse. The king wants to act quickly while Gavril is dragging his feet. The queen isn't too happy with the king either.

Meanwhile, I keep silent. I am part of the family, but I'm not treated like one; they don't deserve to hear my thoughts only to ignore them.

The queen has the nerve to try to use me as an excuse not to give Gavril power which results in the only fight I've ever seen between the king and queen, at least one that looks and feels like a fight.

"It's unfair to her to give him regency and give her nothing," Dalilly insists.

"I agree, but if you're not ready to give them the rulership, then this is the best I can do," Aster counters. "Dalilly, I can't manage it all. You hardly let me do work around here, let alone letting me go to the coast or Grameria across the continent."

Dalilly purses her lips as tight as a padlock.

"If you really felt that way, Dalilly, this would be a coronation not a regency," King Aster continues. "I know it's all frightening, but we have to make a choice."

"Blaming this on the fact these are all risks?" Dalilly's nostrils flare as her eyes narrow with blazing hot anger.

Aster groans in a mix of frustration and resignation rolling his eyes up and to his left, his head following his gaze without any reservation on letting his wife see his reaction and know what it means. "Need I remind you where that's left both of us in the past?"

"Don't you dare, Aster." Her eyes become slits as she glares down at her husband.

"We're not getting any younger, and the prophecy has all the needed components." Aster coughs slightly, flopping his head back against his arm chair to tilt his head up to meet his wife's gaze. "If you believe they need more time, I will respect that, but for him to act for me is necessary this has to happen."

"But not so soon. He doesn't even want it."

"If he didn't want it, he wouldn't accept it."

I glance at Gavril out of the corner of my eye. They're speaking in front of him as if he's not there.

Gavril doesn't speak, a tick going in his jaw I know means he is restraining his temper.

I slip my hand into his to try to help. I know it's hard for him not to let it out in moments like this, but he knows better than I do how little it will help.

It wasn't until I became an official member of the royal family and saw their dynamic more openly that I realized how special it was that Gavril wasn't afraid to let me see his anger and fear that day on the bridge. I might have been the first person he chose to let see it.

Gavril squeezes my hand back, repressing a smile, which makes a bubble of happiness rise in my chest.

However, it still ends as we expect. The king doesn't get the queen to understand; she throws all excuses she can think of to prevent this. I think this could be the first time the queen lost an argument though, because when she runs out of excuses, she stands there at a loss for what to say.

"So, unless you want to give them the throne, I'm going through with it," the king finishes firmly. "I cannot do the job anymore. And this is the only way."

The tension hangs in the air, but not one of us thought for a moment she'd give in. We hoped. But we all knew it was a hope against hope.

"It isn't fair," the queen says. "After the Enthronement..."

"The people are expecting something like this any day now, even knowing I'm alive. I think they expect it more, actually." The king shakes his head hopelessly. "I'm meeting with Count Barsat to arrange the press meeting to announce it, and it will be done by week's end."

"Aster, you overestimate the time for this," the queen says.

"We've underestimated the one prophesied to do what we can't," the king replies and gets up to do exactly as he says he would. "I'm already late."

The queen gapes after her husband as he pushes himself up with the help of his cane and walks out of the room. I can see a million retorts running through her mind, but she doesn't say any of them.

Instead, she turns to Gavril, and from her expression and tone as she says his name, she's going to attempt to explain away why she doesn't want this.

Gavril reads this better than I do. He gets up and bows to her. "I have my own press response to prepare," he says formally and walks out.

The queen's eyes are wide, and her mouth agape as she watches him leave.

I frown, debating where I needed to be. I stand too. "We all know you mean well," I say to the queen, "but the people have waited long enough for the prophecy to show them hope. He's only doing what has to be done. Thank you." For what, I don't know. I curtsy to her and follow my husband.

As I expected, he'd gone to his office, but his staff was not there. He looks just like he did when I saw him on the bridge. That day that felt so long ago, years even though it has not even been a full year. His arms are tense, leaning on the edge of his desk, his amber eyes gazing, unseeing, into its beautiful blue designs. His jaw is tense in pent-up frustrations of years he's struggled to restrain.

This time, there are no walls between us. I walk over and wrap my arms around one of his. He starts a little and turns his head to look down at me.

I smile a little. "You're almost past it," I remind him.

Gavril pushes himself upright with an angry shove. I let go to allow him the space. He starts to pace. "Even if I agree with her?"

"What?" My face falls. Then it clicks. "Gavril, we talked about this. You have to accept it."

"But I can't do this without you. It's not right. It's..." He stops, taking deep breaths that he forces out his nose like a fuming dragon. "I hate that she's using my own argument against me. She doesn't mean a word of it."

"Maybe she does," I try.

"Then she'd agree to give us the throne." Gavril gives me a sharp look. "And you know it."

I sigh heavily. "Yes, I do."

Gavril huffs again and resumes pacing. "I can't do this. I know I have to. And I'll do it, but I just..."

"And it means the world to me you feel that way, but this is what the Enthronement was all about. Everything we've worked for," I remind him, drawing closer to him. It's odd to think that not that long ago, I would have been afraid of doing that, fearing that I would offend him, or that he would strike me. "You can't turn it down."

"I know. I know." Gavril shakes his head in agitation as he paces. "I just hate it."

I smile slightly. "You know. A year ago, I was doing the same thing."

He stops and looks at me in confusion. I smile again and wrap my arms around him. "A year ago, I was saying I couldn't betray the man to whom I was engaged to play a game I didn't want to play so I could fake wanting a spoiled prince who cared more about his wants than his people."

Gavril returns the smile and wraps his arms around me in return. "Oh really? How is that the same?" I hear the tease in his voice that tells me he knows exactly what I meant.

"Well, change out queen for prince and swap me for you and the fiancé is now your wife, is it all that different?" I ask playfully.

"I suppose not." His enchanted amber eyes are studying mine. "So, you're saying though I hate it, I have to betray the woman I love because of a woman who cares more about her feelings than her people for some greater good?"

"Sort of. I'm more saying that it's worth it. I got much more out of it than I ever dreamed." I shrug as if we were talking about arrangements for some frivolous dance rather than our entire lives.

"Did you?"

I smile and kiss him softly. "I really did."

He grins and kisses me back with more intent then again and again. I giggle and return the kisses.

"You're sure it's more?" Gavril teases me.

I run my hand along his jaw. "Quite sure."

He grins mischievously and kisses me deeper, and I let him, allowing him to hold me and support my weight as he guides me back, almost into a dip. I love it when he does that, so classically romantic, right out of a book or play. My prince charming isn't perfect, but he at least has style.

There's a double thunking sound as we both fall back onto the sofa in the room.

"Good grace, you two!" Godwin snaps. He'd knocked and stepped in just as we'd fallen onto the sofa. "Can't leave you alone for ten minutes, can we?"

Gavril throws a throw pillow at him. "What do you want?" he asks.

"We have a press review for handling the press conference before we meet with your father and Count Barsat," Godwin says in an annoyed tone one uses when reminding someone of something they'd discussed many times.

Gavril gives a kind of grunting groan of complaint, like an irritated animal. "Fine."

"We have time later," I remind him, running my hands down his waistcoat as he reluctantly stands up and helps me up.

"And your lady is waiting for you in your office to plan your review as well," Godwin says to me. "She sent Lady Diana and Helena to find you."

"She should have known to ask you too," Gavril teases Godwin as I kiss Gavril's cheek in farewell before I turn to the door in the office that connects directly to mine.

"Look, I am not making this a regular thing. Your bedroom and suite are one thing, but your office, really, Your Highness?" Godwin complains as I open the door and leave them to argue.

"Oh, there you are," Bella says brightly to me. "Everything alright?"

I nod and close the door behind me. "Yes. Sorry, I didn't connect that we were meeting to plan our press response."

"I understand you'll meet with Count Barsat to prepare for the press conference," Bella says. "Though, oddly separately from the king and prince." She sounds annoyed. "I see no reason why."

I pause. "You don't know what it's for, do you?"

"I presume the king is officially abdicating at last." Bella shrugs, taking her seat to the side of my desk.

*Oh no.* I have to tell her. "In... a way," I manage to say.

Bella stops, looking up at me from her comfortable seat, where she'd crossed one leg over the over and leaned back in a way our etiquette teacher would have scolded her for using in my presence.

"What do you mean 'in a way'?" she demands, sitting up. When I don't answer right away, she stands up. "What are they planning?"

"The queen won't abdicate," I say. "So, the king is doing the next best thing. He's making Gavril his regent."

"So, he'll be Prince Regent, and you..." That's when Bella realizes. "No!" she cries so loud I hear the argument between Godwin and Gavril pause abruptly. "They can't do that! Not after the whole Enthronement and what you had to confess. They can't do that."

"I know. But he has no other choice." I keep my composure. "We need to plan how to handle our response to it."

"Gavril can't allow it," Bella objects.

I meet Bella's eyes firmly. "He has to accept it. We'll be paralyzed otherwise."

"You won the Enthronement. You sacrificed everything, not them. You earned this. If anything, it should be the king and queen who have to step back. He shouldn't accept it."

I sigh and shut my eyes in resignation. "It would undo all the Enthronement was for. The sacrifices will be pointless if he doesn't. I had to tell him the same. So, if you'd not press him on it, I'd be thankful."

"You didn't!" Bella gapes at me. "What are you thinking? You can't agree with this."

"No. I don't. But I can't let Gavril reject it just because of the injustice of it. The prophecy is pointless if he's not in power. The king is too ill to handle the ruling of a nation. If he abdicated and she did not, Gavril would be king while I remain princess, and he'd have to have his mother for his ruling partner. We all know that would be far worse. This way, the king is still the buffer between them, and Gavril has the authority to treat with the Japcharians without them looking down on him for being without power. He can now act as king in all choices without prior approval. It's the only choice we have."

"But... No, no, the winner does not get to be treated like this," Bella insists. "Gavril can't let them."

"He has to." Why do I have to debate it with her, too? "Can't you see that?"

"He doesn't. The queen needs to be reminded that her day is over." Bella folds her arms. "Move for a vote of no confidence in her."

"No. We don't need to start a family war." I sigh in frustration. "Don't you dare make a move for it."

"But—"

"That's an order." I'm impressed by how firm and yet easily I say it.

Bella huffs. My heart sinks. She's questioning if I was the best choice to win, I know it. However, I don't address it.

"Can you send for my press team, please? You said you sent them out to find me?"

"Yes, My Lady," Bella says formally with a small curtsy before leaving.

I groan in frustration and fall into my chair. Why does no one see what I see? Maybe I am wrong?

But as soon as the doubt wiggles in, I smack it down.

*No.* I'd been down this road before. I know what I'm doing. This is the only choice, even if I know we all hate it. The real struggle: how to frame it right.

I sit up and arrange my dress before my staff arrives. Although I feel like I should stand, I remind myself that I'm the princess. I'm the highest rank. I needed to respect myself and my office with the protocol.

They all curtsy to me when they arrive.

"Thank you for coming," I say. "We have work to do. The king and prince are meeting with Count Barsat to prepare a press conference to announce that Prince Gavril is to be made the king's regent."

"But not you?" Helena sounds confused.

I simply nod. "Yes. We need to prepare how to handle the press."

"Do... you approve?" Diana asks.

"No," I say firmly. "But I'm not going to stop it. Gavril needs to be given the power, and the king cannot rule full time in his condition. The queen simply will not accept that, so the king is taking matters into his own hands."

"Do you want the people to believe you support it?" Diana asks.

I shake my head. "No, but I do not want to make any statements saying so. There is nothing I can do to change it, nor would I. At this point, more subtle signals on my opinions would be better. I don't want people uprising to demand I'm given power. That would make matters worse."

"Is there to be a public event?" Helena asks.

"I believe it will be kept small, but I would imagine impressioned, at the least, with perhaps only the required court, but that's the discussion they're having in the meeting with Count Barsat," I say, still with that formal tone.

My ladies nod.

"Then we will simply direct all comments to the count. Then your body language, outfit, and part in the proceedings will have to send the message," Diana says.

"Which can be far more powerful. You will not bend to them, but nor do you have to weaken yourself by joining in the foolish squabble," Helena agrees.

"Kasica, you should fight it," Bella urges me.

The looks Diana and Helena give Bella shock me. It's annoyance and a hint of envy. She addressed me far too personally. She is My Lady-in-waiting, my attendant, but I am the crown princess. She brought up an argument and addressed me in a way that is far too personal for a staff member in addressing royalty. I hadn't realized this would be such a problem.

"Bella, I've made my position on this clear," I insist. "I disagree, but my husband deserves and needs the power if this war is to end. I am not debating it anymore. You can't change my mind any more than he could when he insisted he wouldn't accept it."

I look at my other ladies. "And please, there's no need to be so formal with titles if you do not wish to."

"You are our princess," Diana says firmly. "We are honored to treat you with the respect you are owed." The look she gives Bella makes my heart sink and frustration rise up.

So, though I gave them permission, they still think Bella is rudely improper with me. The envy I saw must not be the fact she gets to be so blunt with me. It's likely they just wish they had her job, so they could treat me with the respect they see I deserve.

"But I do want to hear your thoughts. I picked you for these jobs because you have skills I don't. I want your opinions, even if I disagree. Do you think I should fight it?" I try.

"We trust you," Diana says almost stubbornly. "If you believe that is the right course, we will follow you."

I'm honored, humbled. I am careful not to let tears come to my eyes. The faith they put in me is beyond what I deserve, and I want to respect that. I can't let them down.

"Thank you. But I still need help." I smile gently at them. "So, what do you think is the best way to go about making the point clear?"

"It will depend on how they handle the events," Diana says. "Be stiff, try not to be too close to the action either. Show you will stand beside your husband, but you disagree with this action."

"And don't be rude in any way to the king or queen," Helena reminds me. "You don't want to be seen as ungrateful for all they've given you."

"But ensure you carry yourself with power. You have the power, use it," Diana directs.

Bella opens her mouth as if to argue, but the other two give her a look which makes her go quiet with a scowl.

I withhold the sigh that I want to let out. "Very well. We'll have to coordinate a plan once we have more details. I'd like you to keep working on ideas and also see if you can gauge how the people will react. Perhaps we can help curb any uprisings in the making or soothe any fears."

"Of course, My Lady." The two bow their heads to me.

I smile gently and dismiss them. Bella goes to leave too, but I give her a look to direct her to stay.

Once the others are gone, she speaks, "Going to fire me now?"

"No," I say, offended at the idea. "Why do you think I'd toss you off that easily, Bella?"

Bella just huffs and folds her arms, still standing.

"Bella," I stand up, "I just wanted to assure you I'm not angry with you. I do want your opinion. I want to hear it. Just... I still wouldn't pick anyone else. Their respect is something I'm humbled to accept, but I can't do this job alone. I need to hear your thoughts, too. Perhaps in front of others, you can say it differently if you're worried. But I am still the girl who was a candidate with you. You know me."

"I understand." But Bella's formal tone doesn't assure me.

It just makes my heart sink further. "I expected that to take longer. Is there anything else on the agenda for today?"

Bella shakes her head. "Not that I know of. Shall I check?"

"How about you take a break for yourself?" I am sure the way the other girls looked at her shook her, or at least made her angry. "Send for Penelope, please."

"Yes, Your Highness." I don't miss how there's a hint of bitterness to how Bella bows to me before leaving.

Once the door is shut, I grab a throw pillow and scream into it. I feel better after that but still irritated. I really miss Damian right now. Someone to soundboard off of would be so nice. Even Zelda or... someone.

Penelope arrives shortly after. "You called, Your Highness?" she asks.

"Yes, is there any correspondence I should address?" I ask.

"Not currently, My Lady. We're just doing the normal screening," she says.

"Do we have a time to meet with the whole royal press team yet?"

"No, Your Highness. Should I make one?" Penelope asks.

"No. But they should request it very soon," I assure her. "Along with several events. I'm sure Bella will inform you all later, but the king is forced to make the prince his regent as the queen will not give up the throne. I don't like it, but I understand it is the best path forward to keep the peace inside and outside the palace. So, I'd like to coordinate our schedules and press plan as soon as possible. If other appointments have to be moved to make that first, do so."

"Of course, Your Highness." Penelope bobs a curtsy. "If I may ask, why are you telling me?"

"I want to be more one-on-one with you all. It's nice to have everyone's input. I trust Bella, but you came to work for me, and I chose you. I'd like to keep that relationship of trust." I smile at her.

Penelope returns it. "Of course, Your Highness. We're all happy to be working for you."

I pause. "You... agree with my plan?"

"Honestly, My Lady, I've hardly had time to digest the idea. I am not a lady of court, nor do I have any wisdom on that. However, I think you'd make an excellent queen. I'm sure the prince wants you with him more than anything." She smiles gently. "And we'd all like that."

"I'm sure we all would." I sigh.

"Are you okay?" Penelope surprises me by asking.

I blink. "Are you really asking?"

"Of course, Your Highness. Good grace, was that too informal?" she asks in worry.

I laugh. "No. I just didn't expect it." My face falls a little. "I don't like it. My husband doesn't want to do it, but I know for the people it's best. Everyone tells me I'm wrong. But I know I'm not. He'll do it because I tell him he should and it's for the best. But he still hates what it does to me. He knows it will be bad for me, but it's the best we can do."

"Everyone, Princess?" Penelope frowns.

"I'm sure rumors of how Bella says I should fight it will get out." I sigh. "But the rest of the staff I've spoken to trust me."

"Bella does too. She just wants to help and defend you," Penelope says.

I nod. "I know. She always has." I smile a bit, reminds me of how Bella stood up for me when Forsythia and Jonquil would accuse me of being a traitor. "But it may not always come across that way. Thank you." It was nice to have someone to talk to. "But if there is no other work to do, I think I'd like to be left alone for a while."

"Should I get Joy?" Penelope asks.

I laugh. "Actually, that might be nice."

"Of course, My Lady." Penelope curtsies and within ten minutes has Joy, tail wagging, in my office with a toy to play with.

It really helps to just laugh and play with the dog and pet her when she settles down a little more as I sort out my own twisted thoughts.

Dinner is painful.

The queen tries to pretend all is normal, and the king plays along, but it is hard for Gavril. To his credit, he tries, but I can't ignore the stiffness in his jaw and the forced nature of his smiles.

I am more than happy to pull him off to our room to cool down. But it's the only action I can take and the best I can do.

When I set a meeting with my staff to go over how to handle the press conference and how to properly convey the message, Gavril surprises me by being there. Apparently, he'd struggled with his staff to make the time, but he wants to be part of it.

I can't help but notice how my staff looks at him, as if it's his fault. That is something we need to make clear to our staff and the people; he isn't any happier about this arrangement than I am.

"The conference will be this afternoon," Gavril says, "and the event will be the day after next. There will be as few people there as possible, and it will be just impressioned for the public."

"And the press conference?" Helena asks.

"We'll gather them all into the press room. Father will make the announcement. Count Barsat will take a few questions, then the live feed will cut. The goal is to have no more questions from the press after that. Then Father and I have a meeting with the full court to answer any questions they have," Gavril summarizes.

"It's a simpler affair as he's being made a regent and not king," Godwin explains. "The king wants it as quiet as possible."

"Why would he want to do that?" Bella frowns.

"Gives the press less to mess with," Godwin explains simply. "This move is simply a means to help with the upcoming summit that the king is not well enough to attend. The goal is to convince the queen that it's time for them both to step down, and their goal is for it to happen as soon as possible. Whether it will work remains to be seen."

"Is there any way to help the people see he isn't trying to slight her?" Bella asks.

"Not without throwing the queen under the wheel." Godwin shakes his head.

"Someone has to take the blame," Diana says, "and we don't get to choose who that one person is."

"We should," Bella huffs.

"We don't need to make further divides among the people with labels and name calling. The unity among the people now is greater than it has been in the last few hundred years. Let's not break it with something we can control, please." Gavril is giving Bella a pointed look. She returns it with a slight glare.

I stop myself groaning at the looks my staff gives her. I'm uncertain how to handle this whole nightmare with them. The fact she is comfortable challenging Gavril reminds us all that they had dated during the Enthronement as well, but it also reminds the staff she's still not one of them.

"I think being there but being as quiet and reserved as possible should show I stand with my husband but don't agree with this move," I say, changing the subject to the main point of the meeting.

"For the press conference, I would agree." Godwin nods.

"For the ceremony as well." I frown a little.

"No." Gavril surprises me by speaking and being so firm about it. "You shouldn't be there. You being there, visible, even unhappy, will make you look like you'll stand dutifully beside me, even powerless. It will make you look spineless and that you'll just stay in my shadow and do as asked. That is not the image you want, is it?" Gavril is keeping a firm eye on me.

"Of course not, but you're taking on a huge responsibility. I still support you, and they should know that," I insist.

"And you will by being at the announcement, but not for the event itself. It is a clear message of condoning the actions. That is how the press will spin it, and that is how the people will see it," Godwin agrees.

"Even if she is far away from the action, takes no questions, and uses her lovely acting skills to show she disapproves?" Helena asks.

Diana nods. "No, if she's at the main event, it will make her look like the wife who just dutifully follows her husband, no matter what. It will take away a lot of her power without him."

"And I will not allow that," Gavril says stubbornly. "You are the true princess, and that should come with its own respect and power."

I see his point. The fear that had gripped me of being little more than a pretty tag on his arm and bearer of his heirs is real. But not being with him as he accepts it when he so badly doesn't want to... I am the one pushing him to do it, though he hates it. How can I leave him to do it alone?

"But..." I have no argument to make. I try, but there is no argument I can make that would be fair or true. Gavril has a point. I just hate not supporting him like I promised to do.

"This is just about how the people will see it," Gavril reminds me. "Nothing more."

"I think that should be the plan. And she should look more like a queen than the queen does," Diana says. "Make the people wish it was a full coronation. Perhaps that will help dissuade the queen as well as showing Her Highness's strength in allowing it, though it isn't fair to her."

"She should say so," Bella argues.

"I am not causing more of a rift," I state firmly. "No comment, and let them see with my actions, not words."

"She'll look stronger that way," Diana agrees. "It's a stronger stance. Anyone with eyes won't be able to miss it."

"And her missing at the event will send a clear message, as it should." Godwin nods. "Just make sure at the announcement she looks more like a queen than she who wears the crown," he says to Bella.

She remains disapproving but nods with lips pursed.

"Bella, please, you need to understand. This is about sending the message. We aren't pretending to agree with this," I say.

"And we don't," Gavril says with a slight growl to his stubborn tone this time. "I still don't want to accept this." He looks at me. "But my fair queen is right. Without accepting it, we'll be at the same standstill and the whole point of the Enthronement will be for nothing."

"She who passed through all the tests and heartache you put her through deserves better," Bella snaps at him.

I glance at the rest of the staff. My staff have the same disapproving expressions on their faces. Godwin is frowning, but in a different way.

"I don't disagree," Gavril argues back. "She does deserve better. If I had my way, this wouldn't be happening. I wasn't going to accept it."

"Because she's being shy and won't push it." I hear the tone of "like she always does" in Bella's voice.

I fight the anger that rises heat to my cheeks. Yes, I had struggled through the Enthronement, but now I have power. I have authority. I am not afraid anymore. I am choosing this path for other reasons, not the fear of the fight.

"This is not about that," Gavril snaps.

"We all know it is. The people will see this as a slight on her by your parents. And you're going to let them do it," Bella says, "because neither of you will stand up to them."

"That's enough, Bella," I intercede, putting a hand on Gavril's arm to stop him from standing up. "We understand your opinion and respect it, but I've made my choice. This is about not making more divisions among the people. The rebellions have started to quiet since the Enthronement began, and I will not give them the excuse to side with different members of the royal family and create more divides. I will make it as clear as I can in action that I disagree, but I am not going to fight it or try to use any of that to try to get power at the expense of my people. Is that clear?"

"It is clear. I believe it's a mistake to let it happen." Bella gives me a smile, but still shoots a hard look at Gavril. She blames him for letting me take the easy road.

I debate dismissing her from the meeting, but that will only build up her resentment which will cause me more problems down the road.

"I have made my choice. You were hired to assist me in my work, and you have done well at that. Please respect the choice I made."

Bella simply nods, but I know she's not softened towards Gavril. There's nothing I can do to stop it, but I don't know how to calm Gavril when he's ready to leap at her to defend me, which won't help anyone.

"No comment from the press office then," Diana says to get us back on track. "Or her staff." She gives Bella a warning look. "We let them speculate on her actions and why she is missing at the event itself. We should start preparing her attire for that day."

"We should," Bella agrees. "If Your Highnesses don't mind." There's bitterness as she addresses Gavril that way. I'm only slightly comforted that she's not mad at me. She just thinks I'm being a coward again. And I doubt I can change anyone's mind.

"Not at all. I know how long that can take, and you only have until this afternoon." I bow my head to dismiss them.

All three of my staff stand up. Diana and Helena curtsy to me, which reminds Bella to do the same before they leave. Godwin glances at Gavril as I dismiss them, and Gavril gives him a slight nod, and Godwin leaves too, through the door which leads to Gavril's office.

"She shouldn't be so bold," Gavril says the moment we're alone, getting to his feet.

"I know. I can't stop her without discouraging her from giving me her thoughts, and I want the feedback." I frown a little.

"Perhaps it was a mistake to choose a Chosen as your lady-in-waiting. It's clearly causing some friction."

"She's only trying to defend me."

"From yourself and me." Gavril sounds angry.

I sigh. "I know. She'll adjust. The rest of my staff already resent her for it. She was fine until this came up."

"She's not exactly wrong," Gavril mutters.

"She is wrong. You are not wronging me by taking the regency. I asked you to," I remind him firmly, standing as well. "She has no right to judge you for it or be angry with you like you're still her date. She's a lady, but you are the crown prince. She needs to remember the respect due to royalty even when she disagrees. It isn't a dating game anymore."

"Exactly. You're not scared to stand up for yourself, and the fact she still thinks that motivates you, even after you assured her that's not why, is a clear disrespect for you."

"Gavril, you don't have to defend me from everyone who doesn't perceive me as a strong leader the way you do. You'll end up fighting the whole world if you do that," I say placatingly.

"Then bring them on."

I sigh tiredly. "Gavril, please. It's not worth all of that. You see me as far more than I am. And I love that, but you shouldn't gear up to fight off everyone who doesn't adore me like you do."

"At least show the respect the office deserves. I have half a mind to fire her." Gavril starts pacing.

I groan and roll my eyes. "It will be over soon," I point out, taking his arms and stopping his pacing, so he'll look at me. "She is wrong. It is not about me. It's not even about you or your parents' drama. None of that is why you have to do this. I know you hate it. I really do. Ignore Bella. She doesn't understand. That's all."

"She's not wrong. You earned it and will be far better than the queen." Gavril spits the "the queen" in hatred.

My heart sinks. I really don't want to be between Gavril and his mother. It won't fix anything, and she's only trying to protect the one she loves most in the world. What mother wouldn't want to protect her son? She just doesn't see he no longer needed it.

"Please don't make it a competition. I've had far too much of that," I try to joke.

It doesn't work. Gavril holds me tightly. "It's not right."

"And I'm not saying it is." I return his embrace. "I'm saying it's the only good option we have. We'll make her regret it, but don't punish her for it. It has to be done. I know you hate it." I frown. "Which is why I want to be with you."

"Kascia, I understand, but you have to make it clear you don't agree." He lifts my chin so we can meet eyes. "You are right about using actions instead of words. You'll still be with me every step. But if you're there, they'll consider you nothing more than the lady in my shadow. And that I cannot allow. I know you want to help me just as I want to help you, but you cannot be there," he says gently but firmly. "You have to make the point. You'll be standing with me every other time, I promise."

I nod. "I understand. I just... would feel better being with you."

Gavril frowns. "I know. Me too. But you cannot let the people assume that. Even more, you cannot let the other nations who will most likely be watching assume that. You are strong. You don't need me to be the strong princess you are. And separating yourself from this slight against you is the best way to show them. We'll make it through this."

I hug him tightly, and he returns it, resting his head on mine. "No fun for anyone." I let out a weak laugh.

"No. No fun for anyone," Gavril agrees, hugging me tighter. "I love you. With all my heart and soul, I love you."

I smile slightly. "I know."

And I love him more than I ever thought possible. When I let him go, I thought I couldn't love him more. After the wedding, I thought I couldn't love him more. I am learning to accept the truth that there is no limit. It will grow beyond my comprehension more and more.

# Chapter 36

My staff put together the perfect queenly attire. The skirt is full and long with the flutter Damian had mastered, which so few had. He must have taught Bella how. Or maybe he made this one before he left. The top is bedecked with soft crystals across the bodice in stunning patterns as well as the sleeves that cap at my shoulders. The dress ends in a long train fluttering down my shoulders to just above the floor in a queenly cape. The golden color with only hints of Purerahian blue is the cherry on top.

I doubt the queen will top this and look more regal than I do. The sweeping twist they put my hair into is new and helps set me apart as greater than a princess. I am the true princess, and that just means queen-in-waiting, and I am done waiting. My official tiara finishes the look.

Gavril looks me over before we go into the press room. He can't speak. He chooses to kiss me instead.

"You're too stunning for words," he breathes as he pulls back, his fingers sweeping my jaw as if displaying my beauty to himself. "You deserve better." I can't miss the pain in his eyes.

"I know." I go up on pointe to peck his lips. "And I'm proving it."

"I wish there were words to express how much I love you." The pain turns into admiration. "You're truly the true princess. My goddess of the night."

"My gallant star." I take his arm. "Let's get this over with." He nods his agreement, and we step through the entryway to the podium.

The press room is a new room to me. Set close to our entrance is a podium to give announcements from with rows of chairs for members of the press on the opposite side. I can see why we've never used it before. It is small.

Where we stand is mostly in shadow with the others standing closer to the podium. I expect that's to prevent the press jumping at us before they're allowed, but I can see them.

Fabian and Mr. Coppiger sit not too far from each other in the front row. There are only four long rows and only the first two rows are filled and not even to capacity. The preset impressionors line the back.

Count Barsat gets the cue from the king, who is waiting on the king's other side to begin. The count walks up to the podium. He greets the reporters and thanks them for their time before stating the king had an important announcement, and he steps back so the king can take the stand.

Gavril and I step up to stand beside him but stay a little behind. This would give the press plenty of chances to get the images they want as well as show we are with him as he gives the announcement.

The queen is on the other side of the podium with the count. I'm right. Though she wears the queen's official crown, she doesn't match me for regalness. She actually is hardly hiding her anxiety in her lavender dress. Should have picked a darker color.

"Thank you all," the king says. "As you know, I've struggled with my health since the failed attempt on my life. I hardly escaped alive, and I'd like to take this chance to thank the amazing medical team that has pulled off this miracle." He smiles. The jovial nature I know him for is lacking. He's all authority right now. I have to admire it. Gavril learned it from somewhere, even if he does it better.

"But their valiant efforts could only do so much. The day to day of running a nation is wearing on me, and on the advice from my doctors, family, and trusted officials, both royally appointed and voted upon by the people, I have decided I cannot continue to rule full time."

I hear every impressionor in the room click like crazy, increasing the flashes. The press moves closer to hear what he's about to say next.

"To take on the bulk of the ruling, I have decided to appoint my son and heir, Prince Gavril, as my regent."

The room explodes into questions.

"Why aren't you abdicating?" a voice asks.

"Will the queen be appointing a regent as well?"

The questions fly so fast I can't keep track of who asks what. But one thing is clear. No one expected the word regent. They all expected him to announce abdication and a pending coronation. The king keeps his composure though.

"I have fully briefed Count Barsat, who will handle all questions after my statement," the king says firmly, talking over the press. "I intend to fully allow Prince Regent Gavril to rule the kingdom in full force, as if he were on the throne. As a reminder, regency means he acts for me in all things and at all times unless I specifically overrule while in the room. Even when I am not in attendance, he speaks with my full authority. I completely trust him and his ability to look after the nation I've enjoyed spending my life serving. I trust he and his princess will handle all affairs beyond even my grandest expectations, as they have done so far. Thank you."

He finishes and turns away to step down. The onslaught of questions starts again, but he ignores them all as the count takes the podium. The king comes over to Gavril and claps his shoulder, shaking his hand with a proud smile, which he returns, clearly all for the press watching.

The king then surprises me by turning to me. He kisses each of my cheeks, which I return in the familial exchange with a warm smile.

"You deserve better," he says too quietly for any of the press to hear. "I'm sorry." And he stops them from reading his lips by kissing my forehead as he speaks, blocking the view from the impressionors.

I smile in gratitude, though I still don't agree with how they are slighting me. I glance at the queen, who has the nerve to not even look ashamed. She just looks anxious.

"Why aren't the king and queen abdicating?" A member of the press calls to the count as he takes his position.

I don't hear the response as the whole of the royal family leaves, but we immediately go into another small room I'd never seen before which has a large imaginal screen that allows us to watch the rest of the press conference.

Gavril sits turned to me slightly as I squeeze his hands in anxiety, watching, wondering what we'll learn from seeing the rest of this exchange. On Gavril's left, the queen is doing almost the same as me, pale with nervousness as she watches the imaginal and likely squeezing her husband's hand off.

"The queen is perfectly able to handle her current duties. It was not seen as expedient for her to step down when she's been handling the nation's affairs on her own as her husband heals," the count says in answer to a question.

"Is there doubt the new princess is able to handle being queen so soon?" another voice asks.

I can't see any of their faces, and the imaginal sound isn't clear enough for me to pick out who for sure.

"None at all." The count shakes his head with a slight smile. "The nation is at an important turning point, and with all the transitions happening, it has felt a little off balance. We are simply trying to minimize the pain of transition." He points to someone that, of course, we can't see. "Markil."

"Does the queen perhaps disapprove of a former rebel winning the crown and is so reluctant to allow her to rule so soon?"

"As I said, there is no doubt or question about Princess Kascia's ability to help rule a nation."

Did he have to say help? I think he realized his mistake too late too as I notice a slight tick in his check.

"The queen simply has the experience needed to rule her side of things to help smooth the transition." The count points again. "Genia."

"Does this have anything to do with the upcoming summit with Japcharia?"

"Yes, the king's health would not permit him to travel, and that brought up the question if he would ever be healthy enough for such work again, and if not, should he keep ruling in his current capacity? Healing from a knife to the lungs is hard enough without the pressure of a ruling nation.

"As was stated before, there was doubt he would survive, and therefore, correcting the rumor of his death felt dishonest to refute until it was beyond a shadow of a doubt he would recover. The queen has done well handling the nation on her own with the prince's aid since the attempted assassination. This is simply permitting the system that was working to continue thereby allowing some stability to return to the government. This will allow the transition to cement without implementing a bigger change. So yes, it was a large part of what brought about the conversation that led us here. Bevill."

"How do we know you're not covering up the fact the king and queen, now they have seen Princess Kascia as an acting princess, doubt she was the right choice and are trying to minimize her influence to allow the prince to fulfill the prophecy without interference?"

The count doesn't miss a beat. "Because I'm telling you that's not true; that's how you know. Derria."

"If the kingdom is already struggling with a transition, why not just get it all over with at once?"

"The royal family feels it's better to gain some balance and grip on the new landscape before trying to shake it up more. You make sure the diving board is solid before you spring off it into the pool. Sarhai."

"Don't you think Princess Kascia deserves a chance to prove herself?"

"She is not being limited in her duties. Princess Kascia has been and will continue to be a solid member of the royal family. She is already handling correspondence with officials in other nations, was instrumental in assigning the other Chosen girls to solid positions, has almost single-handedly handled all preparations for the upcoming summit and will be attending it alongside her husband in a few weeks with full authority to negotiate. Princess Kascia has been a powerful force for good in her short time as princess and will continue to do so. No one in the royal family doubts that. We all expect good things from her."

"Does this have anything to do with the attempted assassination of the new princess?" a voice asks before the count can call on someone.

"That was the act of a jealous ex-girlfriend who felt she should have won. It has not changed how the royal family or court have accepted the new princess," he says dismissively. "Fabian."

"How are we supposed to paint this as a good thing when the princess the people have accepted gladly is being slighted for queenship, when — from what you say — there is no reason she shouldn't take the throne with the prince?"

The count waits a moment to take a breath, so Fabian goes on. "We can't pretend this isn't some kind of slight, and the people deserve to know why."

Amazingly, no one asks any follow-up questions. All goes quiet save the humming buzz of the devices running the impressions as the count pauses.

I squeeze Gavril's hand so hard it starts to go white.

"Princess Kascia is a strong woman, a true princess, as she proved when she so gracefully admitted her full story though she was under no legal obligation to do so. She has already made changes for good in the court, the palace, and with our foreign relations, though she's only been a working royal for a short time. There is no doubt of her ability. Her abilities to handle even more royal duties had no bearing on the king's choice to make his son regent. I want to make that clear. The king knows the princess is highly capable in her current role and will be in later roles when they are needed. The king fully trusts the princess. And trust me, he made sure I know to tell you all that in no uncertain terms."

"Then why not give her power?" Fabian demands, and the press erupts again.

"Hey! One at a time, I cannot answer all the questions at once. Bevill," the count picks someone.

"Is there rising resentment against the new princess among the rebels for her betraying them, which is the reason for not giving her power yet? Is this stunt meant to prevent the rebels from having more reason to hate the royal family and become more active again?"

"The choice was made with no intent of slighting Princess Kascia," the count says firmly. "I want to make that clear. The king knew he had to step away from full-time service or risk his life. He made the best choice he could for himself, his kingdom, and his family. He is not trying to prevent the princess from taking power. It was simply the best path forward to keep the kingdom stable while lighting his load.

"Now, as you're all just going to keep questioning me and not trusting what I say, I'm going to a meeting where people respect me as much as you do, but at least they will stop pestering when I tell them to. That's a full lid."

The count taps his papers on the wood in front of him, then nods at guards to wrap up the meeting and leaves. A flood of questions follows him as the screen goes dark.

We're all silent for a while.

They had reacted as I expected. The count did his best to defend me, but they're all going to wonder. I swallow hard.

Gavril squeezes my hand comfortingly.

It was done. Now I just have to get through the event.

The hardest part is actually leaving the side room to get back to our offices. The press tries to get to us to ask us questions. They mostly direct their questions at me, asking how I feel and if I requested not to be made queen yet.

I don't answer them. I simply bow my head to them and let the guard keep them back.

Gavril finds it harder. He ignores them more than me until one question clearly hits too close to home.

"How can you take power knowing your wife is being left behind?"

He stops and stiffens. Not even a second passes before I quickly take his hand, and we manage to retreat into the royal offices before the press can push more.

"Gavril," I say, looking at him in concern now we're alone.

He's tense, eyes shut tight.

I frown and embrace him.

He holds me tightly, that hint of desperation returning I'd felt the night he'd told me.

"How can I do this to you?" he asks the question back at me.

"Because you'll make the sacrifice for your people and me. I'm asking you to take it," I remind him. "I'm not hurt by it."

"You are. You just are alright with it." Gavril's frown deepens as tears come to his eyes. "I love you. I hate doing this."

"It will be over soon," I remind him and myself. "Then it's just the delegation to worry about."

Gavril nods, holding me tightly. "I love you."

"I love you too." I kiss him deeply. "Let's ditch the rest of our meetings and have dinner alone. How does that sound?"

Gavril nods. I think that idea helps. He doesn't want to fake contentment to his parents anymore, most of all his mother. I don't know how the king and queen will react, but honestly, I'm finally starting not to care.

The next fiasco strains Gavril's resolve. We're reviewing the press's reactions with the king and queen to come up with strategies to manage it as best we can in the short time we have.

We're gathered in the king's office, sitting around the meeting table as we discuss our options with our press teams when the door bangs open. We direct our attention to the noise as the grand duke barges in.

"How could you not let me in on this?" he demands of the king and queen in one furious look. "I have been able to help you with these discussions before. Why am I suddenly not part of choices that affect my work as well as any of yours?"

There's a beat of silence. I don't have any answer that would help, so keep my mouth shut. The silence is too much for Gavril, though.

He stands and glares at the grand duke. "You are not a member of the royal family, no matter how you like to pretend to be. You may be the third link in the line of succession, but that does not grant you the right to interfere in our planning meetings if you are not invited, Duke."

"I am the grand duke. That comes with power and respect. You seem set to disrespect. This affects the line of succession which I am—"

"Your part in it has not changed one ounce, Duke Aldergone," Gavril snaps.

"I came to speak to the *king*. You're not him yet. Last I checked," the grand duke snarls at Gavril.

"You need to learn respect for your crown prince. I still outrank you, Duke," Gavril hisses back.

This can only get worse. I get up and put a hand on Gavril's arm. He looks at me, his anger at the grand duke still shining in his eyes. But he sighs as he looks at me.

"I request the prince and princess step out as I discuss *your* disrespect for my office." The grand duke glares at us, then looks at the king. "As it's you who has slighted me."

I am pretty sure Gavril had too with his snarling at the grand duke, but I know what the grand duke is trying to do. He's become expert at making the queen so anxious that the king can't calm her, so the king would have to give in just enough to soothe her. He hates to see her suffering from anxiety so. It is a horrible trap.

"I will not," I snap and at once regret it.

"So, you prove why they can't finally retire." The Grand Duke rounds on me next. "Your king orders you to leave his office and you won't? It's not even your office, Princess." The way he spits my title at me is almost an insult.

I shudder as, for some reason, it reminds me of him pressing his body on me in the lift. I fight tears as determination not to let him push me like that again roars up. "So you can manipulate them against us? If you have a true complaint, having us here should not change it."

I step back as the grand duke moves towards me. I swear he is about to strike me.

Gavril shoves him back before he can come more than an inch closer. "Remember your place, Duke," Gavril warns him, tensing to fight if he must.

"That's enough, all of you," the king orders, pausing to cough with how he'd had to yell.

The queen frowns in worry and takes his arm. I know that fear in her eyes. Now the choice has been made, her main concern is not yet losing the love of her life.

"I'm sorry, Father." Gavril bows his head to him.

"I will speak to you on the subject later, Duke Aldergone," Aster says firmly. "You don't demand an audience with me by interrupting a meeting. I will send for you when I'm free." And he dismisses the grand duke.

For a moment, I fear the grand duke won't leave. But after glaring at us, then at the king for a moment, he bows and steps out.

"Little creep," Godwin mutters as the door slams behind the grand duke.

"We should have included him." The queen looks afraid.

"No, we shouldn't," Aster mutters.

"Sorry," I apologize for my outburst in it as I sit down. Gavril follows my lead.

"Nothing to apologize for. You were serving your king as you should." Aster waves it off. "I'll deal with him later. Let's finish here."

I hardly hear the rest of the meeting as they go on. I have so little part in it.

When we're done, I want to leave right away. I get up to go. Gavril stays with me until his father calls him back. I notice the queen has left too. Gavril looks at me to invite me to join, but I would much rather get some air.

He reads my reaction and nods that it's alright for me to go.

I step out into the hall and turn to go into the conservatory, somewhere to feel outside for a moment.

"You better remember your place, Princess." I jump as the grand duke grabs my arm. "You are going to be looked down on by the people and everyone in the court. You don't get to act like you have more power than me."

"Let go of me," I demand, pulling hard, but sadly, I'm not strong enough to break away from him.

"Learn your place, girl, or you won't see your reign come."

"Don't you threaten me. I'm not afraid of you." I glare at him.

The grand duke smirks. "But of course not, Princess. We know your true feelings."

I shudder at the sick feeling his tone brings. The monster has the nerve to lean in, as if to steal a kiss from me.

He gets a knee right into his groin instead. He grunts in pain as he collapses to the floor. I hope I broke it permanently.

I turn to go but stop at a rush of color and the sound of a hard slam. Gavril must have seen something because he's holding the grand duke against the wall by the throat.

"Do that again, and I'll find any excuse to have you executed. Understand me?" Gavril snarls. He throws the grand duke to the floor, takes my hand and walks away.

I am relieved. I embrace him the second we step into his office. He hugs me tightly.

"What did he say to you?" he asks quietly in my ear, but firmly.

"Told me to learn my place." I sigh as I pull back. "That little snake. If Forsythia knew what he wanted to do."

Fire fills Gavril's eyes. "What did he do?"

"Tried to do." I smirk. "I'm fine, thank you."

Gavril smiles. "I'm sure as he didn't have you injured this time."

I don't elaborate. I don't want Gavril to try to let all his anger out on the grand duke. We're at too precarious of a place to do something to him right now. The high king would demand answers when the grand duke is the *end* of our short line of succession right now.

"Tried to sweet talk me is all. Forsythia is the jealous type, you know." I keep it as simple as possible.

Gavril nods with a heavy sigh. "I'll try to mention it next time I see her."

"Which you hope is never." I try to put a positive spin on it.

Gavril chuckles. "Fair enough. I have some... formal briefings I have to go to. More like a lecture that being regent isn't the same as king. Will you be alright?"

I nod. "I will keep busy. Don't worry about me." I can work with Florence, Bella, and my team to prepare how to handle questions about tomorrow.

But that's not what happens. We're just getting started in my office when my mother barges in. Of course, people think they can march in on my meetings. They do it to the king. The slighted crown princess wouldn't be spared that feeling.

"Are you alright? Why didn't you tell us?" she asks.

"Fine, Mother." I miss feeling like she is the one I want to talk to. "Nothing you need to worry about. You're busy, and as a non-royal, it would just make others angry if you were there."

"I don't have to be there. I just... thought you'd tell me." She frowns.

"You have your work to do, and I have mine. When do I have time?" I smile at her. "We can always talk during our lunches, but it's not like we've had one of those."

"Right." Mother frowns. "I understand. Is... why are they doing this?"

"Cowardice," Bella mutters.

I cast her a warning look. "Bella please." She bows her head in apology. "It's far too complicated to go into." I look back at my mother. "But it's simply not time for the queen to step down, is all. What they said in the announcement is correct."

Mother doesn't seem to buy it and hugs me. "Don't let them make you feel you're not worthy of it."

"I don't." I assure her as I hug her back. "Just how it is right now."

Mother nods, looking grim. Then she looks at the room and gasps. "Oh, you're working. I am so sorry. I didn't realize. When no one was in the front... I am so sorry. I didn't mean..."

That's when it hits her. The reality is that her baby is princess now, and she still is just a lady. There are formal boundaries that I am happy to let her cross, but her informality still looks rude to others.

"I had no idea. I'm sorry. Maybe... put a sign or something. I didn't mean to interrupt. I'm so sorry, sweetheart."

"It's okay, Mom." I smile, feeling a million times better with her apology. She finally is starting to understand.

"I'll talk to you during lunch or I'll ask again next time, okay?"

"Please, just ask. I can make time." I promise. All I really need is to feel she understands things aren't how they were. And I think she just learned it.

"Okay." She smiles and kisses my forehead. "I'll see you later then, sweetheart."

"Love you too, Mom." I smile as she leaves. At least something is going right.

Hers isn't the only reaction I am due to receive. At least the next person knocks. I give them permission to enter, and Grandfather comes in.

"If you're busy, I can come back."

"It's fine." He might be helpful. "I'm trying to work out a response plan. You can help."

Grandfather nods and takes the closest available seat to me. "You're sure you're okay?"

I swallow and nod. "As I can be."

I cast Bella a look before she can open her mouth. She wants to ask Grandfather about his thoughts on it. I know she does. I don't want more discussion. I'd made my choice. I'm not letting anyone else try to change my mind.

Grandfather watches the exchange. "Mind if... we talk alone for a moment before I join the meeting?"

His eyes and tone make me uneasy.

"Of course. Would you like to get some refreshments? We will be here a while," I say to my staff. Florence, in particular, looks happy for the break. Bella looks a tad annoyed but does as asked.

I try not to imagine Bella complaining to Florence as they walk. I'm sure they will, though. Staff talk behind their boss's backs. It's just how it is.

"I'm so proud of you." My eyes snap back to Grandfather, who is looking at me in loving admiration. "I don't know how you feel about all of this yet, but either way, you've weathered it with grace beyond your years. Do you plan on fighting it?"

"No." I shake my head. "I... I told him to do it." I explain my thinking and how I know there is no other way.

Grandfather smiles tenderly and gives me a tight hug. "You're so much stronger than you believe, sweet girl."

"Thanks grandpa." I suddenly wish Father would say those words.

"I'd have come sooner, but your father's been... dramatic," Grandfather sighs, pulling back.

"What did he do?" I frown.

"I think he is ready to murder your husband again for allowing this to happen." He smiles with a hint of playfulness. "I don't know if his pride will ever let him get over having to let you marry him. He tries because the prince makes you happy and he loves you. He believes you deserve power, but his pride still struggles."

"Gavril might let him." I bow my head and explain how badly Gavril doesn't want to do this to me. "So... please do whatever you can to make sure he doesn't know more people are mad at him for it, too."

"Bella?" Grandfather asks.

I nod. "And others."

Grandfather sighs. "I'm sorry. This is hard enough without that."

"I'm... I'm right, aren't I?" I burst out like I used to do with Damian. I don't know if Grandfather knows as much as Damian seemed to, but... no one seems to agree with me.

"I think you're doing the best thing in your power." Grandfather nods. "And no one faults you for it."

"That last part is a lie, but thanks." Bella faults me for it. Many do but it's nice he's trying to make me feel better.

"You'll be alright. We'll help you through it. I promise." Grandfather puts a hand on my shoulder.

I manage a weak smile. "Thanks Grandpa."

# Chapter 37

The day of the ceremony, I'm having trouble hiding my feelings. My staff has been stiff with Bella around, and that hurts enough.

Florence, to my surprise, is the most offended. She doesn't hide her looks at Bella, and with how Bella returns them, I think Florence is trying hard to teach Bella how to be staff.

But now we are preparing for this important ceremony, and I'm not a part of it. I feel left out, but it is my choice not to go. I trust my staff and Gavril on the right move to make. It is hard to overcome my sadness, though.

I don't bother dressing up as the public won't see me all day. I do help Gavril get ready, tying his cravat as he buttons his cufflinks. It helps me feel like I am part of it, even if only slightly.

"You okay?" Gavril asks, looking at me in worry. His hands have been shaking, making it hard for him to do his cuffs.

With a gentle touch, I bring his arm down to do it for him. "I'm okay." I'm just not good.

"Kascia, I'm so sorry." And I can feel how he means it from the depths of his soul. "It should be our day."

"Our day will come," I say simply as I take his other arm to do the other cuff. "You look perfect."

He really looks good. His suit is well fitted with a nice collar, the crown prince sash across his shoulder, and the short cape on his shoulders. It makes him as handsome as he was during the memorial when I had trouble keeping my eyes off him.

But not today. The dashing outfit isn't for me to enjoy. It is simply to be proper for his becoming Prince Regent in a few short hours. I'll be watching from a screen. I won't be with him on this important day. I won't be ruling with him.

I fight tears at the thought and put on a smile as I finish. "There."

"Kascia, please..."

"I'm not saying it's not hard." I meet his eyes. It's easier to stop tears when I'm looking up. "I'm saying I can handle it."

"I'd rather be with you," he says in pure longing.

"I'd rather be with you, too. You are the one who explained why I can't," I remind him. "It will be fine. Tomorrow we'll get to the real work together. Not like I can't still be right beside you, as if nothing changed."

"If anyone deserves it being official, it's you." Gavril tilts my chin to meet his eyes. "You know that, right?"

I smile and nod. "Yes. I do. Please, at least try to enjoy it."

"No way in vell will I take pleasure in a second of it," Gavril says with a hint of offense. "I can't enjoy it without you."

"Then maybe I should go," I tease.

"I meant you accepting it with me." He hugs me tightly.

"And one day, we will. We'll share the coronation." I smile, letting myself daydream of it. "It's not forever."

"It's not forever," Gavril repeats, almost like a mantra for himself.

Reinold knocks on the door and tells us its time. I take a deep breath and hug Gavril. He hugs me tighter.

"I love you. My mind and heart will be here with you the whole time," he insists.

"I know." I smile. "I love you."

Gavril has a hard time letting go of me. Reinold walks closer gently and touches his shoulder. He looks so apologetic for both of us, but his compassion is mostly for his prince. Reinold and Godwin are too perfect. I wish my staff were half as good as either of them. Then I'll not need so many.

Gavril nods and pulls back. He kisses me for a moment, trying to assure me of his love and my worth before he pulls back. He can't resist kissing my forehead before his hands let go of mine, shaking with that slightly harder grip he'd give when we were dating. The sign he doesn't want to let go.

He leaves quickly once he does. Reinold gives me an apologetic smile, then snaps. To my shock, three servants I don't know bring in and set up an imaginal.

"I thought you'd rather watch alone. Your staff tried to come in, but I put guards to stop them. Your grandfather has to attend as the official Custod, but your grandmother said she's just a call away if you need her or your mother," Reinold says to me.

I nod, but honestly, I really would rather be alone.

"Oh, and the dog is on the balcony if you want her. She's playing with that ball on a stick." Reinold is not a fan of the dog or any animals, so his joke and invitation mean even more. He set it up so I could be alone or get the dog if I wanted.

"Thank you, Reinold." I manage a smile.

"Anything, My princess." He bows to me. "I'll see you afterward." And he leaves, making the three staff follow.

I swallow and look at the imaginal. It just shows the Purerahian seal, waiting for the event. I immediately decide to open the balcony. As soon as I call Joy in, she bounds inside with all her happy talking.

I take up my spot on the bed, and Joy jumps up. She's a little tired from playing, so she happily rests her head on my lap as I sit back against the pillows to watch.

Thankfully, I don't have to wait long.

I see the king and queen there. The queen looks extra anxious under her proper exterior. I've come to recognize it well, though I'm sure few others can. The king has a small smile, a mix of pride and sadness. The grand duke, a few higher members of court, a few key members of the press, and Godwin and Reinold are there. I also see the king's and queen's attendants.

The ceremony is simple, like a knighting. Gavril doesn't have to put anything on. He already is wearing his official crown. I watch as Gavril kneels in front of his father. Though he hides it well, I can see the anguish in his eyes. He doesn't want to do this.

That's when the tears finally fall, and I stifle my sniffles in a pillow I hold tightly as I stroke Joy. She whimpers in sympathy and licks a few tears away. I laugh a little and kiss her head in thanks. She is proud of herself and nuzzles closer to me.

Thankfully, Gavril doesn't have to do anything more than kneel and say "I so swear" at the end. But when it comes. There's a long pause.

I sit up.

The whirling of the devices fills the emptiness like anxious bees.

*No, no, please Gavril, you have to say it,* I beg in my heart, more tears sliding down my cheeks as I hold the pillow tighter and grip Joy's fur in terror.

The moment holds out too long.

Aster is giving Gavril a look too. I think the queen is about to faint. A little smirk shows on the grand duke's face.

The screen wobbles a bit as if the person manning it hit it a few times to make sure it's working.

Gavril's face is hard to read, but there's a serious battle in his eyes. He can't delay any longer!

"Say it! Sweetheart, please! Gallant star, you have to say it!" I beg out loud. Joy howls as if trying to help me to tell Gavril to do it too.

For a moment, the only sound is my rapidly beating heart.

Finally, "I so swear" slips out of Gavril's lips. I pray no one else noticed how reluctant or resigned it sounded.

I relax and hug Joy tightly, forgetting she doesn't like that.

He did it. Thank heavens he did it! My tears wet Joy's fur and might be the only reason she doesn't wiggle away.

"Then you now, in full force, have the authority and blessing to act as King of Purerah in all things on his behalf," the king finishes with a proud smile, directing Gavril to stand.

He does, and the king embraces his son. I'd never noticed that Gavril is quite a bit taller than his father, more than a few inches, and how much stronger he looks in comparison.

Those in the throne room let out a cheer and throw flower petals or something like it into the air. But all I can see is Gavril's formal smile and nod as he hides how he feels. I see the pain in his eyes.

He's so alone there. I feel so isolated I almost feel as if I'd lost the Enthronement and I'd just watched someone else take my place.

I can't watch anymore. I burst into tears. This is it. I am nothing more than the pretty princess on his arm and bearer of heirs. At least, the latter I can do well.

# Chapter 38

Gavril can't look at me when he returns to our room. The shame in his eyes is too much for me to bear, so I get up to get him to look at me. It is over. I want to speak, make it a good thing, but I can't.

Gavril hugs me tightly. He perceives I've been crying. Joy whimpers and sits at our feet. We spend the rest of the day hiding in our room, taking our dinner there and hardly speaking, just silently comforting each other the best we can with Joy doing her best to make it better.

The next day, the papers are all over the place. The fact I didn't go did exactly what we'd wanted it to. They all wondered why I wasn't and most concluded it was because I didn't approve. The only part that isn't as we hoped is that many, like Bella, questioned how the prince could let them do it to me.

I try to get Gavril to talk about it, but he insists there is nothing to discuss as he gets up to get to work.

"I-it's a rest day," I remind him, feeling a bit discouraged. He planned meetings?

"I still have to address the court. That was the worst part of the timing," Gavril grumbles. "I'll be back as soon as I'm done."

"Shouldn't I be there?" I ask, feeling a bit defeated.

"No reason to make you suffer more," he assures me, kissing my cheek as he puts on his jacket and leaves.

I, on the other hand, feel even worse. At least if I went, even standing there with no new power or authority, I'd feel like I was with him. Instead, he is ruling alone, even with me sitting right there.

I look into my hands on my lap for a long moment, trying to contain it, but I lose the fight and start to cry.

I'm useless. I won and am just as useless as I was when I questioned if I should win. Although I don't doubt it again, I feel worthless and betrayed. Winning means nothing in how I could help the man I loved. I'd wanted that as much as any of it. It was why I should win.

He knew it was me that day on the bridge when I was the one who helped him cope and be strong enough to handle his duty. It is my greatest joy and strength, and the kingdom had stolen it from me. No. The queen stole it from me.

I abruptly force my tears to stop as there's a frantic knock at my door. Once I'm up, I swiftly slip into my study. I can at least pretend I've been doing something important. I hope that will make the person realize I am not in my room and give up.

It doesn't.

The frantic knock comes to my study door. I put on my best acting and tell them to come in. Grandfather comes into the room and looks at me. He's not fooled by my official pleasant smile.

"Kascia, I thought you'd be there. I'm so sorry." And he's hugging me before I can reply.

It makes the tears resume without my control over them, and I hug him back as I start crying again.

"Why win?" I beg the question. "What was the point?"

"You have the power. I would have told him to have you come. I'm sure he thought it would be hard for you to hide the pain there. If I knew, I'd have told him ahead of time. I'm so sorry, Kascia. You're not useless. You'll be right back to the amazing work you do, and in a week, it won't matter as you deal with Japcharia."

"I'm just here to have his children and look good!" I snap. "That's not what... what I signed up for."

"I know. And what happened isn't fair to you. The queen will wise up sooner or later. It's going to be okay." Grandfather hugs me tighter. "It's always darkest before the sun rises."

"It keeps getting darker!"

Damian had said the same before I accepted Gavril's choice to have me as his princess. I didn't know it would get that black again.

"Well, day and night are a cycle, aren't they?" Grandfather asks me. "So, there will be darkest times again, but they are always followed by the light. It will be alright."

"At least I have him." I did win. I am bound to the man I love. And there is comfort in that, even if his duties I should share stole him now and then.

"Yes, and you have good staff." Grandfather pauses as he sees my expression. "What happened?"

I explain about Bella and how it made my staff stiffen around her and how I know what Bella thinks but can't change it. She is only trying to protect me, after all, like she always had as my friend throughout the Enthronement.

"I see. I knew she disapproved but didn't know it was so bad. That is a problem we saw might happen, but it's worse than we thought." Grandfather frowns, still holding me. "But you are her boss. You need to act like it."

"I tried!" I tell him how I told her several times, but it has done no good.

"Hm, it seems she needs to change. Perhaps you could have another lady-in-waiting to help you and help train her. Damian might not have had enough time to help remind her of her place."

"But I want her to tell me her thoughts." I frown. "I don't want to shut her down."

"But you also need to get her to respect you as her boss."

"It's not like she's not following direct orders."

Grandfather sighs. "Well, perhaps the real problem is that she doesn't respect the prince. She was dating him, and now she's not equal with him or you anymore. And while, of course, we treat everyone with respect no matter the station, there is a protocol one needs to follow for those they work for and, most of all, royals. Perhaps it's that she's only ever worked for her family, so isn't sure how to be a good employee yet. I'll talk to her. And if it doesn't work, honestly, Kascia, you can't have someone who acts like that forever. Perhaps you keep her on for the fashion side and get someone else to handle the other aspects."

But I don't want anyone else. The person I want is gone. My grandfather is our court Custod, so he can't handle all of that. And I can't imagine any of the other girls handling it all as well as Bella does. And I don't trust a stranger. Not like I can with the rest of my staff or court liaison who isn't as personal. Too bad I can't just steal Godwin.

"Give it time, though. You have other matters, and for now, I still think she'll do the job," Grandfather comforts me. "Don't get too discouraged yet."

I nod and hug him. "Thanks Grandpa." He's almost like having Damian back. At least he's just as good at talking to me, even if I still miss Damian.

"Anytime, sweetheart." He kisses my head. "I know you like to dance. Would you like to do that with me while you wait for your husband to be free?"

That actually sounds amazing. He smiles; he'll do whatever it takes for extra smiles. He's not shy to try something tricky which makes me laugh.

I'm laughing as Gavril comes into the room. He's beaming to see me happy.

"Oh good, she's making my feet sore. I'm too old for this," Grandfather jokes when he sees Gavril. "Spare an old man."

"Grandpa." I laugh at his joke. He even fake-limps away.

"Thank you." Gavril's eyes are full of sincere gratitude as Grandfather continues to fake the limp past Gavril. Grandfather just smiles and claps Gavril on the shoulder before leaving.

Gavril's eyes meet mine. "I'm so glad to hear you laugh. I feel like I've not heard it in ages."

"Really?" I tease.

"Really." Gavril walks over and hugs me. I smile as he does. "Now it's all back to normal, I promise. You're my go-to for everything. Just as you always have been." He looks around. "You... want to keep dancing?"

I smile mischievously. "Yes, but... not here."

Gavril opens his mouth to ask, but I kiss him hard, and he gets the hint without too much trouble. If I am only good for two things, I am going to be excellent at, at least, one of them.

Will she find her power in time to save her people?
Read The Emboldened

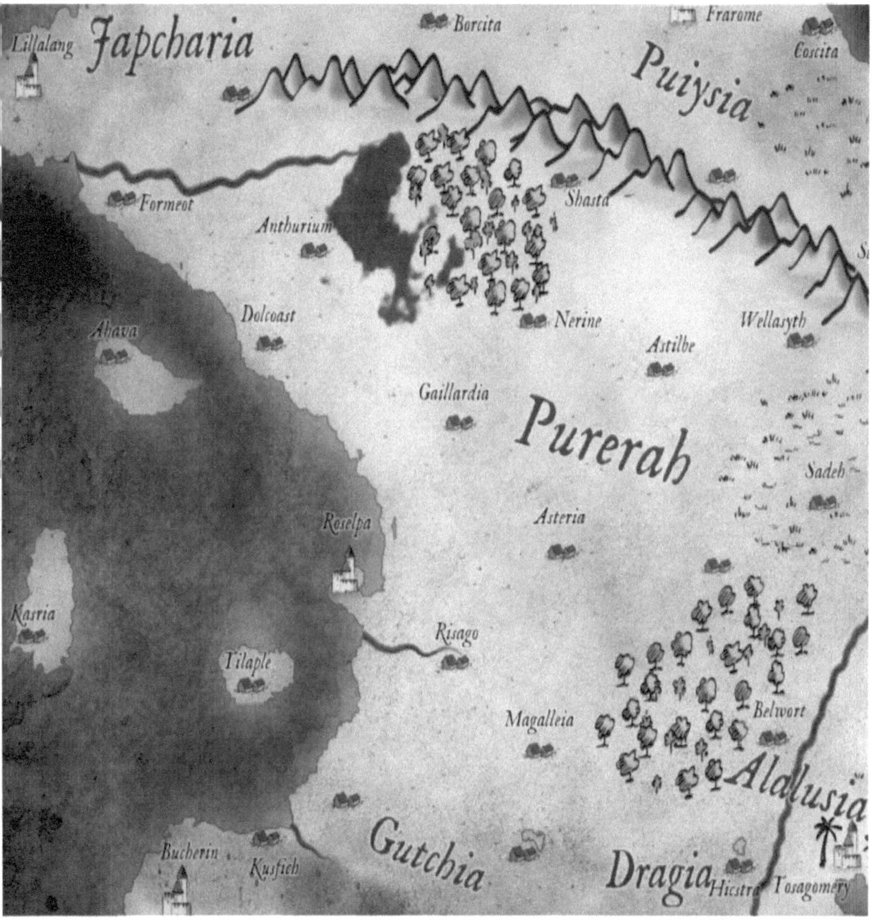

Lillalang
Japcharia
Borcita
Frarome
Coscita
Puiysia
Formeot
Anthurium
Shasta
Dolcoast
Nerine
Wellasyth
Ahava
Astilbe
Gaillardia
Purerah
Sadeh
Roselpa
Asteria
Kasria
Risago
Tilaple
Magalleia
Belwort
Alalusia
Bucherin
Kusfich
Gutchia
Dragia
Tosagomery

# About the Author

When she's not reading and writing, she enjoys, gaming, hiking, swimming, watching YouTube videos, and sitting outside while working on projects. Lives near Mt. Shasta in Northing California and loves the nature there (though she'd like some more snow and rain). She wrote her first 700+ book when she was eleven-year-old and published her first book when she was twenty-one.

Sign Up for her newsletters for updates and exclusive content:

And see sneak peeks, enjoy some memes, and more on her social media platforms.:

Charity Mae Socials